Shadows of My Father

The Memoirs of Martin Luther's Son

~

A Novel

Christoph Werner

Translated by Michael Leonard

Originally published as *Paulus Luther. Sein Leben von ihm selbst aufgeschrieben.* Wahrhaftiger Roman, in Germany in 2015 by Bertuch Verlag Weimar GmbH.

HarperCollins books may be purchased for educational, business, or sales promotional use. For information please e-mail the Special Markets Department at SPsales@harpercollins.com.

HarperCollins website: http://www.harpercollins.com

FIRST HARPERCOLLINS PAPERBACK EDITION PUBLISHED IN 2017.

Library of Congress Cataloging-in-Publication Data is being applied for.

ISBN 978-0-06-284652-5

17 18 19 20 21 LSC(H) 10 9 8 7 6 5 4 3 2 1

Editor's Prologue

On the 7th of March, AD 1593, I was summoned to the sickbed of my friend Dr. Paul Luther, professor of medicine, the youngest and highly erudite son of Dr. Martin Luther. Most recently, and for a handsome salary, he had been personal physician to the administrator of the Saxon electorate, Frederick William. Also, he had looked after the late elector's children and before that had successfully worked as a general practitioner in the city.

As I approached the bed, the famous doctor greeted me in a quiet and friendly manner. Since there were no visible signs of illness, and apparently no fever, I could only surmise that he was simply tired of this life and wanted to join his God.

With a weak but still-audible voice, he said, "My dear esteemed and learned friend, I thank you for coming. In view of my approaching death" (which occurred on the following day, I, Matthias Dresser, add), "I am entrusting you with my memoirs, which I have only recently finished and committed to paper. After my death, I should like you to have them printed here in Leipzig, perhaps even presenting them at the new book fair planned for next year, 1594. I have waited until now to entrust someone with this task so that they would not appear before my death.

"I did that for this reason: I feared my father more than I loved him, and I have remained until today publicly obedient to his religious doctrine and especially to his teachings on the Holy Communion. But even as a student in Wittenberg, I was troubled by doubts about the new church of my father, which, after all, seems to me to be lacking the right Christian love and charity. This doubt has grown throughout my life and has greatly pained me, because I have been forced into conflict between the requirement to appear as the obedient son and my conscience, which told me that the love of Christ, which we should follow, demands something quite different than the enraged hate against the Anabaptists, Calvinists, witches, heretics, Jews, and, generally, people of different faith. In short, I feel a new Babylonian captivity of the church looming ahead.

"And as my inner conflict became greater, so did my doubts, which proceeded so far that the stronger I inwardly questioned the subordination of Christendom under a church organization and the rule of a bishop, the greater zeal for the teaching of my father's I showed outwardly. During my lifetime, I wanted no one to notice what great differences I had with the now-world-honored reformer. One might call this cowardice or at least weakness, but my rise in the learned and aristocratic world would have been impeded had I, in my lifetime, publicly confessed to the deviations from my father's doctrines.

"Even now, in my memoirs, my great doubts have been carefully masked, although the attentive reader will recognize them.

"When I now give you, my friend, this record of my life to be printed and made public, I believe my death will be easier to bear in view of the experience that every man's life is full of lies and blemishes.

"I have already discussed the funeral sermon with Pastor Georgius Weinrich, and it will contain nothing controversial and embarrassing."

After these words, Paul Luther, with a shaking hand, took from the table beside the bed a stack of pages written in a small hand and tied together with twine, which he handed to me. I responded that I would faithfully fulfill his instructions.

Dr. Luther was clearly exhausted. He waved his hand as if to dismiss me and closed his eyes.

And herewith I follow his wishes and make this book available to the Christian readership.

Matthias Dresser, Electoral Saxon Historiographer

Paul Luther's Foreword

Death is certain, but uncertain is the hour; therefore, as Matthew says, be watchful, for ye know neither the day nor the hour in which the Son of Man will come. But the dying man, that is certain, appears swiftly before the face of the Most High.

In preparation for this and in order to clear my conscience, I want now in my sixtieth year to record my life, for one, because I believe that in such a public confession contrition and atonement are included, which as we steadfastly believe are prerequisites for eternal salvation.

And second, I write for my children and grandchildren, that they may derive benefit from my experiences in good and evil. That is my pious hope, though I cannot be certain, because we know that children will mostly behave stubbornly and not follow their parents' instructions despite a generously applied rod.

And third, in the hope of fending off from sinful boredom a larger audience, I have charged my friend, the learned Matthias Dresser, to seek a good-natured printer here in Leipzig. Should, in the end, the quality of my writing art not please, I hope then that my name will be of assistance. The use of my father's fame and prominence for modest commercial purposes I do not consider a crime.

Since there are people who will spread rumors throughout the world that I have not been firm in my Christian belief, I confirm before God and man that I will die in the faith that is founded solely on the saving grace of Christ. At times I have had doubts, but this I have learned from my father: a man must not cease from hammering one's belief persistently into one's sinful heart in order to remain true to it.

As this book will show, I have experienced so many changes in my life that I can no longer be confident in all my recollections, since my memory has grown weaker. Diverse sources—my diary, records, letters, narratives, files, and biographies—have served to close gaps in my recall. Excellent have been the tales of my mother and my honorable eldest brother, Johannes Luther, formerly chancery-councilor at the ducal court in Weimar, who in AD 1575 in Königsberg passed away in the hope of Christ. I also heard much from my brother Martin.

So in God's name I hope to have recorded everything in a Christian manner and according to the truth. Should anything be distorted or falsely embellished, then certainly the Evil One had a hand in it, which would exculpate me. Nevertheless, I beg your indulgence.

CHAPTER 1

. . . tells of the fateful journey to Eisleben, and how my father wanted to frighten the Jews but was frightened by them instead.

It was the third journey to visit the Mansfeld counts, who could not stop quarreling.

Father's concern was his new Evangelical church, but he also wanted to assist Uncle Jacob and his brother-in-law Paul Mackenrot and the other foundry masters and merchants, who were being oppressed by Count Albrecht. My father had always held Mansfeld, his beloved fatherland, as he called it on the journey, close to his heart.

The counts there had long needed more money, so wasteful and foolish were they, as evidenced by thoughtless partitions of estates and pompous courts. They terminated, therefore, the lease of the copper and silver refineries, which were the possessions not of the masters but rather of the nobles. They felt the old masters, working in their traditional way, had not extracted enough copper and silver from the mines and refineries, and this now had become more and more urgent seeing that the cheaper Spanish silver flooded the markets. The old debts of the masters, however, the nobles did not want to assume, which, to their astonishment and anger, caused great fear and opposition. Other grievances had to do with church matters—who, *per exemplum,* had the right to appoint ministers at St. Andreas Church at Eisleben or how the school should be ordered and similar issues.

Father had long suffered from poor health, as we set off from Wittenberg on Saturday, the 23rd of January, 1546, in a covered wagon, which was drafty and jolted us hard. We were, besides my father and myself, my brothers Johannes and Martin; the servant, Ambrosius Ruthfeld; father's famulus, Johannes Aurifaber; and from Halle Justus Jonas. Master Philippus Melanchthon, our venerated but frail teacher, whom my father with great claims upon his friendship had persuaded to accompany him on both previous trips to Mansfeld, was this time too weak to travel in this cold winter weather. Taking into account his small size—he was not much taller than a twelve-year-old boy—this was understandable.

Father had become, through copious eating and drinking, very corpulent—"I eat like a Bohemian and drink like a German; therefore, God be thanked," he said one time—and as a consequence suffered from stones in the bladder and kidneys, gout, buzzing in his ears, and headaches. His blood surged mightily through his body, and his defecation was extremely slow. He often complained that he simply could not shit.

His bodily sufferings were also accompanied by complaints of the head, which never completely left him, and from time to time were increased with new bouts of dizziness and fainting. And in the mornings, weakness of the head and dizziness were frequent occurrences.

Earlier an ulcer had appeared on his left leg, which seemed to heal; as a new outbreak seemed to relieve his head, he followed the advice of a friend, the personal physician of the elector, Ratzeberger, to create a fontanel where the ulcer had been and keep it open by means of a caustic. After that, it appeared that the required equilibrium of the juices throughout the body was for a time properly adjusted.

Because of all this, he was not always reasonable and friendly, and we then had to keep rather quiet. Today I confess I would rather have stayed with our mother in Wittenberg.

My brother Johannes had, a short time before, shown me how through a certain manipulation of the lower body one could experience a very high pleasure, which was now during the entire journey impossible for me to practice. Not until later did it became clear to me that this handling was not a Christian practice, although I am not of the same opinion as Thomas Aquinas, who decreed that self-pollution is an evil worse than intercourse with one's own mother. Also, my experience in medicine has taught me that it is nonsense to say that such a practice erodes the spinal cord or causes softening or dehydration of the brain (so extreme a dehydration that, looking at a self-polluter, one could hear the rattling of the brain in the skull).

One had to concede, though, that the Hippocratists successfully made people suffer from a guilty conscience due to the nasty mixture of self-generated pleasure and fear.

Unlike with Hippocrates, the advocate of spinal consumption, I agree with Galen of Pergamon, namely, that intercourse between the sexes as well as masturbation helps to preserve good health and protects us against evil poisons arising from decaying semen.

Reader, I must give a warning here: that I more often than perhaps you might think necessary give in to the impulse to incorporate the medical findings of my later life into my memoirs, because one can never start too early with the instruction of other people.

So my esteemed father was not feeling well, which was probably why my brothers and I had to accompany him on the journey.

On the following day, the 24th of January, after passing through Bitterfeld, we entered Halle and were given a friendly greeting from Justus Jonas, preacher in Halle since AD 1541, who was the brave first to offer communion under both kinds, and we lodged in his house south of the market.

Now enter events in which I can recognize God's hand only with an effort.

As we drove off the next morning at eight o'clock going in the direction of Eisleben, the Saale River was so wild with torrents of water and floes of ice that the ferryman, because of the great danger to life and limb, especially his own, dissuaded us from crossing the dangerous waters. Also, a return to Wittenberg had become impossible because the Mulde River at Bitterfeld had now risen even higher.

So for three days we lingered in Halle, held captive between the waters.

On the second day in the morning, Father was feverish and completely red and swollen and wanted no breakfast, though on the previous evening he had enjoyed a good measure of the tasty Torgau beer and, consequently, several bowel movements.

What actually took place my brother Johannes related to me later. Here is his report, in which several Jews appear and accuse Dr. Martinus:

> On the morning of the second day of our stay in Halle, my father called Justus Jonas and myself to his bed, where he lay in a fever, sweating and breathing with difficulty, and told us of the following occurrence. He was uncertain whether it had actually occurred or had only been dreamed.
>
> Barely had he fallen asleep on the previous night—after drinking a respectable amount of Torgau beer and Rhine wine, which Justus Jonas had liberally poured and of which I, who counted already nineteen years, was allowed to partake—when there appeared in his room an old Jew, who woke him. He introduced himself as a junk dealer, who between the buttresses of St. Marien Church carried on a trade in used books and old manuscripts.
>
> This man was clothed in a caftan and bade my father to get up and follow him. They went over the market, past the gallows next to the fountain, down to the river Saale. There

the old man led my father downriver to Moritzburg Castle, which had been built on the site of the old Jewish village.

There at the foot of one of the bastions on the east side of the castle, they met eleven men dressed in dark overcoats, standing in a circle. Luther's guide shoved him into the circle, which he himself joined. One of the men then stepped forward and spoke:

"Luther, you have so interpreted the Gospel that the Jews stand under God's wrath and outside his grace and are thus excluded from humanity and the Christian community. 'Therefore their synagogues and schools should be burned down,' you have said, 'their houses razed and destroyed, their prayer books taken away, their rabbis forbidden to teach on pain of loss of life and limb and driven away if they cannot be converted.

"'Safe conduct on the highways should be abolished completely for the Jews. For they have no business in the countryside, since they are not lords, officials, tradesmen, or the like. They should stay at home.'

"Luther, you also said that all cash and treasure of silver and gold be taken from them and put aside for safekeeping. 'A flail, an ax, a hoe, a spade, a distaff, or a spindle should be put into the hands of young, strong Jews and Jewesses so that they can earn their bread in the sweat of their brow.'

"Dr. Martinus, where do you obtain the certainty with which you say the Jews desire no more from their messiah than that he should be a ruler and a worldly king, who would slay the Christians, divide the world among the Jews and make them rich lords, and finally die like other kings and likewise his children after him?

"What, Dr. Martinus, will you reply to God on Judgment Day, when he asks you, 'How have you dealt with my children, the Jews?'"

> Our father knew not how he got back to the house and his bed. With assurance from Justus Jonas, he declared it all a dream in which the Devil, along with the Jews, had a hand, in order to deter him from his great work. And his many ailments served as proof of it.

Such was the account of my brother. Today, it seems to me more likely that the Devil and the Jews had less to do with what had happened than the rich Torgau beer of the previous evening. But the aftereffect of the dream or the experience was soon apparent, as my father called for the expulsion of the Jews from Mansfeld and elsewhere.

Possibly each Christian will form his own judgment, which is not to be too far from my father's teaching, or the teaching of the papist church, depending upon which belief the respective local ruler follows. Earlier, I also thought heathens, Turks, and Jews to be the archenemies of Christianity, possessed by the Devil because they refused to be converted. Now, at the end of my life, I am no longer so sure. We know that my father owed his knowledge about the Jews not to his own observation or examination but rather almost entirely to the book *The Whole Jewish Belief, with Thorough and Truthful Coverage of All the Rules, Ceremonies, and Prayers* by the baptized Jew Antonius Margaritha. This man mercilessly castigates his former fellow believers, and our father had, untested, adopted the evil accusations, as a comparison indicates. Anton Margaritha writes, for example: "The Jews do nothing the entire day. If they need heat, need light, need to milk the cows, etc., they get a poor simple-minded Christian to do these things for them. They famously imagine themselves to be masters, and that Christians are to be their servants, saying they are the true rulers, whom the Christians should serve while they themselves remain idle." It is exactly the same in Father's writing, "On the Jews and Their Lies."

On the same morning, in spite of all his complaints, without breakfast and with the cauterized leg ulcer exuding moisture, my father went to St. Mary's Church, which was still surrounded by scaffolding because it was being rebuilt, to preach in memory of the conversion of Paul the Apostle (which is celebrated on January 25th). He gave a vigorous sermon with dark accusations against the depravity of the Jews as well as the wicked business of the papacy and thundered against the damned Cardinal Albert and his collection of relics, although Albert had been dead since September and the relics long since transported to Aschaffenburg. He complained about the Catholic Church: it had become a worldly, superficial, rich, and terrible power, making the people into helpless servants, presenting Christians with rampant wickedness, horribly distorting and polluting the conscience of the lamentable people.

On the morning of the next day, a message reached us that the Mansfeld counts had sent a hundred and thirteen mounted troops as an honor guard, and they awaited us on the border. Also, the flood and ice drift of the river now allowed us to cross, which we did with three barges lashed together. Our father was, meanwhile, impatient to get to his tasks in Eisleben so that finally, along rough roads, cold and shaken but well protected by riders, we passed through Salzmünde and succeeded in reaching Eisleben.

Here our father immediately became better, like Antaeus, who always received renewed strength when he touched his mother Gaia. I suppose the medicine made from garlic and horse manure, which was prescribed for him in Halle, was probably less helpful, as in my present view the portion of horse manure did not correspond well with the garlic. There was simply too much muck in it.

Shortly before Eisleben, he suffered a dizzy spell but recovered quickly, helped by the knowledge that he would soon be in his beloved fatherland and would be able to assist his dear lords, as he called the Mansfeld counts, in overcoming their disputes. In addition, he believed or professed to believe that the many Jews who lived in the village of Rissdorf near Eisleben under the protection of one of the countesses of Mansfeld had, incited by the Devil, caused an icy wind to blow at him.

"As I drove by the village," he wrote his wife, Käthe, "there was such a cold wind from behind the wagon through my beret as though it wanted to freeze my brain. Immediately after the mediation of the main issues, I must set about expelling the Jews. Count Albrecht is hostile to them and has already abandoned them. But so far no one has done anything. God willing, I will assist Count Albrecht from the pulpit and expose them also."

It seems to me today that in his letter Father was telling Mother what she wanted to hear and thus was cloaking his carelessness, because it has been said that Mother hated the Jews even more than Father.

For he was, as is apparent from another letter, insufficiently dressed for this cold, at times walking next to the wagon, which he did not write Mother, instead writing this: "But if you had been there, you would have said it would be the Jews or their god who was guilty."

On Thursday, the 28th of January, late, we reached Eisleben and took up quarters in the house of the town clerk at the market square, not far from the town castle of the counts. My brother Johannes told me later that it was the home of Dr. Drachstedt and, in any case, the house where our dear father was later to leave this earthly world. That, however, seemed still a while away, for he was feeling well then. He drank the beer from Naumburg and had in the morning three bowel evacuations in three hours, which very much helped his mood. For his entire life, he had had problems with his bowels and constipation, and this was made worse whenever crises in life or faith occurred. When he was at the Wartburg Castle, still not an old man at thirty-eight at the time, he wrote to a friend in Wittenberg: "The Lord has afflicted my ass with great pain. So hard is my stool that I am compelled to use great force to push it out, breaking into a sweat. And the longer I postpone it, the more it hardens. Yesterday after four days I defecated once. Because of that I had the entire night neither slept nor have I until now rested. This is a visitation from God, for he desires that I should not live without a cross."

In fact, the longer I deal with medicine, the stronger is my conviction concerning the interconnection between the soul and the body. Today I no longer wonder at my father's fluctuating physical condition, which accompanied him all his life. For orderly and regular bowel movements are decisive for the balance of the soul and thus for the Christian faith.

CHAPTER 2

. . . speaks of my father's decease and how I felt at the time.

My father, so to say, died twice. The first time was in a lying French article about Doctoris Martini Luther's death in AD 1545, which purported to be a letter from the envoy of His Most Christian Majesty to his monarch.

According to the vicious article, a terrible miracle took place with the ignominious death of Martin Luther, who was condemned in soul and body. It went on that as Luther saw his sickness was severe and death altogether certain, he asked that afterward his body be placed on an altar and worshipped as a god. But through divine goodness and foresight, a miracle took place, causing the people to abstain from such great error, destruction, and corruption the above-mentioned Luther had loosed in this world. So, as his body was laid in the grave, a terrible rumbling and tumult was heard, as though the Devil and hell collided, at which all those present were in a great horror, terror, and fear. All who were there saw the Blessed Host—which such an unworthy man had been dishonorably allowed to receive—hanging in the air. They took the Host and, with all reverence and devotion, transported it to a suitable place. After that such rumbling and hellish tumult were no longer heard that day. But on the following night the turmoil was even greater; therefore, the people got up and with great fear and horror went to the place where the unholy body of Luther had been laid. In this grave, as it was opened, one saw clearly that neither body nor flesh, neither bones nor clothing were to be found. But it was so full of an awful sulfurous smell that all the people who stood there were made sick. Through this, many people improved their lives by turning to the holy Christian belief, to love, honor, and praise of Jesus Christ, and to strengthening and confirming the holy Christian church, which is the pillar of truth.

One can see that the Devil is able to make use of the most sacred words in order to confuse the people. On the day the supposed letter was written and sent, my Herr Father had still a good year to live and thus an opportunity to reply in the following ribald manner:

> And I, Martinus Luther, Doctor, confess and testify with this document that I have received on the 21st of March this angry fantasy concerning my death and have very gladly and joyfully read it. I am pleased that the Devil and his followers, the Pope and the Papists, are so heartily my enemies: May God convert them from the Devil. But should my wish be in vain, then let them go to hell; they have deserved it.

Our father read the letter and his answer aloud at the table and laughed joyfully at the untimely foolishness and blindness of the Papists, which reaction was carefully committed to paper by some of the participants around the table and particularly by Christophorus Silberschlag, who did not fail to add the approving words from some of the students. Silberschlag will speak for himself in chapter 13. By now he is long in the grave.

As we were now in Eisleben, my father sent us three boys to Mansfeld to our Uncle Jacob, as he wrote our mother: "I don't know what they are doing in Mansfeld, probably assisting the Mansfelders in freezing." And signed the letter, "M. Luth. Your old sweetheart."

As the negotiations with the counts, after much effort and delay, which my Herr Father met with a bit of cunning by threatening them with his departure (for which he sent a private letter to the elector's chancellor, Gregor Brück, urging him to order his immediate return to Wittenberg), were a reasonable success (a success that did not last), my father was in a good mood, though he had a premonition of his end when he was unwell. He was firm in his Christian belief, and it took from him the fear of death by promising him eternal life. Thus, once on Sunday Exaudi, the 25th of May, AD 1544, he preached on the resurrection of the dead:

> But there is a winter when we lie in the earth and rot. Though when the summer dawns on the Day of Judgment, our corn will break forth, so that we will not only see merely a blade of green grass or a raised stalk but rather a strong and thick ear. A Christian does not see or taste death; that is, he does not feel it, is not frightened by it, and goes gently and quietly to it as though falling asleep and dying not. But a godless person feels death and is forever afraid of it.

Toward the end of the negotiations, which lasted about three weeks, my father's health began to worsen. Swiftly the two of us, my two-year-older brother, Martin, and I, traveled from Mansfeld to Eisleben, as it was said our father might possibly part with us there. Johannes did not accompany us because he did not believe it was so urgent or simply did not want to undertake the discomfort of the journey.

It had gone very well for us at our uncle's, and Martin und I had several times together practiced what Johannes had taught me. Still, we were disheartened. I must confess that I was of two hearts. The presence of my father had often been oppressive, and I had feared him for the thirteen years my life had lasted so far. Not so much fear that I would be beaten with a rod, which happened often, because father took as his guide Proverbs 23, verses 13–14: "Withhold not correction from the child: for if thou beatest him with the rod, he shall not die. Thou shalt beat him with the rod, and shalt deliver his soul from hell."

More awful to me was his dark scowl or when, as a punishment, he banished me from his sight, which one time lasted three days.

What if he now died? Or if I, or rather we, would from now on live comfortably with our Frau Mother in Wittenberg without him? On our journey from Mansfeld to Eisleben, I remarked carefully about this to Martin and was surprised that he had had similar thoughts. "Yes," he even said, "we, should the case arise, ought not to be too sad because everything is God's will, after all, as Father never ceased to instill in us."

Martin even confessed to me that the thought of being fatherless had a certain attraction if it were not for the concern—in regard to current events and the warmongering—for poor Mother, a wretched widow without rights and a large family to bring up. There were not just the three boys, Johannes (who at nineteen could hardly be described as a boy, though), Martin, and I. Rather, there was Margarethe, a year younger than I, who as a girl would need to be especially supported until she could be transferred to the care and discipline of, hopefully, an eventual marriage companion.

Elisabeth was less than a year old when she died in Wittenberg in the year AD 1528. Magdalena, called Lenchen, at thirteen, my age exactly, died in AD 1542. It had been a heavy burden for my parents when little Elisabeth died. "With what troubled hearts had the child left us, oh, how the misery overwhelmed us," wrote Father for himself and Mother. But especially the death of Lenchen, who to the great pleasure of my parents had been so intelligent and spiritual and had developed a fine Christian sensibility, had been a sorrow to my parents almost to the death. In the end, though, they were ready to accept God's will. God preserve us from the early death of our children.

Now, however, came the real death of our father, at which Martin and I; Justus Jonas; Father's assistant, Johannes Aurifaber;

his servant, Ruthfeld; the castle preacher, Michael Coelius; and a few others were present.

Today I think that Father sensed, or perhaps even knew, that he would not live to depart from Eisleben. His last sermons had a forcefulness as though to leave a legacy, as if he wanted once more to impress in the hearts of the people of his beloved fatherland what he had fought for since AD 1517. With my limited understanding at the time, I was still conscious of how strongly he yearned for the people to remain faithful to the words of God. He sensed that he would soon no longer be there to admonish them and so, accordingly, increased the urgency of his words. Satan and his earthly helpers, all God's adversaries, must be defeated in view of the threats, always growing stronger, of a once again unified papist church, of the Christians in Hungary threatened by the Turks, as well as of the Jews coming forward again, as could be seen at the Sabbath keeping under the Bohemian Christians.

It was the Gospel that my father had at his heart, not so much his own person. Should he die, this would matter only because then he could no longer serve his dear Lord Christ.

So rather than being affected by self-pity, he could even joke, as Justus Jonas in his report to the Most Serene Highness the Elector concerning the death of Martin Luther quoted my father as saying, "After I have helped reconcile my dear lords, the counts, and if by God's will I am able to travel, I will return home and lay myself in a coffin and give to the worms a good fat doctor to consume." He had already one time expressed a similarly drastic statement when he was feeling bad: "I am nothing but rotten dirt, and the world is the wide asshole, so we will soon be separated from each other."

For his entire life, my father saw himself—such is my opinion—not as a destroyer of the church but rather as a renewer, and he rebuked the pope for justifying his office by invoking Christ's words as handed down by Matthew in the Gospel: "And I say also unto thee, that thou art Peter, and upon this rock I will build my church; and the gates of hell shall not prevail against it." He meant instead the pope was a hellhound who threatened the Gospel and the church of Christ. And he himself, Doctor Martin Luther, was a modest tool of God: the new church should not be named after him. "How can I, a poor stinking maggot sack, allow the children of Christ to appoint my name to it?"

On Wednesday after Valentine's Day, the 17th of February, the prince of Anhalt and Count Albrecht, supported by my brother Martin's and my own tearful entreaties, begged our Herr Father to take it easy and rest in his little room, which he finally did. The weeks before, as negotiations proceeded, he had, as Herr Justus Jonas told us, always appeared for lunch and dinner, eaten and drunk heartily, and praised the repast and how everything tasted excellent in his fatherland. His rest was peaceful, his pillows were warmed the way he liked, and he had usually bidden Justus Jonas and Michael Coelius a cheerful good-night, saying, "Dr. Jonas and Herr Michl, pray to the Lord that things will go well for him and his church, because the Council of Trent is raging against him. Could one only chop off all Catholic bishops' tongues."

For the young reader, I will add that the Council of Trent, also called the Tridentinum, had begun one year before the death of our Herr Father and even then demonstrated the following ambiguity. On the one hand, it fought against Father's insistence on justification by grace alone, *sola gratia,* by faith alone, *sola fide,* and by the sole validity of the Holy Scriptures, *sola scriptura.* On the other hand, the council undertook efforts for a renewal of the Roman Church.

That would have been after my father's heart, for well to the end he hoped for a reconciliation of the divided church, though under the fundamental criticism of the papacy, whose highest representative, the Pontifex Maximus, was for him more and more the Antichrist and even the cause of murderous thoughts: "If we punish thieves with the gallows, robbers with the sword, and heretics with fire, why do we not throw ourselves even stronger with all our weapons against these men of sin, these cardinals, these popes, and this swamp of Romish sodomy that incessantly defiles the church of God, and wash our hands in their blood in order to free ourselves?"

During the three weeks, he had enjoyed aquavit and other waters, which he had asked to be sent from Wittenberg, our mother having sent some of it on her own initiative. Now, however, he no longer went to the negotiations, and I was with him in the little room as he, without britches and in his dressing gown, went back and forth and prayed diligently, saying in addition to us brothers and the others present: "I was born and baptized here in Eisleben: What if I should stay?"

My brother put his arm around me, as I began to cry after hearing these words, and my Herr Father laid his hand on my head. I was fearful of the changes that would come, although I was secretly prepared to accept them, for which I felt ashamed. My father could not know that as he laid his hand on my head, and therefore I cried still more, since I was somehow deceiving him.

Before the evening meal, he began to complain there was pressure on his chest, but not the heart, then asked to be rubbed with warm towels, in which Martin and I tried to help by dipping the towels in the wooden vat and wringing them out. They were hot and hurt my hands, but I continued for the sake of my father and also in order to atone for my shame.

Then for three hours he slept peacefully on the daybed. We brothers as well as Justus Jonas, Herr Coelius, the landlord and his wife, and the town clerk from Eisleben watched over him until about half an hour past ten. We then carried him to his chamber and his warmed bed, where we all stayed. After that he slept, breathing quietly. Outside, the night watchman sang his little song warning of fire and foe, which sounded like a reminder from God through the mouth of the simple man out there.

About one of the clock, my father woke up and said to Herr Jonas, "Oh, Lord God, Dr. Jonas, how bad I feel, the pressure is so hard on my chest, oh, I will stay in Eisleben."

We all helped him out of bed, he leaned against Martin and me, went back and forth in the small chamber, and once again desired warm towels, which we applied to him. Likewise, both physicians in the town were called, one a doctor, the other a master of medicine, as well as Count Albrecht and the countess, who tried out everything on Father, the aquavit and the doctor's medicine.

Then Father began to pray so that cold chills went down my back, so near did I feel God being summoned.

"My heavenly Father, eternal, merciful God, you have revealed to me your beloved Son, our Lord Jesus Christ, whom I have made the center of my teaching and my faith, openly, whom I love and honor as my dear Savior and Redeemer, whom the godless persecute, desecrate, and curse: take my little soul to You."

Then he said three times: "*In manus tuas commendo spiritum meum, redemisti mi, deus veritatis.*"

My brother confirmed to me that he then fell back into his beloved German and ended his prayer, "*Ja, so hat Gott die Welt geliebt*" (For God so loved the world).

Then he became silent, I thought he was dying, and he did not answer to our shakes and our calls. Martin looked at me, and it seemed that his eyes mirrored my own relief. Or was it his?

As the countess and the doctors rubbed him with aquavit, rose vinegar, lavender water, and other tonics—at which the countess limited herself to the upper part of the body, though also casting a quick look down where the doctors were busy—my father once more began to answer, although only weakly, with yes or no. Dr. Jonas and Herr Coelius shouted at him and asked, "Dearest Father, you acknowledge Christ, the Son of God, our Savior and Redeemer?"

My father once more answered clearly, "Yes."

I, his son Paul, also acknowledge that I heard it and can testify to it, as did my brother Martin and all those present.

Then his forehead and face grew cold, as I noted when I laid my hand on him. Dr. Jonas did what he could to make him respond, but to no avail, even when he addressed him with his given name, Doctor Martin. He took a gentle breath and sighed and lay with folded hands. So he passed away in Christ, between two and three in the night.

We all broke into tears, so much so that Dr. Jonas could not himself write a report to our gracious elector but with uncontrollable sobs dictated it about an hour after Father's death to Count Albrecht's secretary, who noted it down without much emotion. This was not the first death he had encountered; under the rule of Count Albrecht many a person had lost their lives.

The lore about what happened at my father's death is, understandably, somewhat varied. Even I myself, who was there, had to be reminded by a document from my own hand of what my father had said in dying. I found in the Bible of Lucas Furtenagel, who in Eisleben drew a portrait of my father, made his death mask in wax, and later in Halle created a plaster from it, an entry from me with the date 7th of August, AD 1582, and the place of Augsburg, in which I wrote that shortly before his blessed end, my father had said three times, John 3:16: "For God so loved the world that he gave his only begotten Son, that whosoever believeth in him should not perish, but have everlasting life."

When my father had sighed his last and had clearly passed away, there was genuine confusion and great turmoil. The body was not left in peace, but instead next to the deathbed three underbeds filled with feathers with towels over them were prepared, upon which the body was placed in the hope, as we all wished and prayed, that God would still have mercy upon him and not yet summon him to his throne. Today it seems to me to have been a genuine folly, because the doctors could feel no pulse;

then, however, I hoped for a miracle and feared it at the same time. As it did not occur, the body was left lying for five hours, until nine of the clock. During that time, many honorable townsfolk came and, with tears and much crying, viewed the body. Also we boys received much attention, were caressed on the head and given comforting words, and Father's cousin Frau Gutjahr stuck two pfennigs in my pocket (for which I now know a journeyman carpenter in summer must work a half day or for which one might get a meal in an inn). For her husband, Andreas Gutjahr, who had been indicted for counterfeiting the year before, my father had written a letter to the old Chancellor Brück. He condemned the counterfeiting but wrote that it was a pity that the small forgers were punished while the big ones got away.

I cried as much as possible, more than Martin, because it seemed that it was expected of me. Now that I was fatherless and an orphan, the tears came easily, and my pity for myself was great.

They then clothed my dead father in a new white Swabian smock and laid the body on a bed of straw until a pewter coffin had been cast, into which it was laid. In the casket he was viewed by many people, including nobility, both men and women, who for the most part had known him, as well as a great number of the common people.

My brother and I went to and fro between our chamber and the place of the laying out. I tried as often as possible to kneel at my Herr Father's deathbed, lay my forehead on his cold hand, and cry sweetly, and lo, more pfennigs were slipped to me, of which I gave two to my brother Martin. One could see that I was in a muddle, both internally and externally. Externally by the constant coming and going, internally by a strange mixture of sadness, self-pity, shame, relief, and contrition over the relief, which contrition in its turn seemed to justify me, for which I again felt shame.

CHAPTER 3

. . . is about bringing my father home, how we encountered Mother, and is continued in chapter 4, which tells how my parents met and married.

It should be understood that at the time I could not appreciate the shock that my father's death provoked in Saxony, the empire, and in all Europe. But I felt, rather than understood, above all in view of the noise and unrest that started in Eisleben immediately after his demise, that something big must have occurred. The old evil foe was himself not unaware of it and hastened to promulgate the myth that Dr. Martin Luther, out of despair, had taken his own life. This legend held on tenaciously and is even today adhered to by old believers.

For the rest of us, however, it was important to document all that had happened during my father's death and preserve it in memory, as it was of paramount importance to protect his life's work from the Antichrist and, in spite of the death of its main advocate, to secure and even to raise the Protestant cause in order to help the new Evangelism to ultimate victory. Later I became aware that all the events at the time—the death protocol (which in March AD 1546 was put into print and thus made available for the Christian public by Herr Jonas, Herr Coelius, and Herr Aurifaber by order of our Most Gracious Elector), the death mask, the laying out, the various sermons at certain stages on the return home to Wittenberg, and many other things—were meant to exactly serve the purpose mentioned above.

On the 19th of February at two of the clock in the afternoon, with great reverence and singing of hymns, my father was carried into the main parish church of St. Andrew. We three brothers—my brother Johannes had meanwhile arrived from Mansfeld, a rider having been sent with an urgent message—saw the princes, counts, and other noble men together with their dames and a great number of townspeople walking behind the body. In the church, Dr. Jonas preached a sermon with a warning to our adversaries that this death possessed great power against Satan and his forces and should not give them any premature hope.

I felt at once that Justus Jonas's tone was very belligerent, and he called on the Christian community, after he had told all the details of the honored man's death, not to be downhearted but to remain true to the teachings of the departed and to defend them against all enemies. His sermon was immediately printed and published, and I have it now before me as I write.

Dr. Jonas used the soon-to-be-familiar metaphor of the goose and the swan: at the point of being burned at the stake, the Bohemian preacher Jan Hus prophesied that after him, the Goose (such is the translation of the name Hus), would soon be followed by a Swan, and it would better and more successfully sing. And then Dr. Jonas repeated the message of my dead father about the Roman Church: "Living, I was a plague to you, Pope; in death will I be your death." After the sermon, the casket was soldered up.

Afterward ten citizens watched over the body through the night. The counts of Mansfeld would have liked to have my father's gravesite on their lands, but our Most Gracious Elector had other wishes and refused their request forthwith. Today, with hindsight, the request of the counts seems to me to be rather simpleminded in view of the significance of my father's death for the survival of the Evangelical cause and the disputes in Europe.

So on February 20th, Saturday afternoon after Valentine's Day, a sermon having been preached early, this time by Magister

Michael Coelius, the body was taken, with reverence and hymns and many tears and lamentations, out of Eisleben.

We brothers sat in the shaking wagon but had the honor of being accompanied by forty-five horsemen and the counts themselves. When we, in spite of our winter clothing, with which Mother had abundantly provided us, became too cold, we would get out and struggle along the rough and furrowed road beside the wagon. The tracks in the mud were frozen, and although we often stumbled, our feet at least stayed dry. As provisions for the journey, friendly Eisleben townspeople had sent along bread and smoked sausage, also for everyone a piece of cold roast, and a sachet of salt from the salt market in Halle, all of which we heartily fell to, feeling the sharp hunger that befalls one in mourning.

Johannes told us along the way that those Mansfeld counts who still adhered to the old belief had encouraged the apothecary Johannes Landau to prepare a divergent death report, which was intended to show Father's death as not clearly Christian.

In the evening we arrived in Halle. Ready to receive us, or rather much more to receive my father, at the Klaustor Gate were numerous citizens and women, as well as the schoolmasters, ministers, and the town council. There was such a crowd of people jamming the streets that it took over an hour for the funeral procession to go from the Klaustor Gate to the Market Church of Our Dear Lady. The pewter coffin was brought into the church, during which there were sobs and tears from the congregation. "Out of the Depths I Have Cried unto Thee, O Lord" was sung, a text from the 130th Psalm Father had set to music. He was laid out in the sacristy, and during the night the people of Halle could bid their farewell.

My father, after his homeland of Mansfeld, had loved the city of Halle for the sake of its faith and his friends there: "Oh, Halle, you worthy city, the Merciful God preserve you, so that you do not founder. You have always loved God's word; therefore He will preserve you."

We lodged again with Dr. Jonas, who preached once more. Then we continued on to Bitterfeld, where a squadron of riders from the Saxon electorate under the leadership of two counts awaited us, who conducted us first to Kemberg. There the casket rested in the town church with a guard of honor. In all the towns and villages that our procession touched, the bells rang out. In spite of the great cold, mourning people everywhere walked along with us in order to say farewell to Dr. Martinus, or more accurately his coffin.

Before the Wittenberg Elster Gate, the rector and all the professors of the university had gathered, along with the students, the town council, and the citizenry. All the bells rang out, and we passed by the Black Monastery, our home, along the Collegienstrasse, over the market square, and through the Schlossstrasse to the castle church. In the church the casket was placed on the right of the pulpit, and Bugenhagen and Melanchthon gave the mourning sermon, during which our mother with extreme effort maintained her composure. Throughout her life, people had observed her with jealousy and resentment, which will be discussed later, and she wanted the envious, who believed her now, without Father, to be defenseless, enjoying no triumph.

The pewter coffin was placed inside a wooden one, after which chosen magistri lowered it into the vault.

Johannes, Martin, and I had only been able to greet our mother in front of all the people. She sat with some women and our sister, Margarethe, in a carriage that joined the procession. Now that Father, who was her beloved master and also her protection and shield, was no longer there, she would have to struggle along alone, with the help of the oldest, Johannes and Martin. Before me is a letter that shows so clearly the greatness of her loss. I borrowed it from the estate of her daughter-in-law, Christine von Bora.

Grace and peace from God, the father of our dear Lord Jesus Christ, dear and kind Sister of mine. That you bear a heart-

felt pity for me and for my poor children, I easily believe. For who would not be aggrieved and distressed, losing such a wondrous man as has been my dear husband, who greatly served not only a town or country but also an entire world. Therefore, I am truly very sad that I cannot tell any man the great suffering of my heart, nor do I know myself how I am deep in my soul. I can neither eat nor drink, also not sleep. And if I had lost a principality or an empire, I should not have cared, had I only kept my husband, who was taken not only from me but from all the world by our dear Lord God. When my thoughts dwell on it, I can, from sorrow and tears (which God well knows), neither talk nor write.

When once again I read this letter now, the entire hard though influential and powerful life story of my brave mother returns to me renewed, though she must have felt somewhat consoled by the sympathetic letter our gracious prince the elector sent her, implicitly expressing his great grief at the loss she had suffered.

Dear Beloved,

We do not doubt that you have learned by now that the venerable and highly learned, our dear and pious Doctor Martin Luther of blessed memory, has left this vale of tears in Eisleben on Thursday in the morning between two and three of the clock, accompanied by godly words from the Holy Scriptures, and departed from us, which We have been told and received deeply distressed and aggrieved. The almighty God, We do not doubt, will be gracious and merciful to his soul. Though We can imagine that your dear master's departure will hurt and make you suffer very much, God the Almighty's will, who has so generously and Christianly endowed him, may not be opposed, but it is God whose right it is to order such. Therefore, you should not be too aggrieved but be consoled about his departure, as it is God's will. We are graciously inclined for the sake of your dear master, whom We honored and were well disposed of, to take good care of you and your children and will not forsake you. This We graciously want you to know and to take to your heart.

Duke Johann Friedrich, Elector

Torgau, Saturday after St. Valentine's Day 1546

CHAPTER 4

. . . continues the story of chapter 3.

My father abominated the idea of girls and women being kept in nunneries and said, "I am, however, of the opinion that maids who are forced to live a spiritual life before they can rightly know what flesh and blood is should be extricated from behind the high convent walls, where the words of the dear Gospel are seldom if ever heard these days. The banishment of young maidens is a tyranny and terrible hardship; the weeping of children, who are neither wooden blocks nor dead sticks, must arouse pity in anyone, even if the maidens diligently sing the *Regnun mundi,* pray without ceasing, ask all the saints to intercede for them, fast, confess, and by day and night torture their souls about how to do righteous deeds, as if our heavenly Father lets himself be paid by such."

Already, as she had fled from the Cistercian Cloister of Marienthron in Nimbschen near Grimma in a covered wagon (or voluntarily had allowed herself to be abducted with eight other nuns) and had moved to Wittenberg on the 9th of April, 1523, our mother, despite great sympathy or rather mere curiosity of the crowds of townsfolk and students, must have realized for the first time the enormity of what she had undertaken. For there were other examples of escapes from the convent, for example, the one of Florentina of Oberweimar, whose escape plan came to light and who was punished with beatings and incarceration. Or, even worse, the case of Heinrich Keller from Mittweida, whom

Duke George of Saxony had ordered to be beheaded because he had helped a nun flee from the Cloister of Sornzig or at least had planned her abduction. And this execution at that time was quite legal, as it was done in accordance with ecclesiastical and secular law, which called for the death sentence in such cases.

For the escape, Father had sent a covered wagon for her and the other nuns driven by a merchant and friend of his, Leonard Koppe, councilman in Torgau, who had often brought herring and dried cod to the cloister as Lenten fare.

Among my papers I found a letter my father sent to Leonard Koppe, which has since been made public and shows how he explained the escape of the nuns, justified it, and claimed responsibility.

From this letter can be seen that the nuns had not spontaneously deserted the cloister but had obviously carefully planned the escape. The nuns wanted to return to their families, which, it seems, the families did not want. The nuns, however, had evidently made Father's judgment of the monastic vows their own and were strengthened by secret imaginations of a worldly life. Some of them hid behind the fish barrels, others even in them, as I read in the letter: namely, "in each barrel a virgin," in which they could comfortably crouch, which is why during the successful flight, having had the need to relieve themselves while in their hiding places, they smelled strongly.

Still, as they came through Torgau and arrived in Wittenberg, and after they had bathed and rid themselves of the fishy smell, people asked themselves what to do with them now. The property the nuns had brought to the cloister was no longer there or could not be used. That meant men had to be found willing to marry them, or they would have to be sent back to their families or relatives. But the families were not happy because they had sent their daughters to the convents in the belief that they, for the rest of their lives, had safely and piously been got rid of. As it happened, safe accommodation was found for all the nuns but Mother. For her it took somewhat longer.

She fell very much in love with Hieronymus Baumgartner from Nuremberg, the son of respectable parents. When Baumgartner left Wittenberg, some claimed Katharina von Bora became so very ill from thwarted love (presumably it was, however, the English sweating sickness, *sudor anglicus,* which at the time was going around). Things got so alarming with her that my father himself turned to Baumgartner in a letter: "To Hieronymus Baumgartner, who in piety and education is a most excellent young man in Nuremberg, from your dear friend in Christ: By the way, if you desire to keep your Käthe von Bora, you must make haste before she is given to another who is at hand. She has not yet overcome her love for you. I would be very joyful if both of you were joined. Farewell. Wittenberg on the 12th of October, 1524. Martin Luther."

"If you desire to keep your Käthe"—that can only mean that Baumgartner, so to say, had already had her; otherwise he could not keep her. Apparently that was the picture that people in Wittenberg and also my father had of her and Baumgartner.

The letters and stories seem to suggest that the patrician family of the Baumgartners could have had no interest in their son marrying a poor, runaway, and possibly sinful nun. So for my mother nothing came of this affair other than rumors that she was not a virgin when she married my father.

Father now proposed as husband the Wittenberg doctor of theology and preacher at Orlamünde, Casper Glatz, whom my mother under no circumstances wanted to marry—he was cantankerous. She would rather have had Nicolaus von Amsdorf or, if there were no others, Luther himself. The last name she would have said with a mischievous smile.

But he was not exactly eager to marry, in spite of the good advice he gave others about the advantageousness of marital life. He wrote, "Grow and multiply: that is a divine work which is not up to us to prevent or to permit, but it is as natural as I am a man and even more necessary than eating, drinking, sleeping, and being awake. It is implanted in our nature and kind as well as those parts of the body as are required for it. Man and woman shall be two souls and one body."

So he had urged his friend Philipp Melanchthon to marry, not completely unselfishly, since he thus wanted the famous scholar to remain in Wittenberg. Moreover, a wife could better provide for the hardworking man than he could on his own.

Thus my honored teacher married Katharina Krapp, the daughter of Hans Krapp, a respected tailor in Wittenberg, and was initially not very happy, even spoke in a letter about a day of tribulation and of marriage as bondage sent from God. The modest comeliness of Katharina probably contributed less than Magister Philippus's fear that she would discourage him from his work for the university and the Reformation. Later the marriage improved, and she had four children by him. Economically, things did not go as well for the Melanchthons as they did for my family, and I heard that Mother did not always praise the other Katharina—a situation that was probably mutual. It is also said that Frau Melanchthon was jealous of Mother. If there was reason to be so, it is no longer known.

As was noted, Father was not keen on getting married and did not suffer, as he said, under the monk's vow of chastity. He said later, "With women, I had nothing to do other than a few times in the confession, and there I did not look at them. And other than the natural discharge at night, I was not troubled by sexual lust."

Later he often spoke against the tyranny of celibacy and could quote the church fathers, and foremost Augustine (who still as an old man suffered from emissions), and Hieronymus: "When he felt his blood rushing he struck his breast with stones, but could not beat the maid from his heart." Others such as Francis made snowballs, Benedict lay down in thorns, Bernard so castigated his body that it reeked abominably.

My mother related to me that after the uncertainties mentioned above, which included the fact that Father had previously had his eye on another escapee, Ave von Schönfeld, who in 1523 married the chemist's assistant of Master Cranach, Dr. Basilius Axt (a beautifully drastic name more suitable for a surgeon, however), everything relating to the marriage went rather quickly. There is no doubt she adored the famous man, and as he asked the decisive question, she agreed without any reservation.

Father, by the way, did not lose sight of Ave: her husband, Dr. Axt, would not, without the influence of my father in AD 1525, have become town physician of Torgau and finally, in 1531, the personal physician of Duke Albrecht I of Brandenburg-Ansbach in Königsberg, whereby the family, one would assume, was well off. Twice before, Father had requested from the elector thirty guldens for Axt.

In addition to that, he interceded for her when it came to her parental inheritance, which her brother Ernst refused her because, as a former nun, she was not entitled to inherit. He wrote a letter to the Most Gracious Elector Johann Friedrich: "She, Ave, was one of the first nuns to escape from the cloister, an innocent woman misled to live a nun's life. She is now an honest married woman, so that I think Ernst von Schönfeld is not worthy to be the brother of such a sister. To withhold her inheritance is a dishonor to the Gospel." (And I, Paul, here should add that Father now and then exploited the Gospel for purposes that one can only understand after some lengthy reflection.)

My own research and memories as well as many sources suggest that there were two main reasons and one minor reason for my father's final yet surprising decision to marry.

First, in view of the revolt of the peasants and the excesses mainly of the nobles, a tour through the regions of the rebellion strengthened in him the belief that the end of the world was near, at least his own death. And in spite of the legitimacy of their demands, the peasant mobs seemed to him to be more and more the helpers of the Devil, who wanted to destroy his new Gospel, and he wanted to set an example and outsmart the Devil. He wrote, "And to defy the Devil, I will take my Käthe as my lawful wife so that before I die I will be found in the state for which God has made me, and nothing of my previous popish life with its monkish and nunnish rubbish will any longer stain me."

One can already see here that Father's decision to marry was a rational or a religious decision rather than one based on lust of the flesh, which later did not prevent the emergence of a lasting marital love. My brother Johannes told me that Father had said that marital love is like God's love: "God does not love the sinner because he is beautiful; rather he becomes beautiful because God loves him." So a man does not marry a woman because she is desirable; rather she is desirable because he has married her.

Father said later, "I would not exchange my Käthe for the kingdom of France or for Venice, because she was a gift from God for me, and I in turn was given to her by him."

The second main reason is connected with my grandparents in Mansfeld, primarily my grandfather. As his son in 1505 went into the monastery and renounced a promising secular career by studying jurisprudence, he was intensely disappointed and even said that during the famous thunderstorm in Stotternheim, Martin had been deceived by a specter.

The marriage, Father felt, would after all be a step into the secular world, away from the monkish, a step toward reconciliation.

The additional reason was that my grandfather feared that the events of the times, mainly pestilence and war, could cause the extinction of the family, and my father's marriage, with the hope of children, might prevent that.

It can be seen that on the whole my father had good reasons for marriage: in marriage, he believed, a person follows God's creative will, and the original sin postulated by the church fathers and put on the same level with *concupicentia*, evil lust, through marriage is transformed into something good.

A maid, Father wrote, who swaddles a child and cooks him porridge, even if he is the child of a whore, fulfills God's will much more than all the monks and nuns of the earth who, for all their self-proclaimed holiness, cannot refer to God.

I beg my Christian readers to consider that my mother as the person most affected by these internal and external struggles was *nolens volens* involved, and I only now come to the most dramatic of all the events.

What an outcry arose as my parents' wedding took place! Not just cries from the old church that Luther was a lecher unable to control his urges and therefore needing to have a young, fresh virgin and even a noble little nun. (At the same time, it was said that our Frau Mother had worked in a public house or had been a disreputable dancer.)

And what was the opinion of my father's friend, my venerated teacher, Melanchthon, and with him other supporters of the Reformation? In Greek, on the 16th of June, 1525, he wrote Joachim Camerarius, his friend, who stayed in Wittenberg at that time. I translate for the reader:

> *Unexpectedly, Luther has married the Bora woman without informing even one of his friends in advance of his intention. He invited to dinner in the evening only Pomeranus, as Bugenhagen is mostly called, the painter Lucas Cranach, and Dr. Apel. You might well wonder that in such serious times, when the true believers suffer everywhere, this man indulges and compromises his good reputation. It seems all the worse because right now Germany needs his mind and authority more than ever. This can only be explained in the following way: The man is very easy to seduce, and so the nuns, who stalked him everywhere, have ensnared him. Although he is*

> *a noble and worthy man, perhaps the frequent contacts with the nuns have weakened him and fanned the fire in him. So, I believe, he has been trapped and fallen into this changed way of life at a most inopportune time.*

But then the Magister continued, and seemed to depart from the apparent jealousy:

> *Now what has happened has to be accepted in good nature and is not to be criticized. Because, as I see it, this way of life—the marriage life—although low, is yet more sacred and pleasing to God than celibacy. Moreover, I hope that matrimony makes him more dignified and, through it, he will lose some of the buffoonery that we have often censured. Through many of the missteps of the saints of old, God has shown us that we should use His Word as the touchstone, and not go by the appearance and the personality of a man but rather by His Word alone. And it is also impious, vice versa, to condemn the teaching because of the missteps of the teacher.*

It is a great pity that Magister Philippus, so knowledgeable a man, was unable to see what Father had done in the right light. All the more so as Father had not kept hidden that his marriage had proceeded not out of fleshly love or lust but to reaffirm what he had taught.

This confirms completely the word of King Antigonos, who when asked why he brought a sacrifice to God, said; to protect him from his friends, because from his enemies he could protect himself. Also an example is the statement of the lawyer and legal adviser, Hieronymus Schurff, who had accompanied Father on an earlier difficult journey to Worms: "If a monk marries, so will all the world and also the Devil laugh, and his purpose of improving the Church will fail." My father believed rather that the Devil would cry at his marriage. King Henry VIII of England—of all persons, I might add here—is believed to have sent to my father and the Reformation a devastating broadside in which he insinuated that Father had undertaken the whole Reformation only to satisfy his own lust. This was, of course, before this king broke with the popish church in order to divorce his wife, Katherine of Aragon, and to marry Anne Boleyn. Previously, for his writing of AD 1521, *Assertio septem sacramentorum adversus Martinum Lutherum* (Defense of the Seven Sacraments Against Martin Luther), he had been honored by the pope with the title *Defensor Fidei*, Defender of the Faith. It is pleasing to note that my father had capably responded with his open letter, *Martinus Lutherus contra Henricum Regem Angliae.*

My mother's decision to marry Martin Luther under these circumstances—which could not have remained hidden from her—must have required a great deal of courage.

The couple was consecrated by Bugenhagen, preacher at the town and parish Church of St. Mary's, and then in the presence of the guests was conducted fully clothed to the bridal bed, which had been prepared for them. This is an old custom intended to prove through the successful uniting of the flesh before witnesses, the virginity of the bride. Although only symbolic, this process and what followed in the solitude of the bedchamber must have caused great embarrassment for these two human beings, chaste and untrained in things of the flesh. Father would have suffered even more under these circumstances than Mother, who in the cloister had opportunities, notwithstanding the imminent penalties, to have become acquainted through her sister nuns, above all Ave von Schönfeld, with the desires of love of another person, be they man or woman. Also, there were confessors in the cloisters who knew how to seductively approach their penitents and to give pleasure to themselves and their wards. This was of course done in the name of Christ and grounded in the cloister's pledge of obedience. So one can assume that Mother in the bridal bed would with experienced hands have made the process easier for my father.

What my mother must have gone through moves me even today to great pity and hurt. It was the general belief that marriage between a monk and a nun would bring forth the Antichrist. Though Erasmus ridiculed this belief when he said, "Then the world must be full of Antichrists," it can still be imagined what fears and burdens my mother must have endured, which only found relief for both parents when the midwife handed them a healthy baby boy, not with a twisted foot or a withered left hand. That was my eldest brother, Johannes, born on the 7th of June, AD 1526.

To protect her motherhood from the Antichrist, in whom all Christians are taught to believe, required the most solid faith of my mother and much encouragement from my father in view of the overwhelming rage of all enemies but also of many friends of the Reformation.

My mother heard people whisper that Father was the son of the Devil, who under the guise of a traveling gem trader had gained entrance into the house of a Wittenberg burgher and seduced the daughter. The bishop who spread this rumor from the pulpit did not care that our father was born not in Wittenberg but in Eisleben.

So Mother had to fight the additional fear that she might be married to the son of the Devil. As my mother told me, not without me first taking a pledge that her oldest son would never discover it, she had before the birth as well as afterward often dreamed of the Antichrist, who in many guises met her as the enemy of the Lamb, as Judas Iscariot, as the servant of Belial, as the second Beast of the Abyss with the sign 666, and even—and this was the worst dream—in the guise of a sweet boy, like the Christ Child in the crib, who smiled angelically at her. She revealed to me that she often fearfully checked on Johannes during his childhood and adolescence but saw nothing unusual. For the rest of us children she had no such fear.

The celebration of my parents' wedding on the 13th of June, 1525, proceeded more or less in a hurry, which caused Magister Philippus to complain audibly. The wedding was attended by friends from Wittenberg, Lucas Cranach, Justus Jonas, Johann Apel, and Johannes Bugenhagen. Fourteen days later, again on auspicious Tuesday, the so-called feast took place, to which friends and relatives were invited, most importantly among them his parents from Mansfeld, who all attended church and the feast afterward. Magister Philippus, despite his initial reservations, let himself be persuaded to attend.

My father was very cheerful concerning the feast and wrote to Leonard Koppe, who had assisted in freeing the nuns, "Bring a barrel of the best Torgau beer. I will pay the delivery charge and everything else honestly. I would have sent a cart but didn't know if it would be appropriate, as the beer must be well rested and cold so that it tastes good. If it does not meet these demands, you will be punished so that you shall drink it all alone."

The gifts were plentiful: the good town of Wittenberg gave twenty guldens and a barrel of Einbeck beer; the gracious elector Johann, later called Johann the Steadfast, successor to Frederick the Wise, gave one hundred guldens. And now comes the reason why I recollect all this: I want to show my mother in all her daily cleverness wherein one should consider and remember that she had not long before escaped the closed world of the cloister: Cardinal Albrecht, elector, archbishop of Magdeburg and Mainz, archchancellor of the Holy Roman Empire for Germany (*Archicancellarius per Germaniam*), and thus the most powerful man after the emperor, a great enemy of Father's, the protector of the seller of indulgences, Johann Tetzel, sent twenty guldens for the wedding, which my father angrily rejected because it was obviously a ploy by the cardinal to show how easily Luther could be taken in by money. So the cardinal's servant, who had to deliver the money, was sent away by Father. But below at the front door, as the emissary attempted to escape from my father's wrath, stood my mother and seized the guldens. She was naturally smart enough not to tell Father about it at the time but rather quietly include the money in the household purse.

Reader, I must insert here what made Father later, at the end of the 1530s, particularly angry with the cardinal. But I suspect that the reasons of justice and mercy, which my father gave for his attacks against the man, were not decisive. His concern was his new Gospel, whose sworn enemy the cardinal was. Father simply used the cardinal's apparent infringement in the case that I am about to relate as a palatable reason to rail against him with the crudest words without giving the legal side of the case appropriate recognition.

In January AD 1539 appeared his writ "Against the Bishop of Magdeburg, Albrecht Cardinal," an elaboration of comments already put forth in a sermon, then transcribed and printed, which in a most ruthless manner laid open the bishop's failures.

Cardinal Albrecht had in Halle a trusted servitor, money manager, and builder, Hans Schenitz, also called Hans von Schönitz, with whom he conducted all sorts of unholy financial business. Now the estates in the archbishopric complained of Albrecht's ever-increasing demands for money, which sums they did not want to give before all the approved expenditures had been accounted for. This, Schönitz was anxious to avoid because of the accounting demanded from him, but the archbishop assured him of his protection. Now Albrecht needed money and also a scapegoat, so he sacrificed his servitor and imprisoned him in the castle of Giebichenstein in AD 1534. Schönitz was interrogated under torture and finally confessed, with signature and seal, to having committed theft from the archbishopric. (Shortly before his death, however, he recanted.) For this, according to Saxon law, the death penalty applied if the stolen sums reached a certain amount. He was sentenced, hastily carted to the Galgenberg Gallows Hill, hoisted up, and for two years left hanging there till the wind broke him free. His goods were confiscated to the benefit of Albrecht.

I will not deny that Albrecht later consented to a certain compensation for the Schönitz family—not, however, because he regretted his evil deed but rather because he feared my father and his accusative writings.

Renowned jurists, including Hieronymus Schurff from Wittenberg, confirmed the legality of the archbishop's proceedings and even the death sentence, although this does not absolve him from blame. But the archbishop was not the accused; rather, he was the accuser and the victim of the theft, the latter, however, not without his involvement.

It was said in Halle that Albrecht expressed satisfaction at the gallows death of Schönitz and even sent a servant to convince himself of the successful hanging. They say in Halle that even after hanging and drying in the wind, Schönitz's body bled anew when Albrecht's servants stepped beneath the gallows. Also, at various times mandrakes started to grow under the hanged, and if people tried to pull them out they shrieked horribly as if lamenting the victim's death.

In addition to the theft of money, which the cardinal wanted to punish, and which Schönitz had committed on the cardinal's behalf and for his benefit, there was the thought in his mind that the main witness to his reprehensible ways had to disappear: from Schönitz's house on the market to Moritzburg Castle, an underground passage allowed his servitor to provide a supply of new and healthy virgins for the cardinal's love nest in the Moritzburg Castle. The cardinal was known to be a lustful deflowerer, for which my Herr Father angrily attacked him. The gist of this was that the worthy cleric had spent many thousands of guldens for his whorehouse on the Moritzburg, for which Schönitz was held responsible. But since this money could not be included in the official budget of the archbishopric, Schönitz was unable to justify himself.

Here Father could well and gladly have mentioned the cardinal's precious collection of relics in the Cathedral at Halle, for the completion of which vast sums were needed, which Schönitz must have helped procure. But perhaps he thought his writ "Against the Idol at Halle," which together with the Ninety-Five Theses he had sent the cardinal with the request for the discontinuance of indulgences, would be enough, since his publication was widely known.

I will insert here a small list of what was already there and attracted visitors from all over the empire, because viewing them shortened their time in purgatory through an "overspecial indulgence": a piece of the body of patriarch Isaac; manna from heaven, which once fell in the desert; a piece of the burning bush of Moses, which once every hundred years rekindles; pitchers from the Wedding at Cana and a residual of wine that the Lord had changed from water; thorns from Christ's crown of thorns; one of the stones with which Stephen was stoned; etc., in total well over 9000 relics. These represented a total of 39,245,120 years and 220 hours of indulgences.

It will be clear to every reader that the cardinal could not spend enough hours in sinful whoring at Moritzburg to exhaust that amount of indulgences. But a Polish student who lived with us in our house remarked that it may be true, but one could certainly try.

Many well-meaning people of the highest standing who wanted to keep the peace and preserve the Reformation and also out of personal reasons attempted to dissuade my father from publishing his work "Against the Bishop of Magdeburg." But he had again his qualms of conscience, as at the imperial diet in Worms: "Here I stand, I can do no other," and the document was printed by Hans Lufft.

In the year 1536 in Frankfurt on the Oder, several members of the Hohenzollern family, to which Cardinal Albrecht belonged, gathered, among them Duke Albrecht of Prussia; his chancellor, Hans von Kreytzen; Elector Joachim II of Brandenburg; his brother Hans von Küstrin; Margrave George of Ansbach; and Johann Albrecht, coadjutor bishop of the Archdiocese of Magdeburg, and wrote a letter to Chancellor Brück of the elector of Saxony, in which the latter was asked to dissuade Luther from publishing his ruthless attacks against their relation, Cardinal Albrecht, thus bringing shame on their dynasty.

One can see here what a great force our father represented in Germany when he responded coolly: One should not interfere with his writing but rather better ensure that their family member, Cardinal Albrecht, renounce the debauchery, fornication, and ostentation and similar sins, which sins, not Luther, bring shame to their family. And so the document, as mentioned, appeared and caused a great sensation.

In his fury, Father could not see that Cardinal Albrecht was not purely an evil man. He was a humanist, highly educated and interested in the excellent paintings of Albrecht Dürer, Lucas Cranach, and Matthias Grünewald as well as beautiful buildings, some of which he left behind, among them the new market church of Our Dear Lady, the one in which Father was eventually laid out. And just at the beginning of my father's reformatory activity, the cardinal was open to its ideas to such an extent that he even expressed the intent to marry, in which he was encouraged by my father. Albrecht's goodwill subsided when he realized that Luther's work was tantamount to the destruction of the entire Old Church, whether he wanted it or not.

CHAPTER 5

. . . relates what I can remember from my first years.

Four siblings, Johannes, Elisabeth, Magdalena, and Martin, were born before me, and a year after me, Margarethe, who died in AD 1570 at only thirty-six years old, giving birth to her ninth child. Five years after Margarethe's birth, Mother gave birth to a still-born child and was afterward herself almost dead.

I counted then seven springtimes and can remember how the midwife and the doctor said that Mother was nearer dead than living. She was already forty years old, not an auspicious age to be giving birth. As a doctor, today I say that my parents had probably not taken sufficient precaution when they embraced each other in love, as there is first Onan's method. Though about this Father had ranted in a lecture on Genesis: "To produce semen as the Old Testament Onan, to excite a woman, and the same moment to frustrate her is one of the worst sins." Second would be the suggestion of Soranus of Ephesus (a little older), who recommended that after the ejaculation of the man the woman should withdraw, go into a crouch and sneeze. Additionally, she could try to use a handkerchief to wipe the semen from within her body. This method seems to me to be somewhat uncertain, as sneezing in a squatting position after having physical pleasure is not easy to bring about. Third relates to the use of an herbal bouquet impregnated with various essences, of which there are acacia juice, honey, olive oil, lead ointment, or frankincense. This method has the advantage that if the husband makes the introduction and the removal of the bouquet, taking the proper time, it can easily lead to pleasure for both. Fourth relates to the heating of the testicles of the man through their plunging into hot water before coupling, which should weaken or kill the semen already in storage or in its place of origin. This method is awkward and uncertain because of the preparation of the water and keeping it hot and also does not raise the pleasure of the man for the approaching coupling. Under fifth would be recorded that during lactation the woman is said to be infertile, but at the same time intercourse should ordinarily be avoided because the mother is still recovering. So one can be of two minds about this method.

In recent times there have been coatings made from animal gut, sheep or hog, actually intended to prevent diseases but also pregnancies.

I have again been deviating here somewhat, because I cannot refrain from lecturing and telling people what is good for them, but will now return quickly to Mother. After the stillbirth of the child, she often fainted and became more and more ill. We children were sent out of the room, soon creeping back—unnoticed at first—to the bed. Father did not move from her side, even canceled an important trip to Schmalkalden ordered by the elector, and attempted through incessant prayers to keep Mother alive. Magister Philippus also prayed for her and begged his friends likewise to pray. Everyone knew what the beloved woman meant to Luther and their children. Other friends cared, and the worried elector on the 10th of February sent a deer to her as a gift.

All this concern, including prayers and gifts, along with Mother's own strong will, led in the end to a gradual recovery. A repeated bloodletting on the pale and deteriorated patient, in my current medical view, certainly did not help. She left her room on the 26th of February but could at first only slowly move throughout the house, during which she would have to lean on a chair or a table for support. Only on April 8th could Luther report to Magister Philippus that his wife had finally recovered.

At last the large household, to whose description I will soon come, could resume its regular course. And also the children, not just my siblings and I, felt again the very necessary hand. Besides Father's own children, nieces and nephews were to be found in our family. When Father's sister Katharina, married name Kaufmann, and her husband had died prematurely, the five orphans, Cyriak, Fabian, Andreas, Lene, and Else, had been taken in to our household.

Additionally, there were the four children of my deceased Aunt Margarethe, Father's sister, two other nephews of Father's, and a grandniece of Mother's. The people of Wittenberg shook their heads at the generosity of my parents, who soon had a number of children in their house who were not easy to oversee. Then there was the further addition of Anna Strauss, the granddaughter of another sister of Father's, as well as Hans Pollner, another sister's son. There was also anger, mainly with the niece Lene, who behaved so unreasonably that Father threatened to marry her to a soot-covered foundryman instead of cheating a pious man with her.

One can imagine what turmoil at times ruled in the Black Monastery, so much in fact that Georg Helt from our town disadvised Prince George of Anhalt from quartering at the Luther house because the hubbub was so great that it was detrimental to serious study.

Father, fortunately, had a measure of peace in his study, situated southward in the building in a tower. However, he was angry when the construction of the city wall, which was being fortified, came too close to the house and garden, so much so that at the end of 1541 he wrote an irate letter to Friedrich von der Grüne, the elector's master of ordnance and fortress engineer. I present the letter here in a shortened form:

My Dear Master of Ordnance,

You know that you are forbidden by my gracious Lord from building too close or too injurious to me. Now out of your own obstinacy and iniquity, you buried the middle chamber up to the trelliswork, which without doubt the Devil has commanded you to do.

It is plain to everybody that it is not your wall construction that concerns you but this house. You want to drive me out and drag the princely letter and seal through the mire. Therefore I desire that as soon as you receive this letter you will clear the rubble away from the other chamber, since I do not want it there, and this wish you must carry out immediately; otherwise I shall report you to our gracious Lord the Elector. Now God be with you, and may He make you see the light, because otherwise you will soon go to hell. Your sin and wickedness are entirely your own responsibility, and let this letter serve you as a warning. There have been much worse devils and tyrants than you, but they all had to relent and never saw the sun again.

One can see how Father's anger increases, and he threatens with hell. Since the letter was of no use, and the threat to invoke the prince did not effect any reaction, the damned-to-hell engineer was evidently acting with the approval of the elector, who wanted Wittenberg strongly fortified. Not for the first time did Father use the threat of hell to enforce his purely earthly will.

It was a great relief, especially for Mother, that our Aunt Lene was in the house to assist in the household and help keep the children in hand. She was Mother's aunt and had escaped the convent one year after Mother. She died in AD 1537.

It will be appreciated that so many children cannot constantly behave themselves. I had, for example, a great quarrel with my cousin Florian von Bora, who had taken my knife away and never returned it. I lost the fight and greatly fretted, especially because out of cowardice I had not fought long enough to recover the knife. That was in the summer AD 1542. And then entered my father for me. At that time Florian, together with my brother Johannes, was attending the school of Father's good and trusted acquaintance Marcus Crodel in Torgau to study Grammatica et Musica. He wrote angrily to Marcus that he might give Florian a triple spanking, since he not only had taken my, Paul's, knife but had also had the cheek to claim that he, Martin Luther, had given it to him as a present.

One can imagine with what satisfaction I heard Johannes tell how Florian was vigorously laid upon and with loud screams received the strokes of the cane. Out of sheer friendship to my father, Master Crodel applied the cane in person.

On the whole, my and my siblings' childhood years, in comparison to those of other children, were joyful, disturbed for me only through fear of my father. We had the garden, the yard, the cattle, the bees, the orchard, the fishpond nearby, the many housemates and students, who always tried to keep on the right side of us, many visitors, and many people of high rank, who would pat us on the head and bring gifts along. Also, we roamed with our parents in the region, and Mother would carry along a heavy basket full of food and drink while Father praised God's beautiful nature.

On the way home, when the basket was empty, mushrooms and berries would be gathered. In passing we would meet hunters with crossbows and pikes who had been hunting deer and wild pigs. Other children we encountered on the lanes were unable to go to school because they had to oversee their small brothers or sisters, help at the spinning, tend to the geese, work in the gardens or houses or in their fathers' shops or on the land, run errands, and many other things. At twelve years old, one could already become an apprentice and sometimes by fifteen a journeyman. As an apprentice, one had to work hard in the household of the master's wife and as a journeyman even harder, and most had little hope of ever becoming a master.

I know that I spent these innocent years (I believe I was only six or seven years old) already interested in things of nature and its phenomena. So I could stare long into the hearth, thereby disturbing our Aunt Lene and the cook at their work, and wonder how the wood, crackling and smoking, turned into something else that looked so different from the wood. Could one perhaps convert other material, I asked myself later, and even change it from a lower level to a higher one?

Also, I collected various stones from the garden and the banks of the Elbe River and arranged them according to weight and appearance. Once I took a newly hatched chicken by the neck and held it in the air until it no longer made any movement because it could no longer breathe. I counted in order to determine how long it could remain alive without air. Then I held my breath and tested it on myself. The chick, by the way, lay in the grass for quite a while and did not stir. I blew air into its beak, and lo! it stood up and ran away. According to the numbers, the chick had been able to hold its breath longer than I.

Once a fisherman on the Elbe, instead of throwing a fish back in the water, gave it to me because it was too small to eat. I took my little knife and clumsily cut it open because I wanted to see how it looked on the inside. It was all mushy, but I could at least recognize the swim bladder, which I had already heard about. I attempted to blow it up, but I did not succeed.

My experiments did not always go off lightly. As I one day observed the chickens in the chicken coop and the sparrows, which were thievishly serving themselves in the chicken feed and then quickly flying away again whenever one came near, I wondered why the chickens, which counted themselves among the bird species, did not properly fly. Perhaps they did not have the desire or they had not had the practice.

So I took one of the chickens and quietly stole up to the tower. There in the tower room I opened a window and threw the chicken out. It cackled loudly, fluttered, and hurtled down, landing pretty hard. I got a big fright, descended quickly, took the chicken, which gave me a reproachful look and whose leg pointed outward at a strange angle, and hastily brought it again into the chicken coop. It was not long before Father learned of this prank. He took a cane that hung on the door in the kitchen and took me up into the tower room. He sat down, looked at me sadly, and said, "You are big enough to understand that God has commanded me to punish you. The chicken limps and does not lay eggs anymore, as your mother said to me, and also you have desecrated this room, which for me is full of profound memories."

Then his sadness changed into anger, and without any connection to my prank he shouted, "How can I love you and make you an heir of what I possess or of my spiritual goods? Shitting, pissing, crying so that the house is filled with your noise—shall all this induce me to care for you?" And thus he succeed in increasing his anger and in achieving the proper mood for the punishment. He seized me by the collar, laid me over a table, and struck me with the cane, which on the bare legs especially hurt. I screamed and called, "That's enough, it's enough," until Father stopped. Then he ordered me every day to take care of the chicken until it once again laid eggs. And I did so, turning over many stones looking for woodlice and worms, which I let the chicken eat. It became accustomed to it and came more quickly than any of the others, hobbling and flapping its wings, whenever I went into the chicken coop. However, it never again lay eggs but became fat and was soon slaughtered. So it is obvious the Devil takes one if one is spoiled and not beaten, as Father said.

After years it became clear to me what my father meant by the "desecration" of the tower chamber. He had there his tower experience, as he himself designated it, and I beg the reader's indulgence here for the long quotation, as it contains the spiritual foundation of the new church:

It is true that formerly I was a pious monk and was so strongly attached to my order that I would dare to say: if ever a monk came to heaven through the monkhood, I would be one of them. All my fellow monks could testify to that. If it had lasted longer, I would have tortured myself to death with watching and praying, reading and other work. Because if only a small temptation to sin came to me, I found no consolation, and neither baptism nor monkhood could help me.

Christ and his baptism I had in this way already long wasted. There was I, the most miserable monk on earth, day and night with lamentations and despair from which no one could preserve me.

I not only did not love—no, I hated the just God, who punished sinners as if it was not enough that the miserable sinner was eternally lost through original sin and who through every conceivable hardship was oppressed by the Law of the Ten Commandments. And had God not added through the Gospel pain upon pain, and by His Gospel threatened us with his righteousness and his anger? So I raged in my wild and confused conscience and tried frantically to understand that passage of Paul, Hebrew 10:38, for I was burning to know what St. Paul wanted. Until God showed mercy, and I, who had been thinking day and night, understood the meaning of the words, namely, "The just shall live by faith as God's gift." Here I felt that I was completely reborn and that I had entered through the open gates into Paradise itself, and it seemed to me that I saw the Holy Scripture in a completely different light and had before my very eyes the works of God through which He makes us powerful, the wisdom of God, through which He makes us wise, the strength of God, the holiness of God, the glory of God. And as much as I had hated the righteous

> words of God, so much more now I raised up these sweet words in my love so that those passages of Paul became my gate of Paradise: "Now the just shall live by faith."

My life long as an adult have I never lost the awe for the spiritual and physical pain that my father was exposed to through his quest for the righteous God. And I began to understand, though not to approve, that from these agonies of conscience probably at times arose blind, hateful, and today in my eyes quite unchristian or unevangelical raging against all he viewed as enemies of his work.

Or was this actually unchristian and unevangelical? Father was a very knowledgeable man, though not seldom of crude behavior and talk; was is possible that he did not see the discrepancy between Christ's commandment of love and his own actions? In the next chapter we will see how he did not see this as a discrepancy at all.

CHAPTER 6

... is a significant deviation from the chronology of my report, as it will occur again, but which here is very important because my life was decisively influenced by it.

We will take first Thomas Müntzer and the peasants. In the beginning, as Father on his inspection tour in the spring of AD 1525 was shown the "Twelve Articles of the Christian Association of the Memmingen Peasant Meeting," he recognized the justice of the peasants' cause and criticized their lords without restraint:

> They have established the Twelve Articles, among which are some so righteous that they put you, the lords and landowners, to shame before God and the world. It is, God knows, unbearable so to endlessly tax and maltreat the people. Such filth and turmoil on earth we owe to you alone, princes and nobles, unseeing bishops, mad priests and monks, and now behold that some of the Twelve Articles of the peasants are so fair and equitable that before God and the world you could accept them without shame to your reputation.

He praised the Christian character of the peasants' demands but instructed them at the same time that it is equally wrong to respond to even such ghoulish injustice of the authorities with similar violence. The Christians, so he wrote, fight for themselves not with the sword or the arquebus but rather with the cross and suffering, just as Christ did not take the sword but rather hung on the cross.

What Father demanded here was beyond human. The peasants were maltreated, forced into compulsory labor more than agreed upon in the law of the land, bled white from taxes, had the common land taken from them; the men were put in bondage to the nobles and oppressed by the church with large and small tithes; they always had to remain in the same village, could marry only upon the approval of the noble, and much more. If the harvest was ripe and threatened by rain or thunderstorm, they first had to harvest the noble's land. If wild game came into the fields and destroyed the crop, they had to put up with it.

One can imagine the peasants coming from the noble's fields to find their own field ravaged. One can imagine the young peasant swain who sees a maiden at the village well, falls in love, and may not marry or mate with her. And if finally he is granted the marriage, he must suffer his lord to sleep with his newly married wife and deflower her according to his *jus primae noctis,* or right of the first night. Or he has to give his lord compensation in money.

And all of this, according to my father, they should endure or challenge only with words. I call that requiring something beyond human. The peasants, however, were not beyond human but resisted at times in a very fearsome, brutal manner. The murder of Count Ludwig of Helfenstein and another fifteen knights, who had to run the gauntlet until they were all dead, is still in memory.

This and other events induced my father, who feared for the Gospel, to issue his most outraged invocation: "Against the Robbing and Murdering Hordes of Peasants."

Of course it should not be forgotten that Helfenstein had previously ordered his men-at-arms to slaughter the peasants' rearguard and had threatened the peasants with burning if they did not desist from their siege of the city and Castle Weinsberg.

The malignancy of Rohrbach, who cooked his private soup using the misguided peasants, is proven and drew upon him the terrible punishment of slow burning, as pronounced by the Steward of Waldburg. Many other peasants were tormented and killed although they had renounced Rohrbach and his deeds. Still the nobles showed no mercy and acted as Father had told them (however, even before his missive went out):

> Therefore, dear Lords, redeem here, rescue here, help here. Whoever can, stab, beat, strangle. Should you die here on the field, all the better. A more blessed death you can never gain than to die in obedience to God's words and commands, and in the service of love to rescue your neighbor from hell and the Devil's bond.

Especially severely he deals with Thomas Müntzer, an equally forceful and brutish orator, who enticed the peasants with his vision of God's kingdom on earth and thereby led many to their death.

Father in AD 1525, on his trip through the land, preached in Wallhausen, Stolberg, and Nordhausen, in Weimar, Orlamünde, Kahla, and Jena. In many places he aroused opposition and loud protests and also had to fear for his life because for many people he had become the princes' faithful servant who had betrayed his own Gospel. They wanted, like Müntzer, to erect the Kingdom of God on earth, by violence, if required.

Who would wonder that he found himself full of doom and gloom, especially when he learned that the Electoral Saxon government and also the Wise Frederick's successor, John, hesitated to use force against the peasants? Frederick was at the time at a hunting lodge in Lochau on his deathbed and urged the living: "Go about everything with kindness."

Father feared for his work. Since the divine order was endangered by the peasants, the Christian authorities were obliged to take up the sword and to protect the godly order here on earth. That was the condition for the victory of Christ over the powers of darkness and chaos, over Satan, who wanted to destroy the new Gospel by means of rebellion.

Terrible was the action the authorities took at Frankenhausen against the Müntzer-led peasants, whom he had promised victory. Thousands of people had gathered to him, not only peasants, also miners, craftsmen from the towns, clerks, and clergymen. Five thousand were left on the battlefield, while the princes' army lamented six dead. One sees the inequality of the weapons and might. Luther regretted the many dead but, with Matthew, contended: all that take the sword shall perish with the sword. (Naturally, not the nobles, who as the God-appointed authority were to take the sword.) It were better if all the peasants were slayed than the princes and authorities, because the peasants had taken up the sword without the power of God. His theology told him that the Gospel distinguishes between two realms, one spiritual, which is the Kingdom of God, where compassion and mercy reign, and the other an earthly realm in which rules God's wrath and the relentless need to struggle against evil. And again his demands on the Christians were beyond human:

"Though the bloodhounds and the sows among the princes were ignoramuses, still one must endure them if God chose to plague us through them."

Later it was probably clearer to him that he had proceeded too hard, and he decided to remain silent in such troubled times.

Still, the suffering of the peasants, even if it seemed self-inflicted, did affect him. To Nicolaus von Amsdorf, toward the end of June AD 1525, he wrote with concern that in Franken eleven thousand peasants had been slaughtered, in Württemberg six thousand, ten thousand in Swabia, two thousand in Alsace. So the poor peasants were slaughtered everywhere. Now one must let mercy prevail; otherwise you tear the bag on both sides. However, for Müntzer, whom he considered the originator of the turmoil and a creature of the Devil, he found no mercy, although at a table talk in the year of my birth, AD 1533, he remarked that the death of his false brother, as he called Müntzer, lay heavily on his, Luther's, neck. But then he clarified quickly that he had desired Müntzer's death because Müntzer had wanted to kill his Christ. A curious judgment for, strictly speaking, it contains doubts about the ultimate victory of Christ. Anyway, I do not understand it, being excused since I am no theologian.

As evidence that my father championed the *imitatio Christi* to such an extent that the normal man in his weakness could no longer follow, Hans Kohlhase may be mentioned, an honest man with a sense of honor like a gold balance. Kohlhase took his right in his own hands and attempted to create his own justice because the authorities did not protect him. The junker Günther of Zaschwitz, or rather several of his people, had encountered Hans Kohlhase in front of the inn in the village of Wellaune. Kohlhase was a horse trader from Cölln near Berlin and therefore a Brandenburg subject, who was en route to the fair at Leipzig. They took from him two horses because they believed or claimed they were stolen.

Out of that came a tremendous year-long dispute, which ended with the execution of Kohlhase, who too blindly and with arson and kidnapping and murder had insisted on his rights.

Father wrote about the arson in Wittenberg, clearly with a reflection on the margrave and elector Joachim von Brandenburg, who at the time had not yet converted to the new Gospel and at first protected Kohlhase:

> We live here between flames of fire, uncertain every hour if we will burn down. Some villages in the neighborhood

> have burned, and four times we have had fires in the town. The first consumed four houses. The other fires were passably extinguished. Surely this was caused by an enemy, because tinder, torches, gunpowder, and detonators were found. I have great suspicion that such has happened by the wickedness of Margrave Joachim, and I almost believe this devilry will hasten his end, and his iniquities will drive him to ruin.

Father here was obviously the victim of his own aversion against the then-Catholic margrave, because clearly the latter had nothing to do with the arson, which was committed by Kohlhase.

The execution of Kohlhase took place in Berlin, AD 1540, on the Rabenstein, the city's favored place of execution, through the wheel. The news reached Wittenberg, and though I was but seven years old, I remember the conversation at the table where the divergent opinions over Kohlhase were warmly debated.

In the Year of our Lord 1534, in a letter, Kohlhase had turned to my father, some saying he had actually come secretly into the Black Monastery and had asked Father in person for advice and help. My father had responded in the following way in a letter that was publicly displayed in many places:

> *It is certainly true that you suffered damage and shame and that it is your right to seek justice, but not with sins or injustice. Where you can find justice, seek it, as Moses said. Injustice does not become justice through another injustice. But can you not gain justice, so there is no other advice other than to suffer the injustice. Therefore, if you desire my advice (as you have written), so I advise you to take peace wherever you can, and rather suffer in property and damaged honor than to continue in your current doings.*

It is understood particularly well from this that Father lived for heaven and put God's mercy and Christ's suffering and death for our sins over all mankind's searching after earthly justice. However, it is the example of Kohlhase that again makes clear how difficult, if not nearly impossible, it is to lead such a life. And had he not himself, when he believed an injustice had been done to him, *per exemplum*, through Henry VIII or through the Papists, struck out at them, and threatened them with hell and damnation? But again, I am not a theologian and do not understand the difference.

Especially the peasants' revolt, but also the contention and bickering with Erasmus, Huldrych Zwingli, Bodenstein called Karlstadt, and many others worried my father so that from time to time he believed he should give everything up and, rather than theology, find a different way to earn a living for himself and his family. Therefore in AD 1527 he requested his former schoolmate from the time in Magdeburg, Wenzeslaus Link in Nuremberg, to send him woodworking tools because he wanted to learn the craft. Our mother told us how he diligently used the plane and fiddled with the lathe and rotating iron. After he twice had soundly drilled into his own hand, which brought back his mental balance, he gave up the craft. At home, anyway, I found nothing that was made by my father's hand.

CHAPTER 7

. . . describes how we celebrated Christmas.

Christmas, and the end of the year, was a time full of wonder and also full of fear, however, mostly of wonder. The Lord God did not consider it a crime to let the sun go down so early with everything covered in snow and the land icy cold. Often the Elbe was frozen, and the fishermen had to hack holes in the ice in order to do their fishing. Our father told us that it was not always so cold in Germany so that God must have sent this weather to punish us people. Or perhaps it was the Antichrist in Rome who was guilty.

In the afternoon when I returned from Magister Philippus's instructions with red hands and frozen ears—because even though it was not far, the magister did not keep his house properly heated—then was it so pleasant and warm with the smell of roasting and baking at home. Father was in a good mood when he came down from his study for dinner. He would joke with us, and it was often so cheerful and fun. On such an occasion Father told us a funny story about the fool Albrecht from Torgau, who did not want to go up to heaven because it must be very cold there with rain and snow, but much preferred being in hell, where one could roast fine apples and pears in the heat. And indeed, for a moment I could almost understand the fool.

When dinner was over and our Aunt Lene and the maids had cleaned the kitchen, and the fire for the next morning had been prepared, then the women would get out their spinning wheels and work by the light of the tallow candles, because all the wool must be spun by fastnacht, and in the badly lit kitchen they would tell scary tales like the saga of the Wild Hunter, which I always wanted to hear again even though it greatly frightened me. Did not the saying go that if you were not careful and tried to seek protection quickly when the Wild Hunt raced near, the Wild Hunter himself would dive down, grab you, and take you up with him into his cursed realm?

But if the faithful Eckart went ahead and warned the people, they were able to seek safety. Only one should be sure not to stick one's head out the window from curiosity as the hunt went by. Then one's head would become so big it could not be drawn back in again.

I was very fond of the faithful Eckart because, in another tale, he dealt so gently with the boys and their pitchers of beer, which they had bought at the tavern. Once the Wild Hunter with his raging band went through the town of Schwarza in dark Thuringia. The faithful Eckart went ahead and told the people they must get out of the way. As the army raged through the town, two boys came along. They carried pitchers full of beer they had gotten from the tavern. The faithful Eckart bade them step aside. But the Wild Hunter, who had a great thirst, seized the pitchers and drank the beer. The boys were then miserable, because they feared the beating they would get when they arrived home without the beer. The faithful Eckart, however, said, "Be of good cheer, you boys. It was good that you allowed the Wild Hunter to drink all the beer. Go home now with your beer pitchers, but for the next three days, be silent about what has happened here." So the boys went home, and as they arrived they found the beer pitchers full of beer. And yet, how long can boys remain silent? They soon told of their experience, and from then on the beer pitchers remained empty. Of course, nobody had witnessed such ghostly events, but all had heard people whisper about them.

At other times, I would stare out the windowpane at the clouds being driven across the sky and hope to see my sisters Elisabeth and Magdalene, because it was said that in the Wild Hunter's band, children could also be seen who had died an unnaturally early death. My father would advise me in the strictest terms against such superstition. These tales were only the remnants of an old heathen worship, and the Wild Hunter was just the heathen god Odin, and the old woman Frau Holle riding with him in the wild army was really the goddess Frigg. And my sisters were with their Heavenly Father, where they had been brought by God's will to make them happy.

If my mother was not in the kitchen, having other things to do, the story of the sinful nun and the bridge would be told.

On the 9th of March, 1488, the bridge over the Elbe was almost completely washed away by high water, and the carpenters whom the elector had commissioned to rebuild it superstitiously believed, as a passing monk had warned them, that they must bury a living thing, a small child, on the bank near one of the pillars. And he, the monk, would send them the child. On the next day, as the carpenters were just finishing their work, a wagon, in which a nun and a child sat, came down to the riverbank. The nun gave the carpenters the child, and even though they suspected the child had been gotten by the monk and the nun in a sinful act, they proceeded with burying it anyway. After the bridge was completed, it survived the next flood of the Elbe and other floods to come and thus proved to be solid and stable. But the misdeed of the carpenters brought them no happiness. The elector learned what they had done, put them on trial, and condemned them to death by the wheel. But, he said, since they were victims of their own superstition, to which many were still adhering, he would grant them the clemency of the ax instead. And from then on the nun appeared on the bridge at midnight during every full moon and mourned her dead child. One should take care not to meet her, because her suffering and lamentations are so great that she tries to reduce them by transferring them to others.

That was a frightful tale, and if the maids, for example, had to relieve themselves at night, they would never walk alone across the courtyard to the privy, especially during a full moon. It was clear that neither our mother nor Aunt Lene, both of whom had been nuns and had fled the convent, would be allowed to hear that story or there would be holy thunder brought down on the maids for their foolish chattering. I must confess that I, however, listened gladly to such eerie stories, even though in bed I would have to clutch my brother out of fear until I fell asleep.

Of course we were always looking forward to Christmas, because then the food was especially rich and bountiful. On the 24th of December, which was the end of the Advent fast, liver sausage and sauerkraut would be served, and conversation at the table as well as Father's table talks, which were to become so famous later, would become very lively, because this was also one of his most beloved meals. Though sometimes my mother would have to admonish everyone when the conversation became too animated and the dinner neglected: "Why is it that you keep speaking without interruption and do not eat?" Tempers flared while the food got cold.

Since I collected all my mother's recipes (which made my beloved wife's work in the kitchen much easier), I can lay before you the recipe for sauerkraut.

In addition, you can serve bread in order to fill up the table companions before the proper meal. That will prevent them from finishing the sauerkraut and the sausage too quickly. Our mother often served the young hungry people a large bowl of millet gruel, which they had to eat first.

Sauerkraut: One needs liver sausage, cabbage, white wine and red wine, juniper berries, mustard, and salt. The heads of cabbage are cut into quarters and the core removed, but not too much so that the leaves do not fall apart.

In a large pot, place wood strips first and then small sticks over them so that a grill is created. Pour the white wine in, one and a half inches, almost as high as the grill. Then lay the cabbage quarters on the grill with the cut surfaces under. Cook for an hour, until the cabbage is tender. Take the cabbage out of the pot and cut into strips. Heat the red wine, and add salt, mustard, and juniper berries. Add the cabbage and mix. Put the sausage on top, and place over a small fire until the sausage is heated through.

In the past, when my father was a child, his family would observe a much stricter pre-Christmas fast, but at least they had the mouthwatering stollen fruitcake, and this brings to mind the following story.

Elector Ernst and his brother, Duke Albrecht of Saxony, complained in a letter to the pope about the suffering of the fast time before Christmas. They said there were in their cold lands no olive trees and also very little olive oil imported from the southern countries, which at any rate was too expensive for most of the people. So, with butter excluded for the fast time, there was only rapeseed oil with which to cook. And that was honestly good only as lamp oil or wagon wheel grease or for the production of soap, which, by the way, was already mentioned by the prophet Isaiah. However, rapeseed oil does not agree with their subjects. In short, they begged the pope to make an exception to the fast and allow butter to be used in the baking of the stollen.

And behold, the pope relented. It was Innocent VIII, who shamefully tolerated the prosecution of witches (in this, though, my father was not much better), and who before the papal election took to bribing numerous cardinals and who also was not adverse to simony. In the case of butter, however, he agreed that it would be an act of Christian charity to grant the exception. As a native Italian, he probably thought it was a sacrilege even to cook with anything other than olive oil or butter. His Christian charity, however, did not stop him from making the Saxons pay dearly for this papal butter bull in the form of a tax. The pope wrote: "As such, we are well disposed to accept your request and decree by Papal authority, by the power of this letter, that ye, your wives, sons, daughters, and all your obedient servants may freely and reasonably partake of butter instead of oil without incurring any penalty."

From then on stollen was again delicious, especially if raisins had been baked into it. These delightful cakes had a thoroughly Christian character to us because when we ate them, the shape of the cake reminded us of the Christ child wrapped in swaddling clothes by his mother Mary. As one can see, before my father's work for a new and reformed church took effect, there was this papal tax on each stollen, which was now abolished. Therefore I am of the opinion that the Reformation of the church was not without agreeable consequences, for instance, the tax exemption of the stollen.

With reason this cake, remindful of our Savior, is now called Christstollen, and if this comes from the great city of Dresden, it provides a special enjoyment. By this I do not mean to belittle the good city of Naumberg on the Saale River, where there is documentary evidence that a gift of Christstollen was given to Bishop Heinrich as early as AD 1329. Whether the bishop deserved this gorgeous pastry in God's name is not mentioned.

We children, through Advent and Christmas, had a very intimate relationship with our dear Lord Jesus. All the frills and all the veneration of the saints of the old church were in Father's new Evangelism greatly reduced, if not completely abolished. That greatly affected, for example, St. Nicholas, to whom the 6th of December is dedicated. As bishop of Myra in the eastern lands, he is said to have rescued an entire city from starvation by supplying them with many measures of wheat, which made him the patron saint of bakers. So the people have increasingly revered him, and he even became one of the fourteen Holy Helpers. By the time my father as a young boy attended the Cathedral School in Magdeburg, the Nicholas veneration had become widespread.

But my father preached: "There is no other mediator between God and men than Christ. Therefore, these saints' days are pernicious because they did not only elevate the saints, but they denigrated Christ. We do not say you should not praise the saints, but we want to grant Christ his own right. We were in error when we did not allow Christ to be our Savior but only thought him to be our judge. And the saints would have to come and intercede for us. We have not preached against the saints but against those who have substituted them for Christ."

Since Christ has to be the center of the Christian message and the saints should not come between God and the people, a new role had to be assigned to St. Nicholas by the new church: together with the Christ Child, he was allowed to bring gifts to the children on Christmas and on St. Nicholas Day. But if the children had been disobedient or badly behaved or had been lazy at school, then there were to be no gifts but the cane. This St. Nicholas alone may brandish, because Christ said, "Suffer little children, and forbid them not to come unto me: for of such is the kingdom of heaven." That Christ brandished a cane or carried a sack in which to stick the naughty children is not to be read in the scriptures.

But Christmas was first of all a joyful time, and our father's sermons in the town church helped:

> Today you will hear the story that happened tonight, which is reassuring and joyful. Because the angels in heaven are full of joy, which they impart to us and announce for everybody, though what happened does not concern them, but us. For the preaching of the angels goes: "I am telling you men, not us angels, because Christ was not born for our salvation." The angels are already blessed and have been so from the very beginning. Therefore, we are meant, not they.

> And now imagine how Mary, pregnant with the Christ Child and supported by Joseph, makes the toilsome journey to Bethlehem on an ass. How prudent of Joseph to provide his highly pregnant wife with a ride. Bethlehem lies to the south, like Schmiedeberg, Nazareth far to the north, like Brandenburg. It is a long journey, I believe between twenty and thirty miles.

At this point the people listened almost breathlessly, because from their own lives they could imagine such a journey.

Reader, you might ask me how I know my father's sermons so well. First, on Christmas we naturally went to church, as always, especially if Father was preaching. And second, among the burghers, peasants, students, soldiers, and visitors from other cities, there were always people who carefully transcribed all that was said and soon had it printed. The printers became rich, by the way; Father did not. Thus I have before me printed copies of my father's sermons and so am able to include one of them here.

So, holding their breath, the congregation listened as my father told in detail how the wife of a poor carpenter, greatly pregnant with child and with swollen breasts, could find no help and no shelter. They trudged along in search of lodgings, pulling the ass as they plodded, when Mary's waters broke and she went into labor. Now just imagine the anxiety of Joseph, unable to give his wife any assistance. Finally they were able to find a stable. Here the Mother of God, without a midwife or other help, had to bring the Child into the world. Perhaps Joseph with his carpenter's knife cut the umbilical cord of the Christ Child, and with cold water—they had no fire, no stove, or anything to warm it with—washed the child and dried him off and laid him to his mother's breast. And surely Joseph carried the afterbirth outside and buried it in a nearby field, as was the custom, so that nothing could harm the baby.

At this point a sigh of relief went through the crowd. People of course had heard the Christmas story many times, but through the emotional telling of my father, they experienced it anew. It can be understood that such an art of preaching extracts the money more easily out of the pockets of the listeners and that the collection for the community chest would grow. For out of these proceeds the poor of the city were provided, since the monasteries were no longer there to give them assistance. My father said that the turning to the Gospel and the conversion to Christianity must also reach into the purse, not as a prerequisite for the grace of God, but rather as a consequence.

CHAPTER 8

. . . must be begun here because otherwise chapter 7 would be too long. But, reader, do not despair; it will still be about how we celebrated Christmas.

God Almighty, what guests did we have! Giordano Bruno, the Italian scholar, who also taught in Wittenberg, where I met him in 1586, and who surely could not expect much good from the old church, with his views on the universe, the sky, the stars, and eternity, had related—not from his own experience, but from the tales of others, which I can confirm—how things proceeded in the Black Monastery: "All the world came to Wittenberg—Italians, French, Spanish, Portuguese, English and Scottish, Poles, Balkanese—because here wisdom had built a house and provided a richly laid table for the meal. All in all, there must at times have been thirty or more people who had to be fed."

I think Bruno meant the banquet *in abstracto.* But it is also true that our mother had many to look after and sometimes must have felt she was being pulled to pieces trying to provide everything. She'd say, "I must cut myself into seven pieces in order to be in seven places at the same time and manage seven different things. I must first be farming burgher, second a farmer, third a cook, fourth a milkmaid, fifth a gardener, sixth a winegrower, but seventh I am the doctorissa who for her famous husband has to be presentable and has to feed numerous guests all on a yearly salary of 200 guldens."

When my father would descend from the little tower room, in which we children were sometimes allowed to play if we were not too loud, and settle himself at the head of the table under the curious and interested glances of the fellow diners, he thanked God for his blessings and cast an appreciative glance at his wife. Then she was able to forget her cares for a short while. Still, my mother found it hard to bear when he made remarks on the uselessness and vanity of all human activity, the grubbing of money, and at the same time took a hearty pleasure in the delicious foods and home-brewed beer and princely wines that had been donated to him, which, without the assistance of our mother, the Lord God would hardly have rained on us.

Father would notice her resentment and quickly use words of praise in an attempt to make amends, since he realized that he himself had learned nothing about managing a household. And he actually had no facility with numbers. At the grammar school in Mansfeld, where you were made to wear a donkey collar as a punishment for speaking a German word, they saw no need to teach figures. How weak he was in numeracy is shown by the thank-you letter to Abbot Friedrich at Nuremberg, who had made a present to him of a clock: "Such a horologium is very convenient for me, but I would have to learn from the mathematics in order to get to know the nature and function of a clock. I have never seen the likes of one, have never given such a thing a thought, because the mathematics I do not understand."

He also felt the management of the household must be subject to the rule of the woman and said, "The wife can certainly make a man rich, but not the man the wife. The saved penny is better than the earned. So to be careful with the money is the best income."

It remains a mystery to me even now how my mother, raised from a very young age in a convent, could handle the daunting task of running this household. Her task was not made easier by the care for a learned, famous, complex, and often darkly melancholy man. Added to this was the never-ending construction work; the overseeing of the craftsmen; the bearing and raising of her children; the responsibility for all the farm animals, such as pigs—the swineherd included—horses, cows, goats, and poultry of every sort; the overseeing of servants; the tending of newly acquired gardens (at the Saumarkt and the Eichenpfuhl with beehives and hops); the purchase of building materials, if possible at tolerable prices; and hundreds of other things kept her busy. Father said, "Out of this rotten cloister my Katharina is making a paradise on this dark earth."

He did not make her life any easier when he tried to battle his melancholy through hasty and excessive eating and drinking, which then led again to physical discomfort. One time Johannes, our eldest brother, when he found Mother in the kitchen weeping because of her growing concerns, tried to comfort her by giving her her Christmas present early, a limewood angel figure. In tears, she smiled at him and was again in better spirits.

We children looked at Christmastime differently from our father and, in turn, from our mother, who, together with the maids and servants and helpful Aunt Lene, literally had her hands full with all the great Christmas preparations.

When time came to go shopping at the Christmas market, we children eagerly attended. The Christmas market in our town had taken place since AD 1468, and one could purchase whatever one's heart desired so long as one had sufficient pfennigs and groschens. Father, for his part, expressed no praise for the Wittenberg market: "Our market is shit, and it is also expensive."

We children found it pleasantly noisy and full of color, and the drovers from the entire principality, from Pomerania and Poland, the bakers and blacksmiths, plumbers, coopers, horse traders, barbers, lithotomists and tooth pullers and faith healers, the hatters and hoodmakers, the saddlers and bag makers, the shoemakers and leather belt makers, the tailors, the chandlers, and the wood carvers all offered their wares and handiwork with shouting and yelling. Delicious smells came from the town hall cookshop, where we never ate, though, since Mother was careful with money and said that food at home tasted better and was also cheaper.

There were also cripples to see, and people with mouths purposely cut from ear to ear when they were children still in diapers to confer to them a permanent grin, then allowed to heal; others were given flattened noses that the parents had caused by binding small slats of wood across their babies' faces and so could exhibit them for money.

And then wondrously attired women sat in a tent, their eyebrows coal black and their lips painted red as blood, and clothes worn so that one could see their breasts, sometimes even their nipples, although there was no infant suckling there. Our mother pulled us very quickly past those tents. If we were accompanied by students boarding in the Black Monastery or Father's famuli, then would she become loud and urge us to hurry, because they attempted to pass the open tent flap as slowly as possible. Our maids, carrying the purchases in their baskets, would blush and giggle and then walk past quickly.

The tent of the beautiful women stood not far from the stand of an old woman who peddled eggs. Because of the cold, she had her wares in a basket covered top and bottom with straw. But Mother never bought eggs from her. The maids whispered among themselves that she was a witch and laid the eggs herself.

Also, she was said to be a maker of weather and hail, and if she stared at you cross-eyed, then you had to take heed of your garden and fields. Also, the maids called her the flower witch, because even in the middle of winter she was said to have flowers to peddle. Nobody had seen them, but the rumors went around. It was also said that she would soon be hauled before the town council of Wittenberg, submitted to a torturesome interrogation, and brought to trial. A wonder that she did not leave the city. But perhaps she was not aware of any wickedness and did not know what the people were whispering.

We children would gladly stop for a storyteller or a bookreader, and we especially liked to hear the story from the book *A Diverting Tale of Till Ulenspiegel, Born on the Land near Brunswick, and How He Spent His Life.* The listeners laughed and exulted when they heard how the sly fool got the best of the duke of Celle. The duke forbids Ulenspiegel to step anywhere on his land. Therefore, Till loads a cart with earth from outside the duchy, sits on top of it, and with loud crows of laughter takes the cart in front of the duke's castle, where the duke cannot punish him because he has set no foot upon the duke's land. And even at his funeral, Ulenspiegel gives the duke no rest. He slips from the hands of the bearers and ends upright in the grave. And thus they buried him at last.

Mother purchased presents for many people, for friends, for our servants, for the godchildren of my parents—so many that Father himself could not recall all the names—for us children, naturally, which we were at times sixteen in number in the household. This was accomplished while we were not there, while the servants and maids were allowed to look for something themselves.

On Christmas Day, our father preached two sermons in the city church. We children attended the second service with Mother and were already impatient because dinner was waiting at home. And the presents. And the singing. And the nativity play.

At our Christmas dinner there were various dishes, depending upon what the elector or other well-meaning princes and rich people had sent us as presents, often a deer or a wild pig. Most of all, however, I liked the imitation roast venison and, before that, the spicy beef soup. After that, there were all kinds of stewed fruit, softened dried plums with honey, and various tarts, among them the tasty butter stollen.

After the many dishes had been cleared away, everyone, the entire household included, joined in singing the beautiful song written and composed by my father on the occasion of the birth of our sister, Margarethe, in December AD 1534, "From Heaven Above to Earth I Come," which poetically brings to mind the story of the birth of our Lord Jesus Christ.

This song of our father's—really a children's song with the little manger, the baby Jesus, the little children—which did not follow the strict rules of poetry (as my teacher Melanchthon once pointed out without wanting to deny its heartwarming effect), was soon printed, and now I hear it sung everywhere, even by the Catholics and other old believers. Though my father would certainly have preferred they were converted to the new Gospel.

This song warms your heart and makes you feel happy at the same time. And perhaps, when Father wrote the text and composed the melody, he felt the truth of his saying: "A happy fart never comes from a miserable ass."

Music and singing were for my father vital elements of life, and I have heard him say that if it was not by theology, then certainly by music would he have earned his living. "Music makes people cheerful and contemplative and is a gift of God, for which we Christians should daily thank Jesus. One of the most beautiful and splendid gifts of God is Musica. Satan is the enemy of music, because it dispels many temptations and evil thoughts. Musica is one of the finest arts. The notes bring the text to life. Musica banishes the spirit of sadness. I myself," Father said, "have always been fond of it. Whoever masters this art has a good heart and is capable of most things."

I have unfortunately been little involved in it, although as a child and also as a student, I always enjoyed singing. But later my serious profession of a doctor gave me few opportunities to indulge in it.

After the song had been sung, the sharing of presents began. All of us children had been preparing for this through our Christmas fast, as Father had interpreted Psalm 147 to say, "One should teach the children to fast before Christ or St. Nicholas bestow their gifts." Adults should also fast, not to gain grace and favor with God by this supposedly good deed—that would be a papist idea—but rather to prepare oneself for the coming of Christ. Besides, so said my father in his sermon on works of mercy, everyone should fast in a way that is wholesome. I will not mention that many so fast that they make up for it in drink, that many fast so richly with fish and other delicacies that they would have come closer to fasting had they eaten meat, eggs, and butter. If a man finds that fish causes more wantonness in his flesh than meat and eggs, he should eat meat and eggs and not fish. By contrast, if a man finds that fasting disturbs the head and devastates the body, then he should cease fasting and eat, sleep, and be idle as much as is necessary for his health.

In Father's new belief, fasting took on a different form and meaning and has gradually become less important, which I as a physician regret, because it is not only in the tradition of Christianity, it is also healthful to the body when it is practiced with moderation and reason.

Of course, the fasting period reminds us of the Gospel and the heartfelt story of the temptation of Christ, as is described in Matthew 4: "There was Jesus led up of the spirit into the wilderness to be tempted of the Devil. And when he had fasted forty days and forty nights, he was afterward hungered. And when the tempter came to him he said: If thou be the Son of God, command that these stones be made bread. But he answered and said: It is written, Man shall not live by bread alone, but by every word that proceedeth out of the mouth of God."

"Not from bread alone," said Christ. So at least a man needs bread so that the Devil's challenge—change stone into bread—does not seem to be completely unreasonable. Perhaps Christ here should have answered with more clarity.

We children, who were many at times, received, depending on our age, trumpets, drums, crossbows, hobbies, ginger nuts, honey, gingerbread, dolls, clothes, sometimes a knife to use at the table, writing paper, pens, and books. If then Father's dog, Tölpel, who obeyed no one, began romping around among the presents and causing confusion, our joy was complete.

The maids received linen and the like for their dowries, which they eagerly accumulated in order to be well supplied when they offered themselves to their future husbands, and the male servants mainly received money.

Whether our parents exchanged presents, I can no longer remember.

Then came the nativity play. An angel appeared—one of the girls, provided with a glorious white dress and goose wings—and announced: "Fear not, for, behold, I bring you good tidings of great joy. For unto you is born this day in the city of David a Savior, which is Christ the Lord."

Others of us were dressed as shepherds, singing, "O Little One Sweet, O Little One Mild," as we walked to the manger, which stood behind a curtain. When it opened, we all knelt before the manger and worshipped the sweet Christ Child. In truth, this was but just a little doll, dressed in nightgown and even diapers, but I was so excited that it seemed the Christ Child was even smiling at me. Then we all joined hands and began to sing and dance around the manger.

The living rooms, which in addition to the kitchen were warmly heated while the other chambers remained cold, were decorated with branches from apple and cherry trees, having seemingly died in the bitter winter outside yet miraculously, in the warm rooms, starting to bloom.

Father's famulus, Anton Lauterbach, noted what my father, one Christmas, expressed about all the festivities: "Oh, poor all of us being so cold and dull with respect to joy, which after all has been given to us for our own good. It is the greatest benefit, far surpassing all other works of creation. The singing of the angels announcing the birth of Christ is wondrous and contains all Christian teaching because the *Gloria in Excelsis Deo* is the highest form of worship, which is brought to us by the angels in Christo."

When we finally went to bed on Christmas evening, it was not easy to go to sleep. The Christmas story, the Christ Child, the gifts, the general mood of expectancy we had felt for so long, the stories of the animals that were able to speak on the holy night—which all believe but no one has ever seen or heard—had excited us so that we would secretly gather in one of our bedrooms with the tallow candle burning and nibble on spice cookies, which was forbidden, of course, and tell frightening stories. One of us boys, I believe it was my brother Martin, scared us not for first time with the tale of the unfathomable hole in the basement of our house, the Black Monastery, which led directly to purgatory, he said. If one believed him, there was in the far corner of the beer cellar a large loose stone lying on the ground. If one lifted the stone and put one's ear to the hole, then one heard in the deep an eerie hiss and roar as though from a fire. At night, according to my brother, there comes out of the hole a sooty, coal-black angel of the lower species with small and scorched stub wings who drags sinners from their beds and takes them down to the fire, where, depending on the amount of their sins, they burn for a thousand years because they may not come to heaven with unclean souls.

It gave us a frightful scare, even though one would come straight to heaven after sufficient burning time and thus avoid the eternity of hell. Our sister Magdalena, whom everyone called Lenchen and who unfortunately was soon to die, rebuked my brother Martin for such stories. She said our father had abolished purgatory with the following words: "Therefore purgatory with all its ado is to be looked at as nothing better than an invention of the Devil."

And Lenchen then explained to us what she was taught at an early age, and for which Father would become famous: "When the Lord Jesus Christ suffered on the cross, died, and went for a while to hell, then had he atoned for all our sins. Who now believes in purgatory, like the Papists, doubts the saving effects of Christ's sacrificial death."

Christmas did not end right away. It traveled on through New Year, as we continued to receive gifts and presents and to eat and drink heartily.

What people accept of God's gifts and eat and drink is very important for their health, and as a doctor and a Christian, I recommend my readers to remember that sins against God's creation, our own bodies, begin with an unhealthy eating.

The season determined the bill of fare in our cloister, too. That means in winter there was much preserved food like green kernel, peas, lentils, and millet, dried fruit, nuts, dried mushrooms, also tubers and beets, which in the cellar were kept fresh in sand.

Naturally in winter we trapped birds with lime twigs, including blackbirds, thrushes, finches, and starlings, and we had geese, chickens, and ducks smoked or salted as well as beef and pork. Apart from a few fresh fish that were caught through ice holes in the Elbe and in the ponds, we had to be content with salted or smoked fish, which the fishmongers brought from the coast.

Our mother had always, as she had learned when still in the convent, a good stock of spices such as pepper from the East, salted or pickled garlic, and dried herbs and seeds (which had to be brought from Nuremberg), such as caraway, marjoram, mint, rosemary, sage, borage, and all those herbs that were used in preserving food. And if the meats or fish were a little past fresh, a few sharp spices could make them edible again. Sometimes, however, it did not help, and now and again we got sick. Food gone bad particularly affected Father, who had an especially sensitive stomach and whose rich enjoyment of wine and beer did not help the matter.

A stock of salted bacon and pickled eggs and lard was available throughout the winter. In addition, Mother preserved sauerkraut, pickled cucumbers, and various jams in the cellar. The baker did not get much business from us because we baked our own bread, and we also had the right to brew our own beer. There was wine for the older people, but it was sometimes rather sour and then would have to be sweetened with honey.

The time between Christmas and the New Year was a time of good eating, or rather feasting, and I confess that for me the joy and pleasure of food and even its preparation have never deserted me. I will not now decide whether that did not occasionally outweigh my joy at the coming of Christ.

CHAPTER 9

. . . makes clear that the abundant mention made in chapters 7 and 8 of rich meals and happy feasts could lead the reader to unchristian wantonness or frivolity. As an antidote, it seems fitting in this chapter to talk about famine, drought, and pestilence, all of which I lived through in my childhood or heard people talk about.

Our brother Johannes, the eldest of us children, was only little older than one year when in AD 1527 pestilence befell Wittenberg and the land. God wanted Father at this time to lie prostrate in bed, so sick that he saw his own end and wrote, "My dear son and beloved Käthe, I will leave you nothing, but I have a rich God who watches over the fatherless and is a judge of the widows, as we read in Psalm 68, and this God I leave you. He will support you well."

Our mother was certainly a good Christian, but this comfort from Father did not reduce her anxiety for the future and, if it should arise, her widowhood, especially in view of the malice and enmity toward her in the town, in the land, and even at the electoral court. One need only consider that the renowned Erasmus felt justified in asserting, even publicly, that Johannes was begotten before marriage, then had to retract it when the child came into the world at the proper time.

To trust in God as Father did was Christian, but my mother had already learned in the cloister that one must often help God along, not only through prayers, as Father believed, in order to convince Him the time was right for assistance. In view of His own eternalness, one can understand that for the year, the day, and the hour, He might not have the right sense of proportion.

Now was the time, as pestilence came upon us with the high summer heat. But obviously God first wanted to punish His children, as always, with blood and thunder and sickness. One of His representatives on earth, though, our good elector, different from the loving God, was worried and wrote from Torgau that Luther should quickly move to Jena, as the entire university had done, since the city was still pest free. But Luther persisted and with faith in God remained with his family in Wittenberg.

There were wild rumors about: the Jews poisoned the wells or breathed on people with their poisonous breath. But even then a few asked why it was that numerous appearances of rats with fleas always preceded the plague. This question is not answered even today.

People believed the Black Monastery offered protection and moved in in crowds, among them the parish pastor Bugenhagen.

At this time Johannes, just one and a half years old, was afflicted by a severe fever so that Father himself was almost in despair. At the beginning he was not certain if it was the pest, which also makes its appearance with fever, head, and limb pain. He wrote to Justus Jonas:

My dear Jonas, I don't actually know what I should write. My Käthe remains strong in faith and health despite advanced pregnancy. My little Hans lies prostrate now already eight days with an unknown sickness, it should be the teeth, so one believes. After the wife of the chaplain, there have been no deaths yesterday and today. May Christ help and cause this pestilence to cease. In the suburb of the fishermen, it is indeed already subsiding, and they are beginning again there with weddings and enjoying life as well as possible. Anything certain, however, one cannot say. Because eight days ago the pestilence had almost stopped, so days went by without a single death. But suddenly the wind changed. Within two days, the deaths were twelve a day, though most of them children. The wife of Augustin lay for eight days and longer with an inner ulcer. One naturally supposed nothing other than pestilence, but she recovered again. Margarethe von Mochau lies equally prostrate in our house; one speaks of menstrual sickness but fears the pest.

Käthe and I live now only in one of our rooms, all the rest being filled with the sick and the visitors. Our little Hans lies in my study, where he is unmolested. Pray for his health. Today is the twelfth day he has eaten nothing, and only through drink has he been reasonably nourished. Now he begins again to eat a little. It moves the heart how he wants in his way to be happy and strong but is yet too weak for it. My wife, Käthe, greets you, and knowing that peace prevails on our borders, complains that you do not visit us. Pomeranus also greets you, who in order to purge himself has taken a laxative today.

Today, reader, as I write this, and even assisted by a medical mind, I note that in our investigations of this terrible, if also conveniently biblical, sickness and its possible cure, we have not made much progress.

God in His wrath has used pestilence repeatedly against His own people of Israel and against the Christians as a terrible scourge. First He incited David to count his people, as we read in the second book of Samuel, chapter 24. Then He gave David a choice of punishments for doing the counting as he had been commanded to do, the righteousness of which, in spite of God's order, David was not convinced of. In spite of a warning from Joab, his general, he had been driven by his own vanity and ambition. Of the three possible punishments—seven years of famine, three months fleeing from his enemies, or three days of pestilence—David chose, understandably—although as king, not very caring—the pestilence, whereupon God ordered an angel to stretch out his hand so that He could destroy Israel. The angel complied, and seventy thousand people were killed with much suffering and pain and misery before God repented His sentence and commanded the angel to stop. Would it not have been sufficient if only one thousand or ten thousand had died? In the First Book of Chronicles, chapter 21, also translated faithfully by Father, it is at least Satan who incites David to number Israel.

When today the pestbells begin to ring, the people become ice-cold with fear, because there is nothing worse than to die so suddenly, unprepared, and in this condition to go before God, namely, in the condition of sin. God does not like this at all, that such dingy and unwashed wretches gather before Him and expect to be blessed at once without at least in death having repented. So the wife of Tilo Denes, burgomaster of Wittenberg, could consider herself lucky expiring in Father's arms, surely mildly consoled and prepared expertly for the Kingdom of Heaven.

That was not necessary for the five pigs, which at the same time died in their pens, as they did not need to fear the loss of salvation, although there are various opinions among theologians about the souls of animals, some of which rely on Paul, who wrote in a letter to the Romans: "Because the creature itself also shall be delivered from the bondage of corruption into the glorious liberty of the children of God. For we know that the whole creation groaneth and travaileth in pain until now."

Also in Isaiah 11 is found such thought: "In the new heaven and the new earth the wolf also shall dwell with the lamb, and the leopard shall lie down with the kid; and the calf and the young lion and the fatling together, and a little child shall lead them; and the lion shall eat straw like the ox."

Of pigs and their eternal salvation it is not written here, perhaps because they cannot ruminate like cows and are therefore considered unclean, which again makes them unfit for heaven. Though one must concede that they in a way have cloven hoofs.

But studying *per exemplum* Moshe ben Maimon thoroughly, one finds this need not be a sufficient reason. But at least the loss of our pigs was not a spiritual one. Today I know what Father was not aware of at that time, that pigs are not very susceptible to the rat plague and the human plague but, however, have their own concerns with the swine fever.

We still do not know what causes the pestilence, although it is conspicuous that during the time of pestilence there were always many rats, which themselves died of the pest and then disgustingly lay around. So we are limited in our battle to turning to God and praying that He may spare us and our neighbors—although more us. To this end, pest altars were erected with the pictures of Holy Helpers, as was ordered by our gracious elector, who commissioned Anton Burgkmair from Augsburg with this. Our father, however, said that trusting solidly in God and not in the saints is more wholesome to our health. Also, what was left was the gentle care of the sick and their confinement in their houses, on which were painted pest crosses. Too, as long as the disease helpers had not left the town, the use of the pest needle for piercing the boils, also called bubos, was common. I have later seen, though, during visits to the sick and supervision of barber-surgeons and barbers, that the piercing of a bubo and also the bloodletting hastened the sickness. The purulent content of the bubos would often be emptied onto the dungheap or into the river, and today I think that this helped to spread the disease.

All the people paid close attention to any sign of swelling in the groin or the armpit, of fever or headache. My brother Johannes was, as has been told, spared; not, however, our Black Monastery. Here fell ill the student Jost Honold from Augsburg, a beautiful youth, who had lived with us for three months and wished urgently to live and to study further.

Although our mother was pregnant, she and Aunt Lene bound cloths over their faces, as it is believed that through the breath of the sick one can be infected, and tended to him. They wrapped him in warm blankets and placed warm bricks in his bed to allow him to sweat. As boils in his armpits and groin appeared, they were not fearful of his nakedness, remarking, however, how small, in comparison to the boils, the testicles were, about which they indulgently smiled and washed him with a brew made of vervain and rue. And finally Aunt Lene prepared for him *Chelidonium majus*, or greater celandine, to induce sweating. She cleaned the root of the plant and cut it up small. Of which she put a handful in a half measure of rose vinegar, boiled it down to half, and strained it. In this broth she rubbed three cloves of garlic, as the Alexandrian theriac is too expensive and also not to be found in our town. She gave the sick young man a small glass of the brew, which caused him to sweat for three hours.

Then my mother dried him with warm towels, although one feared for her and her unborn child. Jost had great fear of death, yet lo! the boils disappeared and he recovered. The renowned Dr. Schurff did not want to believe it, but all the people convinced him that the young man could once again look out of his clear brown eyes. Because of this apparent cure, Mother even had to go to the elector's castle, where, however, she could not help the beautiful young maiden, the love-child of the deceased elector Frederick.

In the Black Monastery the maid Lisbeth, two students, and the clerk fell ill and died. Father assisted in the nursing by washing and feeding the sick.

The dead in the city were no longer buried in the cemetery but rather fetched in pest carts and buried in large pits next to the cemetery. In order to purify the pestilential air, fires were ignited in the streets and squares, especially with the wood of juniper, and prayers were said and Jews were hunted.

Finally God relented, the rats disappeared, the dead were buried, and people started to celebrate as usual.

I think today that pestilence is not caused by miasmas of the earth, which are poisonous vapors of the soil, as Hippocrates teaches; rather, I stand with the Italian doctor Girolamo Fracastoro, who attributed the infection to *seminaria morbi,* that is, sickness-carrying germs.

Therefore I also do not hold with the corresponding belief that the burning of fragrant wood is an efficient remedy. Rather, one should kill the rats and keep people away from each other. So was it not beneficial that in many towns the number of church services with entreaties for intercession increased and processions with large numbers of people were organized. It is understandable enough that some magistrates prohibited such gatherings for the duration of the pest, as it turned out that such gatherings contributed to the spread of the disease.

The praiseworthy Council of Nuremberg forbade the procession of the flagellants and had the city gates closely monitored so that no one ill with the pest was allowed to be brought into the city. Also, dead were not allowed in.

My father dealt with the question of fear and the flight from death with the tract "If One May Flee from Death." At first, the preachers and pastors as good shepherds have to stand by their flocks during pest times, as it says in John, chapter 10, verse 12: "The good shepherd giveth his life for the sheep. But he that is an hireling, and not the shepherd, whose own the sheep are not, seeth the wolf coming and leaveth the sheep and fleeth; and the wolf catcheth them and scattereth the sheep."

Other people, he says, who through service or duty are bound to each other should stay: a servant, for example, should not flee from his master or a maid from her mistress, unless it is with the knowledge and agreement of the master or mistress; vice versa, the master should not leave the servant or the mistress the maid unless they are provided for sufficiently elsewhere. Because in all these circumstances it is God's command that the servant and maid should remain bound and obedient. Conversely, master and mistress should provide for their servants. And through God's command to help and to serve, it is true as well for the father and the mother in regard to their children, and conversely for the children in regard to the father and mother to whom they are bound, etc. Likewise, those who are public persons through pay and wages, such as town physicians, town servants, mercenaries, and the like, are bound to the town. They may not flee unless they find other capable representatives to take their places. Experience also proves that those who serve the sick with love, devotion, and earnestness are generally protected from the disease.

This is an observation of Father's that I as a doctor can confirm: few of those who undertook the care or the treatment of pest victims, and were supplied with mouth coverings and watched out for the rats, were infected with the pest. Also, town doctors and pest doctors who bravely persevered and wore beak masks were usually spared, especially when the beak masks were filled with certain flavorsome spices, preferably cloves, although those are very expensive. Fragrance was believed to expel disease-carrying stench. My opinion is that it is not the fragrant filling of the beak masks that protects against the disease but rather the distance from the patient that the beak provides.

The God-appointed authorities, whom everyone is required to obey and who also have special responsibility for public health, must if necessary remain in the city.

Father also warned that one should not take on the care of the sick in order to get hold of their heritage or legacy should they die. That would only, he believed, lead to a quick infection and one's own death. Probably there were cases brought to his knowledge where the caretaker for vile profit accelerated the end of the patient by pressing a pillow on their face, then did not report their death for several days so they could take the provisions that the relations had left on the doorstep and with most of the remaining money or valuable things and devices could leave the house secretly before calling the pest cart.

God evidently holds in His goodness that we small and blind men cannot understand that the pestilence was not sufficient to strengthen our trust in Him and test the steadfastness of our belief and therefore sent the English sweat, or *sudor anglicus,* so called because it first occurred in England.

This testing, which, like the plague, was followed mostly by death, also included newborn children, who in my present-day opinion had not yet been given the chance by our loving God to commit any sins at all but were still buried in the state of *peccatum originale* in their graves or in the pest pits.

First occurred fetid sweat, which soon passed to fever. Then quickly, after one or two days, death. In addition, the patient suffered from anxiety, palpitations, headache, and numbness before God called him to Himself.

God probably also wanted that Father and Huldrych Zwingli in Marburg should not agree on the meaning of Holy Communion. There they had been called by Landgrave Philipp of Hesse, AD 1529, that they might agree on the issue whether our Lord Jesus Christ at Holy Communion is physically present or not. Father insisted that he was, while for Zwingli, the sacrament was merely to be regarded as an act of Christian confession. But before they came to blows, they had to terminate their discussion because of an outbreak of the disease. So the question whether the copula *est* in the biblical sentence *Hoc est corpus meum* is synonymous with *is* or with *means* could not be answered.

Today I ask myself why God and our Lord Jesus Christ allowed the semantic ambiguity of the Latin copula *est,* even though Christ had actually spoken Aramaic, to hold so much importance for us that it would impede the great work of the Reformation of the old church. But God's ways are inscrutable. Father wrote to Mother (do not be surprised, reader, that Father sometimes addressed Mother with the word *Herr;* this he did to emphasize her dominating role in the household and also to tease her a little bit):

> *My kind, dear Herr Katharina Luther, Doctoress, Preacheress at Wittenberg. Dear Käthe, we are in every respect united except that the counterparty holds fast to the belief that in the Lord's Supper we eat plain bread and that Christ is only present in spirit. I mean, God has so blinded them that they have nothing valid to raise.*
>
> *Kiss little Lenchen and Hans for me.*
>
> *Your willing servant, Martin Luther.*

In the end, thank God, the debaters agreed on retaining the chalice for the laity, whereby certainly a great service was done to please God and obtain eternal salvation.

Against the English sweat, the town physician knew of no remedy, and the people died more quickly and more painfully than of the pest. Few survived the sickness, and those who did continued to suffer from palpitations and night sweats. Also, one could suffer a relapse, which had not been observed with the pest.

Reader, I can tell you quite something about the English sweat—how it, for example, raged in England. It had been reported to me by a young man from England with whom I could reasonably converse in Latin. His name was William Shakspeare, and the reasons for his stay in our good town of Wittenberg after a difficult trip over water and land were soon made clear to me.

I encountered him a few years ago, I believe it was AD 1589 at the university, where I took part in a disputation of a doctorate. By chance, we sat next to each other in the auditorium and together left the hall. I invited him to several tankards of wine in the Ratskeller, because I very much wanted to hear of England, which was the first country in the world that had in its entirety broken from the papist church. William quickly came to trust me when he heard that I was the son of the honored Martin Luther.

And now a surprising disclosure. First, he was very well informed about the appearance of the English sweat in his homeland, and second, he told me frankly of his future plans to become a disciple of Thalia, the muse of comedy and idyllic poetry. As if he already wanted to prepare for play-writing, which he strove for besides play-acting, he observed everything around him with sharp eyes and was thankful for any knowledge I could give him about men, their motives, their communications, matters of the heart, if known, and political issues as well as the teaching of my father. He sucked up the world around him like a sponge sucks up water, and I should not wonder if this young man one day achieves fame. Naturally, his Latin was in need of improvement, but it was sufficient for us to communicate about many things.

It seems to me that his stay in Wittenberg was not entirely voluntary, for he hinted that because of poaching from a local noble named Sir Thomas Lucy of Charlecote near his birthplace, Stratford-on-Avon, he was pursued, had flown to the Netherlands, where he became a soldier, of which existence he became weary, so he deserted, coming to Saxony. When the situation in England had calmed down, he would, he said, return home forthwith. I know not what in Wittenberg he lived on, but I believe he had brought a certain amount of money from the Netherlands, which he supplemented by teaching English to several students at the university.

For professional and medical reasons, what interested me mainly was what he knew about *sudor anglicus,* whereby his soaring theater plans were somewhat pushed into the background. The following truths, he related, are generally accepted in England:

The English sweat first occurred in the army of King Henry VII and in some small towns wasted away almost all the residents. In the time of Henry VIII, then still a good Catholic whom the pope had honored with the title *Defensor Fidei,* "Defender of the Faith," the disease occurred again, this time in London, and many fell victim to it. That was AD 1528. The king departed London and fled from the sickness to the countryside. The aforementioned title the king had received, incidentally, for the book, authored together with Thomas Morus, who was not mentioned as coauthor, *Assertio Septem Sacramentorum,* or "The Defense of the Seven Sacraments," was at the same time a defense of the pope against my father's concepts.

Herr Shakspeare even knew that in the autumn of the same year, as the Turks for the first time lay siege to Vienna, they were visited by the English sweat, and their siege army was thoroughly decimated.

The English sweat and the pest sometimes intervened in war events, as is shown in the campaign of Charles V against the city of Rome in the year 1527, now known as the *Sacco di Roma* or the Sack of Rome. As Charles's troops plundered the city, an epidemic now believed to be the English sweat broke out in the Eternal City. Soon some twenty-five hundred Germans died of the disease. The streets were covered with dead and dying. German *Landsknechts,* mercenary pikemen, who adhered to my father's new belief, made a particular point in the city of the Antichrist of humiliating church dignitaries, of committing robbery, and of violating the papal symbols. But God did not allow this to go unpunished, Antichrist or not. Of the twenty-four thousand soldiers who had conquered the city, violated the citizens, tortured, and murdered, only half returned again to the North. The disease had done its work. Unfortunately, Georg von Frundsberg, the wonderful general of the emperor's—who, at the Diet of Worms when my father had refused to recant, had encouraged and comforted him—was so shocked about the insubordination of his army, which had begun when they were still in camp near Bologna, that he suffered a stroke and had to be carried to his castle in Mindelheim, where he soon was to die. My father, who regretted the outrage of the emperor's army, commented, "Christ reigns in such a way that the emperor who persecutes Luther for the pope is forced to destroy the pope for Luther."

I met Herr Shakspeare several times and had every time a most interesting conversation. Then he disappeared as unexpectedly as he had arrived.

With pestilence and English sweat, one might assume there were in the time of my parents and my childhood enough of plagues. But the Lord God had devised something else, for a change as it were, to force his creation to faith and love. Or Satan had made representations to him as he had done with Job, the man in the land of Uz, who was just and good and God-fearing and avoided evil. Perhaps Satan had said to God, "Strike Wittenberg, whom you protected after the pest and the English sweat, and you will see how they depart from the true faith." And God allowed Satan in the year 1540 to enter into some weathermakers and their followers—about which in my chapter about the witches I will write—and these, people believed, prayed to Satan and brought about a terrible drought.

All the fearful sickness, suffering, war, and death seemed to have culminated in our time, and Master Albrecht Dürer from Nuremberg drew these apocalyptic events. He early attached himself to my father and wrote to Spalatin: "It urges me to come to Dr. Martinus and with diligence to portray him and to engrave him in copper to create a lasting memory of this Christian man, who has helped me out of great fears."

Master Dürer, whom I respect above all other Christian painters and draftsmen, fell again into great fear when he heard of Father's abduction, but about the background he did not know anything. In his diary from his time in Antwerp, we can read how he heard about the abduction of Luther but not that he was safely brought to Wartburg Castle. So he feared that he might have been murdered and hoped that God would send another man of equal wisdom who would continue Luther's work.

As it became clear that the Wittenberg Nightingale, as Luther was named by mastersinger and shoemaker Hans Sachs, was still alive and hard at work translating the Bible, he was very glad.

Yes, reader, Master Dürer had carved the Four Horsemen of the Apocalypse into wood in AD 1497 or 1498 and had printed many copies so that it could be purchased by anyone and viewed with anxiety and premonition. From the fourth horseman, who with the others cruelly crossed the land, it is stated in the Revelation of John: "And I looked, and behold a pale horse: and his name that sat on him was Death, and Hell followed with him. And power was given unto them over the fourth part of the earth, to kill with sword, and with hunger, and with death, and with the beasts of the earth."

Death also came many times over Nuremberg, often through pestilence, and in 1494 Dürer fled to Venice, and again in 1506, out of fear of the disease. His first flight to Venice was beneficial for him in the opinion of the scholars because he learned much that enriched his work.

People being by nature obstinate, they often refuse to learn, and since the pest and English sweat were not enough to teach them to recognize God's love, in 1541 He sent a great drought.

I counted at the time seven springtimes. The winter with snow and cold had come and gone, and the snow thaw had swollen the Elbe, which flooded its banks. But just in time, the fields dried off and could be cultivated so that by the end of March, green shoots were sprouting everywhere; the march cups, snowdrops, tulips, and crocuses bloomed; the bumblebees came out of their nests underground; the cattails appeared in the meadows; and alder, poplar, and hazel began to sprout and nourish Mother's bees.

We children roamed over the fields and meadows and sometimes discovered little rabbits in hollows, where they would duck down and remain completely still. Our mother had forbidden us to touch, let alone to pick them up, because then the rabbits' parents would abandon them.

That spring was wonderful, especially for us children, as the weather at the end of March was dry and continuously sunny.

Then it rained no more. From the middle of April it remained dry, the sun already burned hotly, and we could notice concern beginning to show in the grown-ups' faces. Still the crops grew, as there was enough water in the ground.

In May, as it had still not rained, the fresh leaves began to hang limply, and less water flowed in the streams of Wittenberg, which turned into stinking rivulets, and in June one could already see the bottom of some of the wells in the city, so little water had they. It had now been three months without rain, and the roads were dusty. Wearily, because the horses could get barely any fresh feed on the way, the carters brought their wares to the city.

The grass and the feed withered throughout the entire empire, travelers told us, and the wells and fountains dried up. The people whispered that in Schönebeck near Magdeburg, the hunger stone protruded far out of the water. Tradition has it that whenever the hunger stone, a rock in the middle of the Elbe, begins to appear, hard times threaten.

The council ordered that the fire barrels be kept full with water from the Elbe, since through the heat all kinds of fires flared up. Some believed that Hans Kohlhase had returned and was responsible, although the council confirmed and had it published on posters that in Berlin in March he had been broken on the wheel and slowly but reliably put to death.

In August it was clear to all people that there would be a terrible crop failure. The farmers slaughtered their animals, also the milk cows, because there was no more feed. The first hay cut was soon used up so that one knew that by winter there would be little or no feed remaining.

The number of beggars multiplied while the community chests emptied.

The people prayed more and more urgently, beat their breasts, ran to the churches, and cried to God, and many believed, secretly, the Rain Goddess had fallen asleep and must be awakened by a pure virgin. Johannes Bugenhagen, who had recently returned from Denmark, Magister Melanchthon, and my father raged against such superstition.

Many old people seemed to wither and die. We children no longer ran free during the day but rather stayed in the cellar of the monastery, where it was still cool.

Our mother had had the foresight to have the well in the monastery dug very deep so that we suffered no shortage of water. The Wittenbergers came daily to us, the maids with the wooden buckets, to fetch water. But this was just a drop on a hot stone, and the people despaired and began to accuse the weathermakers and demand their punishment so that Satan would lose his servants. I'll record more about that later.

Now, as we children also started to despair, although in the early morning cool we splashed in the Elbe and could even walk through it, our elector had to threaten the traders with punishment if they continued to keep back field crops in order to raise prices. And just as people began to believe God had completely abandoned them, He repented and let it rain, as He had with Job.

There were meanwhile many deaths, mainly old people and children who could not bear the heat as the others, and for them God's repentance came too late. Today I wonder that He had no pity for them, also not His Son together with the Holy Ghost, when even the people felt sorrow as under the eyes of the mother a child was buried in a grave or in the pestpit, which was used for all kinds of dead, pest dead, English sweat dead, and hunger dead.

I have never forgotten the day as dark clouds rose up in the sky and the first drops fell. It is raining, said the people. It is raining, shouted the children, and ran out into the streets, where soon the first muddy puddles began to form.

It rained without interruption for fourteen days, the water in the fountains rose, the streams in Wittenberg filled up, the Elbe flowed full again, and the hunger stone at Schönebeck disappeared in the water. There grew once more grass for feed, and the winter grain could be sowed and would be fruitful, so that all hoped that the shortages in winter and the coming year would not be too great.

The people were cheerful now and believed that God Himself had tired of the plagues, because one can imagine that it also takes labor to be always thinking of new torments, which at the end are regretted.

CHAPTER 10

. . . will discuss the belief in witchcraft and sorcery, as I promised above, and how my father in a Christian manner damned the witches and sorcerers and what consequences this will perhaps have for him.

In AD 1540, as we and the entire empire were dominated by terrible heat and drought (which I have already described), the maids, the servants, and the students living with us in the Black Monastery whispered of a forthcoming public event on the 29th of June, which they under no circumstances wanted to miss. They begged Mother for a few hours off work so that with all Wittenberg they might enjoy the event. We children found out that on that day the weathermaker Prista Frühbottin together with her helpers, her son Dictus and the two knacker servants, Clemen Ziesigk and Caspar Schiele, would be smoked and roasted for two days and so be brought to death, which undoubtedly gave them enough time for prayers to obtain their peace of mind and the fire enough time to develop its purifying force.

We children were not supposed to watch, but I stole out of the house and followed the students to the marketplace, where I hid behind a cart. Later I learned the weathermaker and her helpers had been driven to their execution in this same cart.

They had already been fettered and forged to stakes, and so that they would not quickly die, they had been placed on wooden platforms. One could see they had spent a long time under the torturers' hands, and apparently it was not worth the trouble to set their dislocated shoulder joints, which in other cases the torturers were very skilled in. Now they sat on their wooden seats, a small fire burning under them, and their legs were already covered with red and bursting bubbles. All four groaned and cried pitifully, which the people seemed to like, the louder the groaning, the more joyful the exclamations of the audience. One woman shouted especially loud: "The witch has poisoned our pasture!"

I discovered among those watching the son of our burgomaster, Lucas from Kronach, called Lucas Cranach the Younger, pen and sketchbook in hand.

As I write this, there lies before me a picture that brings back to me the horrific memories that haunt me at night like a succubus. It was carved in wood by Master Lucas the Younger and was at the time widely viewed by the people, who would tear it out of each other's hands in order to greedily stare at it.

Under the picture Master Cranach had printed his observations and remarks, because picture and words together create a greater impact and deterrence. Perhaps he also wanted clear Christian justification for what drove his father and the Wittenberg town council, which his father presided over as burgomaster, to this cruel act.

> The rulers or authorities are to be feared not by those who do good but rather those who do evil. Because they do not carry the sword in vain. They are God's servants and avengers against those who do evil. They wanted these four people who are seen in this picture to be justified and purified by fire on the day of Peter and Paul in Wittenberg for many and varied misdeeds. It is so that an old widow, over fifty years old, and her son, who had succumbed to the Devil, but especially the woman, had courted the Devil and had committed sorcery for several years, created and halted

> storms, made poisonous powders to the damage of many poor people, taught her craft to others, poisoned pastures and thus killed uncounted numbers of livestock of oxen, cows, pigs, etc., which they afterwards flayed to sell the skins just to satisfy their black-hearted and desperate avarice with the little money they could expect. This drawing was done solely to create disgust among the people against all those who do as the witch did, among them beggars, hangmen, knackers, also shepherds and others moving about the land. And any government should take diligent care to protect poor people from harm. May God the Almighty take care of all Christian hearts from the Devil's wiles and temptations. Amen.

The people had fear and called on the authorities, placed there by God, to put an end to the evil doings of the witches. Christian charity, it seems to me, fled from the human hearts not only of the simple people but also from those highly spiritual persons like Father, Magister Melanchthon, the Cranachs, and many others, and natural God-given compassion was not to be found.

I saw how these people smoked and shriveled so wretchedly over the hot bricks and fire, how they cried to God and Jesus Christ and not to Satan for help, protesting their innocence, though under torture they had admitted their bond to Satan, and the old woman her amours and her fornication with the Devil. God—Father, Son, and Holy Ghost—are omnipresent, but here their presence seems to have been very cloudy.

I suddenly felt very sick. Then I fell and only awoke at home as my mother rubbed me with water and vinegar. She scolded me mildly since I became feverish and lay abed day and night with dreams.

Father, because of his travel to Eisennach und his visit to Weimar on the 29th of June, Peter and Paul's Day, could not take part in the justification of the witch and her disciples through torture and fire but admonished his church later in the following words:

> With respect to the sorcerers, I urged you the other day that you say prayers against them, because they have not desisted from us. They have the power of Satan against us, with which to shame us, as befell Job. If he is allowed to spite us here in Wittenberg, we want to pray to spite him. In addition, I urge you not to think that all your misery and all your hardship originate from sorcery.
>
> Often God Himself reprimands His people. But it is easy to recognize the sorcerer's evil actions from those which are God-sent. The sorcerers let bones, hair, gadgets, and other items flow from the pus, as I have seen myself with the wife of the Baron von Mansfeld. These sicknesses cannot be healed through human medicines; the more they are treated, the more violently they rage. Therefore, pray against the sorcerers that they are discovered and have their reward from the torturer.

Father had without a doubt known about the special cruelty of the execution—the damned were not smothered in smoke nor mercifully strangled but rather burned very slowly—but said nothing of it, perhaps because his attention at the time was on more important things than the agonizing death of four children of God, namely, the problem that threatened the Reformation of the church, which was the bigamous marriage of the landgrave Philipp of Hesse, one of the strongest supporters of the Reformation.

As for Father's observation concerning diseases, in which gadgets, etc., flow from the pus, I will not disagree with him but only say that in my medical activity over many years, when I oversaw the barber-surgeons in the puncturing of the boils, never did I see anything similar flow from the festering part of the body.

My father had never made a secret of his hostility to witches and sorcerers; however, sometimes, for a few, he had made a call for clemency or forgiveness. This was used against him by the zealous Papists and other enemies. They claimed he did not persistently enough fulminate against witches and therefore rendered them encouragement. At the same time, they claimed Dr. Luther had, with his usurped authority, all the more spread an excessive belief in witches among the people.

This the old believers led back to his own origin, in which they would have us believe that his mother had intercourse with the Devil, who as a beautiful youth in red clothes often came to the door and spoke to her in a seductive, dark voice, wanting to induce her, after Easter, to receive a wealthy merchant. Thereafter, the changeling Martin was born, and she then quickly married Hans Luder. (Have I mentioned in my memoir that this was the spelling of my father's name when he was young? Only after AD 1512 did he spell his name "Luther," which he derived from the Greek word *eleutheros,* meaning "free.")

Father came to speak about the story and its illogic: "One calls me a changeling and a bath maid's son. But a man cannot be these at the same time, because one is a changeling, the other is a natural child."

Naturally, my grandfather on my father's side had to be sullied by the evil rumor. We know that my grandfather moved from Möhra in Thuringia to Eisleben because of the flourishing copper mining there, which was no longer economical in Möhra. Our enemies contend that he moved there because of an outrage committed on Satan's behalf. Still in Father's lifetime, the defected theologian Georg Witzel, who to his own benefit had been attempting a reconciliation of the religious opponents, reproached Justus

Jonas in a violent dispute: "I could call the father of your Luther a killer or a murderer."

And recently I read—lies have short wings—in a paper that appeared in Paris that my father was the son of a murderer from Möhra. My grandfather, it said, had killed a devout farmer who was grazing horses with the farmer's own bridle. He could have succeeded with that only because he had been given the strength by the Devil, as the farmer was a powerful man and my grandfather was only of medium height and strength.

It should be noted that the flight of such a sinner out of the Electoral-Saxon town of Möhra to the likewise Saxon town of Mansfeld contradicts plain simple logic. Surely the elector's police would have tracked him here. He would hardly have come to his respected position in the local council in Mansfeld if he had been under this suspicion.

Father was of the opinion that behind all the slander stood his archenemy, Duke George of Saxony, who with the denigration of his person wanted to denigrate his teaching.

As a child, my father was naturally more surrounded by belief in witchcraft than we are today, after a hundred years. Still, this belief will continue to persist for a long time.

At table, my father spoke of sorcery during his childhood: "My mother was very much tormented by a neighbor, a witch, whom she attempted to appease with all she had, with friendship and goodwill, because the witch could charm her children so that they would cry themselves to death. And when a preacher publicly rebuked her with words, she bewitched him so that he would die and no earthly medicine could help. She had taken up the earth where he had walked and thrown it into the water, thereby bewitching him, for without this earth he could never again become healthy."

In another table conversation, Dr. Martin told the story of the old woman who sowed the seeds of discord between a wife and a husband: "When I was a young boy, a story went around that Satan, with all his cunning, could not separate two married people who lived together in great harmony and passion. So he brought it about through an old woman. That woman secretly laid a shearing knife under the pillow of each and persuaded each that the other one had wanted to kill them and that each could see the truth in the knife under their pillows. The man found the shearing knife first and with it cut the woman's throat. After that came the Devil and gave the widow on a long pole a pair of shoes. Then she asked, 'Why are you not coming closer to me?' And he answered, 'You are more evil than I, the Devil, because what I was unable to bring about with the married couple, you have accomplished.' So you see what the Devil does with his tools and disciples, making them more wicked than himself."

From my occupation with my father's life, I know that his childhood memories, even though one should not ignore them, were of no great significance in regard to his attitude toward sorcery and witchcraft. Much more had the abundance of examples from theological books, and his later experience with related stories (not his own personal, direct experiences, I must remark here; rather, almost all secondhand). He viewed these through the lens of theology, from which he developed his convictions, sometimes new, sometimes merely a strengthening of old ideas.

He ascribed his physical ills or challenges such as the weather and sickness to the Devil or the Devil's earthly helpers, and consequently, in providing evidence, as we demand it in the study of nature and all its phenomena, he and all theologians were somewhat lacking, being satisfied with the simple assertions as long as they were believed or found in the Scriptures. And what he felt about the law and its enforcers, the lawyers, one sees in the lecture he bestowed on my brother Johannes: "Should I learn that you want to become a jurist, I would plunge you from the bridge into the Elbe and let you drown, and also have no doubt that I would rather justify this sin against God than allow you to become a jurist and rogue against my will."

His parish and his friends but, most of all, our mother he admonished to pray and not be tempted to apply counterspells. Counterspells, too, are sorcery and therefore godless. Therefore he admonished Mother most severely for bringing a healing herbalist into the house, when one of my siblings lay sick to death and the doctor's medicine did not seem to help.

One time he told how Bugenhagen successfully fought against the Devil's milk and butter theft: "The Devil came to the house of Pomeranus so that the woman and the maids worked hard until tired to make butter but did not succeed. Then came Pomeranus, mocked the Devil, and crapped in the butter churn, whereupon the Devil did not steal any more butter."

Now this is indeed a good example of contempt for the Devil, but it also comes near to the forbidden counterspell, where the stolen butter now takes on the taste of Bugenhagen's addition and should spoil the Devil's desire for further thefts. That in addition the butter became unusable for the Bugenhagens, which meant the Devil had in fact reached his goal, Father did not mention.

Father proceeded more strictly in the case of a citizen of Brandenburg who was brought to him.

A man from Brandenburg, charmed by witches, lost all of his worldly goods. He went to a Berlin exorcist, seeking advice. Finally his conscience plagued him, and he begged for comfort. Dr. Martinus answered: He had acted evilly and heinously. Why had he not, for example like Job, persevered and prayed for God's blessing? He said he should repent and flee to Satan no more but rather with serene soul do God's will.

In summation, Father said of witches and sorcerers: "One should have no compassion for them: I would burn them myself. And one should not tarry but rather rush to the punishment. The lawyers want so many witnesses and evidence and despise what is completely obvious. I have had to deal with a marriage problem these days in which a woman wanted to kill her husband with poison; in the end he vomited lizards. Also, he saw lizards coming from her. And though she was interrogated under torture, she did not confess. For these sorceresses are completely mute and despise suffering, as the Devil does not allow them to talk. Such acts, however, are witness enough that one should harshly punish them as an example—which would deter others from such evil deeds."

Here, reader, although only a doctor of medicine and not a lawyer, I must at least point out the following, should the words of my father be put into practice. The entire legal procedure in witch and sorcery matters would be set aside if the confession extracted through torture were sufficient to burn the accused. Where are the witnesses here, and the evidence and circumstances of the alleged deed and all the rest of an adequate trial? And if there was circumstantial evidence, it was of the following kind: the torture cannot be applied infinitely but for its continuation needed new evidence. So clever authorities had the idea that persistent silence in the face of the greatest pain was a sign of witchcraft or sorcery (Father had said that the Devil commanded the witches to silence). In the end, whatever the tortured did or did not do or say or not say, they were doomed.

And, finally, natural causes for the damage had to be excluded objectively before it could be recognized purely as the work of the Devil. That did not go as fast as Father wished, because he was mainly concerned with the spiritual welfare of the flock entrusted to him, the aim of which was to deter evil, not to follow the ordinary rules of justice. Considerations concerning the infliction of terrible, excruciating pain on the tortured played no role because in essence the whole trial with its deadly end was in principle an *executio in effigie* of the Devil, which, however, seemed not to have much effect because his evil doings did not end.

That the torturers and the unjust judges, the city and the rural authorities, the clergy and Father and his friends could by their words and actions damage their own souls, because they acted against Christ's commandment of love and mercy, was not considered, because the godly fight against Satan was everything.

The sorcery and the witchcraft were not limited to herb women, weathermakers and knackers, skinners and executioners, although it was mainly spread among them. No, even in princely houses such as the House of Hohenzollern in Brandenburg, it was not uncommon to deal with Satan's disciples. In this instance, my report does not come easily, because later I was closely connected with the elector of Brandenburg, about whom in due course it will be told.

Joachim I, Nestor, elector of the empire, archchamberlain, and a vexatious enemy of my father's and the Reformation of the old church, had in person dealt with the Devil, as my father said at the table, and also employed sorcerers at his court. One of these had spoken to my father during a visit to Wittenberg in spring AD 1532: "Dr. Lucas Gauricus, the black magician, whom the elector had summoned from Italy, has made me publicly aware that the elector has himself had dealings with the Devil." This black magician had, besides his profession as sorcerer, other qualifications, which were mathematician, astronomer, doctor, magus, and *medicus.* Lucas Gauricus was later to become a bishop and a friend of Pope Paul III. Once, because of a false prophecy, he was thoroughly tortured, the traces of which remained with him his entire life. Even that, however, did not diminish his cheerfulness when prophesying. He continued prophesying, falsely.

I am surprised today at what double standards my father and Magister Philippus and others applied in their dealings with the sorcerers. Dr. Gauricus was not arrested, and if he was spoken of during table conversation, he was held in general esteem. Perhaps this was due to the sorcerer setting up a nativity for Father in his *tractus astrologicus* for the year 1483; that is, he showed the position of the stars at the birth of my father. Also for Magister Philippus he was a scholar worthy of protection, and he praises him in two letters to a friend.

This happened although the black magician had mediated a pact for the elector with the Devil: that he should still live for fifteen years. In summa, the poor man had outwardly lived an impious and godless life, had had alliances with the Devil, and died amid his shameful whoring.

The Devil's pact did not bear the desired fruit, because the elector died in AD 1535 at fifty-one years of age.

For good reasons, the elector was not spared by Dr. Martinus. One story in particular gave rise to unpleasant laughter at table. It was in the year 1525, when the court astrologer, Johann Carion, persuaded the elector to flee to the Tempelhof Hill because a deluge was coming. So the great man went, taking for his noble bodily needs much food and drink as well as his beloved mistress, and awaited the flood. That this deluge would swallow up his subjects was for him not so important, because they were only minor figures. God, however, sent no flood, although there had been adequate sinning at the electoral court; for example, in 1503, most members of God's people, the Jews, had been driven from Brandenburg, and in 1510, thirty of them had been burned in Berlin.

That the elector was an opponent of the Reformation particularly embittered my father. And this prince had, at the election of the emperor, whom my Father in the beginning esteemed and from whom he promised much good would come for Germany, at first wanted to cast his vote for the French king Francis (who had promised him the post of vice-regent). But through the persuasive power of a considerable amount of guldens, he decided to give his vote to Charles. His wife, the Danish princess Elisabeth, a follower of Father's, had to flee to Wittenberg—that was in the year 1528—

which did not endear the elector to Father. Later, Elector John Frederick I, the Magnanimous, ensured that the now-widowed princess received living space in the former religious house of the Hospital Brothers of St. Anthony on the Lichtenburg in Prettin near Torgau.

I have a table talk of Father's lying before me that shows us how he personally dealt with the sorcerers. The talk is about the widely traveled sorcerer and black magician D. Johann Faust, who also practiced his art in Wittenberg.

Anton Lauterbach recorded it in summer 1537 and immediately allowed it to be printed:

> Someone brought up the subject of illusionists and sorcery as the means by which the Devil blinds people. Much talk was of Faust, who called the Devil his brother-in-law, and Luther was heard: "If I, Martin Luther, had reached only my hand to him, he would have wanted to pervert me: but I would not have shied away, I would have reached for him on behalf of the Lord God, the Protector. The Devil uses the service of the sorcerers not against me; could he have gotten me and been able to do damage, he would have done it long ago.

The Herr Father always stressed that God is the Lord over the world and the Devil, and whatever the Devil would cause to happen must be approved by God. Therefore, he had no fear of witches, the servants of Satan, because he believed that God, who allowed the witches' work to exist, also held His protective hand over him.

How Father struggled for the souls in his charge or for those who lived in his town without shrinking before the drastic pastoral threats of penalty is shown, for example, by the student Valerius Glockner, son of the mayor of Naumburg, Viet Glockner.

This young rascal whistled daily a little song, lived in a rich and disorderly way, did expensive whoring throughout the land, and was furthermore also disobedient and not open to corrective persuasion. Consequently, he was severely examined on the 13th of February, 1538, by Georg Major, the preacher at the castle church, and my father, who asked him: Why did he live so, fearing neither God nor man? Thereupon the boy answered impudently that five years ago he had given himself over to the Devil with the words, "I say to you, Christ, I give up my faith in you and want to accept another lord." Dr. Martinus insisted and wanted to know if he had talked more with the Devil and concluded a pact. The student wriggled back and forth, and it was clear that Satan under an assumed name had made him all kinds of promises and had also enabled his loose lifestyle. The examiners showed disgust so that Glockner appeared to regret the pact, and he eagerly and diligently asked for forgiveness. Then Dr. Martinus laid his hand on him, knelt down with the others, prayed the Lord's Prayer, and said, "Lord God, Heavenly Father, Thou hast commanded us through Your Son to pray and have so ordered and employed the Ministry of the Holy Christian Church that we may instruct the brothers who have failed and lead them back with a gentle hand on to the right path. Lord God, we beg You for this Your servant, to forgive him his sins and accept him back into the lap of Your Holy Church, for Your dear Son's sake, Our Lord Jesus Christ. Amen."

Dr. Martin was not convinced of Glockner's expressed repentance and did not believe in such a swift change of heart nor that the Devil would so quickly let his victim out of his hands. Therefore, he pressed him strongly and demanded strict abjuration of the Devil, and when the student seemed hesitant or appeared even a little exhausted and wanted a pause, he was made aware of the consequences if he did not renounce: "You know, Glockner, if we have to report you to the authorities, you easily could be threatened with prosecution because of blasphemy, which is the renouncing of Christ, and with sorcery or heresy, which is the way a pact with the Devil is interpreted. Do you believe you are equal to the torturers when they stretch and impale you and put you to the stake and ensure a fiery death?" There the lad quickly changed his mind and said to Father, "I, Valerius, confess before God and all His angels and before the assembly of this church that I have renounced faith in God and given myself up to the Devil. I am sorry from my heart, will henceforth be Satan's enemy, and will follow God, my Lord, to my betterment. Amen."

One can see here that the participants in no way shared the obsessive and blind belief in witches and sorcery of the frightened people but rather that they subjected the guilty one to church discipline in which they used encouragement and the recognition of contrition before they presented excommunication and punishment. If that is indicative of a Christian approach, I will not risk saying.

But if an alliance with the Devil led to crime, then was Father quite furious and offered to have the witches arrested himself and to burn them if, for example, on order of the Devil they stole milk by having the milk flow into a broomstick, which they then milked at home.

While Dr. Martinus did not doubt the reality of *maleficium,* or malevolent sorcery, he denied the possibility of witches' flights or witches' sabbaths, which Mathesius reported, who talked about these issues with Father. But the Devil at least could make people believe in witches' flights, meetings, and dances; he had particular success in this with women and children.

In general, one should be careful and not believe that all the Devil's work was genuine; much is just illusion, which the Master of Evil is well capable of. He can in no way interfere in God's work against His will and cannot arrogate divine power. To awaken a man from death back to life is for him as impossible as it is to make a barren woman fertile.

Witchcraft is a *crimen laesae Majestatis divinae,* a crime against God's majesty, and therefore is to be punished with torture and death even without the commitment of *maleficium.* This judgment of my father's is, in the opinion that I have now formed after a long life, dangerous because if alone the witches or sorcerers are punished without visible signs of damage done, then their alleged crime can be detected only through the worst tortures.

Well, enough of these frightful deviations from the true Imitation of Christ as a way to salvation.

In any case, after watching the shocking execution of the Frühbottin woman, I lay long and feverishly ill, with terrible dreams. In fact, all my life I have had nightmares, and one of them often recurred to me even as an adult and a professor of medicine.

I dreamed I was in heaven before the judgment seat of God, where He sat in a bright, almost unpleasantly blinding light. Next to Him on the right sat Christ, His Son. An entire row of angels stood ready to guide the accused to the appropriate location according to their sins or virtues; one could also see how some sinners were led away while others, dressed in white and provided with wings, fluttered around behind the judgment chair and exulted and shouted, which disturbed the proceedings. God had to call for order several times.

I noticed that some angels served more zealously than others. One group stayed in the background, staring guiltily down in front of them. I learned they were the angels who had forced themselves on beautiful daughters of men, as one reads in the book of Genesis 1 in chapter 6. God had created the women too seductive, it seems to me, and the female angels in heaven had gotten very celestially translucent and no adequate competition for daughters of men. Anyway, those angels leaped upon the daughters of men, and they bore children, from whom powerful and famous men came into the world. It must have been willed by God, or it would not have happened. At the same time, it did not free them from punishment, as we know. Anyway, God has endowed the woman with great power even over the angels.

I mention this, because I myself have been exposed my entire life to the seductions of women, which for me was an infinite delight but also introduced tangible difficulties. About that perhaps later; now I'll return to my dream.

My time had not yet come, but God had sent an angel messenger who brought me to heaven for a short time to witness the process. It was the trial of God-Father-Son-Holy Spirit versus Dr. Martinus Luther, professor in Wittenberg and reformer.

There stood Herr Father, stripped of all academic and spiritual insignia, naked, pale, and rather fat before God's judgment seat. The angel-prosecutor charged him with two main points. The first was his hostility toward the Jews and all his vicious words against God's chosen people. The second was his cruel and destructive work directed at the witches and sorcerers, who were, after all, also God's children. Charges of similar actions against peasants, Calvinists, Anabaptists, and other opponents had been dropped in order not to protract the process, God truly having other things to do rather than just to bother with Luther. There was, for example, the difficult question to answer whether the siblings of Jesus came from Joseph or were begotten by the Holy Spirit. If the former was the case, one would have to deny Mary's perpetual virginity, which was inadvisable for the Mother of God because then the act of sexual intercourse would have to be assumed, probably even its enjoyment. If the latter was the case, then Jesus's siblings were the direct offspring of God, like Jesus, which would bring confusion to the concept of Holy Trinity.

An English defender had been assigned to Luther, who seemed to approach his assignment with displeasure, which generated a bad feeling in me. I recognized in him the angel who had brought me here as a witness.

His defense consisted mainly of the following. He claimed that Luther's translation of the Bible had brought the Word of God nearer to the people and that he had attempted to purify the church of its evil ways and so make it more pleasing to God. Ergo, his intentions had been good, and he had sought to do the will of God. Also, this had given the German language a form and richness, which God himself had praised for its intimacy and warmth and sometimes preferred to the Latin and Aramaic when conversing with the angels or with his people on earth, which occurred less frequently. When the latter happened, his Son, whose mother tongue is Aramaic, had started to learn German, having already made good progress, especially in the syntax with the difficult sentence structure.

Here God interrupted the counsel for the defense and was really loud: "It carries no weight here what the accused wanted or meant or did for the good of the German language but rather exclusively what consequences his words and deeds had. And here Dr. Martinus"—I was relieved that God at least allowed my father his academic status—"it does not look good for you."

The Lord signaled to an angel standing ready on a small cloud. The angel flew to a door behind which the saved were having themselves a good time, as one could hear by their singing hosanna. He opened the door, and Prista Frühbottin, together with her fellow condemned, her son Dictus and both knacker servants, Clemen Ziesigk and Caspar Schiele, entered the court.

Actually, they had already been clothed in heavenly garments and put back to the state before they were tortured and burnt, but for the purpose of the court proceedings, God had once more placed them in the condition in which they found themselves at death. That seemed to me questionable and had the appearance of an attempt to influence the court, and I wondered if the defense counsel was going to object to this. Still, I knew that the defense angel as God's servant was ultimately dependent upon Him, and I began to think the proceedings against my father might not be fair and neutral.

Dr. Martinus got a terrible fright when he saw those people, but it was not clear whether he was more shocked that they were in heaven or about the condition in which they appeared.

"Look, Dr. Martinus"—now Christ began to speak—"how badly my Father's creatures have been treated, and executed—with your support, I might add. Have you through the study of my Father's words not understood that my Father and I with the New Covenant established the Gospel of Love, to which all actions of my followers, all institutions, all new churches, and all preaching must be subordinated? That the belief in witches and the persecution of Jews have no place within it because they are not based on love? How does it go in your beautiful translation of the letter from Paul to the Corinthians: 'Though I speak with the tongue of men and angels, and have not charity, I am become as sounding brass or tinkling cymbal.'

"Were you, Luther, a sounding brass or a tinkling cymbal when in the lands of the Protestants, where, with your eloquent or tacit approval, more alleged witches were burned than in lands that remained Catholic? Has God not distinguished you above others with intellect and courage so that you can understand what God is all about? How could you not grasp that the Word, the Law of God, is not to be followed in a literal sense for the word's and the law's sake, but only for the sake of God's children? That God is a God of love, and man has made Him into a vengeful, angry, and murderish God? Have you never asked yourself if the Bible, written by human hands, was often changed and adapted to the wishes of the church so that the Word of God might have been altered?"

When my father remained silent, his defender spoke: "I call as witness for the defense Paul Luther, Doctor and Professor of Medicine, if only for a short time, in Jena."

God beckoned me to come forward. I did so, and as Frühbottin and her people caught sight of me, they cried out, shook their charred fists, and called, "This one watched our execution, and because he approved it, he must also be accused."

Thereupon the defender: "My witness, born in the year 1533, saw the burning in AD 1540 as a tender seven-year-old and is hardly likely in any way to be responsible."

Thereon the High Judge: "The witness may speak. And Frühbottin and the others may go."

So it happened. The bailiff angel touched the people, who were once again unscathed and winged as well as dressed in long white gowns, and led them out.

Through my *activitas docendi,* I was accustomed to making speeches *coram publico,* but one does not every day stand before the judgment seat of God, even if only as a witness.

"Highest Court: My father, Dr. Martinus Luther, is a creature that You, God, have placed in his time. And it has pleased You to furnish this time with all the superstitions, beliefs in witches, Jew hating, etc., to which Luther was subject. It would have required much more than ordinary human strength and effort, a godlike love, I venture, to avoid all this. Few could do that. Luther could not avoid believing that his work of reforming the old church was a godly business, though the side effects and consequences have often been so evil. I beg you to understand these motives of my father."

Here called the prosecutor, "Objection. The witness charges the Holy Trinity of God with complicity in the deeds of the accused. That is not permissible."

God, who had looked somewhat affected by my words, then said, "The objection is granted. These submissions are to be deleted from the record. The witness may continue."

I went on, "I refer to the document written by the accused *On the Bondage of the Will,* in which the kernel of the new Gospel of my father's, his alpha and omega, and with it his godliness, is laid open. He himself says:

> This is our aim, that we try to find out what the free will can achieve and how it relates to the grace of God. If we do not know that, then we know absolutely nothing of Christian affairs and would be worse than all the heathens. Because if I do not know what, how far, and how much I can do in relation to God, so would it be to me just as uncertain and unknown what, how far, and how much God can do in relation to me, because God appears in everything. If I do not know the works and the effects of God's power, so can I not know God himself. If I know not God, so can I also not honor Him, praise Him, give Him thanks, and serve Him.

Here was God impatient. He looked at the clerk and ordered him to also strike these remarks out of the record, expressly because they damaged the accused, who here claimed the worshipping man can know God. "And also," God said, "what we have just heard is on the point of being incomprehensible so that even I, God, have trouble understanding it."

He then said, "I order the accused to carefully reread his writings and those of Erasmus of Rotterdam against the background of love and reason and the above-declared correct understanding of God's Word and submit the result in writing before the court. Also, he may defend his view of what he said about Erasmus: 'Who crushes Erasmus squashes a bug, and this stinks even more in death than it did in life.'"

Now Jesus Christ, God's Son, chose to speak once more, and said, "Oh, Luther, reflect, too, on your doctrine of justification. Did you not say a man would be blessed and justified *sola fide*, through faith alone? So you take from God's creation, the people, the possibility to do the Creator's will through their own efforts, through goodness and active love, through their own resolve, and even through sacrificing their own lives. You thus reduce them to blind faith and to obedience to the letter and to a subjugation for which God did not create them. Did you yourself not elsewhere translate my words: 'There is no greater love than this, that he lay down his life for his neighbor'?"

Here God nodded his head and said, "The accused has now an opportunity for justification."

My father looked up, saw God, His Son, and the Holy Ghost as an ethereal haze hovering over them, was long silent, and then began hesitantly. "We are beggars, that is true. Our nothingness becomes especially clear before the throne of God and His Son, Jesus Christ. In the world I was often overbearing and sinful and lost the right path when I believed I had to fight and destroy the enemies of the Gospel of our Lord for the Lord's sake, and all too frequently I made use of the means of my enemies. I have erred, for our Lord is a God of peace, of salvation through love.

"But I pray the court for understanding." Here he raised his hands and called out in despair: "How could I, in view of the confusion of Christians through the thousand years of growing scholastic, papal interpretation and diabolical deception, have acted differently than to forge ahead with gravity and vigor, with bludgeon and grossness? With sword and torture? With regional churches and church order? Does the court believe that Magister Philippus's gentleness toward the papacy would have helped? And may I at the same time remind the court that Magister Philippus was not gentle at all when he congratulated Calvin on the execution of Michael Servetus and urged the death sentence for the Anabaptists. How else should I have kept the true church apart from the false, other than through relentless severity?

"Today I know better. The true church, differently from the false, values the commandment of love higher than itself, its servants, and its institutions. Christ is the Lord of the church, and no one else, not the pope and not any bishop."

Here he stopped, exhausted, then added, "Yes, I was arrogant when I believed I could fulfill the will of God and our Lord Jesus Christ, which we cannot know. Lord, give me peace and grant me mercy."

The judges, after this passionate outburst, showed some emotion. Then the Lord spoke: "I adjourn the trial and will decide later whether Dr. Martinus Luther will go to hell or will take part in eternal life in heaven. Until then is the accused to be kept in limbo."

Always, I wake from the dream at this point and therefore will never discover which decision about my father God had made.

CHAPTER 11

. . . is about anxiety, war and rumors of war, hardships, and death, and how my family fared after my father's death.

As was told in chapter 2, my father died and, with many tears and prayers, was entombed in the castle church in Wittenberg. My mother and we children returned to the Black Monastery and with a few friends and students held a sad funeral feast. It seemed to me that Mother had already begun to proceed more economically, which is to say that in spite of the almost desperate sadness of the situation, she had not lost sight of the daily cares and concerns.

I was now thirteen years old and well tutored through Magister Philippus and Veit Oertel von Windsheim. I am indebted to both of them, the first for a thorough instruction in Latin and Greek and the push toward medicine, and the second, who was himself Melanchthon's student and later graduated in medicine, for an insight into philosophy and the further strengthening of my wish to become a doctor of medicine, first awakened by Philippus.

It should be noted that Father could not have managed his great work of the Reformation without Magister Philippus, though we must not forget that after Father's death he once called the collaboration a regular slavery. His work as a scholar earned him the title *Praeceptor Germaniae*. The reader should take note of this honor—that someone could actually earn the right to be called the Teacher of Germany. For a long time, only Hrabanus Maurus had been so called, the renowned abbot of the Fulda Cloister and archbishop of Mainz, who already as a young man had shined at the court of Charlemagne.

When Philipp Melanchthon in the year 1518 rode into Wittenberg, he was, according to one of his students, small, perhaps sixty inches tall, lean, unimpressive, and possessed of a speech impediment, so that one imagined he was a boy not over eighteen years old, and it must have been a surprise that buried in so small a body was such a great and glaring mountain of art and wisdom.

He was also my godfather. I must note that I did not lack for famous godparents, for which I cannot claim any merit but which on the other hand meant a great responsibility for me; among others, Prince John Ernest of Saxony (from 1541 duke of Saxony-Coburg) and Hans von Löser, Electoral Saxon hereditary marshal, long a friend of my father's. Father was even invited to go hunting at the marshal's castle in Pretsch on the Elbe.

Now Father was not a huntsman and rather shooed the game away than let it be shot. But at least he trotted behind the hunting party on his horse and meditated on the wonderful words of Psalm 147, the interpretation of which he dedicated to his friend: good for a hunter and good to read, as he said. As thanks, he received a handsome stag and a barrel of beer from Pretsch as well as an invitation to the baptism of the marshal's next child. One can see how nutritious the study and wise use of scriptures can sometimes be.

From these two godparents alone, the reader can see what a close connection existed between our family and the electoral house. Whether this had any effects on my later life I still have to relate.

The choice of the godparents was very important to my father, as his baptismal book of AD 1526 shows: "Also should all godparents and all those standing around speak the words of the pastor's prayer in their hearts. Therefore is it proper and right that crude and drunken priests should not do the baptizing; also irresponsible people should not be chosen as godparents, rather sensible, moral, serious pious priests and godparents whom one can expect will treat the matter with earnestness and the right faith."

As the sadness regarding my father's death lessened, my brother Martin and I wanted to begin to enjoy the freedom from Father's sometimes oppressive authority, but an event occurred that nullified our plans. I hasten to add that I had gladly accepted school instruction in any form and continued learning diligently and gladly after Father's death. I particularly liked memorizing and reached quite a high level in it. For my later study of medicine that proved to be very useful, as this is not so much about profound thought and about philosophical insights as it is about the retention of many details, often without apparent connections and independent deductions.

It is true that Mother attempted to sensibly continue the daily business and yet made the mistake in her grief of closing the hostel. After that, the money soon became scarce, so she once again in the summer of the year of my father's death had to take in students.

And then came other concerns. Trusting in God and his elector's favor, Father had in his will manifestly renounced legal assistance—as we have read, he did not think much of this profession—and had shown great naïveté and contempt for legal regulations. The will dated from AD 1542, and it was obvious he wanted the best for his beloved Herr Käthe. Father was in that year often sick so that our house doctor, Dr. Augustin Schurff, a relative of Magister Philippus, frequently came and went. He had only a short way to go because his mouth was often at court, that is, at the dinner table. Father wrote:

> I, Martin Luther, acknowledge with this my own handwriting that I have given all that I own to my beloved and faithful housewife, Katherine, as an endowment or whatever one

> chooses to call it for her lifetime, to manage according to her desire and to her best interest, and this is given to her by the power of this will on the current and present day.

Father recognized the reality, if not always the law (or did not want to recognize it), when he wrote further and sought to establish Mother's claim:

> Third, and most of all, I do not want her to have to care for the children, but rather the children should care for her, hold her in honor, and be subject to her, as God has intended from birth. Because I have seen and experienced how the Devil has inflamed and provoked even pious children against the commandment through wicked and jealous mouthing, especially when the mothers are widows and the sons have wives and the daughters husbands and, in turn, when mothers-in-law have daughters-in-law and daughters-in-law have mothers-in-law.

Our father was aware of the hostilities to which our mother in Wittenberg was exposed when he begged his friends (he here trusted them with more than they were able or even willing to do):

> Also, I pray all my good friends to be witnesses for my dear Käthe and to help pardon and defend her, where jealous and useless mouths want to complain or disparage her.

Even with the assistance of the elector John Frederick, the administration of the will with all its requests and invocations was troublesome. According to the famous lawbook *Sachsenspiegel*, not the widows but rather the children or the nearest blood relatives of the man were the heirs. The widow was also not the guardian of the children but received herself a guardian. Father had neglected to determine that. In addition, this important document had not been officially notarized but only witnessed by his friends Bugenhagen and Melanchthon. So the elector had to graciously intervene and validate the will to Mother's benefit, but he did not resolve the difficult issue of the guardianship. At her request, this was finally accomplished by the elector appointing Wittenberg's captain Hans von Spiegel and her brother Hans von Bora as guardians. We underage children got Father's brother Jacob Luther from Mansfeld and Wittenberg's mayor, Ambrosius Reuter, as well as Magister Philippus.

Thank the Lord that our mother was a strong and brave woman. She gave in very little to the famous men of her time and even, I believe, sometimes awed them. Even when the otherwise always well-intentioned elector wanted to deprive her of her children's education—that is, my twenty-year-old brother Johannes, Father's Hänschen, was to come under his oversight at the court—my mother was adamant that Hans should remain by her and continue his studies, and also Martin and I were to remain with her as well so that—this was the reasoning—the doctor's blessed sons all three be diligently held to chastity, virtue, and learning.

Mother also had the support of Duke Albrecht of Prussia and the king of Denmark, Christian III, whom Justus Jonas had begged to help the widow and her children whenever necessary. The duke and the king quite often intervened for the widow with the elector. So she could—in spite of the opposition of the elector's adviser and former chancellor, a friend of Father's and the Reformation, Gregor von Brück, whose opinion was that after the doctor's death, she should adapt her life to the new circumstances—acquire the estate Wachsdorf in Wittenberg.

Commenting on this, Magister Philippus, whom Brück had asked to be an influence on our mother, resignedly said, "The woman will not allow herself to be advised but must proceed in all things as her opinion and discretion dictate." One sees here the distance between Melanchthon and Mother that existed even during Father's lifetime, and probably Melanchthon's wife, Katharina, was not innocent in this. We know that my mother also had a hearty dislike of Frau Melanchthon.

However, the estate did not become the property of Mother; rather did it pass to us, the sons. Still Brück assumed that she wanted to bring up her sons there "to become squires and loose fellows." The elector, to the anger of his adviser, gave her 1500 guldens for the purchase of the property.

Naturally, the future of her children lay close to her heart, and she believed that without a husband and in these uncertain times, landownership was a certain security. Her trust in God was steadfast, and she saw in Him an important support, but in contrast to Father, she was of the opinion that God especially watched over those who took care of themselves. That appears a little like the teaching of the Calvinists, which our father condemned.

I must here beg for patience because I believe it is important and essential for my life story that the financial affairs at my father's death are presented.

I think today that we were comparatively quite well-to-do, though Mother often complained about Father's lighthearted handling of the money, even his inclination to reject gifts, as the following letter from Father to Elector John Frederick illustrates:

Wittenberg, 17th August, 1529

I have long hesitated to thank Your Grace for the clothes and garments. But I will ask Your Grace humbly that Your Grace may not believe those who maintain that I lack in anything. I have unfortunately more, especially from Your Grace, than I can in conscience accept. Also as a preacher, I should not have in abundance. I also do not desire it because in this life

I do not want to belong to those to whom Christ spoke: "Woe to the rich; you will not benefit from your wealth." In addition, too much will tear the sack. Although the dark red cloth has already been too much, I will out of gratitude and to honor Your Grace wear the black robe, although it is actually much too precious for me. Were it not a gift from Your Grace, I would never wear such a robe.

And in 1545, in November, my father wrote to Elector Frederick in a similar vein, thanking him and saying at the same time that it is decidedly too much: several brands of beer, wine, threescore of carp, lots of other fish including pike—it would have been enough if the elector had sent one piece of each.

It was just as well that Mother had not seen these letters, for she would certainly have become angry and scolded him, mainly concerning the gift of food—seeing that there were sometimes forty or fifty people around our table.

One must also consider the dirty and rundown condition of the Black Monastery and its remaining occupants when Mother moved in. Even the straw mattress on which Father slept was moldy and stank. Mother was well informed about the financial situation of his friends and colleagues, and she would not let it go unmentioned so that he and the table guests would be inspired to give more careful attention to the money.

So said Mother during a table conversation: "Herr Philipp received from King Henry VIII a large sum, 500 gold pieces, and we only received 50. He gets 400 guldens yearly from the elector, and 80 thalers from another source."

This embarrassed Father in front of the others, and I believe he felt a little ashamed for his wife. His answer then was: "But Magister Philippus expends much money for his family and for strangers. He distributes the money. Also, he would deserve that one gave him a kingdom, because he is so important and his work has benefited the empire, the church in Germany, and also abroad."

Mother made no answer to this because Father's reply was too foolish and she did not want to expose him. Because everything he said about Magister Philippus was, for him, true.

In addition to the various land holdings and the Black Monastery, which was provided with the right to brew beer and for Father's lifetime was free from taxes, Father left a large collection of noble cups, jewels, chains, rings, and donated money, which in his will he estimated at 1000 guldens.

His monthly salary of 200, later 300, guldens now fell away. This had been paid directly from the elector's purse because he had no regular position at the university.

The reopened hostel brought in some money, and Mother also received a part of an honorarium in the amount of 50 thalers, which had been granted to Father by the king of Denmark, Christian III. Here had the faithful Bugenhagen provided assistance.

Florian von Bora, my cousin, whom I have already mentioned and who belonged to the household and helped himself generously at the meals, received through my mother's efforts a stipend with which he could study law in Wittenberg.

Immediately after my father's death, the gracious elector had sent a gift of 100 guldens to Mother as a first support. The counts of Mansfeld, whom I did not wish well because they had caused Father to undertake his fatal last journey to Eisleben, donated 2000 guldens, which, however, could not be withdrawn until the summer after his death. The elector had already, when Father was still alive, provided him with 1000 guldens as capital, from whose interest we boys should study at the university. This sum, too, could not at once be made use of.

All this, I am convinced, sounds like a lot of money, particularly to ordinary people like a carpenter journeyman, for example, who had to do a day's work for twelve kreuzers and who could live on one gulden at seventy-two kreuzers for a few days. But alas, God in His inscrutable goodness wanted everything different, and to awaken and at the same time chastise his flock allowed a bloody war to break out. For that he used as his willing tools, Emperor Charles and the electors and estates that had been recently converted to the New Gospel by Father.

In AD 1544 the Peace of Crepy was signed with France, and also the armistice with the Turks was negotiated. So the emperor could turn his attention to the troubled regions in Germany. One can believe that nothing more was in his heart than to reconcile the warring parties, to reestablish the unity of Christendom and, with it, the empire, and to reform the old church in accordance with the Catholic principles and the thousand-year-old tradition. But God did not want that the contending parties should be peacefully united through councils or religious discussions. And so the emperor, with his Spanish army composed of Europe's best soldiers, supported by the pope, who loaned him ten thousand foot soldiers and five hundred riders, and helped by the increasing gold and silver income from America, fought against the Protestant ranks, united in the Schmalkaldic League. The opponents, of course, were all fighting God-fearingly for the best cause.

Soon the situation stood badly for the Schmalkalders, especially when the kaiser succeeded in winning the young duke Maurice of Saxony over to his side. For this he promised him the electorate, which so far had been with the duke's cousin Elector John Frederick, the gracious prince of my father. After that, Maurice was called the Judas of Meissen.

On the 24th of April, 1547, the emperor won the battle at Mühlberg on the Elbe, in which our elector, John Frederick, was taken captive and stripped of his electorate in favor of the aforementioned cousin. Also, Landgrave Philip of Hesse surrendered and was likewise taken prisoner.

In the battle on the Lochauer Heath, as it is still called today, John Frederick had fought bravely even though hindered by his corpulence and not quite sober, which did not help. His troops were surprised by the emperor's soldiers, among whom the Spanish army especially stood out. They crossed the Elbe unnoticed by the elector's army, whose general, the elector himself, with laudable trust in God had just attended a service held in a tent. He had appropriately prayed for victory in the coming clash, but it does not always go according to one's wishes even though they be pious.

The inordinate fondness of our prince for the good beer from Torgau—as if he had divined what was coming—had been audibly dispraised by my father in a sermon held in Torgau Castle and attended by such high-standing persons as the electoral prince of Brandenburg and Bishop Matthias of Jagow. Father asked the congregation urgently as honorable people not to take the drunkenness of the court as an example.

Wars and rumors of wars had already caused Mother in October of 1546 to flee from Wittenberg with us children. With some of our goods in several carts, we traveled through Dessau to Magdeburg. At the time, I could not understand why, without a visible cause, we did this. Johannes Bugenhagen, at any rate, stayed in Wittenberg while Magister Philippus also went away and took refuge in Zerbst. I almost believe that it was he who had advised Mother to flee. Perhaps it had come to his ear that the emperor's general of the Hungarian troops had boasted he wanted to excavate the bones of Luther and feed them to the dogs. And he wanted to cut to pieces Bugenhagen and Melanchthon and completely destroy the town. In addition, soldiers had hanged several Protestant village priests in their own churches, which as martyrs' deaths is admittedly not without merit in God's eyes.

Wolf Sieberger, Father's true helper, remained in the Black Monastery to oversee what had remained.

My fourteenth birthday on January 28th was therefore a quite poor affair. Nobody was in the mood to sing and be cheerful, and I could be happy that my birthday was noticed at all. I at least received a new pair of trousers, because to my shame you could see my underclothes through holes in my old ones. It was clear to me that Mother at the moment had no money for presents, because in order to pay for our accommodations and the cost of the flight, she had been forced to sell part of Father's silver cups and mortgage the rest.

Johannes, our oldest brother, twenty at the time, had to interrupt his studies in Wittenberg, which he was not really sad about. Diligent learning and spiritual exercises were not in his nature, which at the same time did not make life easier for him because he was of goodwill.

Because of the ravages of the war, the university had been severely impaired.

Already in July 1546 the elector had written from Weimar that because of the war the university might look for a place to move to, for example, Altenburg, Zeitz, or Jena. Thereupon the university allowed the students to continue their studies or leave the university.

It can be imagined that an orderly course of study under these conditions was no longer possible. I add here that I was already, pro forma, a student myself since I had from November 1543, at ten years old, been enrolled under my father's wish that I should study medicine.

On the 18th of November 1546, Maurice of Saxony approached Wittenberg with his troops, many of whom were from foreign lands and especially feared. The Wittenbergers burned their suburbs and destroyed the crops in the gardens that lay outside the town walls, on the one hand to provide a clear field of fire for their weapons, and on the other hand to prevent any foodstuffs or useful equipment from falling into the enemy's hands. Though enough remained, and the enemy soldiers, who could not take the town because it was the second strongest fortress of the electoral principality, contented themselves with plundering the surrounding lands. Thus our family lost for the time being not only the town gardens but also the estates Boos and Wachsdorf.

The worst was the loss of livestock, because though one can again grow grain, it is impossible to get hold of young livestock, as the plunderers had butchered and consumed all the mothers.

Provisionally, we stayed in some misery at Georg Maior's, who had also fled from Wittenberg but had connections in Magdeburg, where he had been headmaster. This excellent man and comrade of Father's had taken a wife and produced ten children, who understandably came first in matters of food and clothing.

Our schooling was also makeshift so that, combined with a lengthy illness that I believe had its cause more in my mind than in my body, I was quite in arrears. I was bedridden and felt weak, and the village quack allowed me to be bled (though I already believed this would not help without determining the cause of the illness). I think now that the circumstances of the time—the death of my father, the flight from home, the misery and poor nourishment in a strange place—had all contributed so that I even once more began wetting the bed.

Finally, shortly before Easter 1547, we returned to our home, again traveling over very poor roads, hungry, and often soaked through because the tarpaulin over the carts was not waterproof enough. What our poor mother went through at the time pains me to the heart, although I must say my older brother Johannes gave her strong support. The rumor still persists that Johannes had taken part in the elector's army as an ensign, but I know better. He was with us all during the flight.

We became once again cheerful when we saw the approaching walls of Wittenberg and had no idea that the next disaster awaited us. As mentioned, our brave elector now was used by the emperor as a valuable pawn. The emperor threatened him with hanging, which was proper under the law since he and Philipp of Hesse stood under the ban of the empire unless he would turn over the town of Wittenberg. And so the emperor in May 1547 seized Wittenberg without a fight, although he behaved very nobly and forbade his people, among them especially Duke Alba, who was particularly eager to distinguish himself against the Protestants, to desecrate Luther's grave, which he visited. Later, alienated if not to say enraged by Luther's work, he expressed that in view of the resulting religious and political turmoil in the empire, he should have burned the heretic at Worms, but it was now too late. Since he was an intelligent man, he surely did not want to pour oil on the fire of the religious war, and he left Luther's grave as he had found it.

Our elector had to sign the Wittenberg Capitulation, which meant that he lost the electorate to the Albertine line of Dresden, that is, to Duke Maurice of Saxony. As early as the 4th of June, Maurice was appointed the new elector. The kaiser considered Philipp and John Frederick his personal prisoners and dragged them along on his military campaign. They were not set free again until AD 1552.

The peaceful transfer of Wittenberg, which I consider reasonable because the town was not subjected to plundering and destruction, caused once again the flight of Mother and us children. And again we went to Magdeburg, which this time did not seem secure because of the emperor's victories. So along with Magister Philippus and Georg Major, we traveled through Helmstedt, where at the time there was no university, to Braunschweig. Here we found accommodations at a now Protestant cloister. My mother's plan was to find protection and security with the Danish king Christian III, which Melanchthon quite approved of. Before me lies a very touching letter my mother wrote to the king, in which she describes her plight:

Great, All-Powerful King, My Gracious Lord!

Before anything else, it is my reverent prayer to God my Lord that Your Majesty and all Your loved ones may fare well and that Your Majesty will rule happily ever after.

Most Gracious Lord. After I have had in this year many great distresses and heartaches, of which the first is my and my children's misery at the death of my lord husband, whose death anniversary approaches on February 18th; and following after that these dangerous wars, which are laying waste to the fields of our beloved fatherland with no end in sight to the misery and suffering: is for me in such distress a great and high comfort that Your Majesty has sent both a gracious letter and the gift of 50 thalers for the comfort of myself and my children, also further that Your Majesty promised us to continue Your gracious benevolence toward a poor widow and my poor orphans.

For all this I am deeply grateful and hope that God the Lord, who calls Himself a Father of widows and orphans, may bestow on Your Majesty and Your Royal Wife, whom I call my Most Gracious Queen, together with all your lands and people, all His Grace and Goodwill.

I am again proud of my dear mother. She portrayed our misery and was thankful for the gifts that had been bestowed but expressed no new request. That is more effective than a direct appeal for help. Furthermore, she reminded the loving God of His promise to provide for widows and orphans. Of course, with this she reminded the king that he, as king, is God's tool.

There is also a published note from Melanchthon in which he complains bitterly about Mother's fate, because he had a fine sense of justice:

When the war broke out, she was forced to wander about in misery with her orphaned children under great difficul-

> ties and dangers, and besides the evils which are manifold for widows, she experienced the greatest ingratitude from many who should have been helpful in view of the enormous service of her husband to the church, but had been disappointed instead in a most disgraceful manner.

Duke Francis of Lüneburg cautioned us about continuing our trip to Denmark because the land was full of soldiers.

So we got only as far as Gifhorn in the dukedom of Lüneburg and then returned to Wittenberg at the end of June. Already on June 6th, Wittenberg had embraced the new elector, Maurice, and thus the war came to a temporary end.

This homage to Maurice meant that we, the remaining family of Dr. Martin Luther, had unfortunately now lost our powerful patron, intercessor, and gracious helper, the former (as we had to now regrettably call him) elector, John Frederick, who had always explicitly called himself a follower and friend of Father's. I must add here (because I am what people call a stickler for detail) that shortly before his death he received in the Treaty of Naumberg, concluded in 1554, the right to call himself "born elector."

So had Mother no assistance in a litigation before the bailiff in Leipzig from 1548 to 1550 against a neighbor in regard to our estate in Zülsdorf, which had suffered greatly from soldiers of various nationalities. It had been given to her by my father in 1540 in his will as dowry. The neighbor wanted to dispute her well-known rights in connection to the property. As far as I can remember, Mother had no success with the litigation, which even Melanchthon was unable to help her with.

The estate in Zülsdorf was particularly close to my mother's heart because of the beautiful and painful memories regarding her marriage that were associated with it. The estate lies near Lippendorf, her birthplace, and belonged once to the Bora family. Father often lovingly called Mother "the gracious lady of Zülsdorf," also, "Her gracious lady of Bora and Zülsdorf." He was without doubt a little proud of her noble parentage despite the certain affectionate irony seen in this way of addressing her. The property had cost Father 600 guldens (money that he had thanks to Mother's economic efforts and acumen), and it was said the elector had again added 600 guldens in order to restore the house. Because of Zülsdorf, Mother was often absent from Wittenberg, and when our studies allowed, we children accompanied her—much to Father's pain, which caused him to write sweetly wistful letters. I am happy to possess one of these letters, which attests to the relationship between my parents:

Dear Käthe,

I am surprised that you do not write or communicate, because you well know that we here are not without concern for you since Mainz and many popish-minded nobles in Meissen are very hostile. Sell and buy what you can, and come home. You are much in my heart.

All praise be to God, because we were after all not completely left alone.

There was at first, as mentioned, the king of Denmark, who continued to pay her fifty guldens a year. And secondly, Duke Albrecht of Prussia, not to be confused with Albrecht of Brandenburg, cardinal, elector, and enemy of the Reformation, already mentioned at length. Duke Albrecht was grand master of the Teutonic Order, who was acquainted since 1525 with the New Gospel of Father's and had converted—on Father's advice, for which he was very thankful—the order state into the Duchy of Prussia. His uncle, King Sigismund I of Poland, confirmed his inheritance of the dukedom, for which he became the king's vassal. Albrecht remained a lifelong friend of our family.

Duke Albrecht now—and here I come back to the affairs of our family—founded in Königsberg a university after the Wittenberg model with Melanchthon's son-in-law Georg Sabinus as rector.

The reader will realize how useful connections, relationships, and relatives are for advancing in life.

At any rate, Johannes, our oldest brother, whose jurisprudence studies in Wittenberg had been interrupted, then attended Königsberg with the support of Duke Albrecht, well supplied with Mother's recommendations, who hastened to apologize for possible inexperience and the resulting awkwardnesses of her twenty-two-year-old. Naturally, Magister Philippus and Justus Jonas also provided Johannes with good advice.

In this way, Mother thought our brother was well and safely provided for in order to begin a successful life.

Now it came to pass that Johannes became involved in a dispute whirling around Andreas Osiander about the doctrine of justification as taught by Melanchthon. Osiander, otherwise a respected man of the Reformation, differed with the teaching of Melanchthon on one important point. While Magister Philippus was of the opinion that man, even after the justification by faith, remains a sinner before Christ, Osiander and his friends believed Christ's righteousness would become the essential component for the believer. We see here how such a question, unanswerable really, can once again lead to years of—if not eternal—discord, and how little the combatants were prepared to exercise Christian humility and forgiveness.

New concerns for Mother: in the summer of 1551 she received a letter from Duke Albrecht that criticized the conduct of her son. Johannes had been involved in some quarrels that he would have done well to avoid. So he refused her request to finance her son's trip to Italy or France in order to complete his law studies. He wrote: "We find that Our Gracious Will for him has not served as we hoped."

I have to say that Mother here does not act exactly modestly when addressing such wishes. She probably did not have the correct picture of the academic achievements of her son, who did not lack for diligence but probably lacked the intellect. How he was to supply the latter, I do not know.

But she was then satisfied when the duke, in respect for the services of Father, offered to finance Johannes's further studies in Königsberg or Wittenberg. Johannes returned to Wittenberg, where Mother received him with joy. Here he once again resumed his studies.

This happened in 1551. I was eighteen years old at the time, *studiosus medicinae* at the University of Wittenberg, and was happy to have my brother here, whose support my ailing mother urgently needed.

Now events concerning my life, the town of Wittenberg, and our mother began to hurtle along.

In the summer of 1552, it pleased God once again to punish Wittenberg with the plague, which for our mother had disastrous consequences. However, God acted perhaps with a view toward my fate since the events brought me into contact with Anna von Warbeck, which will soon be told.

The town council of Torgau offered the university—professors and students as well as our family—the Saxon Residence as a refuge. Torgau was a large town and had at the time about six thousand residents, including those living outside the city walls, journeymen, and servants. On the 17th of July, the professors began their lectures in rooms of the disbanded Franciscan monastery.

Mother hesitated because she wanted to wait for the harvest to ripen and store it for the next winter. Much, however, was not harvested as, in addition to the plague, a great drought was added in the summer of 1552. So grain for bread was scarce and therefore all the more expensive.

As the plague moved into the Black Monastery, she resolved to follow the university mainly out of fear for us—myself and my sister, Margarethe. She also knew that only in Torgau could I continue my studies. For herself, she seemed to have no fear. Or rather, after observing an illness in her for some time, I suspected it was exhaustion and physical weakness, a sort of life fatigue, as though in her desire for her beloved husband it was only the concern for her children that prevented her from following after him. She also told me she no longer felt strong enough to care for the plague-infected who would, as her experience told her, be brought in numbers to the Black Monastery because it was believed by many that the *genius loci oder Lutheri* would help in healing.

So in September we moved away again to Torgau, where the council already on the 25th of July had closed the gates of the town to strangers in order to prevent the plague from entering. We were, however, told that for the blessed widow of Luther and her children an exception would be made.

Shortly before the Torgau Gate, after about a half day's hard journey, it happened: we were sitting in the cart and Mother was driving when the horses shied, reared, and threatened to bolt. Mother, as always, made a quick decision, though she was fifty-three years old and not well, and jumped out of the cart before I could prevent her in order to calm the animals. The horses finally calmed down, but Mother in the process was thrown into a ditch beside the road, which in spite of the drought still contained water. As she was soaked through and apparently injured, Margarethe, who had accompanied the accident with a shrill but not helpful cry, and I lifted her into the cart. She moaned loudly and complained of pain in her hip.

In Torgau we took her to a house on the Scharfenberg where she had been offered accommodations. The house was owned by the Karsdörfer family. Michel Karsdörfer had been the ducal cook, although at the time of our arrival he had already passed away. So only his widow and her children lived then in the house, which offered plenty of space.

Immediately behind the front door to the left there was a large, bright room that we had permission to use for Mother. She lay in bed with her face to the window, through which she could see the tower of the elector's—the former elector's—residence.

From then on, her condition worsened. She could only lie in bed, and for three months she stayed in the house, in which more than twenty-five years before, after her flight from the convent, she first met the love of her life, Martin Luther.

I derive a little comfort from the fact that my sister, Margarethe, so selflessly nursed Mother in order not to have her attended to by strangers, and also that Mother was able to witness Margarethe's eighteenth birthday on December 17th, 1552. My engagement, which rightly could be called a good match, she could also approve with great happiness.

She died on the 20th of December, 1552. I sat by her bed on a stool and held her hand until it became cold. Margarethe, on the other side of the bed, could barely see because of the tears. The strange thing for me—only now understandable after having seen many people mourn—was that immediately after the passing away, we were so overcome by a strong hunger that for a while we forgot our sadness and fell in heartily when the widow, in whose house Mother lay and to whom she bequeathed her fur coat and silver, brought us a cold meal of bread, lard, pickled cucumbers, and slices of cold roast, served daintily on two boards with two mugs of beer. Only then could we, to some extent strengthened, return to our dead mother and once again take up our mourning.

Today I am quite certain that my mother, by falling into the ditch and getting thoroughly soaked, died of pneumonia as well as of her terrible grieving. In addition, by the symptoms and attendant pain, the fall had broken her pelvis, and had she recovered, she would never have walked again without assistance. This kind of fracture, after many years, I could verify. Out of respect and consideration for my readers, I will not say more here. The *medici* among you know what I am speaking about.

What the people after the death of my father had failed to provide for Mother, they seemed to want to atone for through honors and tributes.

There appeared at the university a worthy notice from Magister Philippus, which stated:

> During the entire time of her illness she had taken comfort in the words of God, and with the warmest prayers had desired a peaceful departure from this sorrowful life; also she had prayed that God may protect the church and its children and that the pure doctrine that the Lord has given this last age through her husband's voice may be inherited unadulterated by the coming offspring.

With all due respect for Magister Philippus, I must make some objections. Our mother was a pious Christian, without doubt, and I hope to meet her again in heaven. That she, during her last days, was concerned with the purity of the Lutheran teaching and with the fate of the church is—and I, along with my sister, was often by her bed and spoke much with her—a great misrepresentation of what actually took place. She was worried about her salvation, that is correct, but also about whether her husband in heaven would again recognize her: "If my dear master again recognizes me and calls me by my name, and we are together again as we were here below," she said to me shortly before her death in these words. Then she looked with eager eyes at the soaring tower of the residence in the middle distance as though it were an announcement of the heavenly Jerusalem.

She was at the time so very much aged, sick, gray with thinning hair that I said to her that Father would certainly recognize his sweetheart, because in heaven it is not the eyes that speak, it is the heart.

Quite literally true has been the description of her and our lives after Father's death: "With her orphaned children she was forced to wander like an outlaw under the greatest threats. Much ingratitude had she experienced, and that from the very people from whom, because of the service of her husband to the church, she should have expected help. In this she was certainly deceived."

Indeed, Father had changed the world. Many have become rich through his service, from the printers, who were required to pay him no royalties and did not consider it necessary, even after his death, to pay Mother anything for the numerous reprints, to the nobles and princes, who could take possession of church property, which was one of the reasons why many clung strongly to the Reformation.

The university honored the widow of Dr. Martin Luther on the 21st of December, 1552, with a great procession that followed the coffin at three o'clock. My brothers and I of course accompanied it.

She was entombed in the town church in Torgau, where otherwise only members of the electoral court, such as the 1503 deceased Countess Sophie, mother of our elector John Frederick, could find their final rest.

I add that we, the sons Johannes, Martin, and I, for this honor paid three guldens into the community chest. Her tomb received a stone tablet with her portrait on it—I know not who created it or how it was paid for. In January 1552, with the university we returned to Wittenberg.

It should certainly be said that the university, or rather more precisely, the members, students, and teachers, etc., thanked the town of Torgau for its hospitality by performing a comedy by Plautus, *The Captives,* in which we, Luther's sons, took part. In the prologue written for the performance, Wittenberg and Torgau appear as the sisters Leucoris and Argelia. Leucoris deplores the age, which was not favorably inclined toward education; Argelia comforts her. Their father is the Elbe River, and their small brothers are the Elster and Mulde Rivers. A thoroughly heartfelt prologue, which received much acclaim, was together with the whole play intended as an impressive thanks of the students. Later, as the prologue was printed, Magister Philippus inserted two eulogies to Torgau, for which the town council thanked the Praeceptor Germaniae with a keg of beer, obviously an amount that the town thought a fitting equivalent for the praise the famous man had bestowed on it. Mother did not live to enjoy the beautiful play. If she had, she would hardly have been able to witness it since she was all the time bedridden.

CHAPTER 12

... describes what happened after my mother's death and how I became a doctor.

Now our dear mother was dead, and we were truly orphans. But thank God, we were now so far grown that we could be left behind without great concern. Johannes was twenty-six, Martin twenty-one, I was twenty, and Margarethe was eighteen years old.

Mother at her death had debts of 1000 guldens but also the property in Zülsdorf, the sale of which brought in 956 guldens and reasonably took care of the debt.

I will now first tell how we siblings proceeded with the legacy of our parents before I turn to the sweet theme of my love.

Our brother Martin lived on the ground floor of our parents' house, the Black Monastery. He was married to Anna Heilinger, daughter of the Wittenberg mayor. If this marriage was happy, I have my doubts. Martin's wife soon died in childbirth, and I believe Martin was troubled in spirit after that. He did not finish his theological studies and led an unseemly life in my parents' house. I use an example from the year 1563 to illustrate this life I deeply disapproved of, although I did feel sorry for him.

In that year the dukes Ludwig Ernest and Barnim of Pomerania entered Wittenberg University and the Black Monastery, which still at the time had a good reputation as a hostel. The dukes and their attendants lived on the second floor, in the former living room of our parents, and felt very disturbed because on the third floor, contrary to the agreement with the landlord, Martin Luther Jr., there were French, Polish, Swabian, and Frankish students, and day and night they stomped around and made noise. The dukes' tutor sent home an angry note: "Things with Martinus's son have got down to a very bad state; he lives on the ground floor and is reported to be in great poverty, has nothing in the house either to eat or to drink, behaves very flippantly, boozes, and has a lot of riffraff around him."

I must add that my brother, to my shame, expected to be provided for by the other houseguests. This questionable expectation was declined, so he used a key he had duplicated, whereby he served himself directly from their provisions. The tutor of the young dukes swiftly procured another apartment for his protégés. My poor deranged brother died at thirty-four years old in AD 1565 in Wittenberg.

God be merciful to his soul, he was an unhappy man. Our father, who had chosen this son for theology and the profession of pastor, would have been deeply disappointed and would not have understood. At the end of his life, he had already become discouraged in his quest for the renewal of the church, and the failure of his son would have been one of the saddest occasions.

After Mother's death, it was necessary to split the legacy of our parents justly. I was aware that in spite of all my love for my siblings, I could not be too modest. Even if my Anna von Warbeck was well provided with a dowry, I must not fail to add my own assets so as not to damage my status in the marriage.

At the end of June, we met with our guardians, Jacob Luther, Philipp Melanchthon, and Ambrosius Reuter, to share according to Father's will. We brothers received Wachsdorf, which, being a patrilineal fief, we had a right to inherit. Margarethe received two gardens in the Wittenberg suburbs and an orchard on the Saumarkt, which altogether had a value of 500 guldens.

The value of Wachsdorf was higher, and to avoid an unjustified advantage for the brothers, Margarethe received an additional

125 guldens to be equally compensated. This money was to come from the still-outstanding 1000 guldens the counts of Mansfeld had donated, and the rest of the money would be split equally between us siblings. The proceeds from the rental of rooms in the Luther House (as it would soon be called) would also be divided among us. However, Margarethe should take the most valuable or best pieces of all of the domestic appliances of tin, brass, copper, furniture, and silver.

There was some difficulty in explaining this generosity to my Anna. Though, additionally, we brothers did receive—which Anna did not want to regard as just compensation—Father's library, which was estimated to be worth 800 guldens. Seen from today, this estimation seems downright ridiculous, because for a library of books with my father's notes, one would today pay a great sum.

On the 5th of April, 1554, the inheritance contract was signed and witnessed by Johannes Schneiderwien, Magister Philippus, Jacob Luther, and Ambrosius Reuter.

Our brother Johann, to whose experiences with women I will come back in connection with my pertinent attempts with Anna, went into the service of Duke John Frederick, who was released from his captivity, at the ducal chancellery in Weimar and soon received the title of chancery-councillor at the ducal court. He established a household with Elisabeth Cruciger, who had been a widow since 1550 and was the daughter of a close friend of Father's. She also brought a small son to the marriage. Johannes had a daughter with her, Katharina, born in 1554.

A word about our sister, Margarethe. As the reader will remember, she was the sixth child born to our parents, in 1534. She was named after our Mansfeld grandmother, Margarethe. One of her godparents was Count Joachim of Anhalt, who suffered from despondency, temptations, and dejection and therefore during multiple visits from Father to Dessau in the summer AD 1534 had to be consoled. Here Father had the opportunity to urge him to become godfather to the child already in Mother's womb.

Margarethe married Georg von Kunheim in AD 1555, son of the adviser of the same name to Duke Albrecht of Prussia. She had been introduced to him in the house of her guardian, Melanchthon. The young couple lived in the house of our parents, since he had not yet finished his studies. She birthed four sons and five daughters, of which three survived. My sister died early at the age of thirty-six years in 1570 and rests with five of her children in the church in Mühlhausen in the Duchy of Prussia.

At first she was judged not befitting enough by the guardians of her future husband and by Duke Albrecht, but she loved Georg so much and pestered Melanchthon so long that he finally interceded for her with the duke with an emotion you would not normally expect from this rational character: "I surrender to the hope that Your Highness may be filled with compassion toward the virtuous and well-endowed maid and daughter of Luther in the face of such love that surpasses even the most ardent maternal love."

Additionally, there was no denying the fact that it was not easy to ignore the name of the great Reformer, which distinguished Margarethe.

Georg, in 1572, two years after the death of his beloved wife, was married a second time with Dorothea of Ölssnitz, with whom he also diligently procreated. From the marriage came four daughters and four sons.

As when eating a meal one will often, especially as a child, leave the tastiest bits until the end, I only now come to Anna and myself.

My understanding of women at the time was based primarily on ignorance and inexperience, and since until then I had only occupied myself with my own body and the pleasures to be had there, these feelings had something ambiguous, unclear, even mushy-foolish about them.

My brother Martin and I decided soon after our return from Eisleben, as we accompanied our father's body, that if we could obtain such sexual pleasure by ourselves—unfortunately looked upon as sinful—then unimagined heights might be reached in intercourse with women.

Our brother Johannes, who often sought out bathhouses, taught us, however, that too high hopes in this respect should not be nursed, as something very important had to be part of the relationship between man and woman, which is love, which, he pointed out, was not to be found in bathhouses.

Our father had known nothing about one of Johannes's favorite pastimes and would, if he had, have scarcely approved. He had, in his famous treatise "To the Christian Nobility of the German Nation," demanded that the "Women's Houses" be abolished, and he repudiated the argument that reputable wives and daughters were safer if unmarried young men attended those houses. This, Father had written, is an unchristian approach.

Through my anatomical studies as *studiosus medicinae,* I knew about the bodily nature of women and also, theoretically, what must happen in order to completely enjoy them. And what I personally had for this purpose seemed to be of sufficient quality.

That was all well founded, but it did not explain the mysterious charm, the feminine attraction, even when they were not beautiful, that they exerted on me. Was it perhaps their cleverness, not to be confused with dry erudition, which I had already as an adolescent admired in my mother? Their ability to lead the man, without his noticing it, into believing that he was the master? Was it the combination of the more spiritual things with their so-different physique, their apparent nearer connection to God's nature and creativity—which so enticed me that at times I believed I was losing my mind—that made me dizzy when a beautiful girl smiled at me? Sometimes, before I met Anna, I believed that the Devil could well be behind it. Did not the people believe the Devil himself could be seduced by a woman and that it was not always the other way 'round?

Later I was to realize that there were other things that love was made of: an aura of unrealizable hopes, the insatiable desire, and secret tears. For never can one become united completely with a beloved; always there remains an incomprehensible distance, and always in vain a man tries to overcome it. Or he seeks to remedy it by constantly pursuing new women.

Folly, because man and woman were created differently, incompatible to the end. But the desire for complete harmony remains.

And again later, after a long marriage to my Anna, I realized that all that has just been described was replaced by a deep familiarity, a selfless mutuality, and the final wish that God take us to himself, not separately, but together one day. This wish of ours, like almost all others, was not fulfilled. And therefore I sit here alone before these lines and yearn to meet again with the love of my life. Now, in my last days, because I feel that the end is near, it seems to me as if I had existed only as a mirror that receives and then throws back a glow of the beloved, a reflection dark and not of great use.

But at the beginning there was a beautiful and promising woman, Anna von Warbeck, whose sight did not allow those thoughts to come to the surface but replaced them instead with an unordered mixture of longing, feeling, lust, and excessive imagination concerning the joys she had in store for me.

Rumors began to spread while I was studying in Torgau, a whispering and gossiping not only at the market by servants and marketwomen but also in respectable homes, hostels, and the university halls, in which Mother, though lying bedridden with illness, shared that the young Anna von Warbeck would be levied a penalty of several guldens by the council of Torgau because of an offense against the electoral dress code. She wore, it was said, a very beautiful damask skirt with a velvet train and appeared boldly in the town, where such clothing had been reserved for the nobles. It was overlooked, apparently, that Anna was of noble birth though obviously only of lower nobility. It was mainly, as can be understood, the females who vilified the maiden and called on their men on the council and in the guilds to do something about it. Because if the women could not dress as they wished, then certainly a young unmarried maiden who strutted around so insolently should not be allowed to, either.

We students would catch sight of the maiden when she, accompanied by her maid, walked through the town. We admired her slender figure of middle size, got a glance at her brown eyes, and I would often stand with my friends and stare quite openly at her. It seemed to me that though in the main she stared chastely at the ground, she distinctly saw me and tried to conceal a little smile so that I did not know what was happening to me. And a friend of mine, another student of medicine who was familiar with the Warbeck family, told me one evening in the Ratskeller over a beer that the maiden with her parents had inquired extensively about me and the welfare of my mother.

And on a day in the autumn, she actually appeared at Mother's sickbed, bringing nourishing food and wine and spices as gifts, and spent a long time conversing with her, which my mother naturally told me about, and told me openly that she very much liked Anna, who would be a very good match for me. And that she had requested she come again the following week and that I should endeavor to be present on that day and moreover hurry with everything required, because she had not much more time and would gladly see us both united.

My mother had probably wanted to hurry also because she believed the daughter of a noble would not so quickly come my way again. She herself came from a noble's family, and she lost that status with her marriage. So it can well be that she wished the same for Anna, though the latter behaved very respectably toward the widow of the famous reformer but could at the same time not quite hide the fact that she was of noble descent. Even the heart of my good mother had its hidden parts, which made me love her all the more because that was utterly human.

And so it happened that she could still bless our union. We met each other, fell in love, as the English say, according to my acquaintance Shakspeare, and began to see each other as often as possible.

It is not for me to put on paper in too great a detail what happened in my well-heated student's room the first time I succeeded in persuading her to visit me there. I will only say that she was not without experience for her twenty-one years—which I can recommend to all young men, lest they in their ignorance fumble around through impatience—I was at the time twenty years old, so that everything proceeded all right. If she was a virgin when she came to our marriage is nobody's concern; I was at any rate content and loved her as she was. And it all went very quickly then. My mother could yet consecrate our engagement, and on the 5th of February, which I have since designated as my lucky day, AD 1553, we were married in Torgau and later moved to the house of my parents in Wittenberg, where I continued my studies.

Anna was the daughter of the court counselor and vice-chancellor of our elector John Frederick, Magister Veit von Warbeck, whom I never met since he had already died in 1534. I was yet proud of my father-in-law, dead or not, because he had translated the French novel of Peter of Provence and the beautiful Magelone into German. He had given the manuscript of the novel as a wedding gift to his pupil, the future elector John Frederick, and the translation as well. Georg Spalatin, who had become a good friend of Warbeck's, issued the novel in Augsburg in 1535. The book was famous in all German lands and was joyfully received by many of the literate. Maids and lads would have the story read aloud or told again and again because it spoke of such a beautiful and firm love that overcame all obstacles. Especially the boys would swear to their loves that they would certainly act like Peter of Provence and therefore expected of their girlfriends the loyalty of Magelone.

Veit von Warbeck was famous as the translator of the book, and Anna and both her brothers were not less proud of their father and his renown, which also fell on them. No wonder that my Anna after our wedding no longer went with downcast eyes, still gossiped about by the jealous wenches. She did not allow herself to be annoyed, paid her guldens to the council in Torgau only with reservations, and directed a letter to Elector Maurice with the request that since she was after all a noble, she should be allowed to continue to wear the clothing of the aristocracy. This letter I have, with hundreds of other sources, lying now before me, and it touches me to tears by its directness and lovable bearing and charming and graceful writing, done so long ago.

One can now think whatever one wants about Maurice of Saxony, of whom I had previously had nothing good to say, but one cannot think that he had nothing to do. It was a busy time for him. Alliances changed, negotiations with the Roman and Bohemian King Ferdinand, brother of Emperor Charles V, with Henry II of France, with the imperial cities, electors, and relatives—all these took time and strength, just as the paternal care and monitoring of the recently founded and now already meritorious national schools of Pforta, Naumburg, and Meissen, which he had founded. And exactly in this situation he had to deal with the bickering of women and the council of the town of Torgau and Wittenberg University relating to their dress code. And my Anna with her letter was amid of all that. Only later did I remind her—mildly, because she did not love stubborn opposition—of that, and she said that she was then young and foolish and would behave differently today.

At any rate, Elector Maurice of Saxony wrote to the town council of Torgau on the 30th of January, 1552, arguing that Anna's father had been a court counselor of noble origin. Moreover, the garment was a princely gift and sewn before the Torgauer dress code was drafted:

> *Therefore We allow her to wear such skirts honorably and desire that you should also let her do as she wishes and spare her the imposed fine. I further request that you behave toward her in a way that she has no reason to complain.*
>
> *By divine right, Moritz, Duke of Saxony, Elector.*

I add here that Maurice was not the first who had to busy himself with such things. Already in 1546, the year of my father's death, Wittenberg University had complained to our elector John Frederick that the new dress code would place the magisters behind the nobles, because they forbade them to wear velvet trains. The elector expressed himself quite helpless and suggested in the end that the professors should create their own dress code for the university, and he would approve it.

One sees that the electors may choose the emperor and influence the fortunes of the world, but with the dress code, where above all the nature of women prevails, their power ends. So I learned early to absolutely not meddle in any question of my Anna's costume or clothing, whatever the cost.

Anna brought a good dowry to the marriage, though modesty forbids me here from naming its worth, and together with my inheritance and the inexpensive apartment in my parents' house, the Black Monastery, I could without great concern devote myself to my studies. They were the seven liberal arts with trivium: grammar, rhetoric, dialectics; and quadrivium: arithmetic, geometry, music, and astronomy. Latin as well as Greek I had already acquired from my teachers Melanchthon and Veit Oertel von Windsheim before my entry into the *Facultas Artium*. With a bachelor of arts, I concluded my work at the Arts Faculty and began my study of medicine.

Except for arithmetic, I found the fields of study not difficult. I had a good ability to memorize the materials, which then in the Faculty of Medicine especially benefited me in the acquisition of the doctrines and sciences of the ancient scholars. Also I did well in the numerous repetitions and disputations, their main goal being the consolidation of the lecture contents and the preparation for the earning of the first academic degree.

Already in 1557, under the deanship of the renowned physician Jacob Milich, I graduated to doctor of medicine. My doctoral lecture I called "*Oratio de pulmone et discrime arteriae tracheae et oesophagi*," which for the readers who do not feel at home with Latin I translate as: "Lecture About the Lungs and the Distance Between the Trachea and the Esophagus."

The minimum age for graduation in medicine was established as twenty-six years old. The reason was that with the acquisition of the doctor's degree, one might freely practice, and one did not want to demand of the women suffering from illness that they allow a too-youthful doctor to look at their bodies. But because I already had the appearance of a man and was married, they made an exception for me. The other conditions: successful studies including the required disputations, freedom from severe physical disability, and the proof that one had spent a year accompanying a doctor of the faculty on his visits to the sick—a measure that I cannot praise enough because of its great value in the acquisition of medical skills—all of which I had fulfilled. I could also in good conscience make the required oath that I would not take revenge on the doctors and professors doing the testing if I were not to pass the examinations.

Drafting my speech on the lungs, etc., was not too difficult because there were the works of many authors to draw from, which I used without dread and excessive meticulousness. One does not have to name every source from which one draws, and the audience was anyway neither able nor willing in the one or two days of the lecture and disputation to carefully check every reference when above all in a speech they were only fleetingly mentioned.

Much more did they prefer drinking and eating at my expense, which understandably did not cause any wrinkles to depart from the white forehead of Anna. Anyhow, I was no longer surprised that so few bachelors of the arts graduated to a doctorate. Who could pay for it? And, as mentioned, my father in his time had gotten the money for his doctorate from the elector's chest.

It is true that a doctorate in medicine was less prestigious than, for example, that of jurisprudence, which was regarded as accolade, the equal of the lesser nobles. But it was close, and so in relation to my nobly born Anna, I now felt somewhat better.

Therefore, not without pleasure I enjoyed the doctor's privileges. The dress code made that status visible for everyone to see, and in processions we doctors had a distinct front place, as well as being allowed access to the court of the elector. In total, there were thirty distinct privileges for doctors.

When one considers that the first doctorate in medicine was awarded in the year 1280 to Taddeo d'Alderotto, personal physician to Pope Honorius IV, without any scientific merit but rather simply due to his high position, one can see the enormous progress that has occurred in the academic world.

Now I beg the reader for sympathy in regard to my and my Anna's financial situation as I record how, at the time, the university staff and worthies from the town feasted at the expense of newly designated or already-appointed doctors, including me, and what other costs incurred.

Already on the Sunday preceding the graduation, the participants, among them the nobles of the town, council members, professors, bachelors, the beadle, and still other people, were strengthened for the coming ordeal with a dinner that included sweetmeats and good spiced wine.

On the evening of the graduation they were feasted again under the supervision of the faculty, the cost of which was provided again by the new doctor and the quality of which was not intended to bring shame to the faculty. The next day found the group together again, allegedly to eat the leftovers, resulting of course in an expensive banquet. On this occasion the overall bill was to be paid by the host—the new doctor.

In addition to those meals, there were to be provided fees to the faculty, to the president of the disputations, to the professors, the chancellor, the beadle, and the messenger who delivered the invitations to the event. Added to that was the required procurement of the new doctor's hat, ring, and robe.

The most annoying requirement, however, was the bestowing of traditional gifts and honorariums, such as money for wine, gloves (sometimes made from deer leather), jerkins, berets, and cloths to various people because one could never be sure who was to be considered important. In the end, in spite of all caution and care, someone remained offended, and they would pursue one with malice as long as they were able to.

I hear today that the times have somewhat changed and that the doctoral candidate now must commit to a predetermined amount of money not to be exceeded. The list of my graduation costs compiled by Anna shows the irritating sum of 250 ducats.

Not included in the above cost is the payment to a few strong young lads who for the days of the feasting ensure there is order. It would sometimes happen in the past that some students who had not been invited to the doctoral meal, in spite of instructions from the chancellor to remain on those days in their dormitories and rooms, would fall upon the servers carrying food and drink to the meal, or the remaining food to the doctor's room for the next day, and snatch bowls and bottles from them. Also, they sought to force their way into the feast and raise much noise.

In the end, everyone was exhausted and probably happy that the events were over. I can at least say that was true for myself and Anna, who for the most part stayed in the background during the festivities.

We went back to our rooms in the Black Monastery and, getting a warm fire going in the oven, fell into each other's arms and enjoyed the warmth and our newly acquired status. I think also that Anna was not a little proud of me because I sensed she gave herself to me with a special intensity and passion. Perhaps she remembered at that moment that a doctorate in medicine, which, by the way, also applies to jurisprudence, served as qualification for a teaching post in theology, though only at a low level, and saw it as her duty to abandon herself in a particularly pleasing way.

CHAPTER 13

. . . contains Christophorus Silberschlag's confession and is inserted at this point because it is the confession of a lost soul—God have mercy on him—that I only now, as I wanted to continue with my chronology, found among my various documents and sources. It rightly carries the number 13, the Devil's dozen.

Christophorus Silberschlag's confession:

I was seventeen years old and dwelt in my birthplace of Halle on the Saale River when I was called to Moritzburg Castle by the servant of the confessor of His Electoral Grace Cardinal Albrecht. It was a gray November morning with rain and snow falling, and the Saale River was high with raging water that pounded against the castle walls.

It was in the Year of the Lord 1529. My father belonged to the Brotherhood of the Salt Workers, and we lived below the Church of St. Gertrud, which was just being restored, in the Thal, or in the Halle, which the Thal or valley is also called. It is even today a dirty area in which one sinks into the mud if one steps off the narrow boardwalks that lie above it. The small houses seem to push against each other, and the smoke from the wood and straw being burned for the brine boiling hangs in hazy clouds over the dark roofs.

Like most of the salters, called Halloren, we lived in a tiny house of two low stories, dusky hallways with unpaved floors, and a tight close courtyard. The house lay in the middle of alleys, nooks, and blind walks, so narrow that in some places one could get through only with some effort. Yes, one might lose one's way, even though one was a resident of the area.

The cardinal's confessor, who was always addressed as Monsignor, had taken note of my father and made his acquaintance because my father, for the salvation of himself and his family, had made the donation of a small relic for the cardinal's collection. It was the nail from the big toe of the right foot of St. Christopher, Holy Helper, after whom I was named because I was born on July 24th. The toenail had been handed down in my family from time immemorial; it had been brought back from a crusade to Lycia by an ancestor, so the saga goes, where he had bargained it out of a Jew. As a sign of its authenticity, it was noted that it had a highly visible ring of dirt at the upper edge.

In the course of the trade, it was said, a dispute arose in which the Jew was slain. The dispute had arisen because other dealers were offering the toenail of the same saint so that St. Christopher would have had to have at least five feet. At any rate, said ancestor took the toenail without having to pay the price because the Jew was dead. My father therefore believed that a curse lay on the toenail, which made it easier for him to dispose of it as a gift to the cardinal, together with the curse, which naturally he did not mention to the cardinal.

I can now, as I write this down, barely understand why such a fuss was made over a toenail. The fuss would have been justified had it been over the *sanctum praeputium*, the holy prepuce of our Lord Jesus Christ, which he took with him when he rose to heaven and which was transformed into Saturn's rings. But even in that case a mystery would remain, as the Lord's prepuce was often bought and sold, as if the Lord Jesus Christ had had many penises.

I rather side with Dr. Martinus's dismissive teaching on relics and saints' worship, despite the impressive story regarding Catherine of Valois, who in AD 1421 requested that her husband, King Henry V, find her this relic, whose sweet fragrance would ensure a good birth. A sweet-smelling prepuce seems to be reserved for the Lord Jesus; thus the story gains some credibility but cannot at the same time be connected to the Saturn rings.

I went over the drawbridge through the gateway where the monsignor's servant awaited me, past the guards, and straightaway over the courtyard to the room of the confessor, which lay above the castle gate on the north side. In the room a fire was burning in the grate, and the servant provided additional wood before he departed.

The monsignor remained behind his desk as he extended his hand to be kissed. Then I stepped back and remained several feet away. He belonged to the *Ordo fratrum praedicatorum*, called by the people, in short, Dominican, and in secret, *domini canes*, the Beagles of the Lord—for good reasons, as was immediately evident.

I don't know what induced me, but after the conclusion of the conversation I wrote everything carefully down, so it is here and can be read:

"You know, son, why I have called you here?"

"No, Monsignor, and your servant has given me no information about it."

"You study now in the arts faculty in Erfurt? In your second year?"

"Yes, Monsignor. And of grammar, rhetoric, and dialectic I have acquired a good understanding, although in the quadrivium I have fallen somewhat short. But I hope to secure my magister."

"Tell me, son, what do you and your companions do outside the lectures and your dormitory?"

"Monsignor, we have very little time. We do almost nothing but study and learn. Naturally, we spend some time with the fencing master, and we also work at dancing and riding."

"Now let's stop making roundabout remarks. I know of your subversive Lutheran activities, and our gracious elector is greatly irritated to see such subversive activities in the town to which he has a rightful claim.

"You know that Luther and his followers are heretics. And you know also what happens to heretics if they do not recant. And you know very well that the Edict of Worms, on the basis of the Bull of Excommunication from the Holy Father, forbids the supporting or the harboring of Luther and the reading or the printing of his works. Rather, it commands his detainment and transfer to the emperor. You know Luther is an outlaw, and you also know that anyone may kill him."

I nodded.

Now the Monsignor took a small bell from the table and rang it. He said, "Now my servant will take you on a little walk to the lower cellar of the castle and show you something. Then we will continue our conversation."

The servant, called by the bell, reappeared and led me silently through the courtyard. He opened a heavy iron-bound wooden door with a large key, behind which an apparently endless set of stairs led deep into the cellar. He took a torch from the wall and set it alight with flintstone and tinder and indicated that I was to follow him. The air grew damper and mustier, and I believe we were already below the water level of the Saale River.

The servant opened a barred door, beckoned me to pass through, and said, "Right now we do not work on a patient, so you have time to have a good look."

And I saw, hanging and standing everywhere, the instruments. We saw the rack, the view of which seemed to brighten the look on my guide's face. I looked at him questioningly, and he said, "The rack is just the first station, at which I often lend a hand. The first part of the stretching often does the patient good and frees him from complaints of the back so that he is silent. But if he already here confesses, he can go, sometimes healthier than when he came. In the second part he is already taut, and when he is then stretched farther, he begins to talk. Then I must rush to the desk over there and keep the minutes of the interrogation."

At this point I did not feel well, and we went pretty quickly past the other instruments, which my guide did not need to explain—their uses were quite obvious such as the breast ripper, the iron maiden, the studded buck, applied stationary or mobile, the Judas cradle, the pear of anguish or choke pear, applicable both vaginally and anally, the thumbscrew, and several others. These all seemed so horrible that I could not rightly believe that they would actually be used. However, I had a few times in Erfurt seen a man who sometimes begged in front of our dormitory, and some said that his disfigured face was caused by the said pear and called the Glasgow Smile, while others claimed it was the Chelsea Grin.

Possibly many of these instruments were intended just for the territion, that is, the showing of the instruments, as just now in my case. It also should be pointed out that since the papal edict *Ad Extirpanda* of 1252, these instruments could be used for the painful interrogation of heretics, but it was also stated that no lasting physical damage should be inflicted. At the same time, some instruments have been used to increase the penalty, like for example the breast ripper, about which one can read in old criminal law that states the female delinquent shall be led to the usual place of execution, both breasts torn off with hot pincers, to be followed by her execution with the sword.

In any case it was clear why the confessor had arranged this demonstration. When we were once again in his room, I exhibited a lively willingness to talk.

He explained to me the network of Inquisition Mediators, also called IM, that the Holy Office had begun to spread throughout Christianity, and how I would be a small link in the chain.

"My son, you will now continue your studies in Wittenberg and live in the hostel at the Black Monastery with Martin Luther. The payment that Luther's wife exacts as well as other necessary expenses will come from the purse of the cardinal.

"In the Black Monastery you will have ample opportunity to hear and to note down the words of the arch-heretic that he particularly likes to utter during his table talks. However, since he has hardly ever made a secret of his statements, of which many have been printed having barely left his poisonous mouth, it is more important to follow the comments of the other participants at the table and to note them down with names and dates. And for all this, your heresy will not be forgiven, but its persecution will be postponed and even canceled if you faithfully follow through with this."

With that, he pushed a paper across the desk, beckoned me, and handed me a quill and a bottle of ink, which was of a red tint. On the paper was a heading, which I have forgotten with the rest of the content, and remember only that it was a declaration to serve the Holy Office in its fight against heresy and unclean thoughts that did not comply with the doctrine of the Holy Church. I signed it and left soon thereafter for Wittenberg.

I moved into the hostel at the Black Monastery and began to study theology. The participation in Dr. Martini Lutheri's dinner table was an inexhaustible source of information that I carefully took note of. That did not attract attention, for many around the table recorded the words of Luther and the others. I sent my notes to the monsignor confessor in Halle by a messenger who pretended to be looking for work in Wittenberg as a scribe. As has already been noted, these did not concern Luther's remarks, which were anyway known and familiar since many were within days printed, but rather the thoughts of the students, bachelors, and other people at the table, who after completing their studies were to carry Luther's heretic doctrines out into the world. In view of this, the confessor said in one of his secret messages to me, it was advantageous to know what they thought and what they later intended to do in order to either halt them at the outset or at the right time initiate anti-Lutheran movements. Soon came to me great scruples about my untrustworthy activity, because Dr. Martinus often engaged me in conversation, spoke to me in depth about theological matters, and was comfortable with my Christian-Evangelical utterances.

I was deeply troubled by the situation and began to get ill. When I learned that one of the table companions, who, after completing his studies and, trying to spread Luther's teachings in the popish city of Trier and at the same time stop the worship of the Holy Robe, before he could take action and immediately on his arrival, was detained, painfully interrogated, and burned, I completely fell apart. Because I was the one who had reported to Halle about the student's plans.

In his "Warning to the Dear Germans," Dr. Martinus had explicitly written: "What pilgrimages had not the people been persuaded to go on! Only look at the new attempt to screw the believers in Trier with the Holy Robe. It is the Devil who has held big markets in all the world and sold innumerable faked miraculous signs. And worst, with this they have misled the people to trust those signs and thus drawn them away from Christ."

Added to this was that Frau Katharina Luther cared for me in my fever sickness, which made my pricks of conscience almost unbearable.

So I have now written this confession and will seal it and entrust it to Frau Luther before I get a sturdy rope and commend myself to God's mercy.

Wittenberg, the 9th of November, Anno Domini 1536
Christophorus Silberschlag

I, Paul Luther, will not comment on this report but only say how thankful I am that God saved me from getting into a situation like that of Silberschlag. Who can say they would be able to withstand the threat of persecution and painful interrogation by the Holy Office and not become ensnared?

CHAPTER 14

. . . is about death and life as it deals with my funeral sermon as well as with the birth and death of our little son Paul, who was four years old.

Life and death according to God's will belong together; therefore they are told together here.

The reader will have noticed that I appreciate order, the regular course of things, the right and scheduled place, reliability, and punctuality above everything else and that I have been trying all my life to follow these principles myself. Yes, I must confess that I would rather tolerate injustice than disorder and see this confirmed by Ecclesiastes 3:1: "To everything there is a season and a time to every purpose under the heaven."

Everybody knows that disorder and confusion are the result of devilry and that order and beauty are agreeable to God.

In order to keep to these maxims even into my grave, I yesterday received the Reverend Georgius Weinrich, pastor at St. Thomas Church in Leipzig, to discuss with him the sermon to be given at my funeral. And lo! he came well prepared and had written down the full text on the basis of my draft and even had a proof copy printed by Johann Berger in Leipzig.

I at once liked the title page, first, because my father was mentioned and, second, because it contained the prediction that numerous people would attend the funeral:

> Funeral sermon at the Christian and well-attended burial of the Respectable, Honorable, and Highly Learned Paulus Luther, Doctor of Medicine and once Electoral Saxon archiator, etc., son of the highly enlightened Man of God Dr. Martinus Luther."
>
> Who in this 93rd year in true awareness and faith to his Savior Jesus Christ has passed away peacefully and after that in a most Christian manner interred and buried in the University Church of St. Paul.

That I would die this year and be buried in the university church was certain, so only the day of my death and of the burial would have to be inserted.

De mortuis nil nisi bene is regarded as a good tradition in Christendom (though it was coined by the heathen Romans). So my funeral sermon will only mention good things about me, though my life was often enough not free from cowardice, apprehension, and resulting lies.

God the Lord may forgive me. But a funeral sermon is something different and should serve the annunciation of Christ's teaching more than the memory of the dead. It is also meant to convey to the living useful knowledge, which in my case is drawn from my profession, medicine, and its history. And so Pastor Weinrich had written:

> Dear Friends in Christ the Lord. We can read in the histories of noble and famous Romans that it was the custom to build temples for people of high merit in order to honor their virtues and praise their laudable and chivalrous deeds. In these temples were marble columns or statues to help posterity remember them for eternity. Among these temples we find the names of many of the great Medici, who were honored in this way.

> The Greek philosopher and historian Strabo writes about the world-famous Medicus Asclepius, to whose honor a beautiful temple was erected in Tetrapolis, of which the walls were almost completely covered by the names of the patients he had helped recover from dangerous sicknesses.

With this paragraph of the sermon I was quite content and would agree if people dealt with me as they did with Asclepius, even if he was a heathen god (which the good pastor was not quite aware of, but I did not want to correct him and spoil his goodwill) and I only a mortal. It is not quite just, I must say, although helpful for the doctor's posthumous reputation if only those patients are remembered who were healed and not those who under the hands of the doctor said good-bye to this valley of tears.

And even the famous doctors of ancient times must have had quite a number of those. I had, I freely confess, some whom I could not help but had to let them die, though it was a useful and welcome custom to hand the moribunds over to a barber-surgeon, who then had to take the blame for the death of the patient, which of course was important in the case of persons of higher standing.

This did not help the reputation of the profession of barbers or barber-surgeons. Additionally, we doctors had to forgo the bloodletting, the lancing of boils, the setting of broken bones, and the couching for cataract or the removal of bladder stones (which was the work of the lithotomus), since all these treatments were unsuitable to our station. There were still others—midwives, wound nurses, and tooth pullers—under whose care many more people passed away than under that of the doctors.

The sermon mentioned more examples of famous doctors and healings, also those that happened through the heavenly doctor Jesus Christ, as for example that of the woman who, according to

Matthew, Mark, and Luke, had a twelve-year-long bleeding, had seen many doctors, and had spent all she possessed on them.

This latter fact is not mentioned by Matthew but clearly underlined by Luke, a doctor, which I regard as believable.

I call this believable because even today one can observe physicians who enrich themselves through the afflictions and infirmities of the sick—alas, even delay the natural healing process by harmful herbs and essences. Others make healthy people believe that they suffer from sicknesses, imbalance of the humors or fluids, and the like, in order then to pride themselves after a rich fee on a healing, which never happened because there was nothing to heal.

At any rate, "The woman came behind him and touched the border of his garment, and immediately her issue of blood stanched and the fountain of her blood was dried up. And he said unto her, 'Daughter, be of good comfort: thy faith hath made thee whole; go in peace.'"

We must not forget her husband, who after twelve unclean years full of privation could finally cohabit with her again.

I was to be remembered like the good physicians of old, so the sermon went on:

> It is only fair that also our deceased *medicus*, the Honored and Highly Learned Doctor Paulus Luther, is remembered not only because of his Herr Father Doctor Martinus Luther, whom God our Father used as his noble and chosen tool to bring the light of the Gospel out of the popish darkness into the bright daylight.
>
> He is also to be remembered for the skill and ingenuity he displayed in curing many princely and noble people, and he lives in our memory as a gem of our good city.

Here I protested and told the pastor that this was too much praise, and would he please strike that. But he answered that my opinion was one thing, the opinion of my patients and his parish as well as the city of Leipzig and the electoral and ducal courts where I had served, another. If I refused this praise, it would be a reproach to the princes and lords whom I had served, suggesting an inability to have found a good physician. So we left the text as it was. I must say that it was not difficult to persuade me. Who is free from vanity and does not set a high value on the memory of posterity?

Pastor Weinrich then went on to talk about the difference between the spiritual and the fleshly heart, and here he spoke what I as a doctor would not have said otherwise:

> Fleshly hearts search for the greatest good in *bonis corporis,* which means the good of the body, so that there might be strength, beauty, fresh and healthy limbs, and whatever else might grace and adorn the human form. But all this is of short and uncertain duration. As Bernhardus says: "How soon a little fever comes or another seemingly small illness, and gone are strength and beauty, and some are so wretchedly mauled that they are frightened by their own shadow. Beauty and strength of the body are void and fleeting, and the older a man gets, the more he is reduced in beauty and bodily strength."

In all my professional life, I say here in all modesty, I have always sought both health and strength of body and soul because I found that both are connected, and the doctor's mindful encouragement and his bedside manner are at least as important as his medicine.

There followed in this sermon many Christian admonitions and hints, and in the end the pastor came back to my Christian upbringing, my clinging to my father's doctrines, as well as my resistance to many mobs and sects and particularly the Calvinists and Papists.

I was careful not to tell Pastor Weinrich about my doubts and uncertainties with regard to my father's life and teachings. These revelations could not come too early but had to appear only after the publication of these memoirs. Therefore, I left everything as written down by Weinrich, also that in my last avowal before my death, I remain unwaveringly committed to my father's doctrine, that I was *felix in praxi* (which I can affirm), and that I served several princes and dukes, as the reader will learn from my report.

Pastor Weinrich at the end of his sermon tells about my ailment with the following words:

> After he had been ailing for twenty weeks and became more and more decrepit [this is the word the pastor used], he reflected on how he had in all things led a Christian life and how he wanted to conclude it blessedly.

And bade me and the mourners farewell with the following words:

> May he rest in blessed peace, and may we all in our hour of death have a peaceful departure and on Judgment Day a joyful resurrection to eternal life. For this we beg the help of the Holy Trinity God, Father, Son, and Holy Spirit, highly praised forever and ever. Amen.

Verily, there is nothing that I wish more from deep in my heart than a peaceful departure, because there is nothing that I am more afraid of than a protracted and agonizing death, as I often had to witness in my medical work.

Despite all hope of eternal blessedness, I fear the cold death and the uncertainty of the endless time far from all my loved ones and from God. I believe in resurrection, but my rational mind also lets me often enough fall in doubt. What if we simply become earth again, from which we were taken, and remain earth? If all the heavenly promises are nothing but beautiful images?

After the Reverend Pastor Weinrich had left me, not without telling me as a consolation that I would be a worthy corpse and that everything would be done in an orderly fashion and according to my will, I sank back on my pillows, exhausted, and for a while fell into a restless slumber.

My dear son Johann Ernst, since 1587 by the grace of our elector *canonicus* in Zeitz, had been with me since I had become bedridden. He awoke me gently, wiped my feverish forehead with a wet cloth, and gave me warm broth for a drink. After he had left me, I thought about the different nature of my children and how our first child, Paul, was born and how he spent his short life. And what God wanted to tell us when He caused us the deep sorrow and let him die so early.

We lived in the Black Monastery when Anna in 1553 entered my study somewhat self-consciously and said that she had not menstruated for two months. Her joy about a possible pregnancy was not too great because, though we had sufficient means to found a family, I at the moment was just a simple *studiosus medicinae.*

But I got up from my books, embraced and kissed her, and thanked God that He had let us take part in his creative process. And I remembered that this taking part must have happened at the beginning of May, often called the month of delight, because in the time after that I had been indisposed for quite a while.

I at once fetched a booklet from my small medical library that I had taken care to buy some time earlier titled *The Rosegarden of the Pregnant Women and Midwives.* It had been written and published by the town physician of Worms, Dr. Eucharius Rößlin. This book seemed to me to be reliable because it had already been translated into English, French, Dutch, and Spanish. Additionally, it was dedicated to the Duchess of Brunswick and Lüneburg, at whose court Dr. Rößlin had stayed, as he wrote in the foreword, in the year 1508. Also, he had received a privilege from Emperor Maximilian that stated that nobody else, of whatever stand or station, was allowed for six years to reprint, offer, or sell the book in the whole empire.

This term of protection is long over, so the book might be of help to many midwives, expectant mothers, and interested fathers.

Anna took the book and leafed through it. She had a closer look at chapter 2, which was about signs of the approaching birth, though there was still time.

I asked her to take her time reading the book and also to offer it to the midwife, Frau Elisabeth Bauchspieß, who had already stood by my mother, and to talk to her about everything connected with the coming child. It is, regrettably, not to be denied that the business of birthgiving is almost exclusively in the hands of uneducated, although mostly experienced, women, who feel and probe but know nothing about anatomy.

I wished there were a prince or ruler who would order the foundation of a school for midwives, which would certainly help to reduce the frequent deaths of mothers and children during or shortly after birth.

In the following months, I watched anxiously and carefully how the little one grew in the womb of the mother and began to show some movement. At the beginning Anna was often sick, but according to Dr. Rößlin this was quite natural, and so we felt consoled. I had some doubts about the advice to let the pregnant mother drink much wine in order to keep the baby small so that it could more easily pass through the maternal orifice. Fortunately, my wife shared my doubts and drank no wine.

Came autumn and winter, and I was starting to think that Anna would present me with a little Christ Child. But Christmas passed, and finally, at the beginning of January of 1554, it started. I had already gotten the birthing chair, as depicted by Dr. Rößlin, and readied pans and pots so that hot water could be had. Also oil and lard were there to facilitate a smooth passage of the child.

But then I left the chamber and went to the kitchen, because Anna, when her waters broke and the midwife told me that she could already feel the child's head under the birthing gown, which according to the Rößlin booklet indicated an orderly birth, shrieked loud and waved me away, future doctor or not. It seemed to me she did not want me to witness her weakness and pains.

When I was allowed back, the baby was bathed and swaddled and slept in the cradle beside his mother's bed. Anna smiled at me, tired but content, and said that everything went well, including the afterbirth, which had already been taken away.

Everything began well with Paul. I had engaged a clean wet nurse, and he quickly added weight. His mother and our maid watched over him because I did not have much time due to my studies. Our daughter Margarethe was born in the following year.

Seen from today, it looked as if God with our help had provided consolation because in 1558, He took our little Paul to Him. I was already a doctor of medicine, as you could read above, and quite familiar with sicknesses and their treatment. But our child I could not help. He had not been ill when the maid found him dead in his bed one morning. He lay on his belly and had turned his head aside.

Long I was puzzled and thought about his death. Could this position in his sleep have led to his end? I had in my medical practice three cases of unexpected child death, in which the children lay on their bellies with their head turned aside, like our Paul. But I could not find out how this could lead to death. I decided to collect similar cases of sicknesses with their symptoms and note them down in my medical diary so that I could via their similarity conclude what caused the sickness and how to remedy it.

Paul's burial took place in February 1558 in Wittenberg with much participation by the university people, and Magister Melanchthon succeeded in comforting us somewhat by saying that Paul had now joined his grandparents in heaven and had probably become a little angel.

CHAPTER 15

. . . tells of how I came to Jena and what happened there.

When in 1558 I received the offer of a professorship in Jena, I had mixed feelings, which I did not exactly know how to explain to my wife or myself. We were still in mourning for our son. At the same time, the preparatory work distracted me so that I had it better than my wife because I began immediately to prepare my inaugural lecture, which on the 8th of December of the same year I announced on the faculty noticeboard. It proposed to deal with the medical doctrine of Galen, and it presented my fundamental attitude toward the healing art: "*Galeni de constitutione artis medicae ad Patrophilum liber,*" which I, following the interpretation rules of my father's, would translate as follows: "Galen's Conception of the Medical Arts, Written for Patrophilus."

Naturally, I was not a little proud, being twenty-five years old and elevated to doctor of medicine through the already-mentioned thesis, "Lecture About the Lungs and the Distance Between the Trachea and the Esophagus." Therefore I felt myself well qualified to be considered worthy of the title Professor, Teacher of Medicine, at a university.

I said my feelings were conflicted, so after a long conversation with Anna I decided to accept the offer. At first I would go alone, leaving my family in Wittenberg in order to see how affairs developed. How well I did, the reader will soon find out.

"*Ecco la mia bella Firenze,*" our emperor is said to have exclaimed admiringly, as in 1547, after winning the battle at Mühlberg with his Spanish soldiers, he came to Jena with our captured sovereign, the former elector John Frederick I in tow.

As I, in a shaky wagon over bad roads, reached Jena, having come from Weimar, where my older brother, Johannes, the head of the family at the time, since 1554 chancery-councillor at the court of our duke and former elector (presently simply duke of Saxony, who would die later that same year), I was unable to share the emperor's feelings. I came on a dreary autumn day, and the weather in June when the emperor arrived must have presented a more favorable impression. In any case, he had certainly exaggerated.

I have never in my life been to Florence in Italy, though Father traveled there on his trip to Rome in AD 1511 and told us a little of the magnificent city. It was not much, because he was ill at the time. He complained about the dangerous Italian air and the unhealthy water, from which he and his companions were rescued only by the enjoyment of pomegranates. He had to go into the hospital so was unable to explore the city extensively. But I recall from the experiences of which he spoke that a comparison with Jena was unreasonable. Perhaps the landscape on the Saale River was similar to the valley of the Arno, but as far as the small, completely unknown-to-the-world country town was concerned, there could be no question of a Florence-like appearance.

At least in Jena, as in Florence, extensive vineyards were cultivated, which according to tradition had been learned from the Cistercians. However, there has been much ridicule about the Jena viticulture, about which it is said that the vinegar grows right on the vine and the wine would make sock darning superfluous since the wine drew the holes together. But still, the people of Jena drank it with a sweetly sour countenance, and plentifully, and earned their living from the vineyards that ring the town as well as their own little vineyards.

For regular farming the fields did not seem practical because the Saale often overflowed its banks and inundated the low areas, and the mountains surrounding the city were stony and dry. But there were reputable crafts pursued, among them butchers, shoemakers, coopers—which are needed for the numerous wine barrels required—drapers, rope makers, coach builders, etc.

Because now Wittenberg and the university belonged to the new Albertine electorate, and the land ruled by Duke John Frederick had been reduced to a smaller possession in Thuringia, he decided to establish a college and finally a university for lawyers, theologians, and teachers as well as doctors in Jena. The citizens of Jena were not completely happy with the decision, fearing that with student life came all sorts of mischief, such as drunkenness, whoring, nightly noise and disruption, damage to the vineyards, the deflowering of honorable burghers' daughters, and fights with the no-less-combative journeymen. Later there were numerous decrees and prohibitions; so, for example, a student could not carry a weapon, but it was of little assistance because the prohibitions were simply not respected. Also, in spite of the prohibitions, students still disrupted weddings by barging in uninvited, bathed naked in an area on the banks of the Saale called characteristically Paradise, and abused farmers at the market through beatings and theft.

While Duke John Frederick I, the Magnanimous, remained in Jena as prisoner of the emperor, he summoned his son John Frederick, my later lord, to come to Jena and spoke to him about his intention to found a university. There came into consideration the towns of Kreuzburg, Eisenach, Gotha, Saalfeld, and Weida, but finally the decision was made for Jena.

Strictly speaking, the conversation took place outside the walls of Jena, because the emperor required that the former elector spend the nights, except in Halle and Bamberg, in the middle of his troops outside the town since he feared his prisoner would flee or would be freed by his supporters.

After much waiting and many petitions to the emperor, first Charles and then Ferdinand, who as Catholic majesties showed no great interest in allowing an additional Protestant academy in Germany, the university was approved in 1557 and opened in a former Dominican cloister, with the four faculties to teach theology, jurisprudence, medicine, and philosophy and able to accredit bachelors, magisters, licentiates, and doctors.

Our sovereign was, as usual, the first *rector magnificentissimus*, while the *medicus* Johann Schröter was appointed rector. He had been the personal physician to Ferdinand and had, through his influence in the chancellery of the emperor, promoted the university.

And so I arrived in Jena in the dark Thuringian November, wet and cold, and found accommodations in the Helldorf house in the Neugasse.

There I had a room with a good stove and a sleeping chamber. Breakfast was provided by the landlady, who also took care of the heating and the laundry, while I took my main meal in the neighboring inn.

Since everything seemed in order, I could now, I thought, begin an honorable academic life.

My first lecture in what was called "College Building" was well attended. I introduced the students to the lesson plan in the first hour and promised in the following semester to meticulously interpret the philosophy of Galen.

I saw with pleasure how the students eagerly wrote and listened with concentration. They were obviously thankful for the summary introduction; such, in fact, was not usual, and during my time as a student in Wittenberg I had experienced nothing similar. They were also satisfied that I drew attention to the Latin translation of Galen's writings and other Greek authorities, for which the admirable diligence and philological soundness of the first dean of the medical faculty, Janus Cornarius, is to be thanked. Unfortunately, he had passed away before my arrival.

I closed my first lecture in German with some personal remarks. I told them of how my mother's experience in care and healing, as well as my teacher, Magister Melanchthon, had led me to the study of medicine. It was not without purpose. The students would see again that I was the son of the mighty reformer whose teaching the new university in Jena would also follow and for which many students were coming to Jena. Then, for the foreign students, I repeated this little talk in Latin.

I left the lecture hall in a very cheerful mind and ordered a tankard of beer at my local inn, which tasted good to me and had obviously improved since the time Magister Philippus had moved here, along with the University of Wittenberg, in order to avoid the pest. After drinking the Jena beer, he had complained of a violent disposition. That had already happened to him in the winter of 1527–28, when he was in charge of a church inspection. Incidentally, at the time when the University of Wittenberg had been located in the town, the trial of the Anabaptists of Kleineutersdorf near Kahla on the Saale took place, where three people were decapitated on the market square.

It was the only physical encounter Magister Philippus had with the Anabaptists. He personally examined the Baptist leader and miller, Hans Peißker, and advocated for the execution of him and two others. It is still difficult for me to know that there is blood on the hands of my revered teacher.

After another tankard of beer, my above-mentioned conflicted feelings were replaced by a milder mood and a gentle anticipation of the coming period at the Alma Mater Jenensis, and my thoughts were filled with plans for bringing my family to Jena, not divining the painful things the future had in store for me.

In spite of the thoughts of my family, I was open to the promising glance given to me by the barmaid when putting down the beer. She had not particularly struck me upon entering the tavern, but now, after the warming effect of the beer, I found her quite lovely. It is the old saying, which also has a medical nature, that drink can make a woman beautiful.

And when after a while the girl whispered to me that the tavern must close because of the strict town council's regulations and so she had time and desire left for me, the thought of a fresh maiden warmed me more than the beer. But suddenly in a loud voice the landlord called the maiden, who by strange chance was also called Anna, and made distinctly clear to her how she was to behave toward guests, especially someone distinguished like me.

With that I became a little more sober, and I thanked the heavenly God that in the form of the landlord the temptation of carnal pleasure had been made to pass over me. However, I will admit that my thanks were tinged with regret. And I add here that on one of the following days, or rather nights, it came to a pleasant deepening of my relationship with Anna.

I went home elated and looked forward to the coming time. As I lay in bed, well warmed under my eiderdown quilt, and in order to distract myself from the barmaid Anna, I thought over the statutes of the medical faculty at my new university, the "*statuta collegii facultatis medicae in celebri academia Genensi,*" which because of their strict order and great detail were very satisfactory. I also found that the promotion to status of doctor with all ancillary expenditures was about as expensive as in Wittenberg.

Furthermore, I found it remarkable that in the Jena form of the Oath of Hippocrates, the ban on assistance for suicide and abortion, unlike in Wittenberg, was missing. But I decided to abide by the words of my Wittenberg oath.

It pleased me greatly that the Jena faculty took as a model the Hippocratic struggle against the quacks who were trying to impede qualified doctors:

> Among the bogus and presumed doctors are counted cutpurses, soothsayers, village priests, hermits, bankrupters, jugglers, urine prophets, Jews, calf doctors, vagabonds, barkers, executioners, pseudoparacelsists, quacks, ratters,

> devil exorcists, forest dwellers, and such rabble. Because these people, after they spent all their money on spirits, food, and whores, want to misuse the medical profession to make good their losses, they try to sell human fat, marmot lard, theriac, quintessences, hellebore, *Juniperus sabina,* and so on. And added to this are the bogus operations and operators.

The regular supervision of the pharmacies, which was the responsibility of the faculty, was applauded by me, and I decided in my medical activities to uphold this aspect of medical responsibility. My interest in pharmacy and herbalism and for medicinal-chemical problems in general has continued since my schooldays in Wittenberg.

As I awoke the next morning, my good mood continued. My breakfast of bread, lard, wurst, pickles, two boiled eggs, and a glass of beer was brought to my room by the landlady, and it remains even today a fond memory as I lie here old and decrepit in bed—very probably my deathbed, where I am barely able to consume a thin broth. I had just finished a little business with the chamber pot, which after a night enjoying beer was pretty full. The urine inspection that I did at once proved to be satisfactory, so I could decently meet the landlady. I dressed and prepared myself to leave when there was a knock on the door. It was the proctor's man, Fritzsche, and he surprised me with a request from the dean of the faculty to visit him in the early afternoon of the same day.

The dean is not an unimportant person. He secures the seal of the faculty, the statutes, and the faculty book, in which he bona fide enters everything that relates to the faculty and that occurs in it. Surely he would also record the conversation with me, the son of the Reformer. The dean also has to make sure that no one who has not graduated to doctor or who has no explicit permission from the faculty to exercise the healing arts is allowed to practice medicine. The accurate keeping of the faculty book alone requires much time.

The dean is elected on the same day on which the rector is made public. He takes first part in all consultations and meetings, and after him the more senior professors. All faculty members are elected for the position in turn, unless the specific circumstances or conditions require someone older.

The dean greeted me in a friendly manner and asked me to take a seat. After I had sat down, there was a long pause. Obviously he did not quite know how to begin. So he took a detour. "You know," he said, "that there was an exclusion from the faculty recently because a doctor from among the colleagues of the faculty had secretly interfered in the treatment of a patient, although another colleague had initiated the treatment. And, mind you, the urine indicated no danger to life, whereby the intervention would have been justified. With this, I don't suggest that you, Dr. Luther, might do such a thing. Rather, I am reminding all faculty members of the passage in our statute.

"Furthermore, I call to mind that there are three full professors on our faculty, *tres ordinarii professores,* under whom the subjects of study are divided as follows: The first covers physiology, in which the professor is allowed to read Hippocrates or Galen or Avicenna, whichever he prefers. The second covers pathology, the third, therapy; both interpret the writings of the above classics. You see, Dr. Luther, you are, so to say, somewhat superfluous but nevertheless a professor, but classified with the rank of assessor to the faculty, with a correspondingly lower honorarium. You may, of course, continue your lectures and disputations and make the patient visits with the students and also have a seat on the faculty meetings. But you are also free at any time to seek a more lucrative position at another academy, in which we will support you."

The dean must have seen the grieved look on my face, because he hastened to add, "If it comforts you, one might call you *pro-*

fessor extraordinarius, but of course that is no official title. And, naturally, this would not help you much."

Only when I was once again on the street did it become clear to me what I had heard. I scolded myself for being a fool for having been so ignorant as to come to Jena without any precise knowledge of the prevailing conditions in the professors' hierarchy and of the assignment allocations. In the letter in which the position was offered to me, it was spoken of as a professor of medicine, and in my excitement I had not looked into further details.

Still I decided not to give up, rather to ask Anna (my wife, not the barmaid, who against my will I could not easily forget) to be patient for a while and remain in Wittenberg until the financial situation improved and I could support a family. Currently Anna was living with our daughter very cheaply at the Black Monastery. Also, it seemed to me that an academic career with the opportunity of continuing my own education—*docendo discimus*—and also the opportunity to gain practical experience through accompanying the students on the required patient visits was very enticing. After all, I was just at the start of my career with my twenty-five years. So I consoled myself and got back down to work.

I started at the time to consider more closely the properties of the substances and elements, because I was convinced that their chemical transmutation, as it frequently occurs in nature and finally leads to the plurality of the substances as we find it today, is possible. I thought and still believe today that God created a primary substance at the creation and then put rules in effect from which the diversity of the world was developed out of the primary substance and that the main path is from the less noble to nobler.

One had to find and to use correctly the appropriate method, so to say the quintessence, which could be all things and would make the transmutation possible. I was anyway clear that I could hardly here as faculty assessor muster the financial support to begin the corresponding experiments. But perhaps it is possible that the time and opportunity might still come. Meanwhile, I would do the obvious, which was to instruct the students.

Then it happened that on 15th of March, 1559—I have here in my notes unfortunately not listed the day of the week—I was requested by the theological faculty to appear before a commission to contribute to a clarification on certain issues.

It must be added here that the new University of Jena, founded by the will of Born Elector and Duke John Frederick, named the Magnanimous, and his jointly reigning sons, was understood to be the successor of the University of Wittenberg, even to be considered the single true Lutheran university, which defended with fury the strict teachings of the Reformer against the followers of my revered instructor, Magister Philippus, and against him himself. Melanchthon had shamefully—as his opponents said—stayed in Wittenberg and therefore in hostile Saxony instead of following the invitation of our duke and the new university in Thuringia to come to Jena.

The sun had just risen on this 15th of March as I entered the great hall of the university. Today I remember that I sensed what the theologians wanted of me, because I had not been left unaware of the dispute among the Lutherans about the pure doctrine of my father. And of course it was also clear to me that the old sentence of Petrus Damiani, "*philosophia ancilla theologiae,*" had today more validity than ever. This principle of philosophy as handmaiden of theology—also including medicine—ascribed the dominant position of the university to the theologians. And it also ascribed to them the unspoken but self-evident right and duty to guard the truth and Christian character of all teachers of all faculties. And Christian character in Jena meant struggling against any divergence from the theology of my father.

The sun shone through the window at the end of the hall so that at first I could not recognize who sat behind a large table that had come from the abandoned Dominican cloister.

I took a few uncertain steps forward when I heard a sharp voice.

"Come nearer, Dr. Luther."

I approached the table and then was able see who sat behind it. It gave me quite a scare, and I felt how my pulse quickened, and I suddenly had to suppress an urge to rush back out the door to the privy. The relationship between mental excitation, fear even, and tenesmus I was already aware of from the study of the writings of Galen, but now it had practical effects that I had to resist with an effort.

Behind the table sat four people, of whom I recognized the faces of two. I could see on the left side a little table at which sat a scribe with a copybook and a bottle of ink. He held a quill in his hand and appeared quite full of himself.

In the center of the large table was the spokesman, Matthias Flacius, called Illyricus because he came from Istria. He had arrived in Wittenberg in 1541 and had studied under my father and Magister Philippus and not infrequently had taken part in our midday meals at the Black Monastery.

On his right sat Simon Musaeus, who was also well known to me. He had been in Wittenberg from 1545 to 1547. As is known, when he left Wittenberg after the death of my father, I was fourteen years old. I could remember him well because he could not refrain at table from pointing out that though he was of Sorbian origin, he was a good German and Lutheran. Both of these theologians, instead of giving me encouraging looks because of our earlier acquaintance, regarded me severely.

Flacius began. "Dr. Luther, Professor Musaeus and I are well known to you. There now is sitting Johannes Wigand, who next year will start his professorship here in Jena but who, at the wish of our duke, is allowed to appear here as a true believing Lutheran, as well as Matthäus Judex. Both are—in order to put their qualifications before your view—concerned with the editing of a history of the church, *Ecclesiastica Historica,* also named the *Magdeburger Centurien.* Even you as a layman will admit that this history of the restoration of the true faith has to serve to identify the papacy and its church as an aberration and that this can be achieved only by the strictest observance of the principles that your father established."

I nodded in agreement, and the pressure in my anus eased somewhat.

Then Musaeus began: "And for the sake of the unity and purity of our teachings, Paul Luther, we can take no account of our earlier acquaintance. On the contrary, our Lutheran faith, the faith of your father, forces on us the duty to suppress our personal feelings in this matter altogether."

I glanced at the scribe, who was eagerly scratching away with his quill.

I said, after clearing my throat, which I often had to do when I was nervous, "What, worthy gentlemen, has provided me with the honor of this invitation and this conversation?"

Flacius said, "Someone has told us—who that was is of no importance here, only that they are considered reliable and faithful informers—that you, both in your lectures, where you seem happy at times to digress from medicine to talk about general subjects and faith-related issues, and also in private with students and friends, talk in a way that is dangerously close to papistry. So you are said to have referred to the Leipzig Articles as quite reasonable because they speak of a certain reconciliation with the popish church. I quote here from a report of one of our faithful students.

"In his lecture of the 2nd of February this year, Dr. Luther said: 'It is important in medicine to investigate the causes of diseases to which the symptoms point and to evaluate the latter only as signs while one fights against the first. And the symptoms are not always unique to the disease. Also, our new Christian belief interprets the questions whether a priest should wear a surplice, whether the Mass in Latin is also pleasing to God, and whether feast days can be celebrated in the new church without readily indicating popism. One can adhere to the doctrine of justification of Dr. Martin Luther and with it be Protestant but still honor the Mother of God or even renounce the chalice for the laity. For the latter, the medical view is that by drinking out of the same cup, disease is disseminated, which cannot be pleasing to God. Also at times there are pieces of the host in the cup from previous drinkers, especially from the toothless, which reduces one's appetite for the blood of Christ.'"

My privy needs were sharpened by Flacius's words. Quite often I had expressed the view that unless one recognizes in all science that it is the essentials that matter and not the appearances, one remains a bungler. Before I could answer, Musaeus spoke.

"We know of your continuing correspondence with Magister Philippus and must therefore assume that you are in agreement with him and his friends—in agreement that one can be indifferent to the adiaphora since they are not essential to the Christian faith."

Now exclaimed Johann Wigand, who wanted to show himself equal in the strength of his faith, because he was not a professor yet but urgently wanted to become one: "But there are for the true Protestant no adiaphora, no middle positions, to which one can be indifferent."

Now Matthäus Judex had to demonstrate he was the equal of Wigand and therefore repeated and amplified the claim: "Understand, Dr. Luther, there are no indifferent things in the matter of confessional avowal. Who here would reach the smallest finger to the Devil will lose his entire hand, and immediately he is popish."

Now Flacius seized the opportunity to speak again. About Flacius I learned later that he, through his aggressive arguments and coarse speech, the so-called Jena tone, was designated as "Fläz," a word that quickly reached the people of Thuringia and

Saxony and was used for uncouth people, and that he already in 1561 along with Simon Musaeus, Johann Wigand, und Matthäus Judex, forfeited his office, resided then in Regensburg, Antwerp, and Strasbourg, everywhere in dispute with the clergy, and finally by even his strong Lutheran cohorts was accused of Manichaeism, that is, the most impertinent of all the heretic beliefs. After that, until his death, he had to lead an unsettled and insecure life, which served him right, God forgive me these pitiless words.

Here in Jena, however, he sat safely in his position and could fight for the unity and purity of his Lutheran party and pursue his opponents. He succeeded even in the imprisonment and suspension from service of his colleague Viktorin Strigel because of Philippism, but he could not, however, obtain his conviction. And I am convinced that the brave and highly famous rhetorician, Johann Stigel, crowned *poeta laureatus* by Emperor Charles V at the imperial diet in Augsburg, died at the right time and so escaped the new Protestant Inquisition and its main enforcer, the Protestant Control Commission. The latter was not a firm body; rather, depending on local and political conditions, it consisted of alternating members, whose influence and finally even correcting power relied less on police means than moods, trends, fears, and elaborate zealotry. It was an elusive and more spiritual phenomenon that materialized in a specific form as required, intent on maintaining their power and their influence and continuance of their group.

So Flacius said, while I began to sweat, "Understand, Dr. Luther, that in our new doctrine, supported by the love of truth, revealed through Jesus Christ, there is no this-as-well-as-that, rather only either-or. You are, as professor, albeit only in medicine and only in the rank of an assessor, charged with the responsibility for the purity of the doctrine and for the struggle against the popish and Calvinistic influencing of the young. The Papists try to tempt people by making them believe it is easy to get rid of their sins by being absolved by a Roman priest. And this corruption comes under the cover of all sorts of laxness and so-called tolerance, which is represented by Magister Philippus and his friends."

Here Flacius was loud and sprayed some saliva so that I stood up and moved back, which the Fläz misunderstood.

"Yes, step back and repent. We are giving you three days' time to reflect; then you will justify yourself before the entire faculty. Should the justification satisfy the faculty, which you can help by naming us heretical students and faculty members, then would we strongly support that you, as soon as a position is available, become a full professor. Now go."

I went as quickly as I could out the entrance of the courtyard, crapped, and cleaned my pants and rear with the sponges provided.

What had happened to me here? I left the courtyard and decided to organize my thoughts in the presence of God's natural world. Walking, I soon came to the Löbdertor, through which I wanted to escape the fuss of the town. This gate had been rebuilt a few years earlier and carried on an inner section the inscription *Turris fortissima verbum domini*. I drew some comfort from these words, which reminded me of the defiant song of my father's, "A Mighty Fortress Is Our God, a Trusty Shield and Weapon." Stepping over the stone bridge above the water-filled moat, I went up the Haynberg Hill, on which the city had built a gallows as a sign of possessing the *ius gladii* or high justice. I passed, happy that currently there was no one hanging there, though under the gallows there was a fresh mound.

Bushes and trees were still bare, yet there were March cups in the grass and the warm sun had now, at midday, lured some bumblebees and bees. The March cups have a certain effect on the heart, not harmless and therefore to be used only in small quantities to increase the pulse. The bulbs are easily confused with onions, so one should be careful to warn the children. In this sheltered and warm location I discovered on the ground some shoots of goutweed, which had bravely survived the winter. This is good against thick leg veins and gout and contributes to a delicious salad and vegetable. I saw the first little buds of eyebright, useful, as the name suggests, when applied to inflamed eyes. Wild garlic, which also grows in these locations, was not yet to be seen. I sat down, as I often did in the spring, on a tree stump, took my hat off, and attempted to think over my situation and get a clear vision before my eyes.

My previous life, which was still easy to survey as it had not been very long so far, passed before me. I, like almost all men, had passably gone through it with compromises and half truths. In order to gain both my father's—or rather, his followers'—as well as Magister Philippus's good opinions, I had often buried my own true thoughts, which were in opposition to the church, but not to the true Christian faith.

One thing was, and still is, especially dubious to me: the torture and crucifixion of Christ, which was supposed to reconcile the sins of men with God. Even as a youth I had asked myself, Why did God in His almighty goodness not simply forgive man for his sins without allowing His own innocent Son to be murdered? Of course I had never openly expressed this question and am glad that I will no longer be alive when the storm of indignation, and worse, against me will be raised after my memoirs appear. The closer I am to death, the stronger I believe that Christ need not have died on the cross. His words say that he wanted to create the kingdom of peace with man on earth. Already in Isaiah, chapter 11, verse 9, it says, "They shall not hurt nor destroy in all my holy mountain: for the earth shall be full of the knowledge of the LORD, as the waters cover the sea."

Also other thoughts, of whose truths I was convinced, I held close because, after all, one wants to live and succeed.

Now what remained for me, in view of the justification required from me? I wanted to remain a professor or become a regular one, properly paid, and provide for my family. What was required of me was, at first glance, not difficult to comply with, as I knew the teachings of my father (which were so much stricter in comparison to Magister Melanchthon's views) by heart and could easily recite them. But also required of me was the reporting of other heretical persons. I could perhaps evade that and say I did not know of any. Of course, they would not believe me because I had demonstrably been in conversation with some. A small report now and then, if possible empty or even well meaning, I could perhaps hand over. Yet would they not always demand more from me and continually drag me into denouncing my students or colleagues?

While I pondered these perplexing thoughts, I looked up and saw in the distance a man hastening up the hill in my direction. He came nearer, and I recognized my famulus, Thomas. He was quite out of breath when he handed me a sealed envelope.

"Herr Professor, this note had earlier been delivered to your landlady with the comment that it should be handed over to Dr. Luther swiftly. So I rushed out here after you."

Thomas stopped for a moment and wiped the sweat from his forehead. I very much liked the young seventeen-year-old and entrusted him with many thoughts that were not intended to become public. Thomas came from a wealthy yet decent tanner family of Neustadt, which lay on the Orla River, and, having worked for a pharmacist, who had freely shared his knowledge with him, he had come to Jena to study medicine. He had been very helpful to me in the study of plants, had assisted in the investigation into their healing effects, and had generally been an able assistant. He was also a big strong lad, and in Jena it was advantageous in the evenings to have a well-muscled, quick-witted, and fearless companion when traveling through the town. Would the commission also expect me to report on this brave young man?

I asked him to sit down for a moment beside me and broke the seal on the letter. It was from my brother Johannes, councillor at the duke's court in Weimar. He wrote:

AD 1559, 10th of March in Weimar

Highly honored and dear brother Paul,

Greetings in God. Your brother Johannes wishes you good health and well-being. This missive goes forth with a joyful message: His Grace, Duke John Frederick, notwithstanding the theological disputes in Jena in which you seem to be implicated and for which, due to his strong Lutheranism, he is not without responsibility, has decided—read and be amazed—to make you his personal physician. The name of our father, the Protestant attitude of the duke, as well as your good reputation as a doctor of medicine have let him decide in your favor.

He has been especially impressed by the report from a trusted councilman in Jena whom you have helped recover from severe depression and temporary confusion, as well as a persistent bloody stool. That the man is now dead, the duke believes the surgeon is to be blamed, to whom you passed on the sick man for ongoing care. At any rate, the man had passed on his good judgment about you to the duke—naturally, before his death.

A letter from the duke's secretary will soon reach you that will confirm this news. Until this happens, keep it to yourself. But I advise you to settle all your affairs in Jena, notify your family in Wittenberg that you will soon be moving to Weimar, and abstain as much as possible from controversy.

An apartment for yourself and your family has already been rented. You will receive the usual salary of a personal physician, which will allow you to live in a befitting manner, far better than you currently can. With that, I will close, since the messenger for Jena is already waiting.

Your brother in life and in Christ,
Johannes

Thomas, who sat near me, had turned his head aside a bit embarrassedly while I read the letter. After I had folded it and put it in my pocket, he looked at me expectantly. "Thomas," I said then, "this letter says there are some major changes for me ahead that, however, you may not yet be told about. I ask you to go back into the town while I stay here for a while. You will soon discover—and possibly even profit from—what awaits me."

Thomas nodded willingly and took himself off home.

I stayed back, completely surprised by the news from my brother. Yes, it came at the right time because it helped me avoid the difficult decision of my conscience that had arisen from the demands of the Protestant Control Commission.

What actually is the conscience? Is it not the ability to decide what is good and what is evil? The scale, immovable and eternal, that indicates unerringly the rightness or the wrongness of a man's actions and thoughts, rooted originally in the human soul, implanted by God for all time to judge one's deeds? Or does it change with time so that, for example, the requirement of deviation from the strict Lutheran doctrine commanded by the conscience, the indication of heretics to the Holy Inquisition now thought unconscionable, wrong, but by former opinion was justifiable? Or justifiable by the followers of the old church but unjustifiable for my father? So, a dual conscience? Can I choose which one? Does God Himself, who created man after His own image, have a conscience?

If I had not received the letter now in my pocket, how would I, in view of my wishes to progress and rise at the university, have behaved before the commission? The decision was taken from me, my conscience not tested, and yet I was not well, because I sensed how weak I would have been in the coming situation.

It was past midday, and below me in the sunshine lay the town of Jena, which I would soon be leaving. Beyond the Haynberg where the sun sets lay Weimar and the ducal court. In the end, I thought, we all go into the grave, and the conscience, this plague, goes with us. Until then, man must endure, plain and simple, in accordance with his nature. Or as a friend of mine from Trier once said, "You are born, in the end you die, and in between you have to muddle through."

So I stood up and went back into town. My thoughts were lightened by the idea of how I would in three days notify the Protestant Control Commission in writing that I would not even think of appearing before them. They would do all they could to pursue me, considering their zealous nature, but since I was in possession of the appointment through the duke, they could—as my father liked to say—lick my ass, although I admit that medically speaking, there is no therapeutic benefit to be expected.

CHAPTER 16

. . . tells how my family and I settled in Weimar.

At the beginning of the month of April in AD 1559, I moved with my belongings, including my collection of medicinal, pharmaceutical, and chemistry books, to Weimar. This departure from Jena in the light of day after saying good-bye to my colleagues and students was, far from being a flight from danger, rather a deliberate departure to friendlier climes, from quarrelsome theologians to—as I hoped—the friendlier and more open world of the duke's court. At least that is what I told myself. I was very happy and encouraged the horse to speed along. For this I had good reason. On the previous day someone had mentioned that the powerful and influential as well as vain and scheming Basilius Monner, jurist and educator of the duke's sons and not unknown to me, as he had been an acquaintance of my father's as well as an eager supporter of the Fläz, had expressed that one should hold me and let go only when I had sufficiently justified myself.

My good brother expected me at the market square in Weimar, to which I directed my cart. When I arrived, he took the horse by the halter, called to me that I should remain seated, and led the horse and cart behind two magnificent adjoining houses. The house on the right was built and occupied by Antonius Pestel, the duke's secretary.

In the house on the left Master Lucas Cranach spent his last days, and Christian Brück, the duke's secretary, of sad memory, his next to the last before his fateful fall in Gotha. I will tell of that later.

We reached the small Schlossgasse, where a tremendous surprise awaited me. Barely had my brother stopped the horse before a nicely decorated burgher house, and hardly had I descended from the cart, when the door flew open and Anna with our four-year-old daughter, Margarethe, came out. The little one pulled away from her mother and rushed up to me. I kissed her on her red cheeks and turned to my wife. We hugged each other joyfully, and in a stroke the barmaid in Jena disappeared from my memory, or, more probably, I gave her a place rather far back in my thoughts. The surprise made me almost speechless, which did no harm because Anna and Johannes began quickly to talk about how this had all come about and how, before my departure from Jena, the apartment on the second floor of the master carpenter Hagenstolz, who lived on the ground floor and had a workshop in the rear, had been rented and prepared so that we could make ourselves immediately comfortable there. We had a great advantage in that the house was connected to a water supply system, which must not be taken for granted. It acted in the following way, which I will insert here because the connection between water supply and the occurrence of plague and diseases interested me as a physician.

The town master mason was responsible for the water supply, for which he had a pipe master and his assistants. The source well outside the town, several sources in Passendorf, Gelmeroda, the Lützendorf headwaters, the Kirschbachtal Valley, and Wallendorf, provided clean water, a great improvement from the conditions in other towns, which took their water directly from the rivers in which also filth and waste were dumped. Water was here provided to the town through several wooden pipes, mainly to the castle, to town buildings and those belonging to the church, to single residences of higher town and court families, and to inns and local fountains. The location of Weimar in a depression enabled the natural flow of water to the houses and fountains.

We had freshwater in the house, and the sun shone in two places, outside and in our hearts, and still on the same evening we were once again able to participate in the creativity of God. This participation succeeded not immediately but soon so that the following year our son Johann Ernst was born.

My brother told me that I had leisure to familiarize myself with Weimar and to prepare myself for my medical activity, as the duke was currently in Gotha and therefore my first visit would still be a few days in coming. But I would be paid my salary tomorrow morning from the court coffers.

My wife had already been in the town several days and reported all sorts of gossip to me, information it does not harm a new citizen to know. The people reported much that was happening at court, of which the health of the duke especially interested me. Some of his habits were mentioned, which I made note of and was later able to make use of.

John Frederick often marveled over my diagnostic art, because I did not tell him that I discovered certain physical and also mental ills less through my medical ability than through an acquaintance with his daily habits.

Now, reader, I believe it is necessary, since much time has passed and much is threatened with oblivion, to insert an explanation of an enlightening sort about family and the court relationships of the Ernestine Wettins of my time. If I have already mentioned some of these details, that is not a problem because *repetitio est mater studiorum.* My writing will serve, not only to preserve the memories of myself, my weaknesses and moral failures, hereby strengthening the morals of the reader, but also to present the reader with new historical information. Please do not jump over this passage; otherwise much that will be spoken about later will not be sufficiently understandable.

What I am going to write here will not always be praiseworthy. It is true that the dukes and electors were well disposed toward me, but my congenital and sometimes annoying exactitude did not allow me to artificially brighten things when a critical representation was required.

We remember that Elector John Frederick I, the Magnanimous—the later so-called born elector—in the battle at Mühlberg on the 24th of April, 1547, was defeated by the emperor and taken prisoner. His son, called the Middle One, was wounded during the battle.

Led before the emperor, the elector, who had previously fought so bravely, stammered, "Most Gracious Emperor!" But this the emperor rejected gruffly and responded in French because in Spanish, Latin, and German he was only slightly conversant: "This you should have realized long ago."

The Magnanimous, brother of Frederick the Wise, was, like him, protector and promoter of my Herr Father and the reformation of the old church. He was capably educated by Georg Spalatin and my father and, nevertheless, or perhaps even because of it, devoted to tournaments and hunting as well as rich eating and drinking, which was not to the benefit of his girth or his intellectual nimbleness. One wishes almost that his diplomatic skills, especially considering the intrigues of the imperial councillors, would have been equal to his spiritual imperturbability. Unfortunately, not true. He held tight to the Lutheran faith, even when it hurt his land, his dynasty, and himself. Sometimes, I suspect, he listened to his conscience.

He was without doubt wronged when he, still heir apparent, was promised the emperor's sister to marry and the promise was broken. Surely the emperor had fear for her soul because of the now-rampant Protestantism in Saxony.

This injustice, I think today, did not justify him in rejecting the council called by the pope or in considering a competing council or in appointing a follower of the new teaching to the Naumburg bishop's see; it did not justify invading the convent of Wurzen in order to introduce the Reformation or, with the help of Philipp of Hesse, taking the duke of Brunswick prisoner. All of this led, as we know, to his being put under the ban of the empire and his condemnation to death. One may consider here the reversal of fate for the elector's house. Barely thirty years previously, Frederick the Wise could have secured the emperor's crown had he wanted it. But with the fall of John Frederick, the Ernestine ducal house fell into obscurity. It was no longer a significant power among the German princes, quite different from the Albertinian electoral house in Dresden.

Saxony once was a powerful land. Anno 1423, Frederick the Belligerent was successful in the Duchy of Saxony—in being invested with the Duchy of Saxony-Wittenberg as a fief by the emperor and later in gaining the electorship. He was therefore archmarshal, and in the part of Germany with Saxon law he, as imperial vicar, had to administer the land for the emperor should he die and a new one not yet be elected.

In the year of my father's birth, 1483, the dominion of the House of Wettin stretched from the Werra and Main Rivers eastward over the Elbe River, from Coburg and the crest of the Ore Mountains to almost the gates of Berlin. On the Elbe River were the residences of Dresden, Meissen, Torgau, and Wittenberg. From the rocks of the Ore Mountains a stream of silver flowed into the coffers of the elector. Wettin was, after Habsburg, the most powerful German dynasty. But *sic transit Gloria mundi:* in the year 1485 the unfortunate division of the vast holdings and the decline of Saxony began and continued to my time.

Anno 1552, John Frederick was freed from prison and resided until his death in Weimar. With him came Lucas Cranach, who had faithfully comforted him in imprisonment. John Frederick died in 1554, a half year after Master Cranach, who immortalized him in his glorious painting in the attitude of petitioner and silent sufferer.

John Frederick had four sons, of whom three survived. The other, John Ernest, died only a year after his birth.

John Frederick II, the Middle One; John William I; as well as John Frederick III, the Younger, took up residence at Hornstein Castle in Weimar and were my new lords, because they shared the rule, although later I served the Middle One alone, who, after some curious changes and abdications among the brothers, governed the remaining Ernestinian lands in Thuringia from Gotha.

Now I return to us. Anna had the apartment beautifully furnished and had assigned to me a study with many shelves and closets, from which I could look out and see Hornstein Castle, which was being reconstructed.

A door led to a small windowless room in which there was a chimney. "Here," Anna said, "you can have your laboratory." On a stone shelf below the chimney I found beakers, glasses, spoons, and tweezers as well as a hand bellows to kindle the fire. I did an almost unworthy shout of joy as I caught sight of a magnifying glass. Here I must add, to the enrichment of the reader, that this blessed invention can be traced back to the Arabian scholar Abu Ali al-Hasan ibn al-Haytham, or Alhazen, which he made four hundred years ago.

Anna's eyes shone as she showed all this to me and said she had acquired the equipment from the widow of an apothecary in Wittenberg whose husband had died shortly before. I hugged her and thanked God for such a wife, who was sometimes rather strict but in the end dealt with me in a loving and just manner.

On the following evening, my brother and our landlady, Frau Hagenstolz, came to dinner. My brother was widowed. His wife, Elisabeth, the widow Kegel, born Cruciger, whom he had married in 1553 and who had brought a son into the marriage and thus had relieved Johannes from some unnecessary but pleasant efforts, had died soon after the marriage in childbirth. The daughter, Katharina, survived and was now five years old.

We wanted that night to consider our pecuniary circumstances as well as my expected payment in kind and suchlike. My wife was already very familiar with Frau Hagenstolz—one wonders at times how quickly women confide in each other—and so I had no objection to her presence in our family conversation. Also, it seemed to me that Anna was not uncomfortable if our landlady heard of our prosperity.

Johannes said that he—before the official notification—was entitled to inform us of the expected salary and other material circumstances.

Before he could do that, the maid brought in a roasted wild boar. She was a pretty Weimar girl with a pleasant feminine endowment whose ample breasts I noted first and then her sturdy legs—which I caught sight of when she stooped to fetch a knife that had fallen—as well as an inviting posterior. The roast was beautifully arranged and made one's mouth water. Then came sauerkraut and white bread as well as beer. Anna said she had gotten the beer from the Black Bear, although soon we would be brewing our own beer since the house was provided with the brewing right, which Herr Hagenstolz allowed us to participate in. With this remark, our landlady had a look of proud satisfaction on her face.

As appetizer there were, since it was after Easter and we no longer strongly observed the fast, colored refilled eggs, which I had long missed and therefore saw with great pleasure and then ate. The recipe Anna had gotten from my mother, and for the use of all the readers of this biography, I provide it here. Is the man in a bad mood, then, housewife, prepare for him these eggs.

Take 8 eggs, 2 spoons of butter, and a small amount of pepper. As green ingredients, take chopped parsley, lovage, and sage. For yellow, take a pinch of saffron and 2 spoons of hot water. If one wants blue color, take dried and pounded violets.

Blow the eggs out, and lightly fry the egg mixture with butter. Then season with pepper, a little chopped parsley, lovage, and sage, and then color it whichever you wish, yellow or blue. Now feed the egg mixture, which must still be wet, or add a raw egg to it, carefully into the empty shells, impale them on long thin wooden rods, and grill them over embers or in an oven for a short while.

We ate well, and I discovered now for the first time what awaited me at the court. Three hundred guldens a year would be my salary, added to which came the gratuitous use of a horse from the ducal stables to accompany the highnesses as well as for my own private use. The rent for the apartment would be paid by the court, as well as wood for heating and cooking. A garden by the Erfurter Gate would be assigned to us to provide provisions for our household. My brother insisted I be aware of the generosity I received here, because due to the dukes' new conditions, the recent wars, and the loss of a large part of their lands, there was not much money.

In order not to fall into debt, restrictions were enacted in the ducal household, and John Frederick ordered a savings plan to be worked out: unnecessary expenses and superfluous servants and horses were to be gotten rid of and unnecessary spending curtailed, as he had announced. Still, at the time of my arrival at court, there were approximately four hundred people fed daily at fifty tables, which incurred expenses of 46,800 guldens per year. My brother had seen the account books for the ducal cellar and kitchen and added up the figures. The new plan contained numerous restrictions, the dismissal of many servants, and an accurate regulation about how many horses the councillors and the courtiers were allowed to keep. But as already stated, my salary as personal physician and the other benefits were not affected.

Anna showed herself very content with our expected economic situation. She was in financial matters far more experienced than I. Additionally, we could rely on assets that both of us had brought into the marriage. Anna had brought an ample dowry consisting of, among other things, a stately sum of guldens as well as plentiful laundry and dishes, the latter of which would last us a full lifetime if we were spared from disaster.

With respect to my person, Johannes, the oldest and thus head of the family, announced to me that he intended, with our agreement, to sell our parents' house in Wittenberg to the university. He estimated that the expected sum would be near to 4000 guldens, which would benefit our sister, our brother Martin, Johannes, and me. What remained concerning the legacy of my parents, I have already had the opportunity to report.

I had not mentioned that there was a residence in Wittenberg, called House Bruno or Brewer's Hut, which Father had purchased as a widow's residence for Mother. The purchase price was 430 guldens. We had agreed to its sale in 1557 as we, that is, Johannes, Martin, I, and brother-in-law Georg von Kunheim, husband of our sister, Margarethe, had met in Wittenberg.

Since we had been living frugally, and I also in Jena had been going to neither whore nor bathhouse (a single visit to a questionable woman for experimental purposes aside—inexpensive but not very satisfying); and even apart from the barmaid Anna, who of course had given herself for free, we could look at the future, which after all is in God's hands, with clear eyes.

I remarked on this to my brother, who agreed with me.

After our dinner the women began to talk about the drawbacks that the employment of wet nurses for the household brought with it. Frau Hagenstolz stressed that these women of lower status, once they started breastfeeding the infants in their care, made outrageous demands in regard to the food and housing. They demanded that in preference to the other servants, they had to be kept in a good mood, because their bad humor would affect the suckling babe. Many even possessed the boldness to demand that their own child—or even several of them—be allowed into the house, insisting their infants needed to be breastfed, as if a little warm cow's milk would not have been sufficient for them. I dared to interject that I considered it better if the mother breastfeeds her own children, because of the possible transmission of sickness coming from the dirty homes of the wet nurses. Here Anna looked at me sternly and said that I must then also resign myself to an early sagging of her chest, whose delicate strength had so far been a pleasure to me.

At this point, before the conversation could get contentious, Johannes indicated to me that he had something he wanted to discuss that would not be of interest to the women. I looked questioningly at Anna, who nodded at me, which I took as permission to comply with my brother's request.

We once again filled our tankards with beer and went into my study, where a tallow candle burned.

Here my brother said, "Paul, I am happy that you have come to court here in Weimar, which our dear mother would have heartily welcomed. That it was a way to remove you from the life of the university makes me still happier. From my time in Königsberg, I know the intrigues, the squabbles, the jealousies, and the mutual calumnies that are prevalent among the professors. I need only remind you of the disputes, the center of which was Andreas Osiander, who challenged our honored Magister Philipp's interpretation of Father's doctrine of justification. But let's leave it because you have had similar experiences in Jena.

"The medical activities should bring you joy and satisfaction because the gentlemen are friendly and to some extent even obedient patients. They also have—different from the average burgher—the possibility to make use of all the achievements of medicine, even when they are expensive.

"Now I come to my actual point, about which you must keep absolutely silent, although you must be prepared for it. Our duke John Frederick II, the Middle One, is, based on my observation, obsessed by an idea that the father of our lord, the Magnanimous, shortly before his death expressly warned his sons about. The idea is that he could once again bring the electorate back to the Ernestine house. The duke's father, as you know, had the most painful experience in his dispute with the emperor, the empire, and his cousin Maurice of Saxony, and he wanted, after the Wittenberg Capitulation, to preserve his remaining lands and the Lutheran Reformation.

"Now I have observed for some time how the surroundings of the duke, who more and more resides in Gotha, but especially his chancellor, Christian Brück, son-in-law of Master Cranach, strengthen him in the thought of restoring the electorate. I do not have enough influence in this situation to make the duke understand the legal groundlessness of his claims, though I am using every opportunity for this. He has been clearly told he has no claim at all other than in his heart. Only misfortune for the ducal house, for the new religion, and for the land can come from this endeavor.

"My position as chancery-councillor is insignificant, and only the fact that I am the son of the Reformer sometimes results, rarely, in my occasionally being invited to speak with the duke. But the influence of the chancellor is great. In addition, Christian Brück is, since his marriage to Barbara Cranach, who received as a dowry from her father 5,000 guldens, growing ever more arrogant and more despotic, and he has the duke very strongly under his influence. But in the end it is the duke himself who indulges in this vain desire, and his entourage knows that and urges him on.

"As his personal physician, you will often be around him and more often have access to him, and perhaps you can succeed in acting in a moderating sense. And when you realize his ideas are even a sickness, there are possible means that will bring his humors, and with them his head, back into balance."

My brother took a draught of beer and stared at me, awaiting an answer.

At first I did not know what to say. I had just gotten away from the intrigues of Jena in the hope that things would be better in Weimar, only to quickly be made aware that here also affairs might not be so simple.

Of course, there were medicaments that helped alleviate certain quick tempers in general; I needed only think of theriac enriched with an extract of opium. This beneficial remedy, already inscribed in stone on the walls of the Asclepeion of Kos, today also called Venetian theriac, is incredibly expensive and therefore available only to the nobility and other rich people. The theriac for poor people is garlic, and not to their harm.

How well tried theriac is shows in its recommendation by the ancient physicians, for example, by Galen, who is the teacher of us all. While it was recommended by the ancient doctors mainly as an antidote, its scope can be enlarged by adding copious amounts of poppy juice and spirits. Enjoyed in the right amount, it leads the patient to a peaceful, leisurely mood, restrains him from hasty decisions, and makes him inclined to behave temperately to his surroundings. Philippus Aureolus Theophrastus Bombastus of Hohenheim, who called himself Paracelsus, and from whom I learned a great deal, had achieved similar effects with his laudanum.

If a person takes the refined theriac frequently, as with Paracelsus's laudanum, he begins to love it and wants it more and more often. The physician who prescribes it and, with the patient's money, obtains it in sufficient quantity makes himself indispensible to the patient.

These thoughts went through my head while my brother stared at me.

"Johannes," I said then, "you certainly don't want me to administer unchristian prescriptions to the duke that would perhaps weaken his will."

"God forbid," responded my brother with a guileless expression. "I want only that you do everything to ensure his health, and if you now and again have the opportunity to speak a word for political reason, so much the better."

That was a clear retreat on my brother's side.

We went back to the women, whose conversation meanwhile had arrived at the prices at the Weimar market. The conversation went on for a bit, then our guests took their leave. Anna ordered our servant to accompany Johannes with a lantern to his house, which was gratefully accepted. Thanks to the four town guards appointed by the council and to the armed field guards, the city and surrounding areas were quite safe, in contrast to Jena, where at night drunken students often accosted passersby. Still, one could not completely rule out danger, and therefore we wanted to ensure that our guests arrived at home safely.

That night I found it difficult to sleep, while Anna next to me soon closed her eyes and began, as on most nights, softly to snore, causing me to remember that I should—without hurting her feelings, because she did not believe she snored—recommend several cups of nettle tea throughout the day.

The conversation with my brother had caused me to reflect, and I decided not to forget his advice concerning the duke. Meanwhile, if the duke fell ill and his plans stemmed from this disease, I could provide some ingredients that I needed for my version of theriac, as they were mainly anise, fennel, and caraway in addition to abundant meconium. For the last of these, however, I would have to wait until the formation of poppy heads in the garden. I decided to do without the magic ingredients recommended by Mithridates VI, Eupator, namely, duck blood, snake, and toad meat, because to me the effectiveness of the *tinctura opii* was decisive. It filled me with gratitude that in reviving Arab medicine, opium had again gained its rightful place among our medicaments. Charlemagne, hard to believe, had renewed the ban on opium that the old church had enacted. Sickness was a punishment from God, it was believed, and one should not mitigate the accompanying pain through opium or similar means.

Before I fell asleep, I resolved to observe the duke calmly and listen to what he had to say before drawing any conclusions about his state of mind or body. False diagnosis and premature treatment, often at the urging of the patient, have injured many sick, the physician included.

CHAPTER 17

. . . tells how I met the duke and immediately became acquainted with the story of the false Anna, and how we fared in Weimar.

In the month of June, I was for the first time called to Hornstein Castle and introduced to the duke. In the antechamber, the previous archiator of the duke, Dr. Schröter, received me and declared that he would introduce me to my work and make me familiar with the physical and mental sensitivities of the duke. In this way an abrupt and drastic change in the medical care of His Ducal Grace could be avoided, Dr. Schröter said.

Then we proceeded into the duke's presence and made our obeisances. I encountered a vigorous man of middle stature who appeared to enjoy the pleasures of good eating and drinking. His eyes stood out a bit and sometimes had a troubled and distant look and seemed to look beyond the men standing in front of him. Then suddenly, however, as though he remembered that attention was expected of him, he returned to the present and had affable and friendly words for us. He was at the time of our first meeting thirty-one years old, though his outer appearance suggested an older age.

He questioned me about my life and, in particular, about my father and how I had experienced his passing away in God. Also, he wanted to know how I intended to apply my chemical knowledge of substances and plants in my medical treatment. As I was just beginning in this field, I remained vague and said only that I believed in the power of some natural and homemade mixtures that help to cure a variety of diseases and were based on century-long experiences.

His Ducal Grace was pleased and asked if my salary and other conditions were satisfactory, to which I said yes, and then he dismissed me. Dr. Schröter remained with the duke. For an examination, checking of pulse, and the taking of urine and stool samples, I was not given the opportunity. The strange hurry was a surprise to me, but I soon found the explanation in the pressure the duke found himself under at the time because of the false Anna, about whom my brother enlightened me later.

By the way, when I came to Weimar, Dr. Schröter, who in the beginning belonged to the party of the unspeakable Flacius and his followers, had become disgusted with the divisions and bitter disputes between the Lutherans and the Reformed Church and again between the strict Lutherans and the followers of Melanchthon, the Philippists, and he had turned away from the zealots of the Fläz. He tried to influence the duke to curb their impact on the people. Instead of following the Augsburg Confession, there were now hateful preachers and laymen who brought forward hairsplitting and damnation-seeking confessions, concord formulas, confutations, apologias, and similar things, which confused even the most well-meaning Christians.

Instead of the great reformers, there were now theologians involved in furious disputes and in court intrigues or completely ignorant people who previously had been practicing simple trades. *O Luthere,* said Calvin in his *Secunda Defensio Contra Westphalum* 1556: *Quam paucos tuae praestantiae imitatores, quam multas vero sanctae tuae jactantiae simias reliquisti.* I translate for the reader unpracticed in Latin: "Oh, Luther, how few disciples of your noble teachings have come after you, but how many monkeys have heard of your boastful chatter?"

Now back to the false Anna.

I want to tell of this because the story will shed light on the court at Weimar and Gotha and the tribulations that already existed and continued to develop. At the same time, it will be seen that my hope to go from a troubled Jena with its zealots to the peaceful climes of Weimar was not very well founded.

The story of the false Anna, this loose hag, brings to light both the naïveté and the credulity of my lord, Duke John Frederick, the Middle One. Perhaps added to this was a certain mental diminishment, which I unfortunately, through my personal medical activity as well as the best medicines, treatments, and caring conversations, could not remedy. He seemed to me so often needy and childlike and zealous to do everything right and good—at the same time making mistake after mistake—that he quite won my affection, and I decided to serve him truly and if possible to protect him from the worst.

The false queen, Anna, pretended that she was Anne of Cleve and therefore a relative of our three dukes as well as the fourth wife of Henry VIII of England and that she had not, as one read in the news from England, died anno 1557; rather, she had merely given out that she was dead in order to, as a strict Protestant, avoid the persecution of Bloody Mary. She succeeded, she had said, in bringing tremendous wealth from England to Germany, which she intended to bequeath to the dukes of Saxony but first and foremost to John Frederick, the Middle One, to obtain protection, princely housing, and a decent financial allowance. There would be testimonies describing the treasures. Among them were: England's crown and sovereign's orb; a collar with a ruby and other gemstones; 25 tons of gold in crowns; 7 pearl robes; 3 gold pieces; 14 gold chains, which weighed 5000 crowns; 14 girdles and chains weighing 7000 crowns; 24 pairs of armbands, which weighed 2000 crowns; 12 pearl hoods; 14 pearl berets; and 1 necklace with gemstones estimated at 3000 crowns.

I quote from a file from the years 1558 and 1559, which was sent to me by a friendly archivist in the ducal Secret State Archives in Weimar:

> Report concerning the arch-deceiver who told John Fredrick, the Middle One, of Saxony that she was, first, Frau Anna, born of Jülich, King Henry of England's widow, then a countess in Friesland, married Countess of Manderscheid, further a born Countess of Rietberg, further an illegitimate daughter of Duke John of Cleve.

I can still remember what my brother told me of the interrogations of Anna he carried out on behalf of the duke in Gotha and the castle Tenneberg. The duke had finally become wiser after repeated warnings, among them from his brother John William, at the time, in Paris, a general of the French king Karl IX in his campaign against the Huguenots.

The false Anna told the most adventurous tales and lies, which in many places such as Brandenburg, Nuremberg, Wittenberg, and still others had been believed. The duke even visited her personally in Rossla, where she seemed extremely plausible to him because she knew the situation at the Court of Cleve most accurately, or at least spoke most credibly about it. And she sustained the duke's hope by describing her treasures, which she promised to bequeath to him after she had only retrieved them from Nuremberg or another location—she dared not specify where because the Devil nightly threatened to strangle her.

Already on the 3rd of January, 1559, a warning had reached the duke from a clerk, Fritz Ditterich from Leipzig, in which he said that it had been reported by trustworthy people that a woman who had been in Rossla had claimed that she was a born duchess of Jülich and queen of England. She was the same person who already deceived the duke of Prussia, the duke Frederick of Liegnitz, the duke of Mecklenburg, and the elector Joachim of Brandenburg. In Mecklenburg she had stolen silver drinking vessels, and she had cost the Brandenburg elector, where she had been well boarded and maintained, 800 guldens.

Since the clerk was only a person of lower station, the duke was persuaded by his chancellor, Christian Brück, to ignore him as just a tool of Anna's enemies.

As a way to protect her from snares and persecutions, Anna was granted chambers in Grimmenstein Castle in Gotha, where, under the protection of the ducal steward and castellan Bernhard von Mila, she was denied nothing. She secured her position by signing a donation contract with the duke and confirming it through a second contract, in which they both agreed: Duke John Frederick the Middle One should receive 1.5 million crowns; Duke John William, in the event he would become king of England through marriage or otherwise, should receive crown, scepter, and sovereign's orb of England and several hundred thousand crowns in cash; the youngest duke, John Frederick the Younger, should receive 500,000 crowns.

Blinded by the brilliance of these promises, the duke and his entourage did not until the summer of 1559 become mistrustful and investigate various locations, such as Brandenburg, Jülich, and Nuremberg. The duke finally ordered the false Anna to be taken prisoner and interrogated. She continually invented new stories and knew how to confuse her interrogators so that the duke, finally, for the eighth interrogation, ordered his executioner to fetch his instruments and go to Tenneberg Castle in Walter-hausen, where she was brought and where also the rumor spread that she wanted to betray the Grimmenstein to the duke's enemies. How she was going to bring that about, however, no one knew.

As she invented ever-new lies, the executioner bound her to the ladder and stretched her. In spite of the torture, she stayed by her story, invented new ones, and said without being asked that she had not had sexual intercourse with the Devil since his manhood was too sooty for her.

As she became weak and the executioner declared he could stretch her no farther without danger to her life, she was taken from the ladder.

It was never determined exactly what or who was behind this woman. But, although Chancellor Christian Brück expressed his confidence in her to the end and repeatedly attempted to convince the duke of her honor and truthfulness, my brother and I soon had a suspicion. We came to the conclusion that the chancellor wanted to establish a lasting influence over the duke through her. And because Brück also had no good opinion of the duke's wife, Elisabeth, we thought it was possible that Brück wanted to use the false and hypocritical Anna to destroy the marriage, or at least to get Anna into the duke's bed.

There was also another theory maintained at the court. Like every prince, the duke had enemies in Saxony and in the empire, who now saw an opportunity to further diminish his already-restricted sovereignty. And because of his strict Lutheran attitude, they wanted to do damage to him and had therefore used the woman Anna to try and ruin him.

The false queen of England was sentenced to prison for life, but no one knows how long she lived or what she died of. Among the people it is said she was buried alive in the walls of the castle Tenneberg. More serious people believe she was, at the conclusion of the Grumbach Feud, which ended so unhappily for the duke and about which I will write in the next chapter, set free and then vanished without a trace. The whole sad affair was indicative of the avarice, gullibility, and intrigue that an attentive observer could witness at the court.

Still, in the beginning everything went well for my family in Weimar. My duties to the duke were not heavy, first because Dr. Schröter, taking my youth and limited experience into account, was very careful about introducing me to my work. And second, since the Middle One was my only patient and he had little trouble with his health, not much was required of me at the time. I visited him when he was in Weimar about every second day, checked his pulse, examined his urine and stool, and gave him advice about eating and drinking, which consisted mainly of suggesting less meat, wine, and beer.

Joyful events in my family drew much of my attention from the court and the many quarrels there. On the 20th of August, AD 1560, our son Johann Ernst was baptized in the castle church, and we celebrated this event thankfully and extensively. The birth had gone quite easily so that Anna seemed to obtain great pleasure from childbirth, and in 1562 our Johann Friedrich and in 1564 our daughter Anna were brought into the world.

One can see I had time and leisure to lie beside my wife. But because of an unwanted temporary separation and evil political developments, that time soon decreased.

The dukes' father had urgently insisted that the ducal brothers rule their land jointly and harmoniously, which they succeeded in doing only at the beginning.

The brothers, especially John Frederick the Middle One and John William, quarreled for supremacy after it had been settled, following the death of their father in 1554, that the Middle One should be the sole regent of the Ernestine possessions. But now they decided that the duchy should be divided into Coburg and Weimar-Gotha, and every three years the regentship would change, which my brother told me was a completely senseless and injurious decision. The youngest brother, John Frederick III, who was under the tutelage of the oldest at the time, was by nature weak and abstained from the struggle. He always counseled his brothers to moderate themselves. He studied in Jena and died in 1565 at twenty-seven years old.

Finally, John William reigned in Coburg and John Frederick II in Weimar-Gotha. At Grimmenstein Castle in Gotha, John Frederick set up his main residence, which for me meant a very frequent separation from my family since I had to follow him there, and where I subsequently became involved in the affair that was summed up under the name Grumbach Feud. More about that later.

First, I would like to present myself as a physician by reporting a treatment that I carried out on one of the duke's hunters. During a hunt, Duke John Frederick had mistaken a hunter for a wild boar and had shot him in the leg. He was very sorry because in spite of his headstrong nature he was righteous and good-natured at heart, and he ordered me to assist the surgeon who attended the hunter at the duke's cost. The left thigh looked very bad, and the lead shot was embedded deep in the wound. The surgeon and his two assistants strapped the hunter down in order to amputate the leg. Just when the saw was about to be used above the wound, I ordered them to pause. The wound was bleeding at a medium strength, which made the thigh look bad.

I had boiled water procured and the leg properly washed. Then I sent for a wound potion at the chemist's to which should void the effects of the wound on the body. The wound potion was prepared from juniper, cattails, roots of mugwort, and the root of *Dictamnus albus* and then was boiled down to half in three jugs of aged beer. I gave the hunter this potion three times, in the early morning, at midday sufficiently long after the meal, and before sleeping at night, three spoons.

I succeeded in pulling the lead shot out of the wound with my fingers. Now it was customary practice, which I, too, had previously advocated, to clean the wound of the poisons that had invaded it with the shot. This was done with cautery or boiling oils. But I had observed that by doing so, too much healthy flesh was destroyed, the patient was subjected to terrible pain, and the healing process was delayed, if not completely hindered. People knew that and thus said, "Just saw the whole leg off," a treatment the patient often survived and that brought the surgeon no blame.

I told the surgeon to treat the leg with boiled chamomile and carefully dress it and thus stop the bleeding. The patch I myself had prepared in the laboratory so lovingly set up by my dear wife. I later could convince quite a number of doctors and surgeons of the usefulness of this patch and could sell it to them for a nice profit.

To my pleasure and also that of the duke's, the hunter recovered and enjoyed the use of both legs, and it was to be hoped that on the next hunt the duke's motto would be amended from "First shoot, then look."

Of course, I know today that this method of treating a shot wound was not a discovery of mine. I read that Ambroise Paré, surgeon and physician to three French kings, successfully applied it on the battlefield and thereby saved the lives of many wounded. Nevertheless, even today while I write, wounds are being mismanaged with boiling oil and red-hot iron, may God have mercy. New approaches, especially in medicine, come very slowly because doctors and patients hang on to cherished habits and say: what has helped since Hippocrates and Galen, so for a thousand years and more, cannot suddenly be wrong. And these people do not ask whether it has really helped.

The case described above was not my only success, and these served to strengthen my position at court and spread my reputation over the duchy and even as far as Brandenburg. Subsequently, I was called more frequently to high ranking and wealthy people, especially when it concerned a serious wound, and my wife was thankful for the attendant money.

CHAPTER 18

. . . reports on the Grumbach Feud, how I acted there and escaped dangerous consequences.

Reader, in describing what later entered into the history of Saxony and Thuringia and the empire as the Grumbach Feud, I must go back a little. Time goes by so quickly, and much is forgotten, or it is gilded over or darkly obscured depending on the reigning parties' favor or disfavor.

As part of the background, keep in mind that earlier in the empire's imperfect legislation, knights were not only allowed the right of feuding but were actually obligated to fight for their property, their rights, and their reputations as nobles themselves when those values were threatened. There was no question of bringing someone to trial or finding other legal help. The law of the club reigned.

This, however, created such unlimited excesses and such confusion in the empire that something had to be done to halt the unbridled mischief of the knights. Therefore, in 1495 Emperor Maximilian I established the Perpetual Public Peace at the Imperial Diet of Worms. The imperial estates, clergy, nobility, and townspeople agreed, yet the unwritten law of the strongest remained effectively in place, and it was the task of the territorial princes to keep the knights down and bring them under control. The knights saw this as a curtailment of their rights and regarded the princes, bishops, and towns as their worst enemies. Götz von Berlichingen, Franz von Sickingen, and finally also Wilhelm von

Grumbach were the last examples of the rebellion of the knighthood against the growing power of the territorial princes.

Grumbach came from an ancient noble family held in high esteem and provided with ample lands and possessions. He was educated in chivalry at the court of Margrave Casimir of Brandenburg-Culmbach and accompanied the margrave on almost all his travels and campaigns. From that time stemmed the accusation that Grumbach had, in the war against the peasants, first housed the nobleman Florian Geyer but then in a grove had him attacked and killed by his servants. Even Grumbach's enemies were silent concerning the accusation; only one, his most embittered opponent, Bishop Frederick of Würzburg, accused him of that murderous deed. This accusation will stay with him forever, because in view of his inglorious end nobody takes the trouble to free him from it.

As Grumbach in 1540 was again on his estate in Franconia, he successfully used his influence to settle a dispute with the chapter in Würzburg over some estates and forests in his favor and in accordance with the law. In 1544, when a new bishop was elected in Würzburg, Melchior von Zobel, there arose new conflicts caused by the bishop's intrigues and his desire for vengeance because of previous disagreements. Grumbach, however, hid his grudge and lived several years quietly on his estates. He even complied with the request of the bishop when he later commanded one thousand riders in the Schmalkaldic War on the side of the emperor to spare the bishopric from having troops marching through it. The bishop, however, showed little appreciation and, despite all the attempts of Grumbach at reconciliation, pursued him with angry attacks, with questioning the legitimacy of his lands, with delays in the recognition of Grumbach's son as vassal, and with other efforts. In the end, after interminable entanglements with the emperor, the Imperial Court of Justice, Margrave Albrecht of Brandenburg-Culmbach, and hostile bishops, and after recriminations, payments of money, compensations, return compensations, and damning writings from both sides, Wilhelm of Grumbach and his family were totally destitute, figuratively speaking, beggars.

Anno 1558, he decided to regain his rights by force and, with several knights, sought to capture Bishop Melchior von Zobel and force him to surrender what he had unrightfully taken.

On the morning of April 15th, 1558, they assaulted the bishop in Würzburg, but instead of taking him prisoner, they shot dead the bishop and several of his group. One of the culprits made known later that he had been the one who killed the bishop because he would not pay him a legacy. Grumbach had in this murder no direct part but was considered generally—and not unjustly—to be the instigator.

On the 4th of October, 1563, Grumbach invaded Würzburg and forced the town to sign a contract that would compensate him for everything. Here at last, as he transgressed against the innocent townspeople, Grumbach left the path of righteousness and took the way of damnable revenge.

When the emperor in Pressburg heard of this, he declared Grumbach and his followers rebels and breakers of the Perpetual Public Peace and under the ban of the empire without giving them the opportunity to justify themselves according to imperial law by bringing their case before the Imperial Court of Justice.

Although many bishops, princes, and knights supported the claims of Grumbach, the emperor instituted the ban (which, as I said, was not quite legal), perhaps because he harbored concerns that the German nobles would unite and carry on a general war against the territorial princes. Grumbach himself had often boasted of his alliances with the knighthood of the empire. When Casimir as well as his other patron, Margrave Albrecht, died in 1557, Grumbach had to find a new protector who would help him regain his possessions and his rights.

What was more natural than to turn to Duke John Frederick the Middle One, whose family had suffered a similar fate in regard to possessions and honor? Both were struggling to regain their previous state.

As Grumbach personally made his request for protection, the duke at first hesitated because he did not want to go against his duty to the emperor. But at last, because of the duke's sense of justice and righteousness, he was won over to the cause of the injured, persecuted, and abandoned Grumbach. He appointed him his councillor and provided him with a special letter of protection.

The duke and Grumbach became friends, insofar as the difference in their ranks as prince and knight allowed, and it was the beginning of a disastrous relationship in which each was strengthened in his plans, which led to dangerous undertakings and eventually to the abyss.

It happened to the knight as it had happened to Kohlhase, who had also suffered injustice and did not want to submit to it as Job had, fearing God, but rather took revenge, which itself brought with it more injustice. This was accompanied by a transformation of his, Grumbach's, soul, and out of a righteous and equitable man would come a scheming and reckless adventurer who took advantage of the good-hearted and—it must be said—foolish John Frederick for his own purposes. And to help him came Chancellor Christian Brück, who understood perfectly how to influence the duke and use him for his own unworthy and ambitious plans. Duke William had called the chancellor a tyrannical, godless, money-grubbing, and unjust judge who often abused his position. Others said of him that he chased away God-fearing preachers and devastated both regiments, namely, the church and the secular authority in Thuringia, like a sow rumples a field.

A portent of his terrible fate was illustrated by the fact that he once played with a pumpkin, throwing it into the air several times, until it suddenly disintegrated into four pieces.

Grumbach made himself pleasant to the chancellor, whom everybody obeyed and through whom he gained influence over the duke. He quickly found out how much it pained the duke that his father had been forced to cede the electorship and a large part of his land to his Albertine relatives. The recovery of what had been lost was a constant obsession and had degenerated into foolish hopes and superstitious tendencies. And Grumbach—together with Chancellor Brück, who through a regained electoral dignity and recovered lands hoped to gain more power and influence and thus satisfy his excessive ambition—bedazzled, persuaded, and increasingly cajoled the poor but also fame-hungry prince. The three of them believed that with the help of the German knighthood as well as France and Sweden, the Wittenberg Capitulation could be reversed, and at the same time the duke could appear as the protector and savior of the oppressed German knighthood.

My brother Johannes, who, meanwhile, through his skillful behavior in the affair with the false Anna and his smooth handling of the chancellor had quite surpassed the influence of a mere chancery-councillor at court and with the duke, regarded these goings-on with apprehension.

I felt the danger of the duke's dependence on Brück and Grumbach even more, because at almost every consultation with the duke, I had to listen to his ambitious plans, and I had to carefully, on the one hand, not reject them too completely in order not to make him angry and lose all influence and, on the other, try to advise at least a bit of moderation. In the latter, I failed completely, and if I now and then could sense a certain yielding or questioning, Grumbach and Brück, who were often present against my wishes, succeeded in bringing the duke back into line.

Johannes and I feared for the duke, his family, his dominion, and most of all for ourselves, and therefore I decided to take an active hand beyond just my medical activity.

For that, my former famulus, Thomas, who meanwhile had finished his study of medicine in Jena, would be of assistance. He had so far not found a medical position, so it was not difficult to get him to come to Gotha as my aide, pay him a small salary, and allow him to stay in a small room in my home.

My plan was this: if I was going to rescue the duke from his foolish designs, I would have to make his main influence, the knight Grumbach, appear untrustworthy. And it seemed to me that the most effective way to do so was to show that the boy named Hänsel Tausendschön, whom Grumbach was using to pursue his sinister plans, was nothing more than Grumbach's instrument and tool.

Hänsel Tausendschön was a farm lad from Sundhausen near Gotha whose actual name was Hans Müller and who, in the taverns and markets, frequently pretended to be communicating with angels who disclosed to him the future. He was soon known as an angel seer, and the duke, with his tendency to superstition and the miraculous, summoned him.

He came into the ducal office when Grumbach and I happened to be present. I saw the boy for the first time, and Grumbach also greeted him as a stranger. But it seemed to me that something was wrong when Hänsel, who said he did not know the knight, addressed him as Herr Knight Grumbach. The good-natured duke did not notice this but instead allowed himself to listen to a couple of hearty prophecies. Above all, he listened eagerly as the boy said the elector Augustus of Saxony and the emperor would soon die, and an angel had shown him the elector's hat, which John Frederick would soon be wearing. And the boy even took a crystal out of his pocket and allowed the duke to see the hat through it.

My mistrust grew as the forecasts increasingly mirrored the ideas of Grumbach and at the same time reflected the most aggressive desires of the duke, which Tausendschön could never have so exactly known.

Again at home I summoned Thomas to me and made him aware of the court secrets and plans as well as the fantasies of the duke. I told him he should stay on the heels of the angel seer and note with whom he spoke and whatever else might be planned.

After only two days, Thomas gave me a report. He had followed Tausendschön when he came from Grimmenstein Castle and had seen him disappear into the inn called Zum Riesen on the market square. With the help of a few ducats, he had been able to convince the landlord, first, to show him the room in which Tausendschön was staying and, second, to reveal that the money for Tausendschön's room came from a Moritz Hausener, who was unknown to him. But I knew that Hausener was the secretary for Grumbach.

I now instructed Thomas to take a room in the inn. He was to observe the angel seer, note with whom he spoke, and if possible eavesdrop on the conversation. The room that Thomas should occupy was above Tausendschön's room, and an unused chimney traveled up through both rooms. Through a fortunate acoustic design, one could hear quite distinctly what was being said in Tausendschön's room. Thomas kept paper and quills ready and waited for the coming of evening in his room in the inn.

Finally, on the third day, he heard the angel seer open the door for a visitor. There ensued a conversation in the course of which the visitor clearly handed over some ducats and said he should keep his connection and his service to Grumbach secret. Otherwise, he, the visitor, would tell the authorities that Tausendschön was guilty of making magic. And no one would believe that he had learned the magic from him, Grumbach's secretary. Yes, it was these words, and I then knew who the secret visitor was. And finally came the most important discovery: the secretary told Tausendschön what he should tell the duke when he related the next message from the angels, which was to once more predict that he would be the next emperor after he had become the elector of Saxony and the two parts of the country had been united under his rule.

Thomas carefully wrote all this down, noting day and hour, and that was the beginning of a file that I planned to lay before the duke at the appropriate time.

On the next day, Chancellor Christian Brück summoned me. He wanted to know what my servant and assistant was up to, since he had taken a room at the Riesen and at the same time lived with me. I was surprised at how quickly the chancellor's spies worked. Still, I was able to calm him by saying the young man had his eye on the landlord's daughter and wanted to be near her as much as possible. Now the landlord actually did have a daughter of considerable body measurements, so my story was not unbelievable. Nevertheless, the chancellor did not seem entirely convinced. But I was once more sure that Brück and Grumbach were very much under the same blanket and pulling together in their efforts to influence the duke.

At my next consultation with the duke, this happened: Grumbach and Brück with a show of excitement brought Hans Tausendschön to the duke—they did not have to be announced since they had access to him at any time—and asked the fool to speak up. I wanted to take leave, but the duke, who knew my doubts about the prophecies of the boy, ordered me to remain. And then I myself heard the words that Thomas by eavesdropping had noted in the Inn Zum Riesen. The misguided prince became elated and said to me, "Now, Dr. Luther, you have heard with your own ears what the future has in store for me. Not only for me, but for everyone who stays by me. And it is worth the fight. And as evidence that God will help us to victory, he has sent his angels with the black hats." I was silent in order not to bring the ducal displeasure upon me.

A day later I succeeded in being alone with His Grace. I had said to him on the previous day that it seemed to me his eyes were slightly yellowish, and I would apply some eye drops. I hoped God would overlook my small white lie. I employed a dilute of dandelion juice recommended by Otto Brunfels in 1532, with which I had had good experience. By the way, the conclusions Brunfels drew from astrology to medicine did not meet with my approval.

Barely was I in the duke's sitting room, even before I was able to apply my eye drops, let alone raise my actual concern about Grumbach, when the duke showed me a letter of Grumbach's and wanted to know my opinion of it.

The letter was later used in the proceedings against Grumbach and Tausendschön, as part of the official facts, and a copy lies here before me. I include it here:

Written on Saturday after Christ's birth, i.e., the 25th of December, 1563

Your Grace should quickly learn and acknowledge what the Lord God through His little angels has made known: the simplest and lowest of my servants will have to shoot a high lord, whose name they will soon make known. And now I will not conceal from Your Grace that it will be the emperor. Following God's orders, I have today in the morning readied a gun and armed the servant with it, who will now await further instructions from the angels. I feel obliged to tell Your Grace submissively that the emperor had planned to go hunting on Christmas Eve, but something prevented him from this undertaking. So it was God's order that His dear little angels should lead the servant with his gun to the hunt so that he could shoot the emperor straight into the heart that he fall dead at once. Now, as the emperor did not go hunting but God's order had to be fulfilled, today in the morning my servant shot the emperor through heart and soul, and thus he was delivered into Satan's power. This deadly shot, as the little angels have reported, was administered to him in his room. He fell down and shrieked and suffered a lot, and now neither he nor others know how he is, but he is to die under great pains.

The angels, so Grumbach had already told the duke, had appeared to Tausendschön as three-year-old children wearing ash-colored clothes and black hats on their heads and carrying white staffs in their hands, with voices like children. They came out of an underground vault and went back there again.

Now, instead of this nonsense—especially the wearing of the black hats—making the duke suspicious, it had rather served to reinforce Grumbach's and Tausendschön's credibility. I began at this point for the first time to think of the duke not only as good-natured and gullible but also as someone who was not quite in his right mind. And my love and loyalty began to weaken. I decided straightaway to search in my medical books for a means of addressing this madness.

But first I told the duke how horrified I was by Grumbach. This letter of Grumbach's, which speculated about the murder of the emperor, was the highest treason and worthy of death. I also made the duke aware that the emperor was still alive. This objection the duke had also made to Grumbach, but he had only said that such actions were often delayed so that one could only guess why God lets these things happen. And even if it seemed at times like he, Grumbach, had written the angels' note out of his own head and to his own advantage, he yet by his knight's honor declared that everything had been revealed to him from the angels through the boy, and he had allowed no other words to be written.

I implored my princely lord to attend to my assistant Thomas's notes and see the absurdity of the entire story of Tausendschön. Above all, I pointed out that Grumbach's secretary had prompted Tausendschön in his prophesying.

I dared even, with considerable beating of the heart, to say that it was all a plot by Grumbach and the chancellor that served only the pursuit of their own selfish goals. The duke was angry but told me he wanted to use Thomas's overheard conversations to show Grumbach and the chancellor that he had certain doubts. But I should also remember that my servant could have inserted the prophecy in his notes after Tausendschön had done them. With that he looked at me sternly.

I implored him not to tell Grumbach and Brück of my suspicions, or I would fear for Thomas's and my lives, or at least our physical safety. The duke laughed at me and said that for him there could be no doubt concerning their honor and loyalty. With that, he dismissed me. But my fears were based on a terrible event that had recently happened.

The duke's household had employed an old and loyal secretary, Johannes Rudolf, who had seen to it that Chancellor Brück could not acquire the fortress Kapellendorf, which the chancellor never forgot. On a suitable occasion, the secretary was accused by Brück of high treason and was taken prisoner, the accusation being that he had wanted to deliver the fortress Kapellendorf to the enemy, and twice he was so badly tortured that the jailer declared, if he were to stretch Rudolf any more, as the chancellor, who was standing by, requested, he would break like a string, especially since the blood had already spurted from the navel. His innocence was later confirmed by the elector of Saxony and Emperor Maximilian in 1568, after he had been set free. One sees the chancellor had such power that one must truly be fearful, and I confess that I had great fear.

This would become even greater when, two days later, Thomas did not appear as usual to assist me, nor was he in his room. I went to the inn, and the landlord said that on the previous evening two of the duke's guards had appeared and taken him. I started some inquiries on the quiet, but no one could give me any further details. This caused me great concern, because I had involved him in my business and political plans, and I swore if I myself survived this whole thing, I would as far as possible make reparation to his parents in Neustadt if Thomas did not reappear. For a time I did not hear of him again. From then on, I sought a way to escape from the duke's service and the power of the chancellor and Grumbach without damaging my reputation or my family.

Fate began to take its course. In spite of warnings from his father-in-law and the elector of Brandenburg and also the emperor, who actually wished the duke no evil but also could not withdraw his demands and his ban without weakening his imperial reputation, the duke insisted on his own judgment and the protection and accommodation of Grumbach.

Now the emperor lost his patience. On the 13th of May, 1566, Maximilian II proclaimed publicly in Augsburg a renewed and strengthened mandate of outlawry and sent it to the elector of Saxony for wider distribution.

Who in the future would house or hide the outlaws should without further notification become an outlaw themselves.

Before the enactment of this stronger mandate, my brother Johannes had informed me, to my dismay, that he had, with the duke's permission, applied for furlough in order to visit our sister, Margarethe von Kunheim, in Mohrungen in the Duchy of Prussia. Our lord had hesitated to let him go at first but finally had given in, and he departed on the 3rd of May in 1566.

My brother's actual reason, however, was the craving for his new, second wife, Elisabeth von Schlieben, whom he had married in 1563 after spending a year in East Prussia. Ever since his student days, Johannes had forged connections in East Prussia, so one did not wonder that he had married there. His second wife was also a widow, and Johannes told me such widows are ahead of young women in terms of experience and therefore are well suited to become wives.

Now I was alone but greatly relieved because in the coming confrontation the worst would certainly have befallen my brother as councillor and subordinate of the infamous chancellor Christian Brück.

How cloudy my lord John Frederick's thinking had become is shown by his belief that the emperor would abstain from real enforcement of the ban. But the displeasure of the emperor was only strengthened, and so the lands ruled by both brothers were entrusted as fief to John William alone. Still there were attempts, especially from John William, to get his brother John Frederick to relent.

Also the rector and the professors at Jena University, even a legation comprised of the electors of Mainz and the Palatinate, the archbishop of Salzburg, the bishop of Augsburg, Count Palatine Wolfgang of Zweibrücken, Duke Christoph of Württemberg, and a number of counts attempted with serious arguments and reprimands to bring John Frederick to reason. All was in vain, even though they pointed out what he could expect from the emperor's anger, which in the end really happened. The duke sometimes wavered, but Grumbach then would again awaken in him the delusory hopes with an adventurous plan for the duke to once more obtain the electorship: In Westphalian and on the Rhine troops could be recruited, which at first were to plunder the bishoprics on the Rhine, then invade Franconia, rob the bishop of Würzburg of everything he had, drive the elector of Saxony into a corner, and pillage the cities of Mühlhausen, Nordhausen, und Erfurt. At the same time, several regiments would be raised in Brandenburg and Pomerania and with them fall upon the elector and hunt him out of his lands. Then the way would be clear for Duke John Frederick to become elector in Wittenberg and, if he united both armies, perhaps proclaimed emperor.

An event then occurred that was highly detrimental for Grumbach and the duke. Near Dresden, because of thefts, a former servant of Grumbach, Hans Böhm from Freiberg, had been seized. In the interrogation on the 5th of June, 1566, he had said freely and without being asked that he had been repeatedly hired by Grumbach and his crony Stein to ambush Elector Augustus on a hunt and to shoot him. After he had told his patrons about having a cousin in the service of the elector, he said he had been handed by the duke himself and by Grumbach and Stein a gray poison powder with the order to go to his cousin and induce him to get into the kitchen, befriend the cooks, and throw the poison into the food. In a second interrogation, Böhm withdrew the statement. After having been tortured, though, he said his first statement was correct. He held to this statement until his execution.

Shortly afterward, a highwayman, Philipp Blass from Langensalza, was caught and taken to Dresden. He had a long criminal history of inflicting much damage in Erfurt. He had even taken an Erfurter prisoner and charged for his release a goodly sum of money. Duke Augustus of Saxony offered 1000 guldens as reward for his capture. Blass was seized in an inn in Mücheln and was brought first to Freiburg, then Leipzig, and finally to Dresden. He confessed, among other things, that Grumbach had promised him a rich reward if he would help clear the elector out of the way. Duke John Frederick had been aware of the plan.

The duke was deeply hurt by the accusations and rejected them. He said he did not know the people at all. Also, Grumbach and his crony, Stein, proclaimed their innocence. Still Augustus of Saxony was not convinced, perhaps did not want to be, although obviously all was a matter of slander and lies forced from Blass and Böhm through hideous torture.

On July 10th, 1566, under my medical supervision, Prince John Ernest was born. In his congratulatory letter, Elector Augustus once again admonished the duke to follow the emperor's orders—without success.

The bitterness grew on each side, and Grumbach was aware that his life was at stake. And so in desperation he looked to use every means without regard to their illegality or reprehensibility.

Now emerged something that once again gave hope to myself and others who were devoted to our lord. Chancellor Brück fell into disfavor. There were too many complaints received about him, and his own father, Gregorius Brück, had said, "Woe to the prince who lets my haughty, arrogant, and proud son rule over him, and woe unto the land where he is chancellor and has power."

Likewise, the elector Frederick of the Palatinate had expressed the opinion that Chancellor Brück was not worthy to govern a bunch of pigs: Brück was corruptible, had succumbed to gluttony, had set the three ducal brothers against each other, had induced his lord to affiliate with Grumbach, had compared Duke John William with faithless Absalom, and in councils had never allowed the other councillors to utter their real opinions. Then constant entreaties from the duke's father-in-law, Elector Frederick of the Palatinate, and his brother John William finally succeeded in removing Brück from the court. John William wanted the chancellor to be duly tried but found no legal counsel willing to be involved in this thing.

But the duke, in the meantime, had been so ensnared by Grumbach and his cronies that Brück was soon again in favor and was reinstated as chancellor. A rescript from his master expressly commanded the councillors in Weimar that they should regard Chancellor Brück as never having been excluded from state affairs.

Grumbach and Brück were now able to get the duke to strengthen his armament. He looked on all sides to make alliances, ordered all cavalry captains to refrain from going into foreign service, and enlisted new troops.

On the 12th of December, 1566, Emperor Maximilian, who feared a longer delay would cause an uprising by the knights, declared from Vienna that Duke John Frederick was finally and with full legal force to be outlawed by imperial edict.

On the following day, Elector Augustus, as the lieutenant of the Upper Saxon Circle, was requested to quickly execute the ban against John Frederick. He was in agreement with the brother of John Frederick to carry out the order.

John Frederick had not expected such a quick enforcement of the ban. He was of the opinion that the imminent war against the Turks would postpone it, and Grumbach had strengthened him in this thought.

Now the duke had to prepare himself for an attack. He ordered the bailiffs of the castles to provision their forts with beer, grain, butter, cheese, and other necessities. In particular, the duke reckoned on the assistance of the discontented German knighthood, also with France and Sweden, where Grumbach had forged links and where one of his cronies, Mandelsloe, had been sent as an emissary. King Eric XIV of Sweden, however, terminated the alliance when the emperor wrote him that Grumbach had been declared an outlaw.

CHAPTER 19

... is introduced for clarity and continues the previous chapter.

At year's end AD 1566, the duke had approximately three thousand riders and foot soldiers assembled, among them armed citizens and other subjects willing or obligated to fight for him.

How precarious everything was and how reluctantly people now obeyed the duke was demonstrated by the fact that the majority of vassals summoned to Gotha failed to appear. Only about twenty obeyed. The greater number refused the order, because according to the contract between the two ducal brothers of February 21st, 1566, one brother alone did not have the right to convene the vassals, and when they asked Duke John William how they should respond to the order, the answer was, of course, not to obey. It is obvious they were happy to use this as a pretext for sending regrets, because to assist in the face of the imperial ban could quickly lead to disaster.

The duke's small force had to face the much superior power of the empire, and it is indeed astonishing that in the face of this imbalance the duke decided to fight. But one can imagine that Grumbach, for whom it was a matter of life and death, did everything he could to bolster the fighting spirit of his protector. And in all probability he had told the duke that he ultimately did not have to fear for life and limb, having seen the fate of his father, who, though sentenced to death after the battle of Mühlberg in the year of 1547, died peacefully in Weimar.

The duke, who was well secured behind the solid walls of the city and Grimmenstein Castle and well supplied with firepower, was confronted by the emperor's war general, Augustus of Saxony, who commanded almost ten thousand foot soldiers and about forty-six hundred riders. As the reports of the approaching enemy and its strength became increasingly credible, the citizens of Gotha, as well as I, felt great distress. It was clear to me that the duke's cause was lost, and I had to find a way to come out of this without injury. Then, as good luck would have it, my former famulus, Thomas, reappeared. After intense but not painful interrogation, and due to the intervention of my lord, he had been set free. Later I discovered that Grumbach and Brück were probably still reluctant to offend the son of Martin Luther and the duke's personal physician by harming his servant. This was to alter quickly, as we will see.

Now I had my reliable helper and friend back. I drafted a letter to Elector Augustus in which I told him that, though I remained true to my lord John Frederick and thus the House of Wettin, I loathed the actions of Grumbach and his comrades as well as Chancellor Brück, and I requested mercy for myself and my family. Also, as personal physician, I had no possibility and no call to advise the duke. That was, I admit, a certain stretching of the truth, but perhaps it would help me later. This letter I wrote with a sympathetic ink, made from euphorbia or spurge, which Thomas knew how to make visible. The letter was addressed with normal ink to my wife in Weimar so that Thomas could be dispatched with it safely.

Still, I hesitated to send it when, at the end of the year 1566, the order came from Grimmenstein Castle that the townsmen must without delay send their wives and children out of the city. Citizens and council implored the order to be withdrawn because of the cruelty of the measure at this time of year and the proximity of the enemy. But it did not help. On New Year's Day, 1567, the women and children, with little money and clothing, were forced to leave in the bitter cold. I was happy to know that my family was safe in Weimar, although as the family of a court official, they would hardly have been affected.

Grumbach and Brück urgently advised the duke to ensure the loyalty of the city. So he ordered on the 5th of January, 1567, all the citizens and country folk within the city's boundaries to be called to the market square, some of them actually driven there into a circle, surrounded by his riders and arquebusiers. Into this circle he rode with Grumbach, Brück, and entourage and had them swear a renewed oath of allegiance. I could luckily claim illness as an excuse, because some of those who were at the duke's side were soon to suffer a terrible fate.

The people, so obviously threatened by superior forces, and in view of the treatment of some who did not want to swear and said so loudly and were ripped out from the crowd and arrested, finally in fear did as ordered. Thomas, under the roof of the Inn Zum Riesen observed the gathering and said to me that he had clearly seen that many of the people held their left hand behind their backs with three outstretched fingers in order to negate the oath.

When I saw to what measures the duke felt driven, it was clear to me that he could not much longer endure. On the same evening, I gave the letter to Thomas, sat him on a horse, and sent him through the still-passable Erfurter Gate to Elector Augustus in one of the blockhouses that had been erected for his general staff after the completion of the trenches that faced the city. I gave Thomas strict orders in no case to return to the city before he had heard from me and was told to return.

There began now a warlike and unhappy time.

The enemy drew near to the city, shots were traded back and forth, and there were dead and wounded on both sides. A delegation from the elector and from Duke John William demanded once more the handing over of Grumbach and his companions as well as Chancellor Brück. In vain. However, the contents of the demand became known in the city, and it stirred great resentment, because the good city of Gotha and its people were caused to suffer for these few men.

Many lost property because of the ruler's order to destroy the suburbs so that the enemy could not settle there. The gardens before the city were laid waste, and the trees were cut down. He also ordered the mills around the city that had not been destroyed by the enemy to be burned down in order not to be available to the hostile forces. I believe, under the influence of Grumbach, he would have scorched the very earth.

The worst, however, was that the besiegers destroyed the Leina Canal and most of the wells supplying the city with freshwater.

That resulted in the city and the castle, despite a mighty cistern twenty-one feet deep and holding fifteen thousand barrels of water, having such a shortage that, other than the few remaining sweep wells for the maintenance of the people and the cattle and especially for the breweries, it became necessary to fetch water from the moat before the Brühler Gate.

I expressly made my lord aware of the consequences, which followed immediately: There were numerous cases of dysentery and bowel bleeding and also cases of cholera, and many people, after having suffered, most painfully died.

The town physician and I established a hospital under the walls of the Grimmenstein and attempted to bring as many of the sick as possible there in order to separate them from the healthy. The old infirmary, originally intended for lepers, lay accordingly outside the city walls by the Siebleber Gate and therefore was no longer accessible. In addition, I recommended the townsmen boil the water gotten from the moat, but this did not do much good. We were lucky that it was winter and we were spared the plague. Things were bad enough.

An understanding with the besiegers became increasingly impossible because of the conduct of my lord, whose mind seemed now completely clouded, and Brück and Grumbach were the main causes.

When the city was now completely closed off by the siege, John Frederick was foolish to the extreme and took the title of elector and the electoral coat of arms, made use of the same in official letters, on coins—the so-called klippes (for the young reader: these coins, often square, were originally issued under unfavorable conditions, for example, in a city under siege, as here in Gotha)—and on flags, and soon one could read on ducal decrees "Electoral-Saxon Chancellery."

His Ducal Grace must have realized that such action would drive Elector Augustus into a sharp rage. Also, it was completely contrary to the Naumburg Contract of 1554, which the duke had signed and which said that, with the exception of John Frederick I, no member of the Ernestinian line could call himself a born elector. I was now beginning to think the duke was suffering from megalomania, for which I had no effective remedy at hand. Under the pretext that it would give him pleasant dreams, I tried a betonica-nettle tea, but I already knew that this mild herb would be of little benefit. But it also could not do any harm.

Still, during the siege, four thousand of the Grimmenstein gold klippes fell into the hands of the enemy, as they were to be secretly handed over to Mandelsloe, who was traveling at the request of the duke to recruit additional soldiers. And not only gold klippes, but also dispatches about the provisioning, the securing, and the arming of the Grimmenstein and the city of Gotha, and the recruitment of new troops as well as further this plan of the duke. Of course, the news was immediately conveyed to Elector Augustus and furthered John Frederick's downfall.

I had succeeded in my consultations with the duke by all sorts of linguistic circumlocutions not to address him as Your Electoral Grace. I mostly said Your Grace, while Brück and Grumbach and others deliberately used the new title in order to flatter the duke's vanity. That helped me very much later, while for the others it did damage.

The gold klippes, though, which toward the end of the siege were paid to me as my physician's salary, I accepted and carefully preserved, then later I melted them down and used the metal during my attempts at making gold as a reference and auxiliary material.

It was not only the city of Gotha that suffered during this truly unchristian war. The unrestraint of the foreign soldiers around Gotha knew no bounds. Far into the surrounding lands they plundered and robbed, and many localities had such significant damage that many years were to pass before the poor folks were able to recover. Especially bad was the behavior of the Franconian troops. They stole grain; broke windows in cloisters and pulled out the lead; tore up documents and letters; chopped up cabinets, beds, implements, boards, and timber from floors; tore up sheds, stalls, and houses; and carried with them as much as they could. There was some improvement, although not much, when on the 8th of January, 1567, Elector Augustus and three imperial commissioners, Eberstein, Schönaich, and Carlowitz, appeared in camp and threatened corporal punishment for further violations.

For better protection of the lands, Duke John William had set up three roaming patrols stationed in Rinkleben, Ichtershausen, and Eisenach, although they were also of little help.

Now discontent began to grow also among the troops in the city and castle. It is true that the defenders of the castle, unlike those in the city, had enough to eat; still, they had to live in hastily thrown up huts in the bailey, exposed to frost and smoke. Added to that was the considerable doubt that they felt about the cause of the siege. In order to counter that, the duke on the 5th of January, 1567, gathered together all the armed forces in the presence of Brück and Grumbach to demonstrate that Elector Augustus, seduced by the priests of Baal, wanted to suppress the Evangelical religion and lusted for the little piece of land that was left over for the duke after the Wittenberg Capitulation. He admonished the troops to be obedient, recalled them to their oath, warned against mutiny, and consoled them with the promise of imminent help.

Hereupon Grumbach spoke and declared that the strange rumor that war was being waged for his and his followers' sake was fabricated and false. He was instead an old, spent, and weak seventy-year-old man (who nevertheless sat firm and upright in the saddle). He was not the one for whom the duke's army was fighting; they fought rather for the duke himself in order to defend him against the elector of Saxony, who through hatred and envy thirsted for the little piece of land still remaining to their lord under the appearance of following orders of the emperor.

These lies, or half truths, of the duke and Grumbach were soon exposed, as the besiegers shot notices into the city on which the true reasons for the ban and siege were listed. In addition, soldiers before the wall called scornfully to the defenders about the reprehensible, lost cause for which they were willing to sacrifice themselves.

On the 25th of January, 1567, two trumpeters presented the castle guard with a note of request to the vassals, citizens, and subjects of the city of Gotha.

The elector's note, which through numerous copies soon became known, urged the knights, townspeople, and peasantry to follow only the imperial orders. This they could do rightfully, because on the last territorial diet at Saalfeld the emperor had ordered all subjects to be dispensed from all their oaths and duties toward Duke John Frederick. Their lord now was solely John Frederick's brother, John William. They also should surrender the castle to the emperor and turn over the outlaws for punishment. Should they go on following their old ways, they would lose honor, life, and limb and all their belongings. If they failed to comply with this, they would, like the duke and Grumbach, fall under the ban and become subject to the same penalties. It had been determined to take the city by force. Elector Augustus's army would proceed with fire and sword against all the stubborn and exiled outlaws, against the wanton rebels and peace breakers.

The men of the city, naturally, feared for their lives. Presentations were made to the duke that he might renounce Grumbach and his consorts and make peace with the emperor. They would have the same obligations to John William as they had to John Frederick. All was in vain. Whoever contradicted Grumbach was despised and persecuted. Even the superintendent, Melchior Weidemann, employed in Gotha since 1562, who had strongly preached against Grumbach's schemes, was told he should, like others, fear the wheel and the gallows.

To dissatisfaction were added evil omens.

On the 5th of February, when the troops in Gotha had fired a piece of heavy artillery toward Sundhausen, a cannon called the Breme—a gift from the city of Bremen to Duke John Frederick I—exploded into pieces and smashed all windows in the duke's chambers.

Soon afterward, an enemy shell flew into the duke's chambers and passed over the cradle of his half-year-old son, John Ernest, so that it was set in motion.

The townsmen were especially alarmed and concerned about the four-week absence of their wives and children, of whom nobody knew where they had gone. It was generally and finally believed that the cause of the siege was Grumbach alone and that he only needed to be surrendered in order to gain peace.

It was also eerie for the townsmen because the ringing of the bells was prohibited in their city, and just one clock was allowed. At the end of March I learned what the duke and Grumbach had decided in view of the impending defeat. It was so monstrous that I felt no longer any need to remain loyal to my master. The two made the desperate decision to take to the castle all the valuables and provisions in the city as well as the fittest men, then to chase the rest of the people outside the walls and set fire at each of the four corners.

This murderous plan, praise God, could not be executed, but rumor of it soon spread throughout the city so that from then on everybody deserted the duke's cause. The troops in the city and at the castle began to mutiny, and the local council and the city joined in with them.

Now things happened in quick succession.

On the 12th of April, 1567, deputies of the city began negotiations with Elector Augustus, the imperial deputies, and Duke John William. Perhaps *negotiate* is not quite the right word, because in truth it would be an unconditional surrender of the town with abject begging for forgiveness, turning over of the outlawed, the razing of Grimmenstein Castle, and the promise never again to raise weapons against the emperor and the elector. Munitions, provisions, and all silver were to be confiscated, and the duke himself was to be handed over.

At almost the same time, troops in the city and castle seized the castle captain, von Brandenstein. Hundreds of soldiers led him from the castle to the city hall, and on the way he was mishandled with arquebus butts. On being led away, he said to the duke, if he, the duke, would have followed his advice ten days ago, he would not be suffering this humiliation today. This seems to point to the plan to set the city on fire.

One citizen of Gotha told Duke John Frederick, meanwhile, that Brandenstein had planned to sever the castle bridge and burn the armed men in the castle moat with pitch wreaths. After all, they were nothing more than three hundred peasants.

Now the troops and citizens and peasants in the city, whom my Thomas joined, began to search for Grumbach. In the castle, people broke into his chambers but did not find him. Even the duke's room was searched. His scriptorium was broken into, and there they found Chancellor Brück.

"Please," called Brück, "I am not Grumbach, also no outlaw, rather the chancellor."

"That is not a problem, because we want you, too," shouted the rebels. "Out, out with you!"

And as he did not want to go at once, a peasant ran behind him, pushed his gun into his side, and shouted, "Move along, Chancellor, move along. Duke Hans Wilhelm will surely tell you what you have done." And so they took him to the city hall, where he was locked in a special room.

After a long search, Grumbach was discovered in the bedchambers of the young princes in a trundle bed. He was pulled from there and taken to the castle courtyard and, because he suffered gout, laid on three gun barrels. With the cry, "We're bringing the hangman his bride," he was carried to the city hall. On the way, Grumbach became discolored, so that it was believed he had taken poison. "Carry this rogue to the doctor. He has eaten poison and is trying to kill himself."

In front of my house at the castle hill below the Grimmenstein, there arose a loud noise, and someone cried, "The doctor needs to come out and stop the culprit from escaping his punishment."

I went to the door and looked at Grumbach, who had so often put me in fear. He stared back at me pitifully. I said to the rebels, "Don't bring him in my house, but loosen his ropes so that he can get enough air."

It was my luck that I did not allow the man in my house. It could have meant the noose for me for harboring an outlaw. At the same time, I fulfilled my responsibility as a physician to ensure that he once again got enough air. It is said I would not even come to the door but only looked out the window and shouted, "Don't bring this man into my house. He may cure him who made him ill."

This all took place so long ago that I sometimes lose the memory or attempt to subsequently justify my actions. So perhaps it is true what some people have said and my own memory is the false one.

At the city hall, Grumbach was bound hand and foot so that he could not himself even get the necessary nourishment to his mouth and had to relieve himself in his pants. That was, after all, a little vengeance on his guards. In his dungeon, the clergy refused to give him Holy Communion because he was the cause of all the misery and misfortune and therefore unworthy to receive the sacrament.

Wilhelm von Stein, Grumbach's loyal friend, had hidden himself in the duke's armory. The duke did not betray him, although he was threatened. Finally he came out on his own and was taken to the city hall.

Some followers of Grumbach escaped, with luck, right through the enemy camp. They fled to Brunswick and thereby avoided the dreadful fate that awaited the captured.

The angel seer, Hänschen Tausendschön, was locked in a tower. The faithful secretary, Johann Rudolf, of whom the reader has learned, was freed and had the joyful prospect of being present at the torture of his tormenter, Christian Brück, and, if he had the desire, to lend a hand.

After the tumult outside my house had ceased, I thought, like Thomas, who in the meantime had returned against my wishes, that I would remain unmolested.

Then suddenly down below, the door was pushed open and a messenger of Elector Augustus delivered an order to be present at the interrogation of the chief criminals Grumbach and Brück and, if necessary, to prevent by medical expertise too early a death caused by the torture.

This was for me a terrible situation. How could I as a physician and Christian, who has always been averse to the ordeal of torture, comply with the order? I expressed my doubts to the messenger; however, he replied he had been instructed to tell me that a refusal would be interpreted as an attachment to the outlawed duke and Grumbach but that I could show, by following the command, my obedience to the emperor, Elector Augustus, and Duke John William.

What should I have done, reader? Now perhaps you accuse me of lack of courage, but my family needed me. I clung to life and was very afraid.

What then happened to the rebels I can report in all exactness because I was required to be present all the time.

I was horror-stricken, and compliance with the electoral mandate was made somewhat easier when I discovered the following. In a kind of end-time delusion in which a man, if he himself is going to die, wishes to take as many with him as possible, Brück, Stein, and Grumbach had created a list of about sixty unreliable and disloyal people of the court and citizens from the country who should all be executed by the sword. The executioner had been commissioned, and the graves had already been dug. The list with the doomed persons' names on it had been found among Brück's papers.

My name, Dr. Paul Luther, son of the Reformer Dr. Martin Luther, personal physician to Duke John Frederick, had been included in the list, which had astonishingly not been inserted into the proceedings and which neither I nor anyone else have ever seen.

I'll pause here and give the reader time to ponder my situation and to perhaps understand my subsequent actions or, more properly, my inaction.

Now the reader can continue.

On Monday the 14th of April, 1567, in the afternoon at four o'clock began the interrogation of the sixty-four-year-old Grumbach, who had been brought to the castle in a wagon because, suffering from gout, he could not walk.

I insert here that at the wish of the duke, I had previously treated him, although not with much success. My recommendations consisted of warm baths with hay flower additive and a drink made of plantain juice and honey. But he instead ate meat, and he drank far too much beer rather than the clear spring water

I had recommended, so his symptoms did not improve, and both joints of his big toes swelled so much that he was forced to cut holes in his shoes so that he could put something on his feet. I suspect that, because of my treatment's lack of success, a treatment that had helped other patients, he took a dislike to me and tried to influence the duke against me.

Count Günther of Schwarzburg as president, two secretaries, two notaries, a clerk, and a collector as well as an electoral finance councillor directed the interrogation. I was present. Elector Augustus, Duke John William, and Duke Adolf of Holstein were present but stayed hidden behind a green curtain. Adjoining the meeting room was the torture chamber, and through the open door one could see the ladder, screws, Spanish boots, the buck, and other tools as well as the torturers themselves.

Grumbach was initially questioned with kindness but was also shown the instruments through the open door.

He denied everything. He did not have Melchior von Würzburg on his conscience, and he had not advised the duke to name himself the elector. Now the executioner approached Grumbach and stretched this gouty, sixty-four-year-old man for four hours on the rack.

Grumbach's pain was so great that his cries rang throughout the castle. He confessed much and named Chancellor Brück as the cause of his misfortune.

Brück was brought in, and Grumbach faced him. He blamed all on Grumbach and the duke. All that he had done had been done on the duke's orders, and he had therefore found himself in a dilemma.

He eventually fell to the feet of those present, cried, and begged for mercy or at least a quick death in order to spare himself the rack.

This did not help. He was stretched on the rack. Here the secretary Rudolf was present, who not long before had been placed on the rack by Brück. Feignedly, he stretched out his hand and plucked timidly at the rope with which Brück was stretched.

There was nothing I could do. The thought of what Grumbach and Brück had intended to do to me let me endure the procedure.

On the following day Grumbach and Brück were interrogated once more, then Hans Tausendschön, who in spite of great pain insisted that he had spoken with four angels in black hats who had shown him a great treasure of pure gold in Sundhausen, which had been buried by an emperor and was to be raised on Pentecost of this year. Also, the angels had said to him that Duke John Frederick would once again hold the electorate.

Then the jester Hans Beyer and castle captain Brandenstein were interrogated and on the same day, the 16th of April, with the following culprits were condemned to death: Grumbach, Brück, Wilhelm von Stein, David Baumgärtner, Hans Beyer, and Hieronymus von Brandenstein. Hans Beyer, when he was captured, shook his cap and bells, made grimaces to those who grabbed him, and clowned his way to the Inn Zur Schelle where he was held captive.

I was required to be present at the execution on Friday, April 18th, on the market square in Gotha. On the day before, a high scaffold had been erected next to the gallows that was already there. At ten of the clock in the morning, the gouty Grumbach was carried there on an old chair. Before him rode the provost and a law clerk. Grumbach was set down on a bench on the scaffold, where for a quarter of an hour he talked with a priest. Here an envoy on a horse once more read the death sentence. The court preacher, Heinrich Schürrup, asked the people in Grumbach's name for forgiveness and intercession that he might die as a Christian. Then he was undressed, laid down, and tied to a board. Calmly he said to the executioner, "You punish today a scrawny vulture."

The executioner cut him into quarters, tore his heart from his body, and threw it in his face with the words, "Look, Grumbach, your untrue heart." Lastly, the head was cut off from the body.

During the torment, Grumbach remained uncomplaining and also did not cry out in pain.

The process was similar for Brück, whose last plea that before being quartered he wanted to be beheaded was not granted. As he was being executed and his heart ripped from his body, he was heard to scream in a loud voice, "Merciful God, have mercy on me." And when the executioner beat him on the mouth with his heart, he, as reported, screamed long and horribly.

The witness report is wrong. I was a witness and know that a man with his heart ripped out can no longer cry out because he is dead.

Wilhelm von Stein was first beheaded and then quartered.

Baumgärtner was beheaded. Hans Beyer was hanged. The beheading of Wilhelm Baumgärtner created in me such a scientific curiosity that I went up onto the scaffold for a better look at the severed head. I wanted to see if the patient could still feel anything or was capable of saying a word. I addressed the head but only saw a raising of the eyes, and then all was still.

Brandenstein and Tausendschön were hanged a few days later. For Tausendschön it was a terrible miscarriage of justice because he had nothing to do with the conspiracy and unknowingly served Grumbach's purposes. For that, Elector Augustus must justify himself one day before God.

The executions lasted two hours, and six executioners were involved. A farmer from Hausen bought the scaffold and out of it built himself a living room in his house.

Baumgärtner and Beyer were buried, while the bodies of the other three who were executed that day, as the *Constitutio Criminalis Carolina of 1532* prescribes, were stuck on poles and displayed on the busiest four roads leading out of the town. They remained there until they decayed.

On the poles were pinned the following words:

Had Grumbach only stayed on his farm
And never attempted to do any harm
To emperor, elector, and his domain
And with the duke to replace the same
Had he not had the unbridled desire
To take for himself a position much higher
Had land and people not been so distressed
With robbery, murder, and other crimes pressed
So would his body not hang before Gothen
Cut in four pieces to stay until rotten.

Brück's head and quarters went missing after a few days but were soon found by a plowman in Freimar in a sack in his field and delivered to the authorities in Gotha. On the orders of Duke John William, who was at the time in Weimar, the remains were once more put in place on the pole.

Misfortune also met the playmate of my brother Johann and my older siblings in the Black Monastery, Dr. Justus Jonas, son of my father's friend and helper of the same name, who at the beginning of the siege had been sent to seek assistance. He fled to Copenhagen and had been appointed royal councillor there.

But after the elector of Saxony had reported him to the king, he fled, was captured, and was beheaded in his forty-second year.

He was already on the scaffold when he had an exchange with his confessor in Latin, which did not show much repentance.

Even for the outraged and angry emperor, the atrocities and cruelty began to exceed all bounds and became too much.

On the report that was given to him, he wrote in his own hand: *Excessit medicina modum,* which could be translated as "the medicine should not be greater and more hideous than the sickness," a principle we had learned in our medical studies.

CHAPTER 20

... tells how the duke departed Gotha and how I left Saxony with my family.

Now we all stood before a heap of rubble, both in the abstract and in reality. The rule of my former lord was broken, the court was disbanded, and the duke was going to be taken away.

The huge amount of supplies found in the Grimmenstein were not passed on to the guilty yet distressed city of Gotha but rather were taken by Duke John William to Weimar. Rumor had it that there were 15,000 measures of wheat; 15,000 measures of corn; 48,000 measures of oats; 10,000 measures of barley; 800 measures of peas; 2,400 measures of flour; 1,500 measures of salt; 5,000 tons of smoked deer meat; 800 tons of salted meat; 3,000 tons of fish; 1,600 cartloads of wine; 500 kegs of beer; 100 live oxen; a few hundred flitches of bacon; and of ordnance: 3,600 tons of powder; several thousand long spears and halberds; several thousand pieces of armor; several thousand iron and stone shot; and much additional war material.

Of guns, there were 160 in the armory, and 77 stood on the ramparts.

It was my faithful Thomas who provided these figures. Through the landlord of Zum Riesen, he had forged a connection to the cellarer of the castle. But the amounts strike me as truly incomprehensible. Today, I think they were exaggerated, but even so, the castle was well stocked. So well stocked that one can easily see how long beforehand the duke and his evil friends had prepared their schemes.

Even as the city of Gotha began to suffer privation from the siege, the duke thought only of indulging his dreams and had no intention of giving up some of his supplies to alleviate the hunger.

After the transfer of the supplies, the destruction of the castle began immediately without regard to the wishes and desires of Duke John William, who was now sole duke of Saxony (the duchy, not the electorate) and now also of Gotha, which consequently directly belonged to his dominion. A written order from the kaiser regarding the castle commanded: "No stone shall be left on another so that it will serve as eternal memory and example."

In August 1567, the Grimmenstein was blown up and completely obliterated. Grass grew on the hill, and butchers pastured their stock where the feared Grimmenstein had stood, and as time went by it was to become theirs through customary law.

The losses in the city were said to amount to 2,600 people, and outside the walls 4,500. In blowing up the walls, 600 people were killed. May these deaths be held against the guilty at the Last Judgment, also against my guilt-ridden lord John Frederick, whose removal I witnessed or, more correctly, was urgently requested by the elector to attend.

So then on Tuesday the 15th of April, 1567, at midday, I stood with Thomas and others who did not know what the future would bring in the courtyard of the Grimmenstein. The weather was horrible, with hail between patches of sun, then from the east a wall of frightening dark clouds. The sun disappeared, and a truly icy wind blew through the court. Shivering, I pulled my coat tightly around me and held on to my hat with one hand. I felt anxious, first because of the parting from my lord, to whom, in spite of everything, I still felt a connection. It is true I had come to know him as a weak and easily seduced man, but he had also been a good patient who wanted to do what is right, and he had provided for me well. Despite his high education, he held back in medical matters and did not ask his doctor irritating or distrustful questions, as, for example, for the contents of an infusion or the exact effects of a medication.

Second, my future was uncertain, since I did not yet know how useful my letter to the elector had been, in which I had distanced myself from my lord. Too, I was not sure about my own good conscience. Had I not essentially betrayed the hand that fed me? Should I have remained true to him even at the risk to my career, my family, and even my life? Did that fall under a physician's responsibility? Also now, as I am writing this, I still feel discomfort at the memory, which I will probably take with me into the grave. God will judge.

We stood and shivered as there was movement in the small crowd. A wagon covered with a black tarp drawn by four white horses draped in black and with manes and tails dyed red entered the castle courtyard to get Duke John Frederick and take him away.

His wife and children and servant staff stood beside the wagon crying bitterly. Duchess Elisabeth held her beloved husband in her arms and could barely be separated from him. The crowd was still. Two people on the outside made some abusive calls but were quickly silenced. In spite of all the unhappiness their lord had brought over them, the people seemed moved and compassionate.

Before he ascended into the wagon, something unexpected took place. The duke beckoned me over, which in view of my uncertain relationship with the new powers caused me some anxiety. He thanked me for my medical attentions and formally released me from his service. He even said, if it was offered, I could serve as personal physician to his cousin, Elector Augustus. This I found very generous. After all, the elector had been until now his worst enemy.

So much kindness brought tears to my eyes and did not make my conscience feel any better.

With the words, "Now in God's name!" the duke entered the wagon. He had no idea he would never again see his castle and his lands. He probably thought his imprisonment would last only a short time; therefore, as he bid his coachman good-bye, he commanded him to look now for another master, but when he was again free, he hoped the man would return to him.

In the following you can see how unequally God deals out penalties and bounties. While Gotha suffered greatly from the consequences of the siege, and the followers of the duke were terribly punished and left in misery, the duke, though a prisoner, had a comfortable, secure future well attended by a servant staff.

For staff he was allowed to take: treasurer, page, pharmacist, barber, house servant and room heater, cook with two kitchen boys, a cellarer's servant, and a Protestant predicant.

For escorts there were a squadron of riders and four companies of foot soldiers—an impressive number of more than a thousand guards—in which it can be seen that the emperor and the elector were not sure whether the subjects of the duke or Grumbach's chivalrous followers would undertake to free him.

For the duke's maintenance, Duke John William paid the emperor 15,000 thalers annually, which in the summer of 1572 was reduced by 3,000 thalers.

His remaining servants had to swear allegiance to the emperor and promise under oath to in no way advise, help, or encourage their imprisoned lord; also, similarly, to give the prisoner neither nor paper, ink, or writing boards nor to provide him with anything else, be it large or small, not agreed to by the guarding officer. And if they had any suspicions, they were to notify the emperor immediately.

At a stop in Meissen at Albrechtsburg Castle on the way to Vienna, John Frederick, still not cured of his madness, wrote on the wall with a pencil, "It will surely succeed. H.F.H.Z.S. (Hans Friedrich Herzog of Saxony)" But under that in red chalk, probably by the guard commander, had been written, "May the Almighty God have mercy on you."

The duke left behind, first of all, not only his family but also many people with broken hopes and destroyed existences. His faithful wife, who fled first to Weimar with their children, moved to Vienna in 1572 to share his imprisonment. The imprisonment was here more of an abstraction, since it consisted of a small court and a leasehold garden. And he could write and, with the help of a small library, pursue his scientific inclinations.

I confess I had had hopes under John Frederick to indulge my plans of making gold out of base metals. This unfulfilled hope was once more stirred when I attended the interrogation of Hans Beyer.

I will say in advance, I had engaged in various alchemical attempts at gold production in my small laboratory in Weimar, equipped by Anna, but in my short stays there had made little progress.

In Gotha and the ducal laboratories in Reinhardsbrunn as well as at the Grimmenstein, I had been rather passive because I did not want to be counted among the people who exploited the duke's dreams of wealth and money for their own enrichment. I saw very soon what charlatans most people became in pursuance of this delicate task and that the gullible duke repeatedly fell victim to them. His craving for gold had been further stimulated by the news from Dresden, where it was said that Elector Augustus and his skillful adepts were on the track of the biggest and most rewarding of all secrets—the making of gold. Should this hostile cousin, who owned wealthy lands and rich mines, also come into the enjoyment of an inexhaustible treasure of gold?

How I later became involved in gold making and invested much of hand and head is spoken about in its appropriate place.

As the court jester, Hans Beyer, who had almost always been at court and now quickly learned new ways of making faces when he was painfully interrogated, made known: Duke John Frederick had spent over 10,000 guldens on alchemists.

Ten thousand guldens. One may imagine it. The estates, cities, and farms and all taxable people would hardly have wanted their hard-earned money spent on futile attempts at gold making. On the other hand, they also hoped for gold because they believed that if their lord made enough of it, their taxes would be lower.

Every time a gold maker was convicted and imprisoned for his lies and mischief, was painfully interrogated, and often was executed or at least expelled from the country, there were great spiteful cries among the people, who at first had cried "Hosanna!" when the gold maker had been received at court with great pomp, then cried "Crucify him!" when he was unmasked.

The men or, more properly, the adventurers with whom John Frederick forged a connection were Liprand of Güllhorn, ostensibly a Swedish colonel, and his assistant, Valentin Hachenbach. Their trickery, however, was soon recognized, and in their place entered in 1566 Hans Rudolf Plumenecker, Hans Tyrol, and Hans Föhrenschild. And they practiced for a short time their adventurous activities in the ducal laboratory at Reinhardsbrunn.

Among the prisoners in Gotha was to be found also a deceitful alchemist, Matthias Friedrich, who was questioned on the order of Duke William by the bailiff Paul Schalreuther; then, as some people said, the executioner gave the final answer. I know of this last only from rumors. Perhaps he got away.

The preachers Abel Scherdiger from Hohenkirchen and Philipp Sömmering or Therocyclus from Schönau claimed to be able to make the secret philosopher's stone and put it into effect.

They concluded a contract with the duke (6th of November, 1566) and received 760 thalers and 16 lots of pure gold for their experiments, which, however, they could not begin because the siege soon started.

I still had a difficult hour to survive with Elector Augustus of Saxony after the departure of Duke John Frederick. Augustus, duke of Saxony, archmarshal of the Holy Roman Empire and elector, landgrave in Thuringia, margrave of Meissen, and burgrave of Magdeburg, summoned me.

But the fear was unnecessary. He received me gracefully in the castle, let me know that he had received my letter, and wanted my medical advice. He had been plagued for a long time with loss of appetite. And since he was only in his forty-first year, he could not befriend himself with it.

I took a deep breath at this unexpected reception, tried to gather my senses, and ran my collection of medical recipes through my mind. Loss of appetite is well treated with sage. The advantage, I explained to the elector, is that one can use the leaves of the plant, as one picks them, as seasoning for almost anything that comes to the table. The effect, I said, will be apparent within a few days.

The gracious elector thanked me and then dismissed me. It is possible that out of this small medical affair the rumor spread at the time that I had been Augustus's personal physician. That was not correct, and I would also not have liked it. Such a quick change between warring lords demanded an even more flexible mind than I possessed. And, thank God, the elector in those days did not offer me such a position.

With my possessions, I hurried to Weimar to my beloved wife and children, whose number meanwhile had grown to four. So one can see that I, though often in Gotha, still had had time to attend fruitfully to my wife.

My little daughter Margarethe was already a firm young maid of twelve years who, by her diligence in school for maidens, which was conducted in the deaconry house, gave us much pleasure. I want to add here that in 1554 a fifth teacher was hired at the Weimar city school, from which the school for maidens also received benefits. And everything was financed from the common chest, with additional contributions from the city in the form of payment in kind to the teachers.

Johann Ernst was almost seven years old. He had received his first name from his godfather, my brother Johann. Johann Friedrich was five and, as you may guess, named after my lord, the duke. Anna, our youngest, born in 1564, was now three.

After the first excitement and joy of reunion, and after my wife had expressed her satisfaction at my safe escape from the Grumbach Feud, she gave the children into the care of the maid and led me into my study. There awaited me a huge and pleasant surprise in the form of a letter. Not a letter from a vague nobody but rather one from the elector of Brandenburg, Joachim II, Hector from the lineage of the Hohenzollern. I put before the reader's eyes what such an honor implies, because so much is easily forgotten in daily life. But above all, through this I want to make clear how the importance of this letter puts my person in the right light.

There are in the Sacrum Romanum Imperium, the Holy Roman Empire, seven prince-electors, who have the right to elect the German king. For many hundreds of years, the election of the king was made by the entire group of spiritual and secular princes, and the archbishop of Mainz had the privilege of managing the voting process. Later, it was seven princes alone who were allowed to vote. And so it has stayed. With the electoral dignity are connected the arch offices: the elector of Brandenburg, for example, is the archchamberlain, an office of honor, which no longer requires the carrying of the royal chamber pot from the bedchamber.

By their letters of intent about all important imperial decrees, the electors take part in the government. Their power is increased through the Election Capitulations, to which the king before his crowning must swear. Still more important is the privilege of mine ownership and the mining for gold, silver, and iron, whereby, for example, the elector of Saxony is very rich. The electors are treated like kings; they go under canopies, and in processions swords are carried ahead of them. Also, it was for a long time a custom that the emperor went to meet the electors when they arrived at the imperial diet. This custom was abolished under Charles V.

At the crowning of the emperor, they sit alone at a raised table and keep their heads covered with the electoral hats.

For important decisions concerning the empire, the emperor must seek their advice. It should also be noted that the emperor calls the spiritual electors his nephews and the secular electors his uncles. The electoral domains may not be divided or sold and are inherited always by the oldest prince. Also, no elector can own more than one domain. Among these highly noble persons belong the archbishops of Cologne, Mainz, and Trier, the count Palatine of the Rhine, the duke of Saxony, the margrave of Brandenburg, and the king of Bohemia. Because of this, it is no wonder my imprisoned lord had striven to regain his father's place among them.

I was not a little proud and also somewhat vainglorious—God forgive me this sin—as I caught sight of the letter from one of these electors. I broke the seal and read:

Given in Berlin on Tuesday after Decollationis Johannis, Anno Domini 1567.

To the highly learned, our personal physician and dear faithful Herr Paul Luther, Doctor of Medicine.
Joachim, by divine right Margrave of Brandenburg and Elector.

First our greeting, erudite dear and faithful, because we here require you, we graciously desire you, to raise yourself at once and come to us here to join our service, which we deign to offer you with favorable grace.

Archiator of the elector of Brandenburg, of the archchamberlain of the empire! And in the letter both appointment and invitation. My wife, who had read this precious letter over my shoulder, had tears in her eyes from joy. This was now a position for her husband that corresponded with all her innermost desires. I had no illusions about the reasons for this appointment to Berlin. Certainly my medical reputation had traveled over the Saxon border, but I had to mainly thank the name of Luther and my brother Johannes.

As told above, Duke John Frederick had allowed Johannes to go on vacation. But he, despite an increase of salary by 130 guldens and the additional grant of two horses, a servant, stable rent, and feed, had preferred to stay in Prussia, where he for a time joined the service of Duke Albrecht, whose councillor and envoy he became.

Through his good connections and relationships as well as our Luther name, my brother succeeded in providing good positions for himself and me with the elector of Brandenburg. It is to be noted here that this happened at the right time, because Duke Albrecht of Prussia, temporarily under the imperial ban because of his consistent implementation of the teachings of our father and the conversion of the State of the Teutonic Order to the Duchy, was in great difficulty through his declaration against the very strict Lutherans. Everybody wanted to vent their anger on him; the nobility wanted to maintain their privileges against the princes, the theologians of various persuasions wanted to retain their independence and influence, the Polish king wanted to secure his supremacy, and the simple people followed those who most skillfully whispered their message.

In June 1568 the duke, weakened by grief, died of the plague. His worst grief fell on him when his confessor, Johannes Funck, and two other of his allies were sentenced to death for high treason and executed.

CHAPTER 21

. . . reports on our time in Berlin and on gold water.

We had hardly settled down in a beautiful, large house, situated near the River Spree island, where the electoral residence was to be found, when I started my medical activities for the elector and his family. I regularly went to the palace, which my new master had begun building in AD 1538. The elector loved architecture, and he was also inclined to the noble musica. He even sometimes conducted the chant in the cathedral and was an admirer of the other fine arts and sciences, which started to blossom at that time.

His various passions, the court banquets and buildings, and his almost-thoughtless lavishness led to permanent pecuniary embarrassment, which happily did not affect my salary.

Also, his love affairs were not cheap. They grew in number after his second wife, Hedwig, daughter of King Sigismund of Poland, fell and suffered an injury to her belly and therefore had to use crutches as long as she lived.

This, of course, did not contribute to the enjoyment of the marriage, though several times I examined the electoress and tried to restore her belly, which of course was hidden under a blanket while being examined. I had a good knowledge of the lower female anatomy, but under these circumstances neither an exact diagnosis nor an effective therapy was possible. So the elector had to look for compensation, which, according to my observations, he did not really abhor. Womenfolk made it easy for him and crowded around his person and wanted to have children by him, as he was known to provide for them generously. I could understand his feelings. Is there anything more beautiful, more attractive, than a fresh, new woman?

The elector's best-known affair was with the beautiful widow of the cannon founder, a captain of the artillery, Dieterich, born Anna Sydow, called among the common folks the Beautiful Foundress, with whom Joachim fathered several love-children. The Beautiful Foundress was not without ambition and even interfered with state business and appointments. This was to become her undoing after the death of her princely lover. Despite promises to the contrary and strict prohibition by his father, the son and successor of Joachim II, John George, ordered the poor woman to be incarcerated in the underground dungeon of the Spandau citadel, where she died AD 1575. Before her death, she threatened to appear in the future as a White Lady in the Berlin residence and frighten the respective rulers and their courts. She began these appearances immediately after her death and succeeded in terrifying a number of courtiers almost to death. Thank God I was no longer there when that happened.

There are some people in Berlin who maintain that the foundress was walled in, still alive, in the hunting lodge in Grunewald.

Lippold ben Chluchim, the court and finance Jew of my lord the elector, was at the same time, although innocent, imprisoned in Spandau. About him I will speak later.

When I now look back from my sickbed, I can see what a turbulent time it was for me and my family. The religious strife in the land of Brandenburg will serve as an example.

It will be seen at once that those in power, religious or otherwise, had little concern for the common people, who had great fear that they might believe in the wrong faith and therefore be condemned to hell. Since the Augsburg Settlement of 1555 between Ferdinand (the German or, more exactly, Roman king, also king of Bohemia, Croatia, and Hungary, acting for his brother, Emperor

Charles V) and the imperial estates, the principle of *cuius region, eius religio* was to be followed, which simply meant the subjects had to follow the faith of the ruler.

It is not difficult to write the above statement, but what it really meant for the believers was something different.

It had become a truism among the people that a defection from the popish faith would mean eternal damnation. Now suddenly there was the old or even a new pastor in the pulpit who said that was no longer true. Good deeds were no longer the way to salvation; rather, pure faith alone could win it. And what good deeds one had done! And what money had been spent on indulgences, even purchased for sins still to be committed, to be on the safe side!

There were some who had completely ruined themselves purchasing indulgences and were wasting away in the debtor's prison. And all that should no longer be true? Admittedly, the new preacher or even the old one who had been converted to the new faith talked convincingly and made everything less expensive through the abolition of the good deeds and the indulgences. Also, one need no longer keep in mind so many saints, in fact none at all, if you came to think of it. To simply believe was much cheaper. Of course, the church was no longer so colorful, and the preacher in his black robe looked like a dun crow. But that could be endured.

Then the ruler got it into his head that it was better for him to return to the old church and thus be rewarded by the emperor. Otherwise, he his land was taken away, which then was forcefully returned to the old faith, as had happened to the archbishopric of Cologne after the Cologne War. Now the church was again gorgeously decorated, mass was read in Latin—which, by the way, also had its advantages because one could catch up on one's slumber—and good deeds once again gained in importance and again cost money, though the trade in indulgences was attenuated, or rather indulgences were supposed to be given free. But purgatory was again a frightful prospect. One really did not know what to believe in.

Thank heavens such changes back and forth did not occur in Brandenburg, though even here it was not always simple.

For example, during a church inspection the preacher, with the approval of his congregation, refused to read mass in German. Others secretly gathered their sheep in the woods and read the Catholic mass. This was severely punished by the Protestant authorities. The preacher mentioned lost his parish and emigrated to Catholic southern Germany. The parish, of course, had to comply with the new order; they could not all emigrate. Legally speaking there was the *jus emigrandi,* the right to emigrate, but that was available only to the well-to-do.

When the emperor triumphed in the Schmalkaldic War, his soldiers raged in the Protestant lands, laid waste the churches, and even hanged Lutheran pastors in their churches.

Brandenburg, the land of my new lord, was originally a sworn enemy of my father's Reformation. Joachim I, Nestor, brother of Cardinal Albrecht, elector of Mainz, and archbishop of Magdeburg, was a determined enemy of Dr. Martin Luther and was correspondingly quite often thoroughly berated by my father. He has been spoken about previously.

My new master, Elector Joachim II, son of Joachim I and nephew of Cardinal Albrecht, was the first elector who declared himself for the new faith. As mentioned, his mother, the Danish princess Elisabeth, was an admirer of my father and had to flee from Berlin under cover of the night and seek the protection of the Saxon elector Johann. As a boy, I met her in my parents' house, where she lived once for a period of three months in modesty and adoration of my father.

The rage of her husband was immense. He even threatened to bury her alive in a wall if ever he could get hold of her.

You see, reader, walling in, or the fear of it and the legends about it, occur several times in my memoirs, first, because common people often talked about it and, second, because of my profession I often pondered how long a person could endure without food and drink and how they would behave in such a state. When after many years the walls were broken up, one could see how desperately the immured people had scratched and scraped at the walls and attempted to get out into God's fresh air. Though it did not always end like that. Often it only meant—and I think this is what was intended for the mother of my elector—that the person was to be imprisoned for life or at least threatened with this.

With the ancients, the Romans, burying alive was the punishment for vestal virgins who had, during their thirty years in office, broken their oath of virginity. Later nuns sometimes had to suffer the same fate if they could not curb their fleshly lust and ended in the walls of nunneries. There were, by contrast, the recluses, who let themselves become walled in voluntarily to achieve a higher degree of holiness. They had a small opening through which they would be given food and drink. Sometimes, in times of war and unrest, they were forgotten. It was of interest to me how long a person could live without observing the laws of Hygieia.

Back to those who were not immured.

True, my Herr Joachim II had to swear to his father that he would remain faithful to the Catholic Church, but after his father had died in Stendal, AD 1535, and after four years of thorough deliberation, he declared himself for the new belief. He did not join the Schmalkaldic League, though, but like Maurice of Saxony sought a medium position between the Catholic emperor and the Lutherans.

By doing so, he could keep his country out of the struggles, for which I admired him. His son, the electoral prince, was even in the emperor's entourage during the Battle of Mühlberg, and his brother, Hans von Küstrin, had strengthened the emperor's army by joining it with seven hundred riders, which was done according to the imperial constitution. In the Wittenberg talks about—then still—Elector John Frederick as well as in the talks in Halle about Landgrave Philipp of Hesse, he acted as mediator.

It was quite pleasant to serve such a reasonable and moderate prince, if only for a short time, after the excesses of my previous master. In religious matters he proceeded very cautiously. For example, in order not to awaken the enmity of the Catholic party, he retained many of the popish ceremonies in the service. In general, he was good-natured but, unfortunately, succumbed to drinking. Often in the mornings I was summoned to the residence, where I then tried with mild teas and cold compresses to better the aftereffects of the nightly binges. He moaned every time and promised me and himself that he would say good-bye to beer and wine, but in this he succeeded only very imperfectly.

No doubt he was weak. At the same time, he maintained a grand court but forbade his subjects ostentatious clothing and squandering of money. His court theologian, Musculus, real name Meusel, successor to the mild and reasonable Agricola, who had helped set up the Augsburg Interim, ingratiated himself with the elector by means of a book against unnecessary luxuriousness in clothes titled *About the Satanic, Unruly, Dishonorable, Sloppy Trouserdevil and Admonition and Warning of Same.* This title characterizes the man, who was a blustering and strict Lutheran and did not help the new church by his repressiveness in word, writing, and life.

Applauded by him, the elector once ordered three sons of rich citizens, who had strutted around the residence in Berlin in slit baggy pantaloons, for which many feet of cloth had been needed, to be stuck into a publicly displayed cage as a warning against excess.

The elector himself, though, did not deny himself anything and thus ruined the finances of his country. When Emperor

Maximilian II was crowned AD 1562, the elector of Brandenburg came with an entourage of 47 noblemen; 11 councillors, scholars, and doctors; and 452 horses. Imagine the costs alone for the horse feed, rent for their stables in the coronation city of Frankfurt, the stable boys, the harness keepers and harness makers, the farriers, etc. And for all this and much more, the land of Brandenburg, with its poor sandy soil and even poorer forests and meager mineral resources, had to pay.

When in the year of 1569 the elector was invested with the Duchy of Prussia as a covassal, this was of course celebrated in grand style. To the High Mass he rode on a golden-colored horse, clothed in a robe of sable fur decorated with gold pads and expensive cloth. I accompanied him in his entourage on my modest little horse and was quite glad that I did not indulge myself in such foolish necessities. Also, my wife did not force me to appear so sumptuously clothed, though of course she always saw to it that I was dressed properly and in a style befitting my state.

Only once did I succeed in talking to the prince in a moderating way. He liked tournaments and jousts with sharp weapons, where many men were injured, their bones were broken, and sometimes their limbs were cut off. Horses were wounded and had to be killed, harnesses were dented, swords and spears were broken, and the like. The tournament master, who had for quite a time suffered from these losses, created for me a list of expenses with which I was able to influence my lord toward moderation, but, alas, not for long, so that noteworthy economies did not result.

After the Reformation a number of sovereigns in Germany and Europe enjoyed a favorable period through the secularization of monasterial and other church properties. My elector, too, took in considerable sums of money, and though he had to share them with the country's nobility, much remained in his chests. But this did not put an end to the financial problems, understandable considering the expenditures described. Even an excise tax on beer did not help. When the elector died, he left debts in the amount of 2,600,000 thalers.

As with many of the great lords in Germany and elsewhere, it was the Jews who had to help procure money and avert bankruptcy. With this I come, as promised above, to the elector's court Jew, Lippold ben Chluchim, first highly praised and then damned to hell and imprisoned in Spandau with the Beautiful Foundress.

Lippold came from Prague and, with his father and brother, moved to Berlin about AD 1542. This was after Brandenburg was reopened to the Jews in 1539. After some years, he was employed by the elector as doctor, chamberlain, and treasurer, and he proved to be a skilled financial adviser so that he also became mintmaster. About his medical activities I learned nothing, and the elector did not talk to me about them. Lippold also became head of all Jews in Brandenburg.

He was popular at court and with the well-to-do Berliners, because he lent money as a pawnbroker and only took small interest, three pfennigs a week for a thaler. When, after the elector's death, an investigation was started against him, nearly twelve thousand gold and silver valuables still in pawn were found in his house, which, though not illegal, contributed to his misfortune.

The investigation did not reveal any crime by Lippold, and so superstition had to be employed. He was accused of sorcery, of having murdered the elector by poisoning, and also of other things. The people stormed the Jew Yard and the synagogue standing there, and all Jews were banned from Berlin.

Lippold was tortured and through monstrous agonies confessed to having poisoned the elector, which he could not have done, as we will see in a bit. He recanted, was tortured again, confessed again, and finally, in 1573, after having been pinched with red-hot tongs, was put on the wheel and quartered. A mouse that ran from under the scaffold during the execution was seen by the crowd and believed to be the Devil sorcerer who had just left the Jew.

It is probable that those among the Berliners who had pawned their valuables rejoiced, because they would now get their possessions back without having to pay the Jew. The chancellor, Lampert Distelmeyer, returned the pawns, also their promissory notes, to Lippold's debtors without requiring repayment. This was blatant injustice.

I must here note a few things out of sequence. First, the passing away of Joachim II, because it is connected with Lippold, and then something regarding my family and my gold water.

To report that Lippold had nothing to do with the death of the elector gladdens my heart. Unfortunately, I was at the time at the court of Margrave Hans von Küstrin or, more exactly, von Brandenburg-Küstrin, the brother of my lord, when the following happened.

In midwinter, on January 3rd, AD 1571, the elector went hunting for wolves in Köpenick, and as he had drunk quite a lot, he did not pay attention to the icy wind and caught a heavy cold. There was no sensible person in Köpenick Castle who would have recommended him a hot drink, for example, hot and strongly spiced wine, and a bath, hot and with herbs. In addition, he suffered from an effluence on his foot, which for quite a time I had tried to heal, without success. Together with his cold, this led to his sudden death. Now, much too late, I was called back to Berlin from Küstrin by a messenger on horseback.

I performed a thorough examination of my dead master, who was well preserved by the winter cold, wrote a careful report of all that had happened, and recorded also the witness reports of the people present. I could not find any trace of poisoning, and the mere presence of the court Jew was naturally no indication of a crime. It was said he had given the elector, on the evening before his death, a glass of malmsey that had been poisoned. The bottle from which the wine had come had no traces of poison. Also, on the Jew nothing was found.

He was accused of causing the death of the elector because he was afraid he would be punished for the theft of a very valuable gold chain. In truth, he had followed the elector's order and had made gold coins from the chain, with which the elector in his lavish generosity presented his guests on the evening before his death.

Lippold's innocence was clearly proved by my report and the written testimonies of the witnesses so that even Emperor Maximilian II, though without success, tried to persuade the authorities in Berlin to return Lippold's property to his widow. But a legally acceptable trial for the cancellation of the original sentence was not allowed. The following statement was produced at the shameful trial. It had been gotten from Lippold under torture.

> According to the law clerk's record, he confessed that he could ban the Devil in a glass and in a magic circle or any other vessel or figure, so powerful a sorcerer he claimed to be, and force him to do his will.
>
> He could also, with the Devil's help, get into the closed and locked rooms of His Electoral Grace any time, day and night. He had connected himself with the Devil and devoted his body and soul to him. He had poisoned His Electoral Grace so that he had to die. Also, he had bewitched a black hen and buried it in the mint so that no coins could be made anymore.

I had hardly finished my autopsy and dictated my findings of the causes of the elector's death to the clerk when a messenger came from Küstrin with the news I should come at once. The margrave was dying, ten days after his brother. I was very sorry because the margrave was a diligent and economical prince whom I greatly respected, and it had occurred to me several times to leave Berlin, move to Küstrin, and offer him my services. Of course, I would have had to persuade my wife first, and I do not think that would have been easy. Now circumstances had spared me the decision and also a possible argument with her.

Both princes died when I was not present, and so I could do nothing to help them. But thank heavens this did not harm my reputation as personal physician, as we will soon see. Perhaps my absence was even favorable, because their passing away could not be blamed on me. But, of course, my feelings were mixed, and I was greatly saddened because they were fine men and had always been good to me.

There is a legend that the elector shortly before his death was my guest and that he in one big gulp emptied an entire silver cup that King Gustav Wasa of Sweden once presented to my father. This is really just a legend, and the death of the elector happened as described. However, this kind of talk showed how close I was to the elector in the eyes of the people.

It is true that the elector, before he died, ordered that two massive gold chains be given to me as a present for my good services. When a member of his staff presented them to me, I hesitated to accept them in view of the miserable finances of the land. I also remembered my father did not like to accept expensive gifts and always said that the Lord God would stand by those who trusted in Him. While I considered this and hesitated, my wife made clear her opinion with a simple look that quickly helped me to decide. I accepted the chains and thanked His Electoral Grace in many words.

Much dying occurred at the time, and the Jews suffered badly, but in my family we had a blessed event. On Palm Sunday, AD 1569, our youngest child, a little boy, was born and baptized in the Palace Church with the name Johann Joachim. Godparents were Elector Joachim II; his daughter, Magdalena Elisabeth, widowed Duchess of Brunswick and Lüneburg; and my brother Johannes and our uncle Jacob, brother of my father, who was in his eightieth year and died AD 1571. One can, by the way, see that my wife and I, when naming our children, did not forget the advantage of the child or the christening presents. I do not think this is wrong or unseemly.

Not more than one year later, there was another very joyful event in our family. Our elder daughter, Margarethe, married. At first I hesitated to agree because she was so young, fifteen years old. But my wife, Anna, called me foolish and pointed to the well-developed and visible state of maturity of our daughter as well as the good match that was offered. The bridegroom was Simon Gottsteig from Magdeburg, who was the mill overseer of the administrator of the prince-archbishopric of Magdeburg, John Frederick of Brandenburg, grandson of my lord, Joachim II, and his wife, Hedwig of Poland. I was now connected to the Hohenzollern as I had been earlier to the Wettins, to whom I was to return one day.

To my greatest sorrow, Margarethe died one year ago, my only consolation being that my dear wife, who left me alone AD 1586, did not live to experience this. Margarethe was only thirty-seven years old and left several children, who, thanks to the position of her widower, are well provided for. Because the administrator of the archbishopric mainly resided in Halle or went hunting in the Letzling heath, Simon's range of responsibilities was quite large as overseer and main bailiff.

Now I am coming to my gold water, the invention, or rather improvement, of which I regard as my most important achievement in Berlin and still today fills me with pride.

Soon after I had begun my service as archiator of the elector of Brandenburg, I started to seriously occupy myself with the manufacture of *aurum potabile*. This problem had been of interest to me earlier, but time and circumstances of life, as I have described them, had prevented me from doing systematic alchemical work.

Gold, or *aurum* or *rex metallorum* or whatever it may be called, is the purest, most durable, densest, heaviest, most valuable, and most excellent of all metals and can be called their king. How near, then, must be the assumption that it has a curative effect better than all other substances, like a king who surpasses all other people. The noblest metal must logically and necessarily have the strongest effect if—and that is the decisive condition—it can be administered to the human body in a form in which it can exercise its beneficial effect best.

Gold is essentially determined by the purest and most mature quicksilver with a pure and solid sulfur heated so strongly by the power of the sun or subterrestrial fire that they cannot ever be separated from each other, and that is why gold is stable in fire and all sorts of *aqua fortis.*

The last statement, which is shared by all alchemists, had been bothering me for a long time. If it were possible, by alchemical methods, to make an *aqua fortis,* or let us call it *aqua regia,* that could dissolve gold—absorb it into its liquidity, as it were—then one could, principally, drink it. This *aqua regia* is naturally of enormous power and sharpness and has to be diluted correspondingly so that it does not do damage but can exercise its healing effects.

Gold water at the time I am writing about was, in my opinion, not effective or not effective enough. It consisted of the tiniest gold particles, really gold dust, suspended in a drinkable liquid, and naturally it left the body in the normal and natural way as all other food.

It should be clear that the extraordinarily stable and noble gold, other than iron, quicksilver, and other metals, cannot be digested and taken in by the body vessels.

I do not hesitate to admit, though, that even administered in this way, it is not without effect, as I could observe with some patients. All the more grew my conviction that the effect of *aurum* would have to be incomparably greater if it could be incorporated in the body like other substances—digested, so to speak, and built into the body. The famous Paracelsus said about this: "Of all elixirs, gold is the highest and most important for us, because it can make the body unbreakable. *Aurum potabile,* or drinkable gold, heals all illnesses; it renews and reconstructs."

Even now, at the end of my life, I cannot give up my secret. I will hand it down to my grandchildren, who can benefit from it. The recipe is in a safe place and will be made known to my progeny in due time.

I will say the following: after many experiments, distillations, rectifications, and calcinations, I succeeded in making my *aqua regia,* or king's water, and dissolved gold into it. I diluted the solution so far that it became drinkable and then made a liqueur from it, which tasted very good and had the best healing effects. The elector granted me a privilege license for the manufacture and sale of my gold water, which soon got a good reputation and even better profitability.

CHAPTER 22

. . . brings me, my family, and the reader to Dresden.

In these my final days, I find myself more and more reflecting on how much the happy circumstances of my life are due to my own merit or are simply the result of lucky accidents. Such as how after the Grumbach Feud I found myself in a new position, happy again—a change for which I consider myself and my family fortunate. As soon as Joachim II and his brother, Hans von Küstrin, had entered eternal life, a message from the chancellor at the electoral court in Dresden, Georg Cracow, reached me saying the elector was thinking about an engagement of my person as his personal physician. My wife was beside herself with joy, and I, too, not forgetting the necessary manly refrainment from emotion, became quite elated. Had I known how they later dealt with Georg Cracow, I would certainly not have been quite so joyous.

There was still another reason we were looking forward to a possible move to Dresden.

As reported, Duke Albrecht of Prussia had died in 1568 of grief and the plague, grief because in Prussia a fanatical Lutheran named Heshusius together with a self-seeking party had won the upper hand so that there was no home for Christ's true evangelism. Albrecht's son Albrecht Frederick was only fifteen years of age when he succeeded to the title and was completely under the tutelage of the new councillors, who had been forced upon his father, and the son soon found himself in a deep depression.

It was feared that the mean-spirited zealots, after an expected unification of Prussia with Brandenburg, would also gain influence in the electorate. Remembering my experiences in Jena, it made me afraid.

Another point: the son and successor of my lord, Joachim II, who was on the whole a good-natured if lavish prince, John George, was an intolerant, severe, and parsimonious master, who treated the Jews in the electorate and, above all, in Berlin evilly and did great injustice to the court Jew, Lippold. I was afraid that nothing good would come to my family in Brandenburg-Prussia and was all the more eager to accept the appointment from Elector Augustus in Dresden, which dated from the 20th of July of the Year of the Lord 1571.

Elector Augustus of Saxony, the reader will ask: Is he not the one who dealt so badly with your former lord in Gotha and took such gruesome revenge on his entourage? And now, Paul Luther, you are going to join his service?

This I respond to with the following reasons.

First, my lord, John Frederick, had formally dismissed me in Gotha and left it to me to go into the service of Augustus of Saxony, and, second, I, head of a family of five, was looking for a new employer whose reputation and wealth should at least be equal to my former one. What should be here so remarkable or cause me pains of conscience? Do we not all seek first for a good livelihood and contentment before we start examining our conscience? Is it not so that a good livelihood is the precondition for the possibility of such an examination? To put it another way: the poor peasant who has to fight for his daily bread does not have qualms of conscience because all his time and energy is spent struggling to survive. To put it still another way: Necessity knows no law. Admitted: my necessity was on a relatively high level, but does that mean it mattered less? Anyway, we moved to Dresden, which I did not regret during the first years.

Dresden is a beautiful city, and the Elbe River, which in Bohemia is named the Labe River and is already a powerful watercourse in Dresden, gives the city its characteristic imprint through its broad and fine meadowed banks. The river passes Wittenberg, too, and therefore I was quite familiar with it, like an old friend.

The residence lies on the left bank of the river, while on the other side, reached by a stone bridge, is Altendresden, which was not unified with Dresden until AD 1550 by the elector Maurice.

This bridge, when I arrived, took my breath away. It is a stone arch bridge with originally twenty-four pillars and twenty-three arches, of which four arches had been filled with earth and were hardly visible at all. The length of the bridge is eight hundred paces, and nobody knows of a longer arch bridge in the whole of Europe. A drawbridge connects the two sides and is constructed of timber, for a good reason. In case of an attack, this part can quickly be burned down and so made unusable for the enemy.

Trade and commerce thrive in Dresden, and on the Elbe River one can see the merchants' barges and the nobles' pleasure boats. Not far to the southwest, silver ore is mined, and in the surrounding fields there are abundant crops and cattle, and the forests teem with game. On the slopes of the Elbe Valley good wine is grown, particularly since Elector Augustus in 1560 imported Hungarian vines for the improvement of the Saxon stock.

The city connects the trade of the east and west, and its importance has grown since Constantia, first wife of Henry the Illustrious, brought a valuable relic, a piece of Christ's cross, to Dresden, which attracts numerous pilgrims, who all want to eat and drink and be well accommodated and so help trade and commerce thrive in the city.

The city achieved its prominent status when, in 1547, the electorship was transferred to the Albertine Wettins, and Duke Maurice of Saxony became elector. Now Dresden was the capital of an electorate, which added significantly to its development.

My new master, Augustus, duke of Saxony, archmarshal and elector of the Holy Roman Empire, landgrave in Thuringia, margrave of Meissen, and burgrave of Magdeburg, ruled over a great and wealthy principality, which he knew to administer wisely.

There were several things especially to his credit: the decision to receive the industrious Dutch who had fled from Spanish suppression, the improvement of the roads and the coinage by concentrating the mints in one place in Dresden, promotion of the Leipzig Fair, the exemplary cultivation and management of the ducal demesnes, and the support of pomiculture as well as cattle breeding. He himself wrote the *Little Fruit and Garden Book.* Also, he began laying the foundation of collections that show examples of human activities in important fields.

His main fault was a narrow-minded religious attitude, which was caused by his worry that the Ernestinians might again claim, even by force, the electorship. Throughout his entire life he sought an alliance with the Habsburgs and carried on a fight with the Calvinists. This will be written about later, when the influence of such developments on my life will be presented.

We arrived in Dresden almost like gypsies with bag and baggage in three wagons. It was a fine, sunny, and not-too-warm day in July in 1571. The roads between Berlin and Dresden had been rutted and dusty, and it took us seven long days of travel to complete the journey.

The guards on both sides of the frontier between Brandenburg and Saxony showed themselves impressed by the orderliness of our passports, my past position in Berlin, and my future position at the court in Dresden so that they just glanced superficially into our wagons.

Our horses could draw the heavy wagons only at walking speed, with which we were quite content. Our children, the eleven-year-old Johann Ernst, the nine-year-old Johann Friedrich, and our seven-year-old Anna, enjoyed the journey. Sometimes they rode on the broad backs of the heavy horses or jumped from the wagon—which each time alarmed their mother—and ran on the meadow beside the road. When the horses stopped and were fed and watered, they plucked grass and put it into the nosebags of the horses.

Little Anna was the first to get tired, because she was small and tender, and she lay down on the sacks and blankets in the first wagon, which was meant for our transport. We spent the nights in wayside inns but slept two nights in the covered wagon. The first night was disturbed, not far from Finsterwalde. We heard wolves howling in the distance, which made the horses restive. The wagoners took turns keeping watch and tending to the fire. The two boys, anxious to appear brave, waved their wooden swords and scared their little sister with tales about wolves who preferred little girls for their food or even carried them off live. My wife had to intervene strongly to make them desist.

In the meantime, I patrolled the wagons with a heavy stick and my sword and felt important protecting my family.

Toward midnight the howling stopped so that finally we went to sleep. In the morning our servant surprised us with a hare that he had caught in a snare, slaughtered, and disemboweled. We roasted it and thus had, quite unexpectedly, a hearty breakfast of roasted hare, bread, and clear water from a little stream. In addition, the children had gathered sorrel and early blackberries, which served us as dessert.

The little stream was very useful as my wife, chastely behind a blanket hung between two trees, and then the children could have a thorough wash. Where the stream formed a bay and had a gravel ground, the wagoners bathed the horses, curried them, and watered them.

We reached Dresden in the morning and could immediately move into a house in the Kanzleigässchen, which was provided for me as archiator.

We had hardly moved in when I was summoned to the castle, because the fourteenth child of the electoress Anna, the boy Adolf, born on the 8th of July, had fallen ill. I was called to his cradle before I was even introduced to the elector or his wife and the court. At first sight the little infant proved to be very weak, and I recommended to go on feeding the child breast milk from the wet nurse and in between fennel tea. A herb woman, in whom the ducal couple set great hopes, I tried to keep away from the child. He recovered a bit, but in the autumn he was again very ill. The herb woman had succeeded in sneaking in and giving the child a medicine of lion's manure with droppings of doves and deer, mixed into his pap, also little cakes called *manus Christi* with fresh aniseed oil, infusion of lime tree blossom, a certain kind of root, and fresh honey from Lithuania.

I must confess that I did not protest against this detestable medicine strongly enough, as I had just come to the court and did not want to jeopardize my position with the parents. I prescribed dandelion pap and small doses of theriac, but the child died in the following year. The parents really were ill fated, because of the fifteen children the electoress gave birth to, they lost eleven in child- or babyhood.

CHAPTER 23

. . . describes what we met with in Dresden.

After I had been introduced at court and my wife had also made the acquaintance of the ruling couple, we soon settled down in Dresden. The children quickly got to know our neighbors, mostly court people, and liked playing on the banks of the Elbe River. It naturally was inevitable that they also befriended the children of the menial court staff, such as cooks, maidservants, grooms, stablemen, servants, barbers, craftsmen, gilders, silver polishers, and others. From them they acquired much useful knowledge about life in the city, the markets, the booths and stalls, etc., with which they entertained us at dinner and quite often made us laugh.

They quickly learned to speak our beautiful German language with the Saxon-Dresden pronunciation, which Anna disliked, but she did not succeed in preventing such contacts. For life on the streets was too interesting. One could see and hear jugglers, buffoons, revolting deformities, beggars, dancers, tightrope walkers, traders, all kinds of wayfaring people, soothsayers, fire eaters, and ballad mongers. The latter made even me stop sometimes when they recited news and ghoulish stories from all the world.

My wife had a lot to do, not so much in the way of household chores as in supervising the children, the cook, a maidservant, a stableman, and my servant. In spite of that, she seemed to me to be quite content, so I could devote myself extensively to my work at court.

My new master, Elector Augustus, was from the beginning fond of me, which was a surprise, as I had been a faithful servant of his Ernestine relative and opponent, Duke John Frederick. In truth, my life long I have wondered how people could like me, because I am actually a weak person, not easy to be fond of. I myself have always found it difficult to put up with myself, and now that I will soon pass away, I can do so with a heartfelt sigh: God, I thank you that finally I have gotten rid of myself. With this, I do not mean to say that my life did not have beautiful, even irretrievable and unique, moments.

But such thoughts did not move me at that time, and I eagerly threw myself into my new tasks, which were: bring order to the organization of apothecaries in Dresden, practice my medical duties at the court, and—a task that became more and more important—engage myself in the art of gold making, which, together with His Electoral Grace, I did to a growing extent.

Dealing with the apothecaries began when one day Electoress Anna summoned me.

The page knocked on my door very early. It must have been about seven of the clock. Because it was still dark, he carried a lantern. We were at breakfast when he arrived, and I had to ask the young man to wait in the hallway until I had dressed myself suitably to my station. We went to the residence, crossed the courtyard, and, passing the guards, entered the ground floor, which had four wings devoted to the ducal economy, the storage and safekeeping of goods, the kitchen, and the accommodation of the servants. Also, there was the silver chamber and the court tailor's shop, which I was allowed to make use of, naturally for adequate payment, for the making of my court livery.

In the western wing behind heavy oak doors there were green-painted rooms, which served as the treasury. Already, one year after my arrival in Dresden, this secret safekeep of the duke was called the "Green Vault" and was actually not really very secret. Everybody knew what was locked behind those doors.

We went up to the second floor, which accommodated the ducal family. Here the page led me to Her Electoral Grace's study.

She was sitting behind a desk on which there were, properly arrayed, all sorts of papers, writing materials, and an inkpot. The electoress was dressed very modestly; she wore, except for two rings on her fingers, no precious stones and appeared well prepared for what she was going to disclose to me.

Born Anna of Denmark and Norway, she was called by the people Mother Anna. She had been interested in medicine, botany, and pharmacy all her life and, too, was herself quite a good, competent physician, though of course not very scholarly. She had invented a stomach plaster against hypochondriac melancholy, which became very famous, also certain antidotes and an eye wash, which I often prescribed for my patients.

I did the required obeisance before the princess, who nodded at me graciously, said God be with you, and beckoned me to come nearer. A lady-in-waiting, whom I had not seen yet and who later was introduced to me as Countess Elsa von Grauenfels and looked her name, stood to the left of the princess and near to the window. She was silent during the talk, just listening and observing.

"Dr. Luther," said my mistress, "it is quite to my liking that you will from now on adorn our court with your eruditeness and knowledge of medicine and pharmacy. I want to make claim to your services in a further matter. My husband has already given his consent. And I hasten to say that he, too, will want something more from you than just your medical services. And this can have interesting and far-reaching consequences for you.

"But now to my request. Since my arrival in Dresden, I have noted a lamentable lack of apothecaries in our city. There is only one, the Old Apothecary, and perhaps you have seen the state it is in. The laboratory is dirty, the assistants are unfriendly and ignorant, the stock is unordered and part of it moldy, there is no well-kept apothecary book, and people increasingly complain to the council and the elector about bad, ineffective, and even health-endangering medicaments that are also too expensive. This I want to remedy with your help. Your predecessor, Dr. Peucer, a very knowledgeable though sometimes doubtful man, was unwilling to spend his time on these things, as he was more interested in geodesy, astronomy, and mathematics. You, I seem to recall, have known him since his time in Wittenberg."

I made an affirmative bow and was surprised at what the electoress knew about me.

"At least," she continued, "we should put into practice what the highly famous and noble Emperor Frederick had demanded and ordered. Do you know these regulations?"

My interest for everything historical has always been strong, and naturally I had a thorough knowledge of the *historia medicinae et pharmaciae.* But my prudence, or should I say cunning, told me to give the impression that the electoress told me something new. At the same time, as archiator I could not be without any knowledge in this field. So I did not answer her question directly but nodded knowingly to her revelations.

Her Electoral Grace now started on a veritable speech, and it seemed to me that she was not making it for the first time. Later I learned that she had for quite a time been involved in the improvement of the pharmacy assistants, midwives, and herb girls.

"You know, Dr. Luther, that a properly equipped and maintained apothecary is of the highest importance for the whole *ars medicinae.* Without apothecary, without pharmacy, no medicine.

"A big step forward in Europe for the healing and pharmaceutical arts was made when the glorious Emperor Frederick II, who not without reason was called *Stupor Mundi,* or the Amazement of the World, ordered all people in his Sicilian realm who wanted to become physicians to study at the Schola Medica Salernitana, the first medical school in the known world."

Here, I found, I could insert something without angering the electoress and still show my knowledge. "Yes," I said, "Salerno, where the last Ostrogoths in AD 555 surrendered to the troops of the Eastern Roman Empire."

Obviously this was news to the electoress, but she did not let it be known and went on: "The emperor ordered that an anatomical college be added to the medical school and corpses be provided for dissection. Those could be had in abundance, as the emperor was not squeamish with his enemies. In the interest of anatomy, to his credit, he in many cases dispensed with torture, which would disfigure the bodies and thus confuse the anatomist.

"You are well aware yourself, Dr. Luther," she interrupted her educational speech, "that even today corpses for anatomical purposes are difficult to come by."

I resumed my nodding, stronger than before.

"The noble Staufer, to which dynasty Frederick belonged, had achieved great things for the apothecaries by demanding in his medicinal order of AD 1241: 'There must be no common business of physician and pharmacist. Physicians may not possess pharmacies and are not allowed to trade medicaments.'"

Here she gave me a sharp look, as if she believed I would sell medicine and thereby bypass the apothecaries.

Well, to be honest, this happened now and then, because my *Aurum potabile,* or gold water, as well as later my *Unguentum de nitro,* or nitro-unguent, as well as the fine *Magisterium perlarum,* or master mother of pearl, which I sold as saltpeter salve and master powder, were very profitable, which I did not want to share with the pharmacists. Also, I did not want to share the secret recipes with others.

Master powder and saltpeter salve were excellent against many complaints, as were many drugs that I extracted from plants by means of spirit. As to the master powder, I could observe with many a patient that the name alone, which did not contain any indication of its composition, effected an improvement.

Thinking about these things, I probably looked a bit distracted, because the electoress said rather loudly, "Dr. Luther, do I still have your attention?"

I responded quickly, "Of course, Your Grace," and forced myself to listen to her intently.

"On the other hand," said the lady, "pharmacists were not allowed to treat patients. The authorities were required to monitor the preparation of the medicaments, and the pharmacist had to buy impeccable raw material, to make all recipes as the doctor had ordered or as prescribed in an up-to-date book of medicaments. He had to visibly show the price and composition of the medicines, to offer them to the poor at reduced prices, to act solely for the good of the patient, and to prove his expertise with a certificate as well as master the Latin language, and so on.

"But alas," the mistress sighed here, "how long it takes to put into practice such reasonable regulations. Look at the apothecaries today and observe the itinerant traders in medicines, and you will see how much is still lacking from the implementation of the orders of the famous emperor and how much we still have to do.

"We'll start," she then said, "tomorrow morning with a visit to the Old Apothecary. Please be there in front of it at exactly ten of the clock, and await my litter."

With this she dismissed me.

This talk I took for a good beginning of my work, and I felt sure of the goodwill of the electoress. I had before heard about the great influence she exercised on the politics of the elector, such a great influence that people at the court whispered to each other the impudent word of *gynocracy*. What this led to will be reported.

The visit to the Old Apothecary next morning caused quite a stir. I stood in front of the door on time, when the litter bearers put down the litter with their mistress. People stopped, gawked, and jostled, and the guards who accompanied the princess had to clear the way for her into the apothecary.

Here we found exactly what Lady Anna had described the day before. The laboratory was unaired and dirty; light could hardly penetrate the small uncleaned windows; and the assistants were unwashed and uncombed. It was obvious that no one had notified them of our visit.

The electoress, to whom of course the assistants behaved servilely, ordered her amanuensis to write exact minutes of her orders and then said she expected me to check on the state of things within half a year.

Everything stood in absolute disarray. The oak bark used for hemorrhoids was in a wooden box beside the *Pasta regalis.* There were tins, flasks, phials, mortar and pestle, *aqua destillata* in an unclean wooden barrel, camphor oil, nutmeg balm, diaphoretic salve, henbane extract, plasters, horn spoons to fill in powder, and herb bouquets as well as fat from hanged people, urine, breast milk, and other *animalia* in addition to the magic powder of the unicorn. It was a miracle that under these circumstances the apothecary could do business at all.

In addition, the apothecary traded groceries, spices, spirits, or *aqua ardens,* which the chemist distilled himself and could produce for sale—a privilege that had been granted to the apothecary since Johannes Huffener founded it and that had to be renewed yearly. The electoress told me quietly in an aside that she was considering not renewing it but instead granting the privilege to the Court Apothecary being planned and over which the court alone, and no longer the city, would have jurisdiction. Then, to my surprise, she added in good German: "Apothecary is apothecary, and schnapps is schnapps."

The electoress ordered the *separanda* to be put on a special shelf and to be labeled as such. Under this were subsumed all substances that had a strong effect and could, when wrongly dosed, be dangerous, such as *Lilium convallium,* or lily of the valley, which can be either poison or medicament and, when prescribed correctly, helps against falling sickness. Another one, more importantly, is the Spanish fly.

This latter medicine has caused much damage because people believe that much medicine means much benefit. This powder is by no means just an *aphrodisiacum;* it but leads to a man's longer-lasting erection and also to a swelling of the woman's parts. Many well-to-do men had been hauled to my house whose erection had changed into a veritable priapism, which I could help only with the assistance of a barber-surgeon and his sharp lancet. If one waits too long, the member can get gangrenous and fall off completely. But if the surgeon steps in in time, the patient can be healed, often though without ever suffering from an erection again.

The electoress gave the apothecary numerous orders, which the amanuensis noted down carefully.

If you look today, as I am writing this, into the apothecaries in Dresden and elsewhere in the electorate, you begin to feel better as soon as you enter, and you are inclined to forget about your illness. The assistants are friendly and knowledgeable about pharmacy and the manufacture of medicaments. On the shelves you find cleanly labeled pots, boxes, and flasks; from the ceiling hang leather bags with spices as well as bundles of herbs, dried or fresh, the season allowing.

On the large table you can see the orderly arrayed spoons, mortars, spatulas, sieves, and all instruments needed for the making of medicines. On the left, perhaps, you will find a counter for the sale and a desk for bookkeeping; on the right there is space for all devices, distillators, barrels, glasses, alembics, cooling hoods, and ovens with several openings, all of them needed for the preparation of medicaments and also for alchemy, as well as a hearth for the preparation of decoctions, the thickening of juices, and the manufacturing of electuaries.

A special place is reserved for the awe-inspiring *Tabula smaragdina*, or Emerald Tablet, or rather a copy of it in the form of a book fixed to the table by a chain. The original was found by Abraham's wife Sarah in the grave of Hermes Trismegistos, the god of, among others, alchemy and astronomy. In it you can read in mysterious words how microcosm emerged from macrocosm and how knowledge of this process is the key to many riddles of nature.

Thanks to the efforts of Electoress Anna and myself, the authorities now control the apothecaries and their keepers. The books are checked, the medicaments are reviewed for their age, the general cleanliness of the laboratory is observed, and the honesty with regard to prices is paid attention to.

The number of people who fall ill or die after taking the medicines prescribed by the physicians and sold by the apothecaries has declined greatly.

Later, in AD 1581, the elector ordered the court apothecary to be built at the Taschenberg Hill as well as a test house, which served as the laboratory for the court alchemists. I could make use of both of them, being allowed to experiment, distill, rectify, and calcinate in the pharmacy and carry out my alchemical experiments in the test house.

CHAPTER 24

. . . deals with gold.

It has been stated that I was on good terms with the electoress, and I hoped it would be even better with the elector. But I have to say, both of them made it a policy to associate with the sort of people who did not make it easy to exhibit the best qualities of my character. This was especially true in religious matters. Instead, they reinforced my inclination to say what others wanted to hear. And in this I developed considerable skill. In short, in some situations and affairs I had to hide my true feelings and act against my conscience in order to protect myself and my family from the intrigues of the electoral court and the duplicity of state policy.

But first I am going to record how the elector, with my assistance, planned to become rich and powerful. Or still richer and more powerful. Richer and more powerful through the art of gold making. The experiments required for this he and I carried out until his death in AD 1586.

The reader should understand that since my time at the university, I have been intrigued with the idea of making gold. And even though I have long had doubts about the possibility of accomplishing it, my hopes in the end prevailed, and of course I attempted it.

One morning in the spring of my second year in Dresden, when I was already well installed and sufficiently provided with money, the elector summoned me to the castle. I was led into his cabinet, in which a table was laid with cold roast venison, white bread, and red wine.

We were alone in the room, when the following talk took place.

The elector: "It is early in the day, but I think it does no harm to have roast, wine, and bread for breakfast."

As I did not utter any medical reservations, the elector helped himself and asked me to follow his example. I had had breakfast at home with my wife, but to keep my master company, I also took a bite. But I asked for permission to have water instead of wine because I wanted, I told my host, to keep a clear head in view of the disclosures to be expected from the princely mouth. This the elector accepted with benevolence. Before helping himself to the roast, he took a large gulp from a golden chalice encrusted with jewels. I had for a drinking vessel a tall glass. The sun had barely risen; its first rays shone through the leaded glass window and caused the chalice to sparkle.

His Grace continued: "Dr. Luther, when you were still in Gotha on the Grimmenstein, for which, as you know, I don't bear you any enmity but rather take it as a sign of faithfulness toward the House of Wettin, you heard of my experiments here in Dresden to make gold. I was encouraged by the adepts who promised me quick success, but except for causing expenses, they have made little progress. Therefore, I had them all deported. A number of them went to other courts, where some of them are still cheating their new rulers. One of them, though, who lied too impertinently and asked for always more gold instead of making it, I had to have arrested at Königstein Castle, where he now sits, a bit wet but well deserved, or rather stands upright, because he is chained to the wall and has much time to think about his art.

"Now tell me what you think of the doubts that can be heard among the people and even at my court about the art of making gold. My police tell me that even among the poor people in the inns and at the markets it is rumored that instead of spending money on making gold, a sovereign should rather give it to the poor. And well-to-do citizens say I should instead lower taxes."

Me: "I believe in principle that it is possible to make gold in the laboratory. But you need a small amount of gold as a starting substance." Here I saw the elector knit his brow, so I continued quickly: "One needs some, a small amount of, gold, which I could myself provide for the purpose of the experiment and so would not burden Your Grace's treasury."

The elector: "Dr. Luther, you are a man to my liking. And the first to offer such a pleasant prospect."

Me: "Of course, this does not mean that my—or, may I say, Your Electoral Grace, our"—here he nodded gracefully—"experiments will not cost anything. Costs will arise for laboratories, instruments, gadgets, tools, assistants, running costs of the process, heating materials, also literature about gold making. All this is not to be had cheaply. Moreover, an officer of Your Grace's lifeguard with a detail of soldiers should be in place to watch the laboratory day and night."

His Grace: "This can be afforded, and in comparison to what the former gold makers demanded, it sounds inexpensive."

Me: "Now, I would like to tell Your Grace something about my basic philosophy and beg to appraise it or have it appraised."

His Grace: "Speak up. You know that I have occupied myself for quite a time with the problem and without boasting can say I have some knowledge in alchemy. Trust that I can follow your explanations.

"But first of all, I want you to answer the following question and thus check on the legitimacy, as it were, of our plans before God. It is not the first time that I put this question to myself and others. Now I hope to receive a satisfying answer from such a famous scholar as you and, moreover, from the son of an even more famous father. The question is: Does man not interfere in a forbidden way with God's creation when he so basically changes substances created by Him?"

When the elector said this, it began to dawn on me for the first time what kind of faith he adhered to. He was on the way to strict

Lutheranism, which, as we know, is connected to permanent and deep self-examination of oneself but above all of others. I knew to proceed with caution. I still remembered my arguments with the zealots in Jena.

I answered: "Your Grace can rest assured. I believe God has gifted us with logic and thinking in order to work for His praise and to replenish the earth and subdue it, which also means to be allowed to further develop God's creation. Your Grace may only think of the many fields in which man has changed nature—how he breeds animals to his good use, changes the field crops that they bear more fruit, picks ore, diverts rivers, irrigates deserts, drains swamps, and, to mention an example from my field of knowledge, even looks man, the lord of the creation, God's image, into the head and there drains blood or water."

And then I added, "My Herr Father has always praised reason and its use as a gift of God."

To be honest, I could not remember if Father had really said so, but it seemed to fit into our conversation, and it seemed to allay the elector's fears, and he indicated I should go on.

I said, "Logic and reason as well as the teachings of many scholars of old—and with this I am coming to my philosophy of gold making—tell us that God created the world in the form of a primary matter, the *materia prima* of Aristotle, which has transmuted since the day of creation to today's manifold forms and substances. This has happened over thousands of years, in the hottest processes in the inner earth, in the volcanoes, in the hot springs, in the celestial bodies. Also, the influence of the orbits of the stars, their positions to each other and to the earth, must be considered when one looks into the transmutation of the substances."

"Halt," the elector called out, "and let me say myself what you certainly have in mind. And if I talk reasonably, you will see that you have found a worthy adept. So, if I can in my laboratory shorten this thousand-year process, I should come to similar results."

"That is so, Your Grace," I replied, "but perhaps somehow more complex than Your Grace deigns to assume. There are quite a number of accompanying conditions that have to be regarded in the shortened reproduction of the process."

"I know," the elector interposed. "Your predecessors have always maintained the importance of the stars for gold making."

"And there they were not wrong," I continued. "Above all, the sun, the moon, and Mercury have to be taken into consideration, and their positions in relation to each other and to our earth."

"This means," said the elector, "our undertaking can only succeed at certain times of the year, and to calculate these is the task of astrology."

"That is so," I answered, and went on: "We must take the most fundamental, impartible source material, similar or, if possible, equal to the primeval matter of Aristotle, and strip it of its present character in order to be able to invest it with new forms, properties, and structures. So we will obtain a nobler, more refined material and, at the end of our not-simple processes, the noblest, purest, most invulnerable, most valuable matter on earth."

"Gold!" cried the elector enthusiastically. "And what," he asked, "is this source substance in your opinion?"

"Quicksilver or *mercurium* or *Argentum vivum.*"

"And where," asked His Grace, "do you think you will find the necessary amount of quicksilver?"

"Cinnabar, or dragon's blood, from which the name stems, is present in nature in large amounts. It is heated, and the quicksilver escapes as waft or spirit and is caught, cooled in glass tubes, and thus recovered. Then, of course, it must be rectified carefully, because smallest additions can falsify our result."

"You have," the elector said, "made no mention of the *Lapis philosophorum,* the philosopher's stone, which is, according to all gold makers, indispensable."

"Your Grace has, in your wisdom, hit upon the essence of the whole procedure."

He looked quite cheerful, and I congratulated myself on my choice of words.

"It is correct," I continued, "that for this process of purification, transmutation, and perfection a decisive medium is needed, and this was given the name by the ancient scholars that Your Grace has just used. That means that even if I can create the right conditions in my laboratory and find the right moment with the help of astrology, my success depends on finding the *Lapis*. And here, I believe, I am on the right way."

"So you have this *Lapis?*" asked the elector.

"Yes and no," I replied. "Different from what most adepts believe, this *Lapis* is, in my opinion, no material substance but a concept, an idea, a spiritual influence. And these I look for, not in nature, but rather in the firm belief that through deduction and inspiration, transmutation can be accomplished. The search for the philosopher's stone, as it has been pursued by people for so long, is therefore in vain.

"The alchemist can here be compared to the physician. The latter heals the sick, first of all, by causing them to believe in their recovery. The optimistic attitude of the doctor, his prudent and understandable encouragement, his apparent and continuing efforts for his patient, his altruistic attitude (I wish it were so) help the prescriptions to take effect. So it can happen that substances that seem to have no influence on the body and seem to pass through it apparently unchanged still have a healing effect as long as the doctor can make the patient believe so. Just as the doctor starts the chemical processes in the body by his spiritual influence, nature works in the same way outside the human body."

Here the elector bade me to stop. Obviously, my disclosures affected him strongly, and he felt the need to calm down. And really, as I asked him for his wrist and felt his pulse, it seemed quickened. The sovereign stood up, went to the window, and looked out on the Elbe River. He beckoned me to his side. The mighty river, the main artery of the city and the country, flowed broad, powerful, and yet calm.

"Look at the river," the elector said. "It will with certainty reach the ocean, and I wish that we with the same certainty reach our goal. Go on."

"I want to say that the transmutation from the less noble to the noble can take place only when the alchemist concentrates his mind and directs it to the desired result in the same way as the doctor does with his patient. And this whole process is the long-sought-for philosopher's stone. As I said, the primeval substance of our laboratory work will be quicksilver and the decisive force mercury, the speediest planet in the vault of heaven.

"Its day is the *dies mercurii,* Wednesday, which we must not forget. It is then important to find the day of mercury's highest efficacy for our tests. Wednesday received its name from Woden, as the Old English called the god Odin. It is the day of the skilled magician and wanderer and represents as well the ability to change. It is also the day of wisdom and self-sacrifice. Overcoming death, Woden is transmuted into a new world, from something less noble to something more noble.

"Gold, now, whose celestial body is the sun, we add in small amounts to quicksilver, and it is taken in by the latter inseparably; it shares its nobleness with it so that in the end this basic element transmutes to gold.

"Now we must succeed in designing our process in such a way that quicksilver, keeping in mind all the accompanying circumstances already mentioned, incorporates gold in smaller and smaller amounts, forming itself into a growing percentage, and in the end is completely transmuted to gold."

"And for this," said the elector, "we have ordered a well-equipped laboratory to be built in the basement of our residence, in which we, you and I, will try our best."

"Your Grace," I said, "I must ask you for the strictest secrecy concerning our chemical experiments and recipes as well as of all test conditions. Therefore, only the three of us, Your Grace, my assistant, and I, will be involved in the work."

The elector did not mind that I made him a worker in the laboratory because he was so happy about the idea that he would soon be abundantly provided with gold. He dismissed me in his most gracious mood.

I left the castle, crossed the great bridge, and walked downriver on the towpath in the direction of Meissen. My feelings, my conscience, were in a turmoil, which I hoped to calm by a long walk.

I had deceived the elector. It was correct that I, despite occasional doubts, believed in the art of gold making. But my foggy remarks about the philosopher's stone were what they were: foggy. I had found it necessary to make the process for successful gold making sound as difficult as possible, requiring extended periods of time as well as the propitious circumstances.

The processes in the laboratory, the heat, additives, instruments, etc., and first of all the position of the stars cannot be put in question for long and can be checked without difficulty by alert masters such as the elector and his controllers.

But the spiritual influence, called by me the *Lapis philosophorum*, is more difficult to grasp. Here, should a test fail, I could more easily say that this influence was simply not yet strong enough or wrongly directed or the like. Because instead of what I told the elector, I believed in the *Lapis* as a substance, a matter, and to find it seemed to me the most important step toward gold making. I was already thinking of such a substance, which till now had never been mentioned by an alchemist and never been described in a book. To find this substance, which was a celestial one, I now considered my most important task.

I had several reasons for deceiving the elector. First, I wanted to keep the secret to myself in order to make, at the given time, gold for my private purposes. The time was not yet ripe; I did not have enough capital and independence for an adequate laboratory.

Second, I knew that the elector would, like every sovereign in the empire, use the gold to increase his power and strengthen his divine right, not foremost for the well-being of his country. With the help of the gold, he would try to put himself above the law to the detriment of those who seek their right before court.

And third, I was certain the secret of gold making would not stay a secret for long, having a guard or not. It would come out, gold would be produced in big amounts, and its price would sink.

I looked at the river, saw the boats as they were towed upstream, saw the fishermen on the banks and the silhouette of the city. The scaffolding on the castle was visible because tearing down, rebuilding, and extending were once again in progress. As long as I was in Dresden, work on the castle and the resulting changes never stopped. People on the other side of the river seemed to me unimportant and small, and the plans of the elector void and empty and partly sinful, my deceiving him therefore partly excusable. My conscience was calmed, and I started on my way home.

CHAPTER 25

. . . is about religious strife and human weakness.

Anno Domini 1572 winter arrived early, and already in November ice formed at the banks of the Elbe River. My wife ordered the rooms to be heated unsparingly, since we did not have to be thrifty with firewood and hard coal from Zwickau, which was delivered to our house as part of my archiator's remuneration.

One evening there was a knock on the door, and a messenger of the electoral chancellor Georg Cracow delivered a letter for me.

I went into my study, in which a tile stove, fired from the hall, spread a cozy warmth. There I sat on the stove bench and broke the seal.

It was a short letter that invited me to visit the chancellor next day in the early morning when there were few people on the streets. I was to see him not in the residence but in his house on the Old Market. And would I please burn the letter at once and tell nobody about its content.

One can imagine that I hardly closed an eye during the night. Almost every hour I heard the voice of the night watchman, who demanded that the people watch their fireplaces.

I got up about five of the clock the next morning and started on my way, without having had breakfast. It was dark, though some snow had fallen so that I could recognize my way. An icy mist rose from the river and lay heavily over the town. The first fires in the hearths were lit, and their smoke mixed with the icy haze from the river and made breathing difficult. I took a detour and went along the Elbe pathway before I turned right to the Old Market. Possible observers should not see where I was headed.

On the market I looked around and could see the first lightened windows in the large houses of stone which that had been erected by the rich citizens. Since the great fire of 1491, by order of the town council and the elector, most of the houses had to be built of stone. Almost half the buildings of the inner city had been destroyed by that fire.

I passed the big trough in the northeastern corner of the market and reached the house of the chancellor, in whose room on the second floor I could see light.

A maid opened the door. With a lantern, she went ahead up the stairs that led to the study of the chancellor.

Chancellor Georg Cracow welcomed me with a serious face. I put coat and hat on a chair beside the door and sat down, as he indicated, at the big wooden table in the middle of the room. He sat opposite me. A candlestick with a burning tallow candle stood on the table. That did not so much lighten the room as give it a conspiratorial atmosphere.

I owed the chancellor thanks because he, among others, had recommended me for the position of archiator of the Saxon elector. He had married the daughter of Johannes Bugenhagen, friend and helper of my father's, so I knew him well. His lectures as a professor on Roman law in Wittenberg had attracted many students, and I had also attended some of them. Cracow had been close to my honored teacher, Magister Melanchthon, and shared his theological views; in some instances he even went further and approached the doctrines of Calvin.

"Dr. Luther," the chancellor began straightaway and in a serious voice, "you have certainly heard about the bloodshed on St. Bartholomew's Day in Paris."

I nodded.

The news of the bloody night in Paris on the 24th of August of that year, 1572, had spread like wildfire over Europe. Thousands of Huguenots, the followers of the reformer Calvin in France, had been slaughtered during the night before the Day of St. Bartholomew and on the following days in Paris and other places in France. People also called this massacre the Paris Blood Wedding, because only a few days before, Henry III of Navarre, later Henry IV of France, had married Margaret of Valois, the sister of what were to become three French kings. Despite this relationship, Henry barely escaped the fate of the other Huguenots in Paris.

Georg Cracow said, "The religious and above all the political ambitions of the Huguenots in France are not favorably regarded by our elector. He is not only our elector and, as such, responsible for the political unity of our country; he is also bishop of the Lutheran Regional Church in Saxony and thus responsible for the religious unity of the land. I have tried to convince him that the Calvinists' interests are purely theological, especially with regard to the Eucharist and baptism, and that they in no case strive to conquer part or all of the stately power in the country, as the Huguenots in France do. Moreover, he is still not sure of his electorship. He is afraid we Calvinists might become stronger and help the Ernestine branch of the House of Wettin to regain the electorship."

When the chancellor said "we Calvinists," I was not surprised. His convictions were not secret, and their effects were felt everywhere. He was the elector's Most Trusted Chamberlain and favorite and had proved to be indispensable in the talks during the conquest, or rather surrendering, of Gotha. Here he had fought unrelentingly for the interests of his prince. So it seemed for a while. He used his favored position for the spread of Calvinism in Saxony.

"Why, Your Excellency," I asked, "do you trust me with this talk about these important political matters?"

"Because," replied the chancellor, "yesterday I met in the Privy Council with a new quite unexpected coldness, even hostility, on the part of my master, who so far had been well disposed toward me. He did not allow my remarks to be included in the minutes and also did not so much as look at me. My Lutheran opponents in the council were, in contrast, allowed to do all the talking. This, Dr. Luther, will end badly. And because I know that you have good connections to Magister Philippus, who in the end was quite open to the doctrines of Calvin, I would like to warn you. Though there will probably be no Blood Night in Dresden, some of us will be in great danger."

"Can Your Excellency," I asked now, "advise me how to behave so that I and my family don't come to harm?"

Thereupon Georg Cracow regarded my sadly. "This question," he said, "no one can answer except yourself. In fact, only your conscience can answer this question."

The next day but one, Chancellor Georg Cracow, Most Trusted Chamberlain of the Elector, reformer of the law in Saxony by his cooperation on the Constitutions of Elector Augustus, which helped to renew the legal system on the basis of Roman law, professor and rector of Wittenberg University, participant in famous imperial diets and religious disputes, was arrested on his estate, Schönfeld, near Dresden, was taken to Pleißenburg Castle, and was subjected to torture.

As a consequence of this, he died in 1575. Some say he took his own life. A deadly sin. But who dares condemn here, when the poor delinquent is threatened with repeated torture and unspeakable agony? It is also said that shortly before his suicide he was heard to pray and ask God for forgiveness for his imminent sin in his dungeon.

It became known that the elector felt greatly deceived because the chancellor had advised him wrongly and had not represented his interests adequately.

A further arrest was that of Caspar Peucer, mathematician, astronomer, and medicus and my predecessor as electoral archiator. In 1552 he had acquired the title of Licentiate of Medicine under the guidance of Milich in Wittenberg and was therefore well known to me. In Dresden he was regarded as the leader of the Philippists and was denounced as a Cryptocalvinist. What made things worse for him was that beside his eruditeness, he was equipped with the ability to injure people with his sharp tongue.

And here I am coming to a second reason for the arrests. A mockery about the gynocracy, or female rule of the electoress, was found at the court, which gave the elector enormous offense and accelerated his change from the Philippists to the Lutheran hard-liners. The Philippists allegedly had contributed to this lampoon. And it also became known that Caspar Peucer had written somewhere, “Let us first get Mother Anna; then it will not take long to win over the prince.” With that he meant they would entice the electoress away from the Lutherans.

Peucer was detained until 1586, most of the time at Pleißenburg Castle, where he had ample time to practice his art of writing. He composed a chronology of his experiences in the dungeon, which was printed later as *Historia carcerum et liberatonis divinae.*

Fear and terror ruled thenceforth at court and in the city. People asked themselves who would be the next to be struck by the elector’s wrath. Some out of fear even left the country. To celebrate their victory, the Lutheran zealots had a medal coined with the inscription: “In memory of the victory of the true faith over reason.” All that is left for a comparatively reasonable person after reading such a sentence is continued speechlessness.

The reader should put themselves into my situation.

I kept quiet and did not attend court until the elector summoned me. It proved to be advantageous that I had occupied myself during this time in the laboratory in the castle cellar with making gold.

When I went to see the elector, I remarked a company of foot soldiers with arquebuses in the yard of the residence lying around a number of fires. The guards at the gate and the entry to the residence were reinforced, and even before the rooms of the elector stood his guards. So much iron and so many weapons made me feel quite sick on my way to my lord.

When I stood before the elector, I felt like a defendant about to be questioned, though the prince had not yet uttered a word.

Then he began: "What, Dr. Luther, do you think about the Calvinists, Philippists, and the other people who do not strictly follow the teachings of your father? I know you had connections to Magister Philippus, and I have been informed about the intimacy between you and Chancellor Cracow, who at the moment sits in the Pleißenburg and is being interrogated. My agents told me that shortly before the detainment of Cracow, you paid him a visit. And let us say that after sufficient encouragement, he confirmed your visit."

My heart stood still.

How was I to answer? It was clever of the elector to speak of the teachings of my father. With this, he called me not only to his but also to my father's duty.

It was clear that for the elector I, too, was under suspicion. Now it was only me and my family that mattered. I must not even think of an intercession for the arrested, though I felt near to them or they were my friends. I would only harm myself. I was not sure about how I stood with the elector. Should I, despite everything, try to bring him around and ask him to go easy on my friends? I was the son of the famous reformer; this was not to be forgotten. But would that protect me sufficiently?

I saw my beautiful house in Dresden, my dear and still-attractive wife and lover, Anna, and my children before my mind's eye. I thought of my lucrative position at court and the promising alchemical tests in the basement of the residence. But above all, I saw the instruments of the executioner, the red-hot irons, the thumbscrews, the Spanish boot, and the iron maiden.

No, I decided in my heart, Cracow and Peucer and the others had exposed themselves to danger on their own volition. Why had they not, when there was still time, endorsed the changed faith of the elector, which was easy to recognize, kept their mouths shut, and paid court to the electoress instead of using their conscience as an excuse for their Philippistic or even Calvinistic views? They then would still be in their old positions, enjoying courtly life. One could distinctly recognize that the elector, with his growing might and stronger position in the empire, would be less inclined to tolerate deviations from his own faith and political attitude. In the streets the people whispered to each other the saying: "The prince, the prince is always right . . ." and here they stopped, looking furtively around.

My heart raced when I now answered the prince. I must sidetrack him, must direct his interest to something else and make him forget his question. Perhaps that would help me to avoid a straightforward answer.

"Your Grace, may I first congratulate you?"

The elector asked, taken by surprise, "On what?"

Whereupon I said, "Yesterday we made an important step forward in our alchemy. I could reduce the amount of gold that incorporates the mercurium and still retain the solid form of the noble metal. Of course, further advances and constellations are now required to give the gold the chance to impart its properties indissolubly to the quicksilver."

I must say here that my information to the elector was meant more to keep his good grace than it was a real research result; we had not, in the laboratory, come as far as I maintained.

His Grace was enthused. "Let's have a look at once. And you must show me a sample of the—how shall I say—near gold so that I can show it to the electoress. Because then," he added in a hushed voice, falling back into the old topic, "it will be easier to convince her of your indispensability as archiator and alchemist. But you must, before her, take an unequivocal position against the abuses of the Philippists and the hostile ideas of the Calvinists."

So it happened, and the noble couple kept me at their court in honors and in the coming time displayed further and increasing goodwill, thanks to my persisting good behavior.

God forgive me that my own good was more important to me than that of others. But at home in the privacy of my room, I prayed for the hunted and above all for the tortured chancellor and also read in the prohibited books of Calvin. But at court I raised my voice a few times against deviators from the elector's thinking.

CHAPTER 26

. . . depicts how the Devil tempted me.

I wish to point out to the reader how strong a power a woman can exert on a man if he does not protect himself sufficiently against such temptations.

The woman is a child of God like the man and yet different. God has endowed the woman with a power of seduction that is almost devilish, though I see that this is a *contradictio in adjecto,* yet not if one knows that the Devil, too, is God's creature.

In one of the earlier chapters I mentioned that I have often succumbed to the allurement of women. One example may suffice, because these memoirs are meant not to induce the reader to try out what I will be describing but to protect him against such temptations by means of my bad example. One case, however, must be included because I want my memoirs to be as near to reality as is feasible.

As if I had not enough anxieties in Dresden, I found myself in the following predicament.

At the time of the elector's conflict with Philippists and Calvinists, when my position at the electoral court had been somewhat consolidated, I met, in the summer of 1573, the wife of the captain of the castle guard, Bernhard von Greiffenhagen. Her name was Johanna von Greiffenhagen.

She was accompanied by her maid and, as I later learned, confidante, Magdalena Herfurth. Johanna was still young, eighteen years old, and had not long been married to Bernhard, an old war-scarred battle horse. He was ten years older than me, that is, fifty years old. She was distantly related to the electoress and despite her youth a friend of the forty-year-old Anna.

In passing we greeted each other in the castle court, when I heard hurried steps behind me. I stopped, turned, and saw the maid hurrying toward me. "Dr. Luther," she said out of breath, her chest moving up and down, "my lady begs for a word with you."

The lady had turned toward us and obviously expected me to come nearer to her. This I did.

"What can I do for you, My Lady?" I queried.

"Dear Doctor," she addressed me confidingly, "I would like to ask you for an interview in a medical matter. Tomorrow after breakfast my husband will be away in the service of the elector in the hunting lodge of Dianenburg, and we can talk undisturbed."

That the young woman wanted to talk to me in the absence of her husband stimulated my imagination. That she, moreover, suggested the morning, increased the stimulation. Did not my experiences and the teachings of Hippocrates and Galen tell me that in the morning the driving forces of the man are stronger than during the long and wilting day? Was it possible that Frau Johanna had heard, let alone experienced, this despite her youth?

Before I started next morning on my way to the castle, I had a thorough wash and also rubbed a small amount of patchouli on my chest. The latter I did, I admit, shortly before I left the house. I wanted to spare my wife unnecessary disquietude. As I loved her, I always tried to consider her feelings. The washing itself was not suspicious because I always took great pains to be fresh and clean before I went to the residence.

When I entered the domicile of the captain, Johanna's confidante, Magdalena, received me and led me to the chamber of her lady and friend.

To my surprise, the latter was still in her nightgown, which was visible through the open morning gown. Magdalena left the room, though I was not sure that she did not stop to listen immediately behind the door.

"Dear Doctor," Johanna commenced, "I have asked you here about a very delicate matter. It concerns my husband as well as myself. You know he was a widower when he married me last year. I will admit that with this marriage I followed more the wishes of my parents and the encouragement of the electoress than my own inclinations. My experiences with men have been small—in fact, did not exist at all or were only gathered from books. The electoress alone advised me before the wedding night and told me not to be afraid. I was just to surrender to my husband, which meant lie still, open my legs a little, and wait for the thing to come. As it would be dark in the room, the sight of my husband need not frighten me."

Here she paused and looked at me, obviously surprised somewhat herself by her openness. I was moved by the young woman, and *nolens volens* something else moved. I noted it with a measure of anxiety but could do nothing about it. A new and fresh young woman is like a spring for a thirsty man having lost his way in a forest, irresistible. Its bitter additive is only tasted later.

On her face while she was speaking, I could see a mixture of slight embarrassment and mischievous coquetry.

She went on: "When now my husband came to me and hoisted himself on me, I closed my eyes and wanted to let things take their natural course. But nothing happened. My husband, who, by the way, smelled strongly of the roast venison and wine from which he had generously eaten during the wedding dinner, fumbled about with his hand at his belly and moaned quietly, but nothing happened. He put his hands on my breasts and kissed them, but again everything remained as it was.

"I did not know what I had to do. Then he took my hand and moved it down until I felt something that I had seen once in an anatomy book. It must have been my husband's private parts, or whatever they are called, at which I probed and felt, but again nothing moved. I knew at least that for a successful cohabitation, a certain size and form are required.

"At that moment he again heaved a sigh, turned to the side, and fell asleep."

I was surprised by these revelations. The old fellow had a beautiful young and delicious woman in his bed and failed to enjoy her.

"Dear Frau Johanna," I now began, "I assume that you want me to do something for your husband so that he in an orderly manner can fulfill his marriage obligations to you. This won't be easy—in fact, it will be almost impossible. I confess that I have rarely seen as strong an aphrodisiac as you yourself. Even I . . ." Here I stopped. What went on in me? The young woman had looked at me in such an enchanting and needy way that I got quite warm around the loins.

"No, don't misunderstand me, dear Doctor. I am not concerned with the implementation of my marriage with an old and scarred man."

"But what then could you wish for?" asked I.

The young woman now truly blushed and did not know how to go on. She rang for her maid, Magdalena, and ordered a decanter of wine and two glasses. "I hope you won't decline a glass of wine," she said.

In the meantime, my suspicion of what she desired became a certainty. And I saw that she needed to fortify her courage for that. Every understanding reader knows that for a man, there is nothing better than to be seduced by a young woman, one who does this not for a living but out of an irresistible mental and physical need.

I succeeded in concentrating my thoughts on my duties as a physician, which are directed at the welfare of the patient and fulfillment of their wishes, which sometimes may include physical effort and dedication.

I observed how Frau Johanna added a few drops from a vial labeled *Tinctura opii* to her wine. This she did, not furtively, but quite openly and without any explanation or excuses. Her matter-of-fact attitude seemed to indicate that she was preparing herself for things to come.

"I don't believe"—Frau von Greiffenhagen took up the interrupted thread of the conversation—"that my husband, even by such a high medical art as you are said to have at your disposal, can be brought to a stableness required for his married duties. As you know, I am not his first wife, and he had no children with his last one. He told me at the beginning of our marriage that it was his first wife that the Lord God had stricken with barrenness."

"This, by the way," I interjected, "is an excuse used by many men to hide their own infertility or incapability."

Frau Johanna gave me a grateful look and took another few sips from her glass, which seemed to help, because she no longer appeared embarrassed but chatted on while looking me in the eyes.

"I am now," she said, "coming to the core of my request to you as a physician. Help me so that I do not have to wither away as a virgin but can, by having children, lead a more fulfilled life. Be fruitful and multiply, the Bible says, but how can this happen under the circumstances I described?"

Now this I liked very much. She used for her charming desires God's word, and in this way she demanded my duties not only medically, as it were, but also religiously. If I were to do as she wished, there had to be clarity between doctor and patient.

Therefore I asked her, "Would you, Frau Johanna, that I myself, with my own person, remedy your suffering or, let's say, your matrimonial deficits?"

I thought it suitable to sustain an atmosphere of the right medical behavior by means of using scholarly words, though the talk and the things to come created in me such a blissful pleasant anticipation far beyond the normal work of a physician that I decided to drive our talk forward a bit and thus ease the situation for my patient.

Of course I saw that something extraordinary was developing, because a physician must have the gift of anticipation. And if now—rarely enough—work and pleasure turned out to be a unity, I could not, just to avoid a sin, leave a woman without assistance in her predicament.

And should I here really commit a sin, I had to regard this as a sacrifice for my profession. The Lord may forgive me as He forgave David when he, out of passion, allowed Uriah to be slain by the enemy. He not only forgave him but even let him become the father of the blessed King Solomon and ancestor of Jesus Christ. King David was driven by his carnal desire only but I by my desire and at the same time my duty as a doctor.

Johanna answered my question by taking my hand and leading me into her bedchamber. There she threw off her morning gown, took off her nightgown, and stood before me like the beautiful damsel Abishag, who was laid beside David so the king might get heat.

This I did not need. I got rid of my clothes, lauded secretly my precaution that I had washed and applied fragrant salve, and went to Johanna, who in the meantime had laid herself on the bed.

I went to work very tenderly because I did not want to frighten the maiden or even cause her pains. But lo! I did not meet with any resistance as I came in unto her.

My pleasure was so great that I for the moment was not surprised when the maiden from the start uttered short lustful sounds instead of tensing herself in expectation of pain. Nor did I wonder that I, though I did not look very thoroughly, could not detect any traces of blood on me or the bedsheet.

The surprise came after two days.

The electoress summoned me.

"Dr. Luther," she said, "my maid and friend, the wife of Captain Bernhard von Greiffenhagen, has confided in me and told me what you have done, allegedly in the course of your medical duty. Witness to this is her chambermaid."

I, of course, was utterly taken aback by this as well as apprehensive and not a little frightened.

The electoress regarded me rather coolly and went on: "Johanna told me that by your tender skill she rather enjoyed the act, which—as she is my friend—I count in your favor. Though it is true that her husband in certain decisive moments is a failure, the story of her virginity is an invention, which you should have noticed, being a skilled lover and a doctor. But we know that in such moments, generally head and reason do not rule a man but rather the member with which he sins."

In the meantime I had regained some confidence and composure. The words of the electoress seemed to indicate that we could come to a mutual understanding, but for the time being I preferred to remain quiet.

She went on with decisiveness: "I will not talk about the affair, nor will my husband, the elector, learn about it. I have ordered Johanna and her maid to keep their mouths shut, too."

I summoned up courage and began to thank the electoress. Because imagine if the captain, who was known for his vengeful jealousy, or, even worse, Anna should learn about the expanded administration of my medical services. Or worse, if the elector, who was known to hold high moral standards—not so much for himself as for others—would be informed.

Amid my expression of gratitude, the electoress interrupted me. "I have not quite finished," she said. "For my generosity I expect from you the strictest loyalty in all matters of the Lutheran doctrine, which means the faith of your father. This should not be very hard for you."

"Your Grace," I replied, "is very noble, and I will follow all Your Grace's wishes as a matter of course."

Now, reader, you know why I up to the death of the elector and his wife in the years 1586 and 1585 neither left the court nor deviated in any way from the faith of the court.

Circumstances in Dresden were not always untroubled, but I was forced to endure them. I could not seriously consider leaving (though I often thought about it), because the elector cast a long shadow, far beyond the borders of Saxony. So I humbled myself and tried to make the best out of my and my family's life there. As I enjoyed the favor of the ruler and his consort, as mentioned above, life was tolerable, and I got used to hiding my true feelings, which I recommended to wife and children, too.

As I today lie here and with difficulty put pen to paper, I am still amazed at what intrigues women are capable of through the exploitation of their seductive powers and of the corresponding weakness and folly of men. At the time I swore a holy oath not to fall again into such a trap, but it did not help much.

CHAPTER 27

. . . describes how we fared further in Dresden.

If you, like my wife, I, and our children, obeyed the God-given regime and did not deviate from the views of the elector's party, and if you did not audibly but only secretly praised the deviations of other people, you could live quite well and comfortably.

Admittedly, some people did not live comfortably, by which I do not mean the poor. Those have been having bad lives from the beginning, because it pleased God to create the poor and the rich. And the poor should count themselves happy, as their hopes to acquire eternal blessedness are infinitely greater than those of the rich, because Jesus says, "It is easier for a camel to go through the eye of a needle than for a rich man to enter into the kingdom of God."

No, I am speaking of the well-to-do, the burghers with property, business, and trade; the master craftsmen, the farming townspeople, and the usurers; the clergy from a certain hierarchical stage upward; and the courtiers and others.

If those people remained loyal and quiet and did not spoil the elector's and electoress's good mood and the general peace, if they did not constantly examine their consciences and inquire about who sat in the dungeons and what was the most correct belief and did not demand to read adversarial, that is, Calvinistic, books, they could enjoy life in Dresden.

And people who did not require unconditional honesty or try to leave the electorate without permission of the elector had no need to be unhappy in the principality of Saxony.

I did well with my medical practice. My salary at the court was substantial and paid regularly, my ointments and drops sold well, and gold making in the elector's laboratories appeared to progress. That is to say, it did not actually go forward visibly, but it yielded intermediate results that were good enough to keep the elector contented and hopeful.

My wife was well connected in Dresden and had found enough friends so that she did not suffer from boredom. Let me for the benefit of all husbands include here: Do not allow your wives to become bored. If this happens, the way to harlotry is not far.

Moreover, my wife agreed with me that generally we should become close only to people who tolerated our attitude in regard to policy and the religion of the state.

As I will relate forthwith, such an attitude was soon rewarded.

My reputation, or shall I immodestly say my fame, had spread in Saxony and neighboring lands so that several universities tried to lure me to a professorship at their medical faculties. Of course, this reached the elector's ears and caused him to issue an order that was meant to keep me in Dresden. It reads as follows:

By Divine Right Augustus, Duke of Saxony, Elector, etc.
Highly Learned, Dear and Faithful Councillor:

For inevitable and important reasons, We can no longer tolerate that one of Our councillors or servants is in some way or other bound to a university in Our land. We therefore urgently, seriously, though graciously demand that—insofar as you want to remain in Our service—you as soon as possible send us in writing the renunciation of such academic obligations. We will then notify the university, and please mind well that this letter and demand is caused by Our highest necessity. We remain your most gracious Prince and Lord.

Torgau, February 15th, 1579
Augustus, Elector

To: Paul Luther, Our highly learned, dear,
and faithful Archiator and Doctor of Medicine.

Clearly, it would have been very unwise to resist such an urgent and also honorable request.

There were other things, which I will add here in summary.

Because I complied and supplied the elector with the statement requested, a veritable cornucopia was dumped upon us—or at least the elector believed so.

From this my sickbed, it seems to me that he unflinchingly believed in my successful gold making.

First. As I had resolved to remain servant and councillor of the prince, my salary as archiator was increased, and I was promised that I would receive a percentage of the gold made in the future.

Second. The elector invested me as joint owner with some properties in the town of Dohna. Here he followed the request of my uncle Clemens von Bora. This fief had once been a burgrave's free estate, meaning that it was not taxable. This sounded good, but in fact this fief brought me neither happiness nor profit but only unending quarrels with the relatives of my mother, who had become impoverished. But of course the elector had meant well.

Third. Equally well meant and, moreover, lucrative was that the elector made me the first receiver of a prebendary of the cathedral chapter of the town of Zeitz, which later was to go over to my descendants.

Fourth. AD 1577, my house in Dresden was signed over to me as my property.

Fifth. The climax of all these honors was to be AD 1581, the donation of the cloister estate Sornzig near Meissen. I am writing "was to be," because it never got into my hands, though the elector personally had legal arguments with the Meissen cathedral chapter.

Sixth. Our son Johannes Ernst studied jurisprudence in Wittenberg successfully. In AD 1581, at twenty-one years of age, Johannes Ernst, at the instigation of the elector, was elected *canonicus* of the Zeitz cathedral chapter. This position paid so well that from then on I need not worry about his future life. From the provost and senior of the chapter I received a letter that made my wife and me very happy. In short, the letter told us that Johannes Ernst, because it was the elector's will, was to become a *canonicus* of the chapter. For the entering of his name in the chapter's roll, we had to pay a fee of ninety-four guldens.

Of course we sent the sum immediately and thus, to our relief, did not have to undertake the burdensome trip to Zeitz.

Verily, the canonicate paid well so that our son was even able to go on longer travels and could visit interesting and curious sights. Nevertheless, I hope that he takes good care of the money, because he needs it if he wants to find a wife. To our regret, he was much too hesitant in this matter. A wife brings order into one's life and as a rule—I am saying "as a rule"—protects one against temptation.

Seventh. On November 15th, 1584, our daughter Anna was married in the ducal hunting lodge in Nossen with the blessings of the elector. We, the parents, were very much relieved, as we had started to doubt that she would find a good husband because she put great emphasis on social status, good looks, and character.

She was now twenty years old and, as my wife assured me, still a virgin. The reader will understand that, despite certain liberties I was taking, I set a high value on the honor and purity of my own wife and daughter. I regard it as both wonderful and moving if at the end a woman can say of her husband that he was her first and only.

Obviously, Anna had found the right match. It was Nikolaus Baron Marschall von Bieberstein from Oberschaar at Arnsfeld. My wife, Anna, born von Warbeck, was quite proud of this marriage and the well-sounding title. During the marriage celebration, she walked proudly among the noble guest because she felt she was among her equals.

The barons of Bieberstein in the thirteenth century held the hereditary office of marshal and chamberlain with the margrave of Meissen, and in the end the office became part of their name. Tradition has it that the family had their origin in Halle on the Saale River and was founded by the Salzgraf—which was quite a reputable office among the Salters—Norbert von Schladebach. I felt at home with my daughter's husband, as his origins reminded me of a place with which I felt—through the fate of my father—somehow connected.

At Arnsfeld I possessed an estate that I had leased, though the income was nothing to speak of. But there is no denying that this was a further sign of our well-being.

Not small, though, were the costs of the wedding and, naturally, the dowry of the bride, which, thanks to the efforts of my wife, will certainly last until the old age of the couple.

My wife and the high standing of the bridegroom as a baron demanded a generosity that I was somewhat unwilling to show. But finally I could not resist the constant arguments of my wife—one could sometimes call it nagging—and in the marriage contract signed over 1000 guldens to my daughter, that is, in fact, to her husband.

Here among my papers I can still find the bills I had to pay for Nikolaus Marschall's nuptials with Anna Luther.

A word about Johann Friedrich, our youngest son, born in Weimar in 1562. He married Magdalena Ziegler from Nürnberg, who died of childbed fever when their first son was born.

His grandparents from his mother's side looked after this grandson. Our son, a jurist, did not marry again and therefore could not take care of the child and keep him with him. Not long ago he moved in with his sister Anna in Arnsfeld, which I think is a sign of the good understanding between them.

CHAPTER 28

. . . in which much dying occurs and a little gold is made. My father once again appears in a strange way.

All things considered, my elector was not a bad sovereign. Certain dishonesties do, however, have to be admitted, as, *per exemplum*, the annexation of the County of Henneberg, which Augustus carried out by exploiting the guardianship of the sons of Duke John William of Saxony-Weimar. In addition to what I have already mentioned, the first postal service was introduced in Saxony; the Court of Appeal as well as other useful institutions were opened, such as the Privy Council and the Supreme Consistory; and an overall tax authority was founded. Saxony flourished; industry and trade and, with them, tax collections increased. Unfortunately, in regard to the Saxon attitude to the empire and confessional matters, the traditional narrow-mindedness prevailed.

As has been said, the elector had an admirable wife, whom he held in honor, though he had several liaisons and fathered a love-child, a girl named Katharina Sybilla, of whom I was the first to be notified.

Katharina Sybilla was well provided for and disposed of in an advantageous marriage. The electoress forgave her husband for good reasons. Unlike us common mortals, the lords and princes, often have to marry out of dynastic considerations and not out of love, and this is not unusual among them.

The electoress, however, even if she had wanted to, could not take such liberties. Her husband made her pregnant continuously so that in the end she gave birth fifteen times and thus had no chance to cultivate harlotry.

From AD 1550, when she was eighteen years old, until 1575 she gave birth every two years, often every year, so that one should not wonder that at fifty-three she was worn out and weakened and died on October 1, 1585, hopefully in God, but certainly in irreconcilable enmity against the Calvinists.

I tried my best to ease her dying, and I think that she would have had to suffer longer, weak and bedridden, had not my medical art, though involuntarily, I admit, sped her departure.

To strengthen her heart, I had prescribed her an extract of *Digitalis purpurea,* or purple foxglove, which obviously was overdosed. The electoress, after taking the medicine, became agitated and quite cheerful and was on the point of jumping out of bed, but then as quickly she faded and died. The reader can understand that I promptly poured the residue of the medicine away and washed out the glass thoroughly and decided not to apply this medicine in the near future. Rather, I determined to prepare new dosages and test them for the time being on poor patients out of the court.

The elector recovered surprisingly quickly from this loss and, to my astonishment, was not too distressed. Already on the 3rd of January, 1586, three months after the death of the princess, he married the twelve-year-old Agnes Hedwig of Anhalt, daughter of Prince Joachim Ernest of Anhalt, who adhered to the Calvinists and supported the Huguenots.

Therefore, I believe that our strictly Lutheran elector was driven by an abnormal lust when he married the child. When I caught sight of the bride for the first time, I saw a girl with a quite infantile body but a rather sensible face. Also, she was quite relaxed when the court accompanied the couple to their bridal bed, while the elector himself seemed to be in a rather agitated state.

Nobody knows what happened in the bridal bed. But everybody was surprised when next morning the above-mentioned Caspar Peucer was released from his prison in Pleißenburg Castle. The court was convinced that this could have resulted only from a successful wedding night and, consequently, the equally successful intercession of the bride.

Soon, reader, I will write about the next death but, before that, about gold.

Despite what I had told the elector about the material existence of the *Lapis philosophorum,* I was convinced of its existence. In the search for the stone, my father came to my aid, so to speak.

One day—it was in October AD 1585, shortly after the death of the electoress—I walked across the market on my way to the palace. My mood was gloomy, since the death of the electoress had wakened some doubts about my professional capability. In principle this is all right, because doubt leads the way to new insights in the art of healing. But today my gloom arose from the fruitless doubt that gnaws many of us and causes man to question his suitability for his profession and even the value of his whole life.

The October day, however, was not gloomy at all but was warm, the Elbe meadows still green and the leaves only just beginning to become golden. This improved my mood a bit, and I looked around me. A herb woman sat under a tent roof behind a table. This was surprising, as normally herb women do not hide under tent roofs. I became curious and stepped closer. She was old, wrinkled, and gray-haired. But her eyes were bright as in a young woman. Also, she still possessed some front teeth, though singly spaced. Her headscarf covered half of her head and was knotted under her chin. On the little table a cloth was spread, under which, it seemed, some things were hidden.

I suspected at once that she was a soothsayer in the guise of a herb woman, who here in Saxony could not openly practice her trade. I pretended to believe her guise and demanded, pointing to a stick from which herb bouquets were hanging, a bunch of poppy heads. She handed it to me, I paid the required groschen, and I turned to leave.

"Dr. Luther, I have something for you."

Surprised, I stopped and turned around, because it was a man's voice uttering these words. There stood a young man, perhaps twenty years old, dressed like a student and making a bow. He beckoned me to the back of the tent, which was separated by a blanket.

"How do you know me?" asked I.

"This is a very long story," he answered. "Let me please first introduce myself. My name is Victorius Radschläger."

"Go on, tell me."

"When your Herr Father on the 2nd of July, AD 1505, experienced mortal fear in a raging thunderstorm on an open field near Stotternheim, in order to find protection from the thunderstorm and dry his clothes, he asked for help in a farmstead. This farm belonged to my great-grandfather Hermann Radschläger, who had the second sight. He also was a secret seeker for the unearthly, fairies, wood nymphs, specters, sprites, and the like. He believed if one met them, this could mean good luck or bad luck, depending on when one met them and how one behaved in the situation. He had in his house a number of strangely formed stones, roots, ossicles, plant remains, horns, and such things. There was even the withered testicle of a unicorn among his collection.

"My great-grandfather believed that these things had been created by spirits of nature or left behind as a sign to show the finder the way. There was also a piece of the tail of a werewolf and the handkerchief of a revenant, already used. About the latter, my great-grandfather was not quite sure whether it had perhaps belonged to a *nachzehrer,* which is a kind of vampire in North

Germany feeding on dead human bodies, or an *aufhocker,* who is also a kind of vampire of varying appetites.

"Within the collection was the left hand of a bogman. One of Great-Grandfather's neighbors once had brought the whole bogman from North Germany and sold it piecemeal to a chemist. The medicine made from it raked in a lot of money, though its efficacy against nightmares, once attributed to it, has not been brought down to us, or one considers the passing away of the people after they had taken the medicine as a positive effect, since naturally they can no longer have nightmares."

Here the young man seemed to me to be rambling.

I asked him, therefore, to go *in medias res,* which he immediately understood. I was astonished, and he told me that he studied medicine in Jena and had been acquainted with the herb woman, whom he called Aunt Barbara, since his early years. She had taught him many useful things about plants and their medicinal benefit.

"What," I asked him, "have you got for me, and how come you know me at all?"

"Let me, Dr. Luther, continue my report; then the questions will answer themselves.

"When the thunderstorm had subsided and the guest, who had introduced himself as Martinus Luder, had traveled on, my great-grandfather and his grandson, my father, went to the place at which, the student Luder had told them, he was almost struck down by the lightning.

"Now I follow the records of my father, who kept a diary all his life and let me have it in trust on his deathbed."

With this, the young man took a stack of yellowed sheets from his bag, which were bound together by a twine and protected by two little slats, like a book cover. "From now on, we hear my father speaking," he said, and began to read:

Beside a tree that was cut in half and partly charred, I saw something twinkle in the burnt grass around us. I was just trying to grasp it when my grandfather took hold of my hand.

"Careful, my boy," said he; "this seems to be a sky stone. Perhaps this is the lightning the Luder man had seen falling from the sky. Don't touch it."

Grandfather took me by my hand and led me to a fallen tree trunk in safe distance from the sky stone. We sat on the trunk.

"The phenomena and things of nature down here and in the sky," he now said, "are not simply as they appear to the naked eye. Mostly they are signs and symbols and occur because they want to tell us something. For this they choose days, times of the day, and positions of the stars, which in their turn are of significance. Moreover, they let themselves be seen only by persons who are aware of their significance and who know how to respect the holiness of all the things of nature. And I believe we—you and me and our family—belong to this group."

I was only ten years of age, but I felt the magic of my grandfather's words and resolved to keep them in my heart and trust them to this paper.

"What day is it today?" asked Grandfather, though he certainly knew.

"Today," I said, "is the 2nd of July, AD 1505."

"You see," said Grandfather, "day and the hour are of importance. We are in the zodiac of Cancer, to which since ancient times the god Mercurius is assigned. The 2nd of July is an important day.

"On the 2nd of July at noon, half of the year has passed. On the 2nd of July in the year 311, Miltiades became bishop of Rome. Under him, who was not yet called pope, the

> persecution of Christians in Rome ended. And today is Wednesday, *dies mercurii.*"

Interrupting his reading, the student said, "Today one can add that the famous Nostradamus died on a 2nd of July." Then he continued reading.

> "These important coincidences allow us to assume," said Grandfather, "that the sky stone was meant to give us a sign. And also Martinus Luder. Now let us with care and respect take up the stone."
>
> This we did.
>
> "Look here," said Grandfather, "a sign. It is the symbol of Mercurius. Do you see the circle with the cross below and the wings above?"
>
> Something similar I could indeed detect on the stone, formed by little iron-gray strands.
>
> "This stone," Grandfather said, "came to us from Mercury."

The student stopped reading again and said, "Here is the stone." Like a magician, he suddenly had in his hand a stone, and I did not know whence it had come.

I was so surprised that I took a step back.

"No, wait," said Victorius, "the stone is yours, and after I finally found you, I can follow my father's order. He had said, 'This stone belongs to the great Reformer, and I hand it to you so that you can give it to his heirs, because he is no longer among us.'

"This happened when my father lay on his deathbed and I had hurried over from Jena, where I was a student at the university, to be near him. In Jena I was also told where I could find you, Dr. Paulus Luther. And now I am glad that I have finally done what I was told."

With this, he handed me the stone, roughly the size of a fist.

I got into a strange mood. The voice of the student, who talked about what he had planned for his life, came to me from a great distance. It seemed as if the stone exuded a great force that spirited me away from the present and the people. For a moment I did not know where I was.

"Dr. Luther," I heard the student say, "come around."

I awoke from my distance and looked at the student.

"What do you want for the stone?"

"Nothing," he said. "It is yours by right. And its effect, which I notice by your reaction and which my father predicted for the rightful owner, is proof of that."

I thanked him, bade farewell, and left the tent.

On the market I could see the usual bustle, but that day my only interest was the stone. I hurried home to my laboratory, not the one of the elector but my private one, because what I wanted to test nobody should know.

I threw off hat and coat, asked my wife and the servants not to disturb me, and locked myself into my laboratory. Here I took a hammer and knocked off a small chip from the stone. This I hammered on an iron plate until I had a fine powder.

How I won from this powder the *Lapis philosophorum,* I cannot entrust to these records. I stored the recipe safely, and after my death my youngest son, Johann Friedrich, will get it and store it safely, too. It may be said, though, that this powder helped me to make a small amount of gold without the powder becoming less. Its mere presence and close contact with the less noble metal, which need not necessarily be quicksilver, was sufficient.

Now the reader will ask why I did not make enough gold to become rich.

In this I did not succeed because I could not exactly repeat the conditions under which I had made the first batch. And as much as I tried, distilling, rectifying, calcinating, mixing, and shaking, as much as I included the positions of Mercury and moon and concentrated my mind and my will on the success of the experiment, I failed. Now I hope that someday there will be an alchemist and astrologer among my descendants who is able to recreate the right conditions for making gold with my powder. Therefore, I leave the powder and the recipe behind. Of course, I did not tell the elector about my little success.

At the moment he would not have been interested anyway, because he had time only for his new wife, with whom he wanted to be together day and night, though he had already reached his sixtieth year.

On a cold January day about two weeks after his marriage, I plucked up courage and tried to warn him against excessive copulation. We were alone in his study, which was well heated. Outside lay a thick layer of snow, and an icy wind blew around the castle. The Elbe was almost completely frozen, and the ships lay still in the harbor.

I felt the prince's pulse and put my ear to his bare chest, which was completely covered with gray hair.

"Your Grace," I said, "knows that Your Grace's heart is no longer what it used to be. I notice that it does not beat regularly, and Your Grace's pulse is too quick. This can also indicate a weak heart. If now Your Grace meets your wife daily in the heat of love, this can be very taxing."

Here the elector turned pink in the face, got agitated, and said, "I hope you are not going to prescribe to me that I do not cover my wife anymore?"

Here I add that the elector was a horse fan, who liked to borrow his words, including the intimate ones, from horse language.

"No, Your Grace, in no way," I responded. "I would only advise to reduce the number of the coverings. Perhaps Your Grace could be happy with three times a week. More is dangerous for Your Grace's heart. Your Grace knows how the heart races shortly before the highest pleasure and how quick the heart beats during such. Moreover, we must not forget the tender age of the electoress."

The elector made an indignant face.

"No, Dr. Luther," he said, "this advice displeases me very much. It is your task as my archiator to take care of my heart and strengthen it so that in all affairs of state and also in love it is up to its tasks. And the electoress is well."

With this he dismissed me, not in his most gracious mood.

Is there not the saying that a man's mind is his kingdom? So at home I mixed a heart-strengthening drink. For this I took leaves, blossoms, and fruit of hawthorn and prepared a potion. Also, I added an extract of blessed milk thistle, *Silybum marianum*, which in fact is usually used against liver complaints. But I thought that the white spots on the leaves, which originate from the milk of the Virgin Mary, would have a favorable effect on the entire health of the elector.

What good was this?

On the 20th of February, 1586, Elector Augustus of Saxony died. I was summoned to the residence, but it was too late. In the bedroom cowered the frightened young electoress beside the bed on which the dead prince lay. He was naked from the belt down, and she told me haltingly that her master and prince, lying on her and in copulative movements, suddenly went limp, fell to the side, took one last gasp, and lay still. I was hurriedly sent for, but already in the anteroom the secretary told me that the prince was probably dead. And so it turned out.

I was only moderately upset, because this is an agreeable way to pass on, yet I was concerned for my insecure future. Would the successor keep me as his personal physician?

The young electoress recovered rather quickly from her fright. As her dowry, she was given the castle of Lichtenburg near Wittenberg, but she did not make use of it. I lost sight of her somewhat, then I heard that on the 14th of February, AD 1588, she married the widowed Duke John III of Schleswig-Holstein-Sonderburg, forty-three years old, who was in a sense a relation of hers as he was the brother of the deceased electoress Anna. Now the young widow—we must not forget that she was still only fifteen years of age—had a husband three times her age, though younger than her first. Into this marriage she brought the handsome sum of 3,000 imperial thalers, which certainly was happily accepted by the duke, who was not very rich.

This marriage turned out to be very fertile. The duke was well trained and in good shape, as he brought with him into this marriage fourteen children by his first wife, some of them being older that the young duchess. She did not hesitate to try to emulate her predecessor and gave birth to further nine children.

This year of 1586 was an *annus horribilis.*

My dear wife, Anna, died at fifty-four years of age on Saturday, the 15th of May. We had been married for thirty-three years, and losing her took away all my zest for life.

Now, as I sat by her deathbed surrounded by our children, who had come running to support their mother, I was overcome by such grief that I could not help weeping and sobbing endlessly.

My faithful wife had gone with me through all heights and depths of life and dangerous times and had stood by me in word and deed. She died without lamenting and, thank heavens, without pain. The last weeks had been hard, because as Anna suffered and was weakened from a fever, I could not find the cause and therefore could not fight it effectively.

I closed her eyes, put a hymnal under her chin to support it and thus keep her mouth closed, and put her hands one above the other. My children kissed her on the forehead a last time, then we left her to the care of the undertaker's women.

Now I was alone, a widower fifty-three years old and hardly any longing for either life or love. My only wish remaining was to live the rest of my life with integrity and the hope that I would depart without fear or pain.

CHAPTER 29

. . . lets the reader know that I leave Dresden and go to Leipzig.

Not at once, it should be understood. The successor of my elector Augustus was his sixth son, now called Elector Christian I. The other sons had all passed away.

The succession of Christian was accompanied once more with religious changes, all of which caused his subjects and me to become bewildered.

Christian kept me as his personal physician but did not make my life as his archiator easy, because very early he succumbed to alcohol. This prevented him from properly seeing to the affairs of the state, though his father had from early on trained him to govern the principality. The new elector preferred hunting, a pastime during which I was required often to be present.

I did what I could to keep him away from bottle and tankard but dared not insist too much, because then, though normally a good-natured person, he could get nasty. All I could do to alleviate his stomach complaints was to prescribe him summer savory, *Satureja hortensis,* already recommended by Hildegard of Bingen, to be added as spice to his meals.

But as soon as his sour stomach was better, he grasped the chance to take to the bottle again and that even more intensely than before. At the beginning he tried to persuade me to join him in drinking, but as a rule I could ward him off by pointing out my duties as a doctor.

In alchemy—particularly gold making—he believed less than his father and therefore left me alone in this respect.

What helped my mood and relieved me somewhat was his attitude on religious issues. He hated the bickering of the theologians about the true doctrine, which had poisoned the rule of his father. In this the Lutheran zealots and the Philippists, followers of Melanchthon, were at each other's throats fighting like devils. He even enacted a law against such squabbling.

I cannot emphasize enough how fed up I was with all this, the back and forth, the never-ending struggle about trifles backed up by threats to destroy each other.

A word about the so-called Formula of Concord, or *Formula Concordiae,* which Christian's father had initiated and which Christian rejected as thoroughly as he did the unchristian exorcism in baptism. He was helped in this by Christian Johann Salmuth, newly appointed court chaplain.

The *Formula Concordiae,* also called the Bergic Book or the Bergen Book, was originally devised to bring about an agreement between the strict Lutherans and the followers of Melanchthon, but it made, at the same time, any reconciliation between Calvinists and Lutherans impossible.

In the electorate of Saxony, all pastors had to put their signatures to this formula. And the saying went around:

Sign, dear pastor, sign
Then you can keep the parish thine.

Of course, everybody signed. I would have signed too to keep my job.

Relief from many of my troubles came from my friendship with Chancellor Nikolaus Krell, who used his influence on the elector to cautiously (very cautiously indeed, since the electoress Sophia of Brandenburg was rigidly Lutheran) to reconcile Saxony to the doctrine of Calvin. Naturally, despite the reasonableness of this approach to religious and church policy, I did not offer my opinion openly, and my conversations with Dr. Krell were always without witnesses.

Krell's attempts to restrain Lutheran orthodoxy in Saxony also were directed against the influence of Habsburg, which he believed was damaging the sovereignty of his country. To this end he tried to befriend good King Henry IV of France, Queen Elizabeth I of England, and certain Protestant princes in Germany. Through Chancellor Krell, I became acquainted with European affairs, for which I was grateful to him.

Our friendship did not seem advantageous for the Saxon chancellor, because in AD 1591, when Christian I had not quite died yet, Nikolaus Krell was arrested and imprisoned in the fortress of Königstein.

The instigators of this unjust and loathsome action were Duke Frederick William I of Saxe-Weimar, who had been appointed regent of the electorate by Christian I, because the latter's son, later Christian II, was under age at the death of his father; the bigoted Lutherans, to whom Calvinists were worse than the Devil; and the elector's widow, Sophia of Brandenburg, who above all wanted to retain exorcism in baptism.

So Chancellor Krell was brought to trial and accused of Cryptocalvinism.

Only a few days ago the honorable Matthias Dresser brought me the news that King Henry IV of France and Elizabeth I of England pleaded for Krell and asked for his discharge and annulment of the sentence. But even that was of no avail. I am afraid Krell, this meritorious man, is in for something very bad indeed, as the new elector is only eight years old and is completely dominated by his mother, Sophia, and the ducal administrator Frederick William from Weimar.

Krell's work would certainly have merited a better recognition than what is happening to him now. He initiated the first survey of

Electoral Saxony, which, without doubt, was of great importance for the administration of the country. It is truly an irony that the castle of Königstein, which under his chancellorship was reconstructed to become a formidable fortress, was the place of his imprisonment.

Several years ago, I was tired of seeing what happened to commendable people, and I moved to Leipzig with my books and my laboratory equipment, where I settled down as a general practitioner for the public. It did me good to get away from court life with its lies and intrigues, the required pliability and also the resultant cowardice.

My patients in Leipzig were normal townspeople, mostly, who were grateful for the attention I afforded them and also did not all the time put my medical advice and treatment in question. Death they always accepted as God's will and not the doctor's fault, which made life easier for me.

Two years later the Electoral Saxony administrator, Frederick William of Saxe-Weimar, invited me to become his personal physician and also to look after the young princes of the late Saxon elector. I was granted a very good salary, which helped persuade me to take the position, though I had many reservations. Also my *taedium vitae* became always stronger, or to say it in simpler words, I grew tired of life. I was not long in my new position, because for weeks now I have been ill, no longer a doctor but a patient myself.

All I have to say is said, and for the expected emergency preceding death I have a large phial of *Tinctura opii,* a poppy juice preparation, ready on my bedside table.

May my children have a happy life with less fear than I had and also more courage.

May God forgive me my doubts and help me to overcome my fear of death. The whispering shadow of the reaper that the poet writes about may promise hope, not terror.

Finis libri finis vitae.

Acknowledgments

I cannot thank Michael Leonard enough for his translation and all the trouble he took to create a text as near as possible to the German original. Without his never-tiring efforts in answering the author's questions and his understanding of German culture and history, this book would never have been published in English.

About the Author

CHRISTOPH WERNER was born in the East German city of Halle on the Saale River and raised as the son of a Lutheran minister. He studied English and German at Martin Luther University at Halle and worked in English teacher training at various universities in East and West Germany before retiring to live in Weimar. He has written four novels and numerous short stories and essays.

CPSIA information can be obtained
at www.ICGtesting.com
Printed in the USA
LVOW08s1423261017
553862LV00006B/94/P